MW00829999

ASHES

OF

CHAOS

AMELIA HUTCHINS

Copyright ©September 2020 Amelia Hutchins

ISBN: 978-1-952712-04-3

This book is a work of fiction. Names, characters, places, and incidents are either the product of the author's imagination or are used fictitiously. Any resemblance to actual persons, living or dead, or to actual events or locales is entirely coincidental.
This book in its entirety and in portions is the sole property of Amelia Hutchins.

Ashes of Chaos Copyright©2020 by Amelia Hutchins. All rights reserved, including the right to reproduce this book, or portions thereof, in any form. No part of this text may be reproduced, transmitted, downloaded, decompiled, reverse engineered, or stored in or introduced into any information storage and retrieval system, in any form or by any means, whether electronic, paperback or mechanical without the express written permission of the author. The scanning, uploading and distribution of this book via the internet or via any other means without the permission of the publisher is illegal and punishable by law. Please purchase only authorized electronic editions and do not participate in or encourage electronic piracy of copyrighted materials.

This eBook/Paperback is licensed for your personal enjoyment only. This book may not be re-sold or given away to other people. If you would like to share this book with another person, please purchase an additional copy for each recipient. If you're reading this book and did not purchase it, or it was not purchased for your use only, then please return to the place of purchase and buy your own copy. Thank you for respecting the hard work of this author.

The unauthorized reproduction or distribution of this copyrighted work is illegal. Criminal copyright infringement, including infringement without monetary gain, is investigated by the FBI and is punishable by up to 5 years in federal prison and a fine of $250,000.
Authored By: Amelia Hutchins
Cover Art Design: Eerily Designs
Copy edited by: Melissa Burg
Edited by: Melissa Burg
Published by: Amelia Hutchins
Published in (United States of America)
10 9 8 7 6 5 4 3 2 1

Other Books by Ameila Hutchins

Legacy of the Nine Realms

Flames of Chaos

Ashes of Chaos

Ruins of Chaos

Crown of Chaos - Spring 2021

The Fae Chronicles

Fighting Destiny

Taunting Destiny

Escaping Destiny

Seducing Destiny

Unraveling Destiny

Embracing Destiny

Crowning Destiny

Finished Series

The Elite Guards

A Demon's Dark Embrace

Claiming the Dragon King

The Winter Court

A Demon's Plaything

More coming 2021

A Guardian's Diary

Darkest Before Dawn

Death before Dawn

Midnight Rising -TBA

Playing with Monsters series

Playing with Monsters

Sleeping with Monsters

Becoming his Monster

Last Monster book -TBA

Wicked Knights

Oh, Holy Knight

If She's Wicked

Book Three -TBA

Midnight Coven Books

Forever Immortal

Immortal Hexes

Midnight Coven

Finished Serial Series

Kingdom of Wolves

Alpha's Claim coming 4/23/2021

If you're following the series for the Fae Chronicles, Elite Guards, and Monsters, reading order is as follows.

WARNING

Warning: This book is *dark*. It's *sexy, hot*, and *intense*. The author is human, as you are. Is the book perfect? It's as perfect as I could make it. Are there mistakes? Probably, then again, even **New York Times top published** books have minimal mistakes because, like me, they have **human editors**. There are words in this book that are not in the standard dictionary because they were created to set the stage for a paranormal-urban fantasy world. Words in this novel are common in paranormal books and give better descriptions to the action in the story than other words found in standard dictionaries. They are intentional and not mistakes.

<u>**About the hero:**</u> chances are you may *not* fall instantly in *love* with him, that's because **I don't write men you instantly love**; you grow to love them. I don't believe in *instant love*. I write flawed, raw, caveman-like **assholes** that eventually let you see their redeeming qualities. They are **aggressive assholes**, one step above a caveman when we meet them. You may *not* even like him by the time you finish this book, but I promise you will *love* him by the end of this **series**.

<u>**About the heroine:**</u> There is a chance you might think she's a bit naïve or weak, but then again, who starts out as a badass? Badass women are a product of growth, and I am going to put her through *hell*, and you get to watch **her** come up **swinging** every time I knock her on her ass. That's just how I do things. How she reacts to the set of circumstances she is put through may not be how you as the reader, or I, as the author would react to that same situation. Everyone reacts differently to circumstances and how she responds to her challenges, is how I see her as a character and as a person.

I don't write love stories: I write fast-paced, knock you on your ass, *make you sit on the edge of your seat wondering what is going to happen next* in the books. If you're looking for cookie-cutter romance, this isn't for you. If you can't handle the ride, **unbuckle your seatbelt and get out of the roller-coaster car now**. **If not, you've been *warned*.** If nothing outlined above bothers you, carry on and **enjoy the ride!**

FYI, this is not a romance novel. They're going to *kick* the shit out of each other, and *if* they end up together, well, that's *their* choice. If you are going into this blind, and you complain about abuse between two creatures that are **NOT** human, well, that's on you. I have done my job and given **warning**.

Dedication

This one is for my ex coworkers in the medical field who talked shit about me and chose to be catty bitches. Look how far that got you. Thanks for the lies, the backstabbing, tossing labs into the trash, and then finding them there by a *'miracle'* even though I'd seen your petty shit coming and reprinted them...(Seriously, people's lives depended on those labs, which makes you a huge asshole)...because I knew you were that ugly inside. I would like to say that I'm a bigger person, and not being petty as fuck, but here I am, being petty as fuck. To the two special women who consistently lied, and were extra catty bitches, I'm thankful that recent circumstances allowed me a front-row seat to see that after all these years you're still in that same dead-end job. I hope you got everything you deserved for lying, scratching, and screwing people over. Maybe one day karma will fuck you side-ways in the nose with a screwdriver, but until then, may the world give you many, many years like 2020 has been for the rest of us. You know who you are, and I hope one day you figure out how to be a member of the team instead of an asshole. Until then, karma is coming for you... But, also, thanks for being such petty bitches, because without you, I'd never have left the medical field to achieve my dream of being an author. The world works in mysterious ways, now doesn't it? I'll think about you often while I am working in my pajamas instead of scrubs. While I'm living out my dreams, and you're still being obtusely obnoxious to get that raise, I'll think of you often. So, like, in the words of Aria Hecate, go un-fuck yourself.

XOXO

Amelia Hutchins, that one bitch you fucked over and life made lemonade and added vodka to those lemons you tried to hand me.

THE MAP OF VISITED REALMS

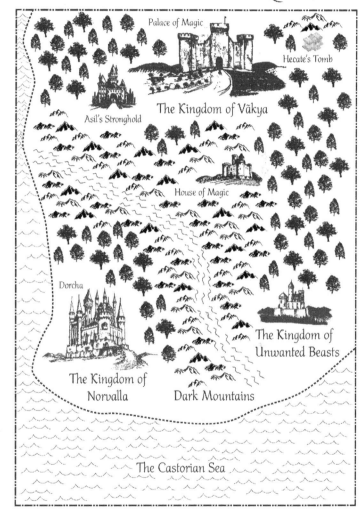

Palace of Magic

Hecate's Tomb

Asil's Stronghold

The Kingdom of Vākya

House of Magic

Dorcha

The Kingdom of
Unwanted Beasts

The Kingdom of
Norvalla

Dark Mountains

The Castorian Sea

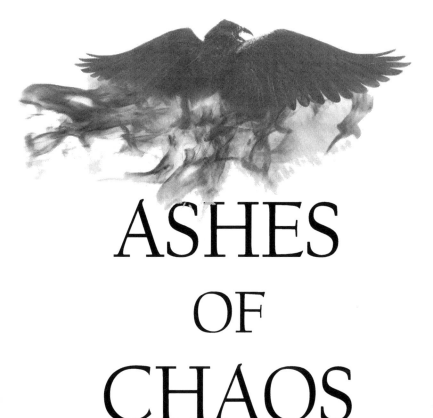

ASHES
OF
CHAOS

AMELIA HUTCHINS

Chapter One

My pulse thundered loudly as sweat beaded on my brow and neck, dripping from me while I pumped my legs faster, harder. The need to escape from the monster hunting me took precedence over everything else happening around me. My body had transformed into toned, sleek muscles because of the endless running from beasts, men, and creatures alike, trying to catch me off guard to rip me apart.

Moonlight was absent in the night skies, hidden behind inky clouds that blanketed the forest into velvety darkness that made every step precarious. I ran from the hunters, knowing I was nothing more than their prey. I slid through the trees blindly, making the headlong run dangerous as my feet crunched over debris and large, jagged rocks tripped me repeatedly, rushing through the terrain.

I could smell the men, their enticing, spicy,

masculine scent calling to the creature within me. She begged for me to stop, to run toward the monster hunting me, and give him what he wanted. Knox was a mountain of a man. His sleek muscles called to me, begging me to get to my knees and worship him and his glorious cock.

He'd been stalking me for weeks, forcing me deeper into the deadly countryside that had hidden enemies behind each rock and ominous shadow. Knox hadn't been lying when he said he'd be within every single realm, no matter how fast I ran, or how deeply I dug into the Nine Realms to hide from him. Here, in this place, Knox Karnavious was an absolute power that no one dared to challenge.

I wasn't ready for him to capture me. I still had so many pieces to move into their respective places that I couldn't allow Knox to get to me. I'd been slowly rearranging things and forcing parts to shift. I made my way in this twisted world that was a giant mess. Not that I wouldn't mind one night in Knox's arms, feeling him moving within me.

Knox wasn't just good at sex. He was a master of manipulation, twisting my body to bend to his touch. He turned me inside out and left me struggling to remember my name when he'd finished. He was a mixture of rippling muscles and sexy tattoos scrawled in a language I wanted to learn explicitly, I danced over the lyrics his body sung.

Growling sounded closer than it had been, forcing me to spin toward the noise. My foot slid through something slick, and my body lurched forward, slamming into a large boulder that sent me rolling down a steep ravine. I cried out, hitting more sharp rocks. I continued to fall down the unforgiving hill. When I finally came to a stop, I laid there, staring up at the darkening sky. Breathing heavily, I took a moment to notice the few stars peeking out from the cloud cover. This world, for all its faults, was beautiful and unreal.

Shouting started from the top of the cliffside I'd just come down, compelling me to move again or chance being at Knox's mercy, and from experience, I knew he had none. Whimpering softly, I lifted from the ground, wincing and hissing, forcing myself to get back into a standing position while taking inventory of the injuries I'd endured.

Blood covered my hands, and my fingers trembled. I reached toward my palm to remove a large twig protruding through the skin. Gritting my teeth, I pulled it out and tossed it to the ground.

Peering down, I noticed my shredded dress sticking to a cut that dripped blood down my thigh, undoubtedly caused by the sharp rocks that broke my fall.

Lifting my nose to the air, I inhaled the male hunting me relentlessly. I had to give it to Knox; he devoted all of his attention to capturing me at all costs. I'd been on the run for months, and every turn I took, he was there. I'd even caught his scent in my sleep, as if he haunted my dreams.

I started forward again, knowing he wasn't far behind me. If I stopped too long, he'd capture and enslave me before I was ready for that to happen. I craved that asshole like a drug and needed him more than the air that fed the cells to my blood.

I should hate him, and maybe I did, but I craved him

even more. I wanted to feel him against me, to hear the beat of his heart against my cheek after the sweat had cooled from our bodies. I yearned to feel his indomitable strength against my softness and feel him pumping into my need with the intensity that was Knox.

I hadn't had contact with my family in weeks, not since he'd increased his efforts to find and claim me. I'd forced my sisters and my aunt to sever their attempts to reach me, forcing them into the tomb that held too many secrets. What I'd found inside that tomb had changed my direction and altered my course, which was how I had ended up hunted tonight.

Light caught my eye, and I slowed, studying the swaying torches that seemed to come from a village in the distance. The choices for my directions were simple; the darkness behind me, or the light before me? The darkness held Knox and his men, which meant I was going toward the light one way or another to escape him.

I paused momentarily, resting my hands on my knees, flinching from the pain the wounds and scrapes caused. My lungs were burning from hours of running. The inability to draw magic within the forest had nullified my powers, draining my strength as well as my energy. I was certain Knox had drawn me into the woods specifically to null my magic. He had thought to bait and trap me, luring me to a place where magic wasn't accessible. He forgot I had feet, and my need to escape him was greater than the need I had to ride his glorious dick.

I loved that dick.

I craved that dick.

Unfortunately, I just hated the prick attached to that

dick.

If I'd been smarter, I wouldn't have fallen into his trap. I'd have sensed it before entering the woods, but I'd never expected an entire forest to be a void for magic. Knox knew this place, giving him one hell of an advantage. He pushed me into the corners, watching me stumble through the trees and down the mountains as he prowled within them, enjoying toying with me.

He'd almost caught me a handful of times already. Once, when I was sleeping, his scent alerted me to his nearness. I fought my body's need as his aroma rushed through me, causing dangerous, dark desires to swell within me. It was as if Knox could sense my body's predicament, having gone into heat the moment I'd escaped him.

I trembled, swallowing down the memories of him studying me from the shadows as I'd tried to force relief to my swollen sex. Another time, he'd found me moving through a crowded city. I struggled to discover if I was even in the realm I'd aimed to visit.

His eyes met mine through the crowd of people milling about, and I'd stood rooted to the spot, craving the taste of his kiss against my lips. The heat in his stare liquefied until my sex clenched with a carnal need that threatened to allow my creature to grasp control of my mind. That would have been a catastrophe.

The creature that slumbered within me was working against me. She wanted Knox, and it wasn't just desire; it was a primal need that had me waking up in the middle of the night, screaming for him until I was hoarse.

I would wake on my feet, standing in the midst

of nowhere with no memory of how I'd even gotten there. I knew it was my creature, and I knew who she was hunting. Luckily, Knox hadn't been close any of those times, or I'd be in chains at his feet, looking like something out of *Star Wars*, but less sexy.

Stepping into the shadows of the village, I shivered. The sensation of black magic slithered over my body, alerting me to the dangers awaiting me here. I'd felt it several times since being on my own in the Nine Realms.

Not once had it been a good omen, since black magic indicated death and foreboding. Silently, I stepped over the salt line, trembling with the power of the warding spell that slipped against my skin, sparking magic to my fingertips.

A blanket of darkness covered the village, but I could still make out the destruction. I walked further toward the center of town. Flags of all shapes and sizes blew in the breeze above the doors of each house I passed.

Frowning, I moved closer and peered at a door, seeing it marked in blood before I noticed droplets dripping onto the earth. Lifting my eyes, I slapped a hand over my lips, stopping the scream before it escaped through them. What I thought was a flag, swaying in the darkness, was a woman.

She hung upside down, her throat slit until her head clung to her body by a thread as her dress whipped in the wind. She dangled by a rope wrapped around her feet, secured to the cottage's chimney as her blood painted the ground crimson. A shiver of trepidation slid down my spine. I backed away against the house across from hers.

Something wet dripped onto my cheek. I brought

my other hand up to wipe it away. I peered up into yet another woman's sightless eyes. I fought the tightening in my throat as bile churned in my stomach.

Scanning the other cottages, I found more women strung up, draining their blood into the ground below them, flowing into shallow trenches in the earth that lead deeper into town, creating a stream of blood.

I whispered a spell to shield myself, becoming invisible to the world around me. I slowly withdrew the potion from my pocket to enhance the spell I'd cast. Tipping my head back, I chugged it as I stared into the lifeless woman's cloudy eyes. She was young, too young to have lost her life. She blinked, and I gasped loudly, unable to stop the noise from ripping from my lungs.

A scream ripped through the night, forcing my attention further down the road. I stifled my fear as a shiver snaked down my spine. I closed my eyes, inhaling deeply as I fought for calm, slowly inching to the center of town.

Music wafted toward me, and my brows creased in confusion at the noises that sounded like revelry. How could there be celebration while dead bodies hung from chimneys like sacrifices?

I paused at the mouth of the darkened alley, noting that my hair rose along my nape. Growling stopped me, causing goosebumps to form on my arms as another shiver made its way up my back. My lips trembled, studying the forms concealed in shadows, heading in my direction. Fighting not to tuck tail and run like a bitch, I clenched my teeth to keep the chattering noise from waking the dead.

Gasping, I watched as huge dire wolves moved toward me. Once they were near enough to where I stood, I relaxed ever so slightly. I took in their appearance from the light of the torches swaying in the wind. Red glowing eyes studied me, and I fought the hot tears threatening to break past my rapidly blinking eyes as I tried to hold them back. Bones protruded from their faces, appearing as if someone had kicked them in death before raising them from their grave within Hecate's tomb.

"Oh, you sweet babies," I whispered, carefully lowering to my knees as the dire wolves bared their deadly fangs in warning as they walked toward me. "Who brought you here? Who would be so selfish to disturb your rest?" I cooed to them as their ears lowered, noting the drool that escaped from their mouths. "Come to me, my sweet darlings, and allow me to ease your pain and send you back to your sleep."

Dire wolves raised from Hecate's tomb, or even in the surrounding area, were a terrible sign of what was happening here. They don't rise on their own. Someone must summon them from their tomb, calling them here for a purpose. No one except a Hecate bloodline witch would hold the right or power to control them, let alone summon them from their grave.

The fact they were dead and disturbed from their promised rest, protecting Hecate during her eternal slumber, was definitely not a good sign. Dire wolves were ethereal in life and could only reanimate if someone from the Hecate line performed death magic. I could sense they were here to guard something sinister.

Knox's scent rolled through me, the spiciness of it causing my body to heat with need. Closing my eyes,

I harnessed the hungry bitch within me who preened, taunting me with the fact that eventually, I'd lose my battle. She promised me I'd weaken in time and go to him to stop the need driving me.

My sex clenched, and the image of his eyes holding mine prisoner as he drove his magnificent cock into my body, caused a needy moan to slip past my trembling lips. My hand lifted, covering my mouth as a soft purr fought to escape, calling him to me.

According to Aurora, I was entering a breeding cycle that would only end once I'd either had sex or attempted to breed. My instincts were taking over. The creature inside of me needed the beast that was within Knox. We needed him to catch us and do what he'd promised; fuck me so damn hard that I'd never need or want any other man so long as I lived.

Bastard.

I hated that Knox was so smug about the fact that he knew what I was and suspected what I would become. He held it over my head, goading me. He'd left items around for me to find, notes asking if I needed assistance getting fucked or if I had any interests in a quick fuck-and-duck, using my own term against me. He had no idea how badly I wanted to leave him a pair of my panties with my scent soaked into them, showing him just how close he was to the mark. The problem, I was breeding. I couldn't chance getting pregnant while fighting witches as I cleaned the house of Hecate, alone.

Since I was so young, Aurora had faith that I wouldn't be able to get pregnant because, well, sometimes, mixed-species struggled to achieve the biblical act of creating life. She sugar-coated the shit out of it since my body was a mixture of fire and tension that kept me in a frenzied state of sexual frustration. The worst part I'd discovered about being in a breeding cycle? I couldn't get off without him to help me. It wasn't an orgasm my body craved; it was him, and what his body alone could offer mine.

The wolf neared me, sniffing the air as I lifted my bloodied hand with the palm up. "That's it, baby. I vow that I won't hurt you. Show me who brought you here, interrupting your promised and deserved sleep."

The wolf snarled but stopped abruptly as his nose touched against my palm, cold as ice. I winced, taking in his blood-red eyes that bespoke of the pain he'd endured being awoken from death. Whoever disturbed their sleep was selfish and uncaring that they'd caused the wolves to suffer needlessly.

I watched as the wolf nuzzled my palm, the relief from my touch, driving him closer to me. He bowled me over, and I laughed silently as he burrowed his head into my hold, finding comfort in my arms. Others moved closer until five decaying dire wolves sat around me, touching me. My hands slid through their fur, ignoring that clumps of fur and skin fell off as their tails wagged with happiness.

I sliced through my palm, slowly letting them lick the blood as their saliva mixed with it, strengthening them while allowing me to see who had brought them back from death. My head spun as my eyes closed. My third eye opened to show me dark, shadowy figures slitting throats and torturing women while sightless-eyed men stayed behind the inky silhouettes. A dire wolf stood beside each shadow as hands silently stroked them to calm their unease.

Screaming ripped me from the image, cutting it off as the wolves bowed their heads, growling at something behind me. I stood, peering into the shadows before I smirked. I lifted my nose, drinking in the scent of masculinity that danced through me. Knox was close, too close. I turned toward the screams, closing my eyes. I swallowed hard, ignoring the need that rushed through me, hot and dark.

"Get'em, boys," I hissed, stifling a laugh before I stepped deeper into the shadows. "Do no harm. Only play, my loves."

Turning toward the screams mixed with laughter, two sounds that didn't belong together, I moved in their direction with my heart racing loudly in my ears. The hair on my neck rose. I listened to the snarling wolves while men screamed, and a smile spread over my lips.

Knox deserved the wolves' anger for hunting me until I was so exhausted I didn't even remember what it felt like to sleep. There were much better ways to exhaust me, and chasing me wasn't it or fun. I knew his game was to wear me down until I made a mistake that would allow him to capture me without a fight. I didn't intend to let that happen, not at any cost.

Chapter Two

Knox wouldn't enjoy the wolves, but he also wouldn't hurt them. Technically, they were already dead, but the problem with dead dire wolves was this; if you killed one after its true death, it would multiply during regeneration. When Hecate first discovered this anomaly, she allowed the witches to use this knowledge to manipulate the wolves, creating an army of thousands. Living dire wolves were rare. Therefore, Hecate allowed the mated pairs to roam freely within the tomb to breed, maintaining the line.

At the sound of Lore screaming like a woman, I winced and canted my head, pausing. I could hear Lore, Brander, and Killian, but I couldn't hear Knox, even though I knew he was behind me.

I shivered as the sensation of being watched settled on my spine, thankful that my invisibility spell was still working. My eyes swung toward the mouth of the alleyway, finding it empty. Worrying my lip with my teeth, I exhaled as I greedily drank in Knox's scent before dropping my head back, trembling violently with need.

Forcing myself to ignore the scent of the primal male that promised carnal pleasures untold, I moved toward the center of town. Rounding a corner, I came to a dead stop as my stomach churned, and chaos danced in my mind. Men and women swayed on their feet as their bodies dripped blood from gashes slit deep into their flesh.

The scene was grotesque, and the vileness mixed with carnage had me swallowing past the saliva in my mouth, threatening to release the contents of my stomach, which I'd been lucky to find. Food wasn't something I could waste since I needed the energy it would give me to escape Knox. Food was fuel, and without it, Knox would surely catch me.

My back brushed against a stone cottage. I backed away from a couple that nearly trampled me. They barreled through the village, blindly, tearing each other apart with their bare hands and whatever they found lying in the road, doing anything to ease their sexual urges.

I covered my mouth, stopping the scream that bubbled up, tightening my chest while they went at one another. Blood splattered the wall near my face, and I closed my eyes, trying to block out the sounds of their bodies slamming together against the house as they fucked and moaned loudly. Clearly spelled, they were mutilating each other for someone else's entertainment.

Cruel laughter turned my focus to the dark shadows across from me, watching the couple as they feasted on and fucked each other, slowly stripping their lives away in the process. Feminine voices cheered the male on, laughing when the woman screeched as he parted her legs too far, and bones crunched as he repeatedly slammed his body into hers.

The woman's teeth ripped into the man's throat, tearing the flesh as he moaned and snarled, pounding into her body, harder and faster until she screamed her release. The couple was driven into a frenzy using sex magic while the shadowed figures continued to cheer and utter encouragement.

Slowly, I side-stepped toward the doorway of the nearest house, carefully to not disturb the dirt and gravel at my feet. I forced myself to move away from the splattering blood that painted the stone cottage from their frenzied coupling.

Turning my head, I watched as other couples slowly joined the morbid dance of death, oblivious to their surroundings. Blood turned to ice in my veins, growing sluggish as it pumped through my body, and I shivered. Disgust raged within me, realizing the people in this village served as living sacrifices for the wicked creatures still hovering in the shadows.

The entranced couples danced an ancient ceremony once used to induce mass suicides as sacrifices to Hecate. It was one of the darkest rituals she'd performed, and long ago outlawed because the spell could spread without warning, causing entire villages to become inflicted by the mysterious lure of the magic.

Entering the stone cottage, I quickly tore a piece of fabric from my dress to wash away any traces of blood that might have splattered on my face. I jumped as a loud bang sounded against the house's wall, followed by loud cries of pleasure mixed with pain. Taking a deep breath, I nearly choked on the coppery smell of blood that hung heavy in the air, and I closed my eyes, pushing the back of my hand against my lips as I fought the need to throw up.

It took effort not to get sick as the pained sounds of coupling continued outside. Every single person who had lived inside this village was dead. They just wouldn't succumb to death until the shadowy figures had finished playing their game. There was no need for this spell to linger, but the spell casters were enjoying the pain inflicted on the villagers, enjoying their suffering as their forced copulation fed the spell.

Grabbing onto the handrail, I climbed the darkened staircase, compelling myself to move faster before I heard another body hit the ground in death. I searched each of the darkened rooms, peering out the windows into the torch-lit night. I searched for a view of the courtyard. Window after window, all of them faced other windows and stone siding to the cottages next door.

The last room I entered had a perfect view of the monstrosities playing out in the courtyard. I settled into the shadows, observing the scene as dark figures wearing masks depicting demons and hideous beasts, danced around the couples continuing to encourage their participation. Long daggers glinted in the torchlight, ending life after life of those that didn't dance fast enough, or hadn't been pleasing to watch. Hecate, the goddess, demanded the most beautiful and purest men and women to mate, coupling to offer a child for her altar.

I'd never actually seen the dance of death playing

out, but I'd read about it a thousand times. The House of Magic told us about the evilest, vilest enchantments, whispering to us in warning of spells and dark sorcery that we couldn't allow practiced. The house itself was a vessel of magic, a calling to be pure of the darkness and bathed in the light of true magic. I was always eager to hear the tales and learn, much to my sisters' chagrin. They found it boring and tedious to listen to a house.

This was the third town in which I'd found all the inhabitants dead. The dance was a new touch of carnage, but the dark figures inducing the magic weren't. Each village had shown an escalation of violence, their acts growing viler as the spell grew more potent and more ominous.

This spell was smothering and powerful, forcing my skin to pebble and my soul to recoil. I knew the difference between darkness and light, having been tested for both types of magic after my mother declared to my teachers that I was a practitioner of the dark arts. I knew how each felt and what the magic of the light offered to avoid the darkness. The magic in these villages was darker than any other I had ever experienced.

I wanted to examine the horror unfolding, needing to sense what was at work after I stumbled across the first town. The Neanderthal chasing me made it difficult to manage, though. Each time I entered a village, Knox was hot on my heels, forcing me to take in what I could quickly before I had to portal out or chance getting caught. He was making it extremely difficult to do anything about the current state of affairs in my house. I portal-hopped until I was partially drained, slaughtering an entire manor of witches, escaping by the skin of my teeth from the last realm I'd visited.

I was growing more exhausted every day, worn down until my body was a mass of burning muscles. Resting my head against the window, I noted the dark figures were placing their victims into a pattern. I blinked, scrunching up my nose, frowning, and fighting the urge to vomit. I peered down at the scene below. I was forcing myself to look past the carnage to examine the shape that the masked figures created with their victims' corpses.

They arranged the bodies in a large pentagram pattern, draining each person of all blood and bodily fluid before placing them on the ground, posing their faces, forcing cloudy eyes to stare sightlessly at the midnight sky. Their arms stretched above their heads, touching the fingers of the body above them, connecting each of the victims to create a grid of power fueled by their sacrifice.

My heart pounded in my ears, echoing each beat as I trembled violently. Closing my eyes, I tried to concentrate, searching through memories for where I'd seen this pattern before. Feeling a twinge in my leg, I opened my eyes and frowned. I bent down, running my nails over the cut in my thigh that itched as the skin healed.

Thinking back, I recalled seeing pictures in a book depicting a similar design. The book filled each page with morbidity, and atrocious patterns of human corpses, giving me nightmares. To witness it happening in person was much worse. It was the shit of horror shows that even the most creative of minds would have had trouble bringing to life on film.

The illustrations showed men and women spelled

to slaughter one another. The victims had to be willing to die for the sacrifice to power the grid. Spelling the victims provided a way to cheat the process, ending their lives without argument. The sexual incantation used was then amplified, turning it into a weapon to drive their victims mad with the need to take their pleasure by force. They created sexual monsters that felt no pain or remorse, only boundless pleasure until they died from mating or self-inflicted wounds.

Chapter Three

I stared through the window as the masked figures set ablaze the bodies, and my breathing stopped. I watched the Hecate insignia burning dimly on the remains of the many victim's heads and chests. Each palm also carried the mark and was placed touching another, sealing the circle and igniting the grid as a sacrifice to Hecate, increasing the coven's power.

Adult bodies created the outside circular pattern while smaller victims formed the five-pointed star in the middle. As I studied one male's face, his eyes shifted, holding mine as his body slowly burned, and I clamped my hands over my mouth as tears slipped from the precarious hold I'd had on them.

Not everyone set on fire was dead before the flames had reached them. In horrified silence, I listened to the screams of the dying as they burned to death before my eyes. I trembled with the force of my emotions, unable to stop the tears that burned in my gaze.

I wanted nothing more than to jump to their aid, but the reality was the moment the villagers fell under the spell, it sealed their fate, and nothing would change that fact. The only thing I could do now was study and to learn more about my enemies so I could avenge all those sacrificed in my grandmother's name.

As I silently cried, evil shadows danced hypnotically to the screams of their victims. The masked figures laughed at the dying as their flesh sizzled and burned, sending the putrid scent high into the night. I noticed other flames lit in the distance, and suddenly, the entire area glowed with hundreds of similar circles made from remains. The fire created a burning pathway that flowed outside the village, deep into the countryside as if lighting the way toward something, or worse, *someone.*

Calming my emotions wasn't easy. Inside the Nine Realms, everything about me was enhanced, including my senses. My sense of smell was unreal. My hearing had amplified to the point that a twig, breaking miles away, echoed within my ears. The need to mate hadn't merely increased; it had intensified until even my nipples ached when Knox was near. To say it was ridiculous was an understatement, but that's how I knew when he was near, how I sensed him before I ever saw him as he continued to chase me.

My body knew Knox, desired him, and craved him deeper than I craved the need to do what I'd come to the Nine Realms to accomplish. I'd used potions and spells, all to no avail, because it was a primal need and something that wouldn't be ignored or shut off.

I leaned against the wall, closing off my emotions. I tuned out the debauchery happening outside. The victim's screams were dying down, which meant death was finally claiming them. I rubbed away the tears, deadening myself to the senseless loss of life, knowing that I'd come upon it too late to make a difference. Nothing I could have done would take away the dark, oily magic fueling the men and women to slaughter one another.

I wasn't that strong, nor did I house the right magic to fight against the spell. Not yet, at least. *Soon.* The witches outside stopped laughing and talked excitedly, in a rushed, worried speech. I frowned, moving back to the window.

Peering down the road, I spotted Knox as he stepped into the village and unseeingly moved through the scene. My eyes narrowed as he and his men continued toward the courtyard, stepping *through* the bodies. I blinked, rubbing my eyes. I watched the hooded figures slowly slinking toward him, Knox seemingly unaware.

Son of a bitch! Knox and his men were within a layer of the realm. I turned my attention back to the masked figures, but they showed no signs of alarm. They could not see Knox and his men, so how was I able to see them? Knox came closer into view as a hooded figure emerged from the crowd, looking directly at him. Removing the mask, a woman scowled angrily at Knox as she reached into the layer of the realm, sliding her fingers around his wrist, causing him to jerk back in pain. Anger snapped through me that they'd dare touch what was mine.

Power unleashed within me without warning. Power like I'd never felt before slid through the masked figures closest to me, until they recoiled, screaming as it burned their flesh, just as they'd done to their victims.

"Tit-for-tat, bitches. That monster is mine, and only mine." My eyes slid over their burning bodies, a smile lifting my lips as the rush of magic rippled through me.

Black eyes slid to my position in the window, and I realized I was no longer invisible. Shadows swayed around the woman's body as she released Knox, giving me her full attention. The figures all moved closer, coming toward me as one. I sent a warning shot of pure, untethered light magic at them. They recoiled since dark magic couldn't handle light, something we were taught very young.

Once you embraced the darkness, it sucked out your soul and then your beauty. You became a cold, undying, horrifying monster. Skin withered and wrinkled as it stole the witch's beauty, leaving her a decaying vile husk of a thing that no one trusted, or wished to be around. It made you into a witch's worst nightmare, unwanted and ugly.

The stronger the witch, the longer she could hold onto her outer shell, but even the strongest witches eventually fell to the darkness. I watched as the woman and the masked figures vanished, removing the victims from my vision, becoming shadows, drifting on the wind before ashes drifted into the night.

Turning my attention back to Knox, I smirked at the confusion playing on his face. Ocean-blue eyes lifted and locked with mine, before turning to look around to find what had touched him. Death had touched him and sought to take him without his knowledge. Like I'd let them hurt that asshole, not when I enjoyed our cat-and-mouse game, even if he was exhausting me effortlessly. I was still winning.

Knox didn't waste time as he entered the house, marching toward the room I occupied. I pulled a portal to me, opening it as his heavy footfalls started up the stairs. The moment he stood in the bedroom doorway, heat rolled through me, and my body grew pliant with need.

Knox's gaze slid down my body. His eyes turned heavy-lidded and filled with lust. My reaction to his proximity wasn't normal. It created a violent need that stormed within us both. There was normal lust, and then there was the raw, intense lust that drove us, pledging violent sex, bone-jarring, leg shaking, unending pleasure that his eyes promised me. He didn't need me to speak because he knew my answer without asking the question.

Knox was primal, and everything within him matched perfectly, and I matched him. My gaze held his, screaming for him to end the chase, begging him to slam me against the wall, part my legs, and make me cry his fucking name. His lips curled into a grin as he inhaled deeply, watching me through hooded, seductive eyes. I shivered with the need my expression begged him to give.

This man was brutality mixed with virility. He was darkened desires that left no inch untouched when he consumed you. The need that rushed through me was razor-sharp, etched in violence that I needed him to give me. The more hostile Knox got, the hotter I burned with a need for him to take me. I didn't understand it, nor did I even care to look deeper at what we were.

There were ordinary people, and then there were us.

People flirted. They gazed shyly at each other,

sparing brief glances and smiles, exploring looks or other shallow things about one another. I'd watched my sisters lure men in a thousand times. The steady flutter of eyelashes, or the cute little smirk that said, '*Here I am, fuck me.*'

Knox and I didn't do that. I looked into his gaze, and I saw his bare bones. I felt the carnal need to get on my knees and worship him as he destroyed me. We went to war in bed, visceral need driving us to go deeper. Together, we're both volatile and destructive. We could ruin worlds by coming undone without walls to protect them from us.

He stepped forward, and I trembled violently, which didn't go unnoticed. Knox noticed everything about me. He knew that I arched my spine for him when he got too close. He saw my nipples pebbled against my top, and those fucking lips slid into a knowing grin. He isn't oblivious to the signals my body exposed. If I were a song, I'd be the one he wanted to replay on repeat.

Knox didn't speak, but the purr escaping those sinful lips rumbled through me. It reverberated off my clit, bounced to my nipples, and slid to my womb, awakening it with the promise of fulfillment. His eyes told me he'd enjoy breaking me, and mine said to bring it, daring him to dance with me. Knox's mouth opened, revealing serrated teeth, causing my jugular to pulse with the need to bare my throat to his beast.

His nostrils flared, inhaling my scent as his body rippled with power. His chest rose and fell with silent breathing, and yet I knew it wasn't rage rushing through him. It was need; a need so raw and undiluted that I smiled, unable to stop it from spreading across my lips as my eyes fluttered closed while I drank his scent deep into my lungs. I loved his smell, the dark spices mixed with male, driven by that deadly hint of darkening desire that caused my body to clench with anticipation anytime I caught a whiff.

"Aria," he growled huskily, slowly letting his attention slide down my battered body. His eyebrow lifted, telling me he wasn't happy to find me hurt.

Those sexy oceanic-depths slipped back to lock with mine as he held his hand out, no doubt expecting me to be struck stupid enough by desire to place mine into his. I smirked, watching as his body rippled with something deadly, reminding me that this man was more beast than human.

"Knox, you smell… delicious." I bounced on my feet, needing him to slam his body against mine as he wrote his tag of ownership within me. I didn't dare take my eyes off of him. The moment I did, he'd have me pinned against the wall, with that glorious cock of his buried in my heat. I'd be screaming his name like a prayer I couldn't say enough times until we became nothing more than beasts in human clothing.

It wasn't need.

It was a primal demand.

I wanted him, and he wanted me.

I was the sickness; he was the cure.

I was the chaos, and he was the storm.

Together, we'd destroy each other and enjoy every moment.

Knox had hurt me, and I'd hurt him. I didn't care if it was wrong. It wasn't about anyone else. It was just how we met as beasts on a need so primordial that others wouldn't understand or even process that we were just... right when others would say it was wrong.

"Do I?" he asked, narrowing his eyes on me, dropping to my hands where my nails had pushed free. "Why can't I smell you?"

"Because you're not even on the same level as me right now," I chuckled darkly, canting my head to the side, watching as he stepped forward. I stepped back, slipping through the portal to stand in a meadow filled with glowing flowers.

"You know that I will catch you eventually," he growled through a deep rumble, unable to hide the lust entering his tone. "I tire of this game, little girl. When I finally catch you, that look burning in your eyes will become a fire that will leave us both in ashes."

"I keep waiting for you to catch me, but you never do. If you tire of the game, you change the game you're playing. You don't get mad at the other person for your failures," I taunted, trying to force him to come through the portal.

The desire to ride him had me wired. It was as if being this close to Knox made me into something else. I could feel his eyes, their scorching trail of heat as they slid down my body. My skin prickled, acknowledging every inch he surveyed.

Knox smirked wickedly, watching how I moved like an addict craving a fix, bouncing from foot to foot with pent up energy. Lust created need while his eyes promised me pain, sending excitement burning through my veins. His nostrils flared, trying to figure out what was happening to me as he licked his lips. I purred at the memory of that tongue buried in my body as he purred back, sending vibrations rumbling through me from within, hitting my clit. His tongue skills were something ordinary creatures probably hadn't mastered or even realized was a thing.

Knox knew every erogenous part of me with carnal knowledge. He knew he could get violent because I liked it when he did, needing his bruises that came from the way he savaged me. He could bruise my hips, leave handprints on my thighs, and still, I begged him to fuck me harder. I let him wreck me, and I'd wrecked his ass right back, giving him blow for blow in the bedroom until we were both nothing more than empty, exhausted shells gasping for air. His smile was predatory, as if he remembered the same night, the exact fucking moment as we stared at one another.

"I always catch my prey, Aria. This isn't a game for me. When I catch you, and I will, you're going to know why I'm the fucking King."

"Is that so?" I whispered, pushing my hands down my dress as his heavy gaze followed their trail. "I'm a needy bitch, so either do it already or stop talking. You seem to always taunt me, and yet you never follow through. You want me, and I want you. The thing is, I'm not willing to sell my soul to the devil to get the things I want from him. Don't get me wrong, Knox. You're deliciously wicked in bed, but you're not the only cock in the Nine Realms. Now, are you? You want me because of what I have and what I can do. The thing is, you have no idea what that really is. You will soon, and when that happens, you'll probably decide that I'm too dangerous to keep alive."

"You're not dying, Aria. I won't allow that to happen. You are mine. The other men? They won't satisfy that need burning in those pretty eyes. They won't destroy you like I do, nor would they even satisfy that hunger you feel when replaying those memories of our time together through that pretty head of yours. You're lust, and I'm carnage. You're a beauty, but that hides that vicarious bitch that's itching for you to release her.

"You're fucked in the head, just like me. You're bare-bones that unleash the moment you discard those clothes because without them, you shed your humanity and give in to the monster you truly are. You and me? We're kindred spirits that come together and shed our fucking skin and go to war against one another. It's glorious, and you fucking know it, don't you? Just now, you imagined me pinning you against a wall, driving into you until the only name you know is mine. Didn't you?"

"I'm imagining someone else doing something similar, yes." I teased, but he knew the truth. His eyes smiled, calling me out on the lie as I caught his scent. Fighting to remain in control, I shivered with the need to throw him down and make new memories with that thick cock of his.

He knew that only he could fix the ache that throbbed through me. He let me lie to myself, knowing that only he could take me to bed and show me both heaven and hell, making me choose hell because we were both sinners, and we would end up there together. Somehow, that thought didn't bother me. I didn't care, so long as

Knox was there with that glorious cock for me to ride straight past the gates and on through eternity.

"I marked you, and no one else would dare touch you. So, when you go into heat, and you will go into heat, you'll come to me. I'm sure you'll try to fight it, but you're too fucking young to do that yet." Knox stopped in front of the portal, inhaling deeply as a sinful smile played on his lips. "How hard are you already fighting it, Aria?" His head canted to the side as his eyes slid to obsidian. "I'm going to mark you again so fucking hard that you never want to leave me."

I swallowed, and his scent caused my mouth to open, releasing a moan of need before I slammed the portal closed. The sound of his laughter sliding through the portal as the fabric of the world closed was unnerving. I dropped to my knees, exhaling and inhaling slowly to get control of my body. Knox was dangerous because even though I knew I shouldn't want him, I did. My basic genetic makeup didn't have emotions. It didn't get angry. It was like my creature—basic needs driven by a monster that never grew tired or sated from hunger.

This wasn't what I expected.

It wasn't what I'd planned on happening.

Knox was mucking everything up, even though technically, me being in heat wasn't his fault. However, I still blamed him because he was an asshole.

Dark witches had messed with things that they shouldn't, calling up dire wolves from Hecate's tomb and using forbidden dark magic. I never thought I'd enter the Nine Realms and discover that Knox had told the truth, let alone to figure out he'd sprinkled a lot of sugar over the details of what was going on here.

Whatever was happening, I had to stop it before dark witches slaughtered more innocent people. The only way to do that was to get ahead of Knox and find witches who weren't playing in the middle of this mess. Someone powerful was leading deadly, evil witches onto a very dark path that they wouldn't survive. I would make damn sure that happened.

First, I had to figure out how to shake the alpha male gnawing on my butt cheeks and nipping at my heels. I spun as a shadow moved over my shoulder, staring up into the other male's eyes that pushed my every damn button on purpose.

"Hello, Puppy," I muttered, standing up.

"I'm your escort tonight, pretty girl," Dimitri stated softly, offering his elbow as I slipped my hand through it, resting my head on his shoulder.

"Well, then, escort me, handsome."

Chapter Four

Soraya, Deep within the Kingdom of Vãkya in the Palace of Magic

Standing in the line of witches chosen to serve Ilsa, High Queen of Witches, I swallowed against the need to spew my lunch, or what little I'd held down after watching body after body added to the large, unending human grid we were building at her behest.

Slowly, my eyes moved to my sister, hearing her eternal scream, calling my name, Soraya, echoing on repeat in her mind. I couldn't save her from what was coming. I hadn't been strong enough to prevent this evil bitch standing before us from taking my sister, so instead, I joined her coven to save myself, and I've done horrid things to reach the notice of the high queen, doing whatever it took to get here.

Instead of finding my sweet baby sister, I'd found a mindless follower in some kind of stasis serving Ilsa unquestionably. Julia was only a mere twelve moon rotations around the Nine Realms, too young to be this lost within the darkness so soon. Whatever Ilsa was doing, it was sucking the life from the witches at an expedited rate, allowing dark magic to take everything from them too soon. It was pure, undiluted evil that was swallowing the young witches whole.

Scraping sounded against the marble floor, reminding me where I was and in whose company I stood. Turning toward the sound, I examined Ilsa, positioned beside the large window. Her cruel, blue eyes scanning the endless miles of corpses, creating an enormous, winding power grid that fueled her infinite reign of terror. The hair on my neck rose as Ilsa moved her cold, dead gaze to the witches entering the room.

"We have a problem," Kalan announced. She was one of the witches sent to murder an entire village to add to the grid, spreading wide into the Nine Realms.

Ilsa tilted her raven-colored head, glaring at the newcomers. She nodded toward the shadows while her magic flowed endlessly through the room, slithering against our flesh. It was a warning, the power raw and smothering to those within its reach.

"I don't feel the power that should have added to the grid, Kalan." Ilsa turned toward the corner, nodding her head again slightly, and my eyes narrowed as I inspected the empty space.

A tremble of unease trickled down my spine as magic pulsed thicker in the room until my body threatened to bend and yield to the woman before me. Kalan's blackened eyes turned, noting the witches who stood silently while Ilsa decided our fates.

"That's the problem, Mistress. We were interrupted before we could seal that grid and add the magic to your amassing powers."

"By whom?" Ilsa hissed, her blackened teeth clenching as my stomach churned with the grotesque visual her character and person had become.

"We don't know who she is, but her power was… different. The magic she unleashed as a warning was unlike anything I'd ever felt."

Ilsa turned her dead eyes toward Kalan. Sweat beaded on my nape from the coldness of her stare. Hatred boiled to the forefront, and Kalan's failure sent my lips twisting into a wicked grin. Ilsa's mouth pulled back into a tight snarl that vibrated from her with displeasure.

"Explain to me what happened, you idiot!" she screeched, her hands balling into fists as her body slithered, turning to face the group of witches who had failed her.

I buffed my nails on my skirt, watching as Kalan and her group tensed from the force of Ilsa's full attention directed at them. Magic suddenly filled the room, a sign that more bodies were added to the grotesque grid that stretched all around the Palace of Magic. Steeling against another shiver, I watched as the blackening ooze of putrid magic pulsed through the witch's veins.

"We added the dark magic, just as you instructed, Mistress. I'd just finished the last of the spell when King Karnavious entered the area, moving through it, seemingly oblivious to our presence. I grabbed his wrist, and the moment I did, another witch sent her magic rushing through us with what I assumed to be a warning that he wasn't to be touched. It would have ended there, but her magic unraveled the grid's power, and something happened to the souls."

Ilsa tipped her head, turning to look over her shoulder as power pulsed faster and harder through the room. Anger and pain rose in my throat, and I forced it down with a veneer, giving nothing away that would show the fear and trepidation that arose. The anxiety of what was to come wrapped around my heart, tightening my throat with emotion.

"You said she took the power of the grid, easily? You allowed her to cast without guarding the grid?" she snapped, her spittle spraying over Kalan's face.

"It was unlike anything we'd ever felt. I figured it was more important to return to you and report back with what we had found first and foremost."

"You thought wrong," Ilsa growled. Her hands unclenched as she stepped aside, moving back to the window that overlooked the grid.

"We have failed you, Mistress," Kalan whispered, her obsidian eyes narrowing to slits as Ilsa turned toward the shadows once more, tilting her head as if she could hear something that none of the rest of us could. "We will move to attack another town and finish the grid."

"No, you will not."

Dark magic rushed through the room, causing nausea to swirl within me. My body clenched, and I fought to keep from spewing up what little food had been given to me as one of Ilsa's disciples. My attention moved to the witches, noting the eerie, utter silence that filled the air as panic and disbelief crossed Kalan's expression.

Kalan's hands lifted before her, and her mouth opened as blood expelled from her lungs. My body trembled with the atrocity of horrors unfolding before me. Hands became ashes, black lines spread through them as flesh turned to flecks of embers that flowed through the room. Ilsa opened the window, moments before Kalan's fiery parts slid past us to escape upon the wind.

One witch from Kalan's group howled, her body a mass of glowing lines that looked as if she'd drunk lava, and it was escaping through her veins.

A witch beside me screamed, her fear overriding her need to survive. Everyone in line stepped back to reveal the guilty party in our ranks. The witch who'd shown her fear, jerked forward by invisible hands, her body making odd scrunching noises before it dropped to the floor, ripped apart as her deafening scream echoed in my ears.

I didn't move or even blink as Ilsa watched us from her vantage point beside the window. My fingers remained flat at my sides, showing no reaction. No emotion whispered through me, or any outward sign of the screaming echoing through my head as the body before me continued to bend until only the crunching of broken bones sounded. The screams died away, and then Ilsa moved, slowly walking to stand directly in front of me as the scent of burning, rotted flesh singed my nose.

"Fearless, and yet so beautiful," she whispered.

Blackened fingertips touched my chin, forcing my heart to thunder in my chest. I held it together, praying for my heart to slow to a steady beat. I thought of the meadows where I'd once played with my sisters.

We'd spent hours on our backs, gazing up at the sky, guessing the shapes that each of us could find within the puffy clouds that filled the blue skies. The rapid beating tapered off, slowly returning to a steady beat as Ilsa's lips curved into a smile. The scent of decay and death caused my eyes to burn as the stink from her heated breath fanned my face.

"What is your name?"

"It is whatever you wish it to be, Mistress," I announced, standing statuesque straight.

"I didn't ask you what I wanted to name you. I asked you what name your mother graced you with, Witch."

"Soraya, Mistress," I stated without looking into her eyes. I looked through her, knowing she hated it when her acolytes looked into her decaying form.

"Tell me, Soraya, what do you see out there?"

She smiled at me as more power entered the room, jerking our bodies from the sheer force of magic to find that Ilsa had removed the dead witches from the room, adding them to the power grid outside. Ilsa grabbed my hand, forcing me to the window as my heart jackhammered against my ribs, worried about her intentions.

Oily shadows appeared around the victims comprising the grid. We called them The Dark Ones. They were creatures completely consumed by dark magic that had taken control of them in life, flowing through them in death. Venomous clouds of magic oozed around them, poisoning the air as they moved the corpses around, connecting hands or other body parts to the next in line.

It wasn't just a toxic cloud surrounding them, though. Damned souls and the souls of those added to the grid lived inside the clouds of mist. Revenants created the macabre fog with the dead's graying faces, reaching toward the witches tending the human power grid. To those of us close enough to the darkness, we knew what crawled within the blackened cloud.

The Dark Ones had nearly captured me once. Their twisted gray corpses with poisonous teeth and long, grasping claws were created to capture the living. The dead's withered husk had seized my leg, leaving poison that seeped into my pores, fighting to subdue me so the dead, mindless beasts could feast upon my living cells.

The condemned souls of The Dark Ones exist trapped within perverse, dark magic, forming swirls and wisps that drift in the thickening fog, reaching out toward their victims like smoky fingers. Still, I could hear the unholy eeriness of their voices as they screamed and cried out for us to join them in their void of nothingness.

Witches that had displeased Ilsa wore coverings over their faces to hide bits of bones revealed from the boiling of their flesh. Their punishment was to stand close to the revenants, allowing the wispy fingers to caress their skin. Bile pushed against my throat, burning. I fought to conceal my weakness so I wouldn't become her next victim, adding my magic to her power grid.

The odor released from the cloud surrounding The Dark Ones consisted of death and rotten flesh that clung to their souls in the afterlife, of which they could never escape or know peace, so long as Ilsa lived. That was the fate given to the acolytes who had displeased her, no matter how minor the offense.

These witches thought they served Ilsa well, but revenants would consume them in that unholy mist if they displeased her again. Their corpses spat out and added to her power grid, making the ultimate sacrifice, forced to serve her for eternity.

Many others had displeased her or failed to answer her summons to give in to the dark magic. Ilsa slaughtered them for their unwillingness to take what she so freely offered. You helped the mistress either by becoming a dark witch or by adding your power to her grid.

Focusing on the scene below, I saw that the grid spread out miles beyond the horizon, further than my eyes could see. Bodies covered the ground in circular patterns, even where the sun rose over the mountain, and in the sweeping valley that settled into a wide-mouthed gorge. All the grids were directing power to the Palace of Magic, no longer called the Palace of Light, once Ilsa had assumed control. No light reached these walls, shrouding the palace in darkness and offering only a cold, restless death.

Ilsa cleared her throat, and I realized I had yet to answer her question. I continued to gaze out the window.

"I see absolute power, which is yours for the taking, and rightly so, Mistress," I turned toward her and away from the grid she forbade us from admiring too long, in the event we thought to reach for the power it exuded.

Ilsa's smile was cold, curving her lips, sending dread and trepidation rushing through me. Her hand lifted, touching the amber curls that hung in rivulets down my shoulders. Ilsa stepped closer, her eyes holding mine while challenging me silently. I felt the need to hold her stare as if something more was happening here.

"Hecate's line has returned."

"So it is rumored, Mistress," I answered firmly, somehow managing to stay upright past her rotting corpse's debilitating stench.

Ilsa's scent was thick and eye-watering, like a chamber pot filled with rotten shit while surrounded by the dead who had suffered an ailment, dying before emptying its contents. Unblinking eyes held mine, searching for any sign of weakness, but I'd long ago had it beaten out of me.

You didn't expose fear to your enemies, or those you served. Her jaw clenched tightly, unnerved by the inability to cower me before her. She turned again, staring off into the corner before nodding once firmly.

"I have a job for you, Soraya. I do hope you won't fail me. Such brazen courage before your mistress could be grounds for punishment, but I find your strength to pretend that you're not terrified, intriguing. Come, I would speak to you away from the ears of the other acolytes who would listen to our every word. I'm about to make you a legend, sending you to a king that has a fondness for those who have yet to turn to darkness." She peered out the window once more.

My heart slowed, trained to hide fear and emotion since the day I'd been born, half-witch, half-shifter. When my mother refused Ilsa's dark magic, she abandoned us, leaving me alone to raise my younger sisters. She had known her life would end at that moment, and her attempt to hide us in the Realm of Light had failed since Ilsa had conquered it, claiming it as her own.

I swallowed, hating that Ilsa held power over me. My eyes slid to the line, running briefly over my youngest sister, Julia, who stared forward, eyes pooling with darkness. My heart clenched, knowing that I would lose my sister unless I found a witch stronger than the one I served. Steeling the emotion her emptiness caused me, I plastered a wicked smile on my lips, turning to look at Ilsa.

"I am yours to command, Mistress. Becoming a legend sounds wickedly nice. How may I please you?"

I'd be whatever Ilsa needed to remain close to my sister, even if I lost my soul in the process.

Chapter Five

Aria

My eyelashes fluttered as I lounged on the stone that overlooked the large hot springs in which Dimitri bathed, washing the blood off of his hands and arms. He wasn't ashamed of his body in the least, or offended that I stared at his ass with what he assumed was hunger. Instead, I compared it to Knox's masculine, perfectly muscular form and found Dimitri lacking.

"You could join me. You know you want to," Dimitri chuckled, and I snorted, rolling my eyes toward the vivid blue sky above me.

Birds sang in colorful trees, snatching insects out of the sky every once in a while when they'd get too close. The forest we had hidden within was lush with greenery and colorful flowers that moved around the trees, pulsing with life. I studied one bird, a smile playing on my lips, watching as the flower behind it bloomed. The flower lunged, closing around the bird, sending feathers drifting down from the limb. Shocked, I sat up, feeling a pang of regret for the bird and making a mental note not to piss off the trees with flowers.

"You do realize you're just going to get bloody again, right?" Frowning, I lowered my gaze to the witches we'd captured in the town just outside the forest. They had murdered all the villagers and had used their corpses to create the power grid when Dimitri and I found them.

"Unless they start talking," he muttered, nodding toward the struggling witches and their severed limbs still twitching on the forest floor.

Strolling out of the spring, Dimitri paused and shook the water from his hair, making sure I had plenty of time to notice the impressive erection he didn't even bother trying to hide.

Moving to where I sat, Dimitri leaned over to place a soft kiss against my cheek. Since I'd saved him from certain death, he'd fought the attraction he felt for me, but it seemed harder to ignore each time we ended up somewhere together. It wasn't hard for me. On the contrary, I easily ignored Dimitri's scent and presence. My body didn't get heated, but admittedly, I found his flirting cute.

It spoke volumes since I turned into a raging sexual fiend every time I was near Knox.

I'd discovered a lot about myself and just how fucked up I was since entering the Nine Realms. I knew that I wanted Knox and that no other male would soothe the ache I felt between my legs, or my clenching need. I hated it, but he'd dug himself so deeply within me I couldn't rip his claws out.

Dimitri hadn't given up hope that I'd succumb to his seduction and flirted mercilessly with me. His hands grabbed and parted my legs as he settled between them, cupping my face as he studied my eyes. I watched his tongue snake out, wetting his lips, noting the lust that danced within his pretty blue eyes.

"Can I kiss you?" he asked, watching as I puckered my lips, scrunching my face before I exhaled slowly.

Leaning forward, I let his lips brush against mine and waited for the burning need to tear through me. I craved the primal need. The violence the kiss would rip from me, reminding me I wasn't human at all, no matter how I looked. It never came.

With Dimitri, it was cute flirting.

With Brander, there was a little heat.

With Knox, he melted the flesh from my bones, revealing the monster beneath the skin I wore. He scorched me down to my rawest form. Knox exposed bones, melting away my human genetics as he showed how deeply he intended to take me. Bare-bones, primitive need, driven by animalistic instincts that demanded we go hard, fast, and the monsters slumbering within us felt our mutual connection.

Dimitri pulled back, narrowing his gaze on me as he frowned. "You're not kissing me, are you?"

"I was," I muttered, using my foot to push him away. I moved to collect my knife from where it sat just out of reach beside the witches.

It wasn't as if they could reach it anyway since I'd removed their arms. Dimitri was quiet, so I peered back at him, noting his stiffened spine as guilt washed through me. I knew he was attracted to me, but Knox's warning echoed through my head. If my creature surfaced in response to Dimitri's wolf, he was burnt toast. I missed toast. The food in the Nine Realms was lacking, to say the least.

I crouched down, moving my skirt out of the way of the bloodied witch, and watched as she opened her mouth, preparing to scream.

"You could make this easier on yourself and just tell me what I want to know," I offered. My eyes slid to another witch secured to a tree, watching me with fear etched in her expression. "You're next," I taunted.

Dimitri leaned against the rock I'd abandoned, watching me through thick, dark lashes. He waited for me to slice the dagger through the witch's side, opening a large gash in her flesh as blood began seeping into the ground. She struggled to escape me, using the stumps of her cauterized elbows to scoot out of reach. There was no escape, just like there was no escape for her victims in the village.

"Could you love him?" Dimitri asked offhandedly, causing my heart to race with the answer as he scoffed. "You will be nothing more to him than an enemy with flesh in which he finds release, Aria. You deserve better than that," he growled low, unimpressive to the monster within me.

My beast didn't even acknowledge Dimitri, other than peeking out, rolling over, before going back to sleep. It terrified me that he was right, but then what did I want from Knox? I liked his dick. I enjoyed his touch and the rawness of him as we went to war with each other's bodies. Did I see a future for us? No. Ghosts that he couldn't let go of yet broke and haunted him.

Dimitri bent down as his mouth changed, revealing long canines. He ferociously tore into the throat of the witch on the ground, lifting his glowing, sapphire, alpha eyes toward the other tied to the tree. The potent scent of urine assaulted me, and I grimaced, covering my nose from the offensive stench. Death was messy and disgusting.

"Where is the Keeper of Lightning located?" he asked, creeping toward the witch on the tree as I studied his physique.

Dimitri had thick tribal tattoos on his arms, and wolves and skulls decorated his waist, torso, and back. His thick, dark hair brushed the tops of his broad shoulders, yet unlike Knox's body, I didn't itch to touch it or his tattoos. Dimitri was virility and masculinity mixed into how an alpha should act and look. His body promised pleasure while his strength told of security. So why wasn't I attracted to him? I felt nothing when I looked at Dimitri, other than an appreciation for his masculinity.

Dimitri narrowed his eyes and growled, licking his lips as he stalked closer to the witch who had yet to answer his question.

"I don't know!" the witch screamed, continuing to lie.

"Cut off her feet," I ordered, hoisting myself up onto

the rock, as Dimitri turned, peering at me from over his shoulder, piercing me with a pointed expression. "You made me cut up the other one, and then you killed her. That one drank hemlock, and I'm not getting close to her in case she pisses herself when she dies, too."

"Everyone pisses themselves when they die, Aria." Dimitri placed his hands on his tapered hips, frowning as the witch gasped. Her blackened teeth were rotten from using too much dark magic. "I hate killing women."

"She's not worth your pity. She was murdering two men when we caught her, so she is definitely not from the same class of women I'd respect. I don't identify her as being anything like me, so instead of thinking of her as a woman, just stick with the fact that she's a murderous witch that isn't worthy of mercy or pity."

"That works," he snorted, grinning wickedly at the witch who had whimpered.

The area surrounding us rippled with magic, and I turned as Luna, Kinvara, and Aine appeared without warning. Smiling at their sudden arrival, I jumped from the rock and moved to hug Kinvara tightly, and Aine smirked, hugging me from behind, sandwiching me between them.

"I have missed you guys so much!" I admitted, pulling back as Kinvara narrowed her eyes and scrunched her nose at me.

"What smells like piss?" she asked, her eyebrows pushing together as she eyed the offending body that lay unmoving in the high grass. "Yuck!"

"Is there a reason your dick is out, Dimitri?" Luna

asked, glaring murderously at him before she let her scathing gaze slide down his body.

Luna had been moodier than usual. Everyone was walking on eggshells or avoiding her as the moon got fuller within the Nine Realms. Dimitri spent his nights with Luna, but still pursued other females willing to soothe his need to mate. He was the basic man-whore of the group, the only man actually, and I still didn't care or feel an attraction to him.

A scream pulled me from my thoughts, and I looked to see Luna slicing her claws through the throat of the witch tied to the tree, removing her head from her torso. Hissing vehemently, Luna cradled her hand, burning from the hemlock in the witches system. Moving into motion, I grabbed Luna, pulling her with me into the water while avoiding her hand.

"She drank hemlock, dammit," I groaned, carefully helping Luna wash her blistering arm. "Are you okay?" Luna lifted her haunted eyes as she nodded.

"I don't know why I did that," she whispered, shaking her head. "I'm going back."

"I think its best you go back to the tomb," I mumbled, lifting my eyes to the headless witch who had the answers we'd needed.

"To Haven Falls," she returned. My eyes widened before I could prevent the shock from showing on my face.

"Luna, Haven Falls is gone. There's no way for us to return there," Aine stated gently, settling in the shallow water with us. Her eyes held mine as she hugged Luna, comforting her twin. "I'm going to take her back to the tomb."

"You should all go back." I stood, drying my hands on my shirt before turning to frown at the two dead, dark witches. "I'm done here. Thanks to these two, the town is vacant of life. I'll still go back to see what I can find. Hopefully, there will be something there that will point to who is responsible for all these deaths."

I offered quick hugs while a flirting Dimitri stopped in front of the portal to escort Luna away. Glancing at me from over his shoulder, he turned and entered the portal after my sisters, before it closed behind him.

The town, if you could call it that, was empty. No animals moved through the litter and debris. There were no villagers other than the two men that the witches had been feeding on, literally. Dimitri buried them both, offering them what solace we could in death. I erected a crude grave of rocks, placing them over the ground where we'd laid the men's bodies to rest.

It scared me that I was growing numb to death and murdering monsters. I didn't kid myself or give in to the illusion that these witches were anything but monsters. They killed without reason, letting their other half grow rabid and poisonous. The two we'd killed were like Luna and Aine, witch and wolf, and yet they'd been more rabid witch than anything else.

Frowning, I stopped in front of a well full of water; the bucket floating on top. I kneeled, peering into the green, murky water to figure out why the rope had so much slack. Something moved just below the surface, and I leaned in to get a closer look, jumping backward as a scream bubbled up my throat. Stepping to the well again, I looked down, past the hair flowing underwater, into the eyes of the villagers' dead bloated faces. The witches placed them here for safekeeping, no doubt for one of the power grids I've seen all over this realm.

They had secured ropes to their waists, and something heavy on the other end, allowing their bodies to float closer to the top of the well. I glared at the dead, offended that they had sunk where wishes should be made, instead of bodies being laid. Not that I thought the creatures of the Nine Realms believed in wishes. If they had, those days were long gone.

A scent wafted through the air, causing my skin to prickle with awareness. Stifling a groan, I turned, staring over my shoulder into the shadows, searching for the male hunting me. I lifted my skirt, exposing my bare feet as I hurried over the old cobblestone street, slipping into one of the thatched-roof cottages.

I placed a few pieces of spelled, smoky quartz at the doorway to hide my scent, protecting me from others sensing my presence. Slowly, I walked down the stairs that led to a large room filled with journals. Picking one up, I noticed they belonged to the Keeper of Notes, long since forgotten, along with his king, after Hecate banished their entire race for overstepping and going mad.

I heard the sounds of the approaching army, pausing as Knox's scent struck me, forcing my nose to the air as I inhaled deeply. The door above opened, and I moved, rushing further down the staircase that spiraled into the earth, opening to a long, moss-filled hallway with doors lining both sides of the walls. Sprinting forward, I slid into one of the many doorways, discovering a hidden alcove.

Dark, husky laughter haunted me, Knox's heavy footfalls echoing as he slowly made his way down the stairs. I slid behind the wall, backing against a moss-covered doorway. Closing my eyes, I tried to calm my racing heart and emotions. Slowly, so slowly, I lowered myself to the ground, and my legs burned from the strain. Reaching in my pocket, I produced a handful of quartz, placing them on the floor to protect the space I held.

"Aria, I can smell you. You're so fucking close that I can taste you in the air," Knox taunted, his voice coming from every direction at once. The sexy, deep, rich baritone slid through me, creating a storm of need that only he could create within me. I hated and craved him, which was confusing among a mess of emotions that offended me down to my toenails. "Are you afraid? I smell… *fear*." The sound of his heavy boots moved over the moss-covered ground I'd just run over. "I miss the feel of your body beneath mine, and the sweet noises you make when I'm buried deep within your tight cunt. I miss the smell of your hair against my nose when I wake from slumber, wrapped around your heat, holding you close against me. Enough running, Little Monster, I want to taste you dripping down my face. Let me give you what you crave, what we both crave from one another."

He stopped in front of me, his jaw clenching as he inhaled deeply. His oceanic eyes narrowed to slits as he looked at the floor where the moss showed my last footprint stopping.

His body turned, and he stared through me, the crystals protecting me from discovery. The door at my back was covered in thick moss, a tattletale sign that I hadn't gone through. His dark head canted as the men entered the narrow hallway of the alcove. Knox lowered his head slightly, and I held my breath while he looked right into my eyes that widened with worry.

"The rooms over here are disturbed," Killian called from further down the hallway, causing Knox to turn toward him.

When had Killian walked past? How was he at the far end of the hallway without passing me? My attention moved back to Knox, taking in the sleek, rippling muscles beneath his shirt, which did little to conceal the hard-lined contours that my hands wished to trace. No matter how many times I saw Knox, the sheer power and dominance of his presence always struck me.

Relief washed through me when Knox appeared to be moving on, but he paused, slowly turning back toward the door where I stood. He lunged without warning, and I spun, barely missing his hands as he shoved his way through the door behind me. My trembling hands lifted to my lips, holding a scream at bay, and I closed my eyes, relieved that I'd placed the quartz around me to keep my presence hidden.

Knox moved through the doorway, pausing as he turned, inhaling my scent. His nostrils flared, eyes mocking as he stared at me directly, like he could sense me there, but couldn't see me.

"She was just here. I smell roses, and *mutt*," he snarled, turning toward the doorway where Lore appeared, frowning as he inspected the room. "I want Dimitri tracked down and handled. He isn't with the others if the smell of his aroused state clings to Aria like perfume."

"I thought…"

"You thought fucking wrong, Lore," Knox interjected, cutting him off. His tone offered no answer to Lore's question. Nor did Lore persist, choosing to drop the subject abruptly. "Leave it alone. The rats have eyes, and the walls have pretty flowers listening to our every word."

I didn't dare breathe or move my eyes from the room that held enormous, bird-like skeletal remains. I had to refrain from gasping as large, colorful feather plumes glowed with magic. Knox pushed a wall open inside the room, smiling coldly at whatever he'd found. I worried my lip with my teeth, barely standing back as Brander moved through the doorway. Bumping my arm, he stopped and spun to look behind him.

My blood turned to ice in my veins, preparing to run from them, knowing I wouldn't get far with the army outside the house and the men within it. Brander swung his arm, and I ducked just before it would have struck me.

"This place gives me the creeps," Brander muttered, running his hand over his mouth before moving to where Knox stood.

"Get the men in here and have them collect the journals," Knox stated. "She isn't getting what she's after today. If Aria wants these, she can ask me nicely."

I barely managed to stifle a snort as they exited the room, moving back into the long, winding hallway.

The men with Knox gathered outside the doorway. Swallowing, I reached into my pocket, grabbing the remainder of the spelled quartz I'd taken from the tomb. Closing my eyes, I exhaled, moving with inhuman speed. I stepped out of the circle, tossing the quartz to shield the entire doorway leading to the journals.

Ocean blue eyes locked with mine, my lips curving into a victorious smile. I stepped back, tilting my head while his heated gaze slid down my body. Knox and I fought hard, but anytime we caught sight of the other, we looked for injuries, or at least I did. Him, on the other hand, well, he was probably sizing my head up for his throne, deciding what to do with the rest of my corpse.

"That was really stupid, Aria," Knox snorted, his smile all wolf, lifting at the corners of his mouth, promising to draw blood. "How do you plan on escaping a room guarded against the use of magic?" he asked, and the color drained from my face. "Are you planning to spend the night in there?"

I frowned, cocking my head to the side. I sent feelers out, sliding my magic through the room, smiling at him. Knox's magic may not have worked within the room, but mine did. His body moved closer, sending his power slithering over my bare midriff, causing my eyes to grow hooded with need.

"You're moaning, Aria," he announced through a gravelly tone. He leaned casually against the doorframe as his eyes slid over my body, sending thunder rumbling through me, as lightning struck every part of me that came to life in his presence. "Remove the spell and let me ease the tension you're experiencing. You and I both know how this ends. You're only delaying the inevitable by running from me."

"I like the tension you cause me. It's a reminder of how tense I'll be when you remove my head for your throne," I swallowed a moan, inhaling his aphrodisiac scent that fed life to every cell in my body.

"Oh, sweet girl, I had something else in mind for that head. I enjoy that tongue of yours entirely too much to remove it, or the pretty head in which it's attached. I also enjoy how hot you burn beneath me when I am buried within that tight, clenching cunt of yours."

I swallowed hard and loud. Knox had a crude mouth, but damn did it do delicious things that made my legs clamp together at the memory. He smiled with an intensity burning in his eyes that almost caused my flesh to combust and catch fire.

"Stop looking at me like that."

"Looking at you like what?" he smirked as liquid desire pooled between my apex.

"Stop looking at me like you're about to consume me and spit out my bones. It's disturbing because I'm pretty certain I'd enjoy it, up to the point where you left me in a pool of blood and bones." His lips jerked, and his eyes narrowed to mere slits as his nostrils flared at the moisture collecting in my panties.

I absolutely hated the words moist and dripping, yet both words were terrifyingly accurate for describing what he did to my pussy. A mere look, or the sound of his sultry voice like gravel, scraped over every nerve ending until my cunt dripped for him. He was a bastard for knowing how he affected me, and I was a masochist for craving him the way I did.

"Lay down. Spread your legs, show me what belongs to me, and I promise to devour it endlessly for hours. I won't leave you in a heap of blood and bones, but I will leave you boneless, and craving the feel of me buried in that tight, heated sheath that even now clenches from the memory of how it felt stretching while I wrote my name on your insides."

"Damn," I swallowed, and my nipples grew hard with need, pushing against my top's fabric. My spine arched subtly, and my legs tightened together. I hated that Knox knew I was considering his offer. The triumphant look burning in his eyes forced a sultry purr to escape my lungs, finding purchase through my lips, opening as my tongue slid over them. "That was smooth, asshole."

"Not as smooth as that naked flesh that I want to taste. Can I eat that pussy, Aria? I'll even give you control and allow you to ride my face if you promise to let me taste the honey coating your cunt. Remove the crystals and get the fuck on my mouth. You know you want it as much as I do. I can see the need burning in your eyes."

"That's not happening. Though if we're honest? I do miss the feel of you beneath me, stretching me, taking me until every part of my body aches from your abuse. However, we're not being honest, and it isn't happening. I'm the prey, and you're the carnivore that intends to devour me. You're not gnawing on my bones, so stop with your deliciously dirty mouth, because I haven't had a single orgasm in months. I'm a very needy bitch who is experiencing some very hostile emotions about you right now."

"I'm right here, Little Monster. Take that aggression out on me. I'll even let you tie me up if it makes you feel safer."

I smirked at the idea of him bound and a slave to my every whim and desire. However, we both knew it would be more for my benefit because neither rope nor chain would ever contain Knox. I worried my lip with my teeth, causing his eyes to dip to my mouth as they filled with lust and desire.

We both remembered the only time he'd ever been helpless. I'd been on my knees with him buried in my throat and at my mercy. I stepped back as he stepped forward, rattling low and needy in his chest. I purred, knowing he scented the arousal he'd created within me. He was a storm, and I was the land that prepared to be ravished beneath his endless torment.

"Let me in."

"Pass," I smirked, watching the anger rising to fill his gaze as he held mine. "I am so wet right now. Maybe I'll get myself off while you watch. Would you like that?"

"We both know that you can't come without me right now. Your heat is upon you, which means nothing short of me buried within that tight haven will get you off, Aria. Right now, your body pulses with need; a need so deep and extensive that nothing you do will ease the ache in your cunt. You need me. For this, you need me, and only me. You and I both know the truth of what is happening, and yet you think you're strong enough to ignore it. You're not. No one is. You're in heat, and only I will touch you. Anyone else who attempts to ease your aching need will die by either your hand or mine. I care not which of us ends the life of the poor bastard that touches my woman. You're mine and only mine. We both know that, too. You're only prolonging your pain, Sweet Girl. It's inevitable. You can't fight your need any more than you can fight evolution. Now remove the fucking crystals so I can give you what we both need right now."

"Come and get me if you're man enough. Break the wards, and you can fucking have me," I taunted, watching the muscles in his jawline clench as his throat bunched together, his need as great as my own. I smiled, lifting my skirt to show him precisely how drenched for him I really was. "Here's the honey. Let's see how you get through my magic to taste it, Knox. I crave your sting, and yet you're all bark and no bite. Pity," I stated, pushing my fingers through the wetness to lick one as he watched me, his eyes locking onto the tip of my finger as my lips wrapped around it, and I moaned loudly. "Pussy, it's not what you're having for dinner. I taste like you need to fuck me." I dropped my skirt, stepping back as his smile turned cruel, and his features sharpened like he was fighting his creature for control. My fingers moved over the hollow column of my throat, and I slowly stepped back again, showing him that the crystals moved with me. "That's what I thought, pussy."

"Drop your spell and call me that again, Aria. I fucking dare you."

"I'm horny, Knox, not suicidal."

His smile was all teeth, promising blood with his bite. A shiver of unease snaked down my spine, and the temperature dropped as he silently watched me. He didn't move, didn't speak. His eyes told me what he'd do the moment he caught me, and damn if I didn't accidentally want to drop the crystal's protecting me and bend to that iron will he held over my body.

I craved to be beneath him, bending to his superior strength as he wrecked my sensibilities, forcing that animalistic need on me until I was nothing more than flesh and bones that knew no resistance and wouldn't care that he feasted upon them. I trembled, shaking my head to dispel the imagery he was feeding me with his eyes.

"Who's the fucking pussy now, Aria?"

Chapter Six

I stood just out of Knox's reach inside the room. Silently scowling at him, and fighting the need rushing through me from the image he painted in my mind, vividly perverted, right down to the noises I would make if I let him have me. Stepping back, I turned to scan the space that Knox said held information. He was aware I was searching for something, but he had no idea what it was. If he had any knowledge of what I was after, he'd probably laugh at me and tell me I was insane.

Hell, even I thought I was insane for what I wanted to do, or planned to attempt since the chances of my success were a little over zilch.

I scrunched my nose as Knox smiled, folding his arms over his chest while the others patted him on the back as if he'd caught me. He hadn't captured me, nor would he. I turned my back to him, dismissing them all as my eyes slid around the room.

On the far wall of the antechamber was the large, colorful feather plume. I ran my fingers over the glowing feather, watching in wonder as it sparkled brighter as if sensing my magic. Looking to my left, I noticed an entrance to another enormous room and paused. On the table, in the middle of the room, sat a massive bird-like skull with shark-like teeth. Beside it sat a lot of big feathers of varying colors.

I lifted a feather, holding it to my nose, then set it down when I saw what appeared to be a giant nest in a darkened corner of the room. My eyes narrowed, and I tilted my head, studying the materials used to make it. Feathers, blankets, and other miscellaneous items intricately woven together, and upon close inspection, I could see the nest had been well-used.

"What sort of creature is this?" I asked, knowing that Knox was listening to me.

"You tell me, Aria. What is it?" he countered, closer than he'd been moments before. I spun, staring into ocean eyes that were inches from mine. I could feel his breath fanning my lips, and everything within me begged to step past the barrier holding him away from me.

I peered down at the spelled quartz encircling my feet, pressing my lips together before lifting my attention back to him. I drank in the sight of Knox, thirsty for more. His lips curved into a knowing grin as he watched me. He inhaled, and his smile faltered, replaced by a scowl as his expression turned cold.

"You want to explain to me why I can smell mutt on you?" he inquired, lifting a brow as he gave me a pointed look.

"I may have let one kiss me," I confessed, withholding the disappointment of that kiss to myself.

Knox grinned with heat smoldering in his eyes. I didn't need to tell him I'd been disappointed. The smug look in his eyes and the tilt of his lips told me he already knew. I wanted to lie, to say Dimitri bent me over and wrote his name on my uterus, but this was Knox, and he just knew shit. He could smell that I'd simply touched Dimitri's lips, so lying about fucking him, well, it would be pointless since he could scent the lie in my lack of arousal, and something as mundane as my mood.

His expression told me he wasn't worried about Dimitri in the slightest, and mine told him to get bent. Knox tilted his head, and his smirk turned conceited. Fiery eyes told me he was silently considering how he would bend my ass over and show me how he intended to get bent inside me. I swallowed, and his eyes sparkled with the challenge, daring me to lie.

"It could have happened that way!" I snapped, and his head shook slowly.

"Nah, Little Monster. It wouldn't have. You and I both know that I'll be the one satisfying your hunger when you reach your limit." His voice was laden with gravel, scraping over every nerve ending in my body, causing a chill to shiver up my spine.

I loved the sound of his deep, sexy voice when he lowered it to that *come, ride me woman* octave. I swallowed, turning my head to stare into the room behind me. I whispered the spell for light, and candles lit within the room.

I felt Knox stiffen without needing to see him do

so. His heated breath fanned my bare shoulder, and I shuddered involuntarily, sending a carnal wave of lust rushing through me to pulse against my apex. My shoulder throbbed where his mark adorned my flesh, and I felt the whisper of his lips against it, causing my core to clench, as all the blood in my body lowered to my nether region.

Knox's scent was an aphrodisiac that drugged me, more potent than any potion or spell. He projected it on purpose, watching me fight the need to shed my inhibition and abandon my course to do what every instinct within me wanted.

It was an endless fight against doing what my body required, and what my mind knew we should leave alone. Neither could agree, and with every moment I was this close to the man my body desired, I wasn't sure which would win the war.

"I bet Dimitri's lips brushed against yours, and you saw me instead of him. I'm going to guess your creature didn't even stir in his presence because she found him so fucking lacking that she couldn't be bothered to notice him. Your body didn't respond to Dimitri because you need and want the intensity that comes when we're together, and everyone else just falls short and is found wanting in comparison. You and I both know that anything less would be pale and lacking, other than you and me stripped bare, fucking like the savages we really are."

I moved away from him, unwilling to acknowledge he was right. Knox didn't need verbal confirmation. He was cocky enough without me adding to it. We both knew I wouldn't give in to another, and that my creature demanded the biggest, most primal beast would mount us, and that was this asshole prowling around me like a creature that smelled an easy kill.

As I moved, the quartz crystals moved with me, spelled to protect me from anyone, and anything. Quartz alone would serve as heavy protection, but spelled with an enchantment, they became magical stones that guarded me against anyone I didn't want touching me. This meant I'd manually had to add Knox to that list since I wanted those powerful hands on me anytime they were near, even though I shouldn't.

"I'll take your silence as confirmation." He followed me into the room, and I leaned against a table, staring at the formula marked on the paper. "I can help you find what you're looking for," he offered.

I turned to tell him off, frowning as his scent hit me with the force of being struck by a bus I hadn't seen coming. My head dropped back as a moan slipped from my lips. I fought to regain control, dropping my head forward as my attention locked on the wickedly dark smile burning in his eyes.

Knox was releasing pheromones mixed with testosterone to lure me out of the quartz. I smirked, freeing my scent that made the cocky grin on his lips falter. His eyes widened with the realization that I wasn't just horny; I was in season and had concealed it from him. His tongue escaped his mouth, licking his full bottom lip as he silently prowled closer.

Knox's hands landed on the table behind me as he leaned forward, breathing me in as his deep, soothing rattle escaped his throat, echoing through every part of my body. My lips quivered while he watched me, his knowing gaze smoldering with the promise of flames as his nostrils flared. Knox shouldn't have been able to get close to me, yet he caged me against the table regardless of the spelled quartz.

My pulse thundered with need, dropping to his hungry mouth that I desired to devour. If I touched him, the spell in the quartz would end, which wasn't something that I couldn't let happen. Not yet, anyway.

He stood and reached down, hooked his fingers beneath the shirt he wore, lifting it to reveal his body's smooth, sculpted muscles. My eyes lowered to the ripple of muscle clenched in his abdomen, revealing his hard body to my hungry gaze. I loved Knox's body; the subtle curves, the sharp edges. The way it rippled with power as it drove into mine, taking me to heights only he could achieve. He tossed the shirt aside, absently rubbing his large hand across the back of his neck, searching for something.

Slowly turning away, he revealed the hard, tapered muscles of his back that adorned ravens up his spine and shoulders. His broad shoulders dipped into the narrowed waist that vanished into the pants he wore. Those pants offended my senses, hindering the feast my hungry eyes wanted. It took effort to tear my gaze from his hard body, forcing my attention away from the male dripping his sinful scent to fuck with my head and hormones.

A scrapping noise across the floor gained my attention, and I frowned, watching as Knox returned with a large chair. He nodded toward the wide bench seat, his lips curling into a dark smirk as he kicked off his boots and sat, removing his socks.

Knox leaned back, studying me through his dark lashes as my chest rose and fell with hunger, growing labored with the need to climb him and cave to my baser needs. Swallowing audibly, I frowned, noting that he was telling me with his eyes to sit down, instead of asking.

I worried my lip between my teeth, letting my eyes linger on the way his stomach creased in the position he was sitting. His smile revealed white teeth as he noticed how my eyes couldn't tear away from his utter perfection, lifting his arms wide, resting them on the back of the chair. Ignoring the warning burning in his eyes, I paced.

"Sit the fuck down, woman. You're exhausting me," he announced in a clipped tone, his eyes slowly sliding down my body, noting the splattering of blood that marred the wispy white skirt I wore. "I take it the witches in the woods were your kills?" My attention lifted from his muscles, locking with his eyes. "You surprise me. Come, ride my cock. You know you want it, and I'm right here. Use me to soothe that ache."

"Hard pass," I whispered breathlessly, lifting my arm to rub the tension in my neck.

"That isn't the answer I wanted out of you, woman."

"Sucks to be you then, doesn't it?" Knox lunged, and I yelped, swallowing as his lips curled into a predatory smirk.

Chapter Seven

Knox snorted before sitting forward, clasping his hands in front of him. He offered me a wicked smile that promised dark desires as a deep rattle slithered over me. "Well, something is hard." He leaned back, and my eyes lowered to see his cock testing the boundary of his pants, bouncing against the fabric twice. This caused me to laugh in surprise, which made his eyes light up with mirth. "Do you even know what this place is?" he asked, leaning forward again.

I slid to the floor, giving my legs a break from standing. Knox swallowed hard, noting I'd sat on my knees before him. Amusement danced in his gaze at the subtle act of stubbornness, since there was a soft place to rest my ass beside him. I'd decided my knees were a better option. Although it usually displayed submission, Knox knew I wasn't offering that to him. Irony. It was amusing when it played out as it was now.

"I'll give it to you, Aria. You look good from behind

as I am chasing you. But you look much better on your knees before me. You know what would make you look even better?" I smiled, licking my lips while his attention moved to my mouth. "You're playing with fire, and you're not even afraid of the flames."

"Do I look good on my knees, Knox?" I asked, moving my feet out from beneath me. "I think I'd look much better on your face, riding it." I closed my eyes, rubbing my fingers over my strained shoulder.

"You're leaving quite the pile of bodies behind as you move through this realm. I'm impressed with the sheer number of kills, but you're sloppy at best. Eventually, you're going to end up hurt unless you join me, where you belong anyway. You and I both know where this leads, and we know who will win."

I pushed down the pang of regret that came from the fact that I was leaving hundreds of witches dead in each town I visited. They weren't savable, of that I knew, yet it mattered little to my mind that they were vile beings leaving ruins in their wake. I had to stop them, but that came with a toll I carried. It was heavy and smothering. My throat bobbed, tightening, and caused a lump to grow as heat burned my eyes. I pried my gaze from him, looking down at his sexy feet. Who the hell had sexy feet? Knox did, but then I liked every inch of him, right down to his cocky smirk.

Knox had a way of knowing what bothered me, nailing it on the head with a verbal hammer. I slid onto my side, resting my head in the palm of my hand as my elbow touched the cold, marbled floor. A sardonic smile played on Knox's mouth. I watched him stand, moving onto his knees before he spread out on the floor beside me, his body mirroring mine as he faced me.

I swallowed hard as he held my hungry stare. Our eyes remaining locked on one another, knowing each other through a primitive, carnal-lust, on the deepest level a man could know a woman. Sex between us was dirty, primitive, and filled with violence. We unleashed with a mutual need to rid ourselves of the aggression we felt. I worried my lip, remembering the feel of him stretching me full. His body had barely fit within mine, his immensely enormous cock stretching me painfully full, taking up every inch within me. Knox grinned wickedly, like he knew exactly what I had thought of while staring at him.

It wasn't just animalistic.

It was as if our creatures drove the sex to be darker, more aggressive, and I fucking loved it, craving it more than my need to escape him.

Our creatures were primal, matching our need to go at each other hard and without mercy, but then mercy wasn't something either of us would ever ask of the other.

"All the death I leave behind," I swallowed hard, "does it make me a monster you want to kill?" I whispered carefully, studying his face at my words that slipped free. His jaw clenched, and those knowing eyes slid up to meet mine with regret burning deep within. "I didn't think it would be hard to murder bad people. I wasn't wrong, not entirely. It's surprisingly easy to punish those who trespass against the innocent. But I find I've become numb to their cries, which honestly scares me. No one should ever become numb to death, or from taking a life. There's this place within me warning that I may enjoy it too much, which terrifies me the most."

"You either become the hunter or the prey in this world," he swallowed, watching me. "Unless the thing hunting you is much stronger as in our case," he added, drawing his finger into a pattern on the floor. "How many innocent lives have you taken, Aria?"

"None, and I don't intend to either," I whispered through the emotion clogging my words into my throat. "You?"

"Thousands." He watched the narrowing of my eyes as I judged him harshly for admitting something so horrendous out loud. "It is easy to judge what you don't understand. You see a man where there is only a monster. You look at me as if I should care what you think about what I have done during my life. Someday, when you're forced to make the choices I have, I hope you remember that no man craves war. Monsters crave war, Aria. Man craves hearth, home, and a woman to carry his babes in her womb. He wants to watch as she feeds his babe from her breast, growing stronger from their mother's milk. I wasn't born a monster. I was born a man who housed a beast, but once awoken, our monsters do not simply go silent into the night. They're built to wage wars and fight them. I am what your bloodline created, and yet I still crave to see my wife with my son, yet everything within me knows that it won't ever be so. I know war, and I know how to fight it. Have I ended innocent lives? Yes, because in war, there are always those who die needlessly, and those deaths are on us. Losing innocent lives is the price of war and inevitable, no matter how much you try to prevent it."

"Plan for what is difficult while it is easy, do what

is great while it is small," I whispered on an exhale, watching his lips tug into a knowing smile.

"*The Art of War*. You've read it?"

"Several times," I admitted, enjoying the sparkle igniting in his eyes as if he'd found me a worthy advisory simply because I'd read the book. "That's how I judge your moves. You must have read that worn copy a thousand times, with its broken spine and creased pages. The book looked loved and well-read."

Knox licked his lips, inhaling as the muscles of his abdomen rippled with power, drawing my gaze to the tattoos on his chest and stomach.

"Which of Sun Tzu's tactics am I using against you?" he asked in a raspy tone, his eyes studying me as my mind turned over what game he may be playing. "I promise you; there are many in play."

"Thus, the expert in battle moves the enemy and is not moved by him," I smirked, and he returned it with a wolfish smile that promised blood. "If his forces are united, separate them. You have done that. I am alone in this unforgiving land."

"You're not alone. I am here with you. I'm in the shadows, looking over your shoulder, hunting my pretty, ethereal prey as she slumbers, unaware that the biggest monster in all the realms serves as her protector and enemy. You're never alone as long as I hunt you, Aria. I am never far behind you."

I closed my eyes, lowering my arm, frowning as he mirrored me. "If you'd never married, or been in love, and I wasn't your enemy, could you want me?"

His mouth tightened into a hard line, and my brow creased at the pain that flashed across Knox's face. I closed my eyes and felt sleep trying to pull me into a much-needed respite. My chest rose and fell as I sensed his nearness, inhaling the smell of his body.

"I do want you, woman."

"Yeah, to use me as a weapon against those who seek to oppress you and your people? I am neither wanted nor craved by you. I am simply a means to an end. I don't think anyone has ever wanted me, not simply just for me." My eyes peeked open a sliver, and I found him frowning at me. "Don't misunderstand, Knox. My family loves me very much, but I am the strongest player in their game. I know that, to them, I am also a weapon. It would be nice if just one person wanted me because I was worth wanting. Maybe someday, right? When this war is won by you or by me, and you no longer care where I am, I will find a man who craves me for who I am as a person, instead of the power within me. That would be the dream, wouldn't it? To be worthy of one being who just wants me and likes who I am," I swallowed thickly.

"I want you right now, Aria. I dream of the time you spent in my basement. The day you discarded your human skin and let go of those emotions and inhibitions. You shed your morals like snakes shed their skin, revealing the beast within you. I've seen you at your rawest, most vulnerable, yet truest self. You fought me, and I fucked you harder for assuming you had what it took to take me on. You *liked* it and begged me for more. You lost control, and I didn't. You became this beautiful little monster who raged, pleaded, and lifted that sexy ass into the air, urging me forward to take what you so willingly offered. You are a savage. You wouldn't settle for someone just wanting you. You'd want them to crave you with intensity, and fight you when that anger rips through you with savagery. Admit it, that's why you didn't feel shit with Dimitri's kiss. He lacked everything you crave from me. He isn't man enough for you, and the moment you fought him, he'd bow to you, and that isn't what you want from a man. You want someone strong enough to bend you over and pull that hair while destroying your sensibility with every thrust into that tight cunt. You need someone that will dominate you in bed because it's the only way your creature will allow it to happen. Just as mine demands you yield, yours demands to be earned and subdued. It's why she fought me before letting me fuck her.

"You're just like me, Aria, whether or not you like it. We are monsters clothed in a package that eases other's fears because if they ever looked upon us in our truest form, we'd feast on their bones. You and me, we're not created for dreams. We're created for nightmares, and we're okay with that. We're smart enough to know that dreams are sweet whispers of promises that never happen or come true. Nightmares are what people fear most, praying they never unfold into reality. You never forget a nightmare because they haunt you forever."

I swallowed, placing my palm flat onto the floor as a portal opened beneath me. His eyes narrowed to slants. I lifted my head, smirking at him.

"That's where you are wrong. I am someone's dream, and you're my nightmare, Knox."

Passing through the portal, I landed in a field of soft flowers, peering around the space before I moved through the long grass toward the woods. I was exhausted, but that man was frustrating and tiring me out on purpose.

His eyes mocked me, forcing me to hear what his lips didn't speak. He'd taken me right back to that basement, forcing me to relive every sinful act we'd done, right down to the ones that had been painful, and yet I'd roared his name, urging him on. Some shit remained in the dark, and him getting his jollies over his time with my creature was one of those things.

Rubbing my eyes, I studied the terrain, forcing my gaze toward the keep I couldn't breach because of their wards, barriers, and protection crystals. Frowning, I gazed around the field until I found a cliffside, knowing if nothing else, I could catch enough sleep inside before the sun rose.

Chapter Eight

Hands grabbed me, yanking me up from the cave floor where I'd found respite from Knox and his men to indulge in sleep. Ocean blue eyes locked with mine. The smile curving Knox's lip was sexy and bespoke of victory.

He wore nothing more than a pair of loose hanging jeans that clung from his hips. The raven on his hipbone drew my gaze, holding my attention as it shifted, lifting its head, peering at me before opening its beak.

Knox pulled me against his heated flesh, running his hands down my sides. The scent that hit me was overwhelming, turning my mind to mush. His subtle deep purring had my body on high alert. My entire female anatomy dancing and purring in harmony with his as his warm mouth brushed against my shoulder before sinking his fangs into my flesh. Instinct took over, and my body betrayed me as my ass lifted for him.

I didn't care that he'd caught me, or how he'd found me. I needed him to soothe the ache within me. I needed Knox to end the animalistic craving continually pulsing from deep in my soul. I rattled the moment he removed his mouth, noting how his eyes slid down my face, settling on my lips.

"You look like you're starving," he murmured huskily.

"I am. I'm absolutely starving. Feed me, Knox. Feed me all of you," my voice coming out breathy and full of lust sounded as if it belonged to someone else.

The rocky cave floor turned cool and smooth. I looked down to see that I was standing on marbled tiles. Gasping, I lifted my head and surveyed my surroundings. The cave was gone, and in its place was Knox's library. I loved this library.

Slowly, I tried to step away from him, but he didn't allow it. Knox grabbed the bottom of my top, removed it, lowering his head to flick my nipple with his tongue. His sharp fangs nicked the raised peak, and I moaned, calling out in pleasure as dark laughter vibrated through him.

His hand slid to my throat, moving my head to the side as his teeth skimmed the flesh. Knox's loud purr echoed through the room as he kicked my feet apart, running the tip of his finger against my opening. My eyes slid down, finding myself completely bared to his touch. This man undid me, stripping me naked as he made my soul come alive.

He was a fire in my veins that burned without warning, driving my mind to a sizzling inferno that raged out of control. His mouth found mine, kissing me until breathing became irrelevant, and my need for him grew. My heartbeat echoed in my ears, mirroring thunder's sound in an electrical storm with no pulse between strikes.

He pushed me back onto the couch and turned me onto my stomach before licking against my core from behind like a starving beast devouring his kill. I felt him against my pelvic bone, lapping hungrily as he sent my body rushing into orgasm.

The sound Knox made against my sex was a raw, angry noise echoing through his chest and down his body, dancing over my opening as a purr exploded from my throat. A low purr escaped from deep in his chest, pleased to feed me white-hot pleasure, causing me to vibrate and pulse. I came until my body lurched forward to rest on the bed.

My head lifted, and I rose to my elbows, looking down at the bed. Hearing a moan to my left, I slid my attention to the couch, shocked to see another version of me and Knox, his face buried between my legs, lavishing me. I cried out his name like he was my salvation. I watched in confusion, then felt something push against my opening and stiffened.

Peering over my shoulder, I found Knox number one parting my ass cheeks to gaze at my sex. The tip of his cock slid against my opening, gathering my wetness along his shaft, and he groaned, testing my readiness to take him.

The version of Knox behind me was pure lust in the most primitive form. Dark power exuded from him, and I let myself feel it for a moment. In that instant, there was just the two of us. I was a needy ball of nerves driven by desire. He was burning with hunger, ready to devour me, and that was all that mattered.

I felt him entering my body, burning with his invasion as muscles stretched to accommodate his inhuman size. Hands gripped my thighs, spreading me further as he shoved me to the bed, pushing into me again and again. I screamed, crying out loudly at how fully he filled me.

The mindlessness he made me feel was absolute. He picked me up, shoved me against the wall, and lifted me, burying himself within me once more. My gaze moved to the bed where we once were, and yet another version of us was on display. Knox number three pounded recklessly into my body, his ass tightening with each thrust as he entered my heat.

The version of me on the couch smiled in my direction as Knox number two continued to feast on her sex. Her head turned to watch as Knox number one held me pinned against the wall, driving mercilessly into my core as he rattled, creating slick arousal, demanding I take more of him.

"What the hell is happening?" I whispered. Dark wings slid from Knox's spine, preventing me from seeing anything other than him as an orgasm rocked through me.

I felt the library's cold marble floor beneath me as he laid me down and rolled me around. I straddled the glorious beast that held me pinned to his body, impaled by his large, thick cock. I smiled down at him, rocking my hips in a move I knew drove him to the edge of his sanity.

Eyes the color of freshly polished black onyx held my gaze, embers burning within their inky depths as he peered up at me. His hands cupped my breasts, and I whimpered, noting how sensitive they felt.

I looked around the room, noting all the other versions of me were watching us. I moved, clenching hungrily onto him as the orgasm slowly built in my core. My vision blurred, and I started to bend over to claim his mouth, but the sight of my round stomach stopped me cold.

Panic ripped through me, and my hands lifted to my belly, slowly rubbing the swollen flesh. My heart jackknifed, and I whimpered as tiny feet pushed against my hand. Knox touched the babe within me, holding his hand against mine.

"*This is what we will take from him,*" my creature whispered as Knox sat up, cupping my cheeks between his hands. "*This is what he will give us, Aria. This is how we get rid of the cobwebs on our vagina.*" I blinked, frowning. "*You know, this is why we have a vagina. Put it to use, and we're both happy! Don't use it, and it will look like this!*" I stared down, looking at my very flat, very smooth, plastic-looking, Barbie-like flesh between my legs, minus a vagina. On my knees were cobwebs with a spider dangling between my legs. I slapped at it, as Knox snickered very familiarly. "*You deserve it since you don't seem to know how to use your vagina!*"

"Creature!" I snapped, shivering as pain sliced through me, causing me to peer at Knox, who spoke with my voice.

His image wavered until another version of me

was looking into my eyes, holding my face. My eyes searched her face, and I shook my head. Had I eaten something poisonous? My hands tightened, and all around me, the other versions of Knox and me moved closer. I stared into the eyes of Knox number one as he moved his mouth. Sounds echoed in my ears, and yet I couldn't make out the words.

I gasped as pain entered my awareness. I felt the oily touch of dark magic and whimpered. My eyes slid to my belly, finding it smooth and flat once more. A tremble of unease slithered through me, wrapping around my throat as panic entered my mind.

"Wake up, Sweet Monster," Knox whispered, standing in front of me.

He forced me to move, pushing my double out of his way. His hands clapped against my cheeks with his claws extended. Knox shook me forcefully as I cried out, alerted to more than his angry scream. His face morphed into that of a monster, his tone urgent and immediate.

"Wake the fuck up! Now, Aria!" Knox shouted, and I whimpered as something struck me, hard.

My eyes snapped open, revealing black-eyed witches surrounding me. Blood caked my face, both dried and fresh. My blood painted the white skirt and top I wore, and I could feel bruises and cuts aplenty over my body. One witch smiled crudely, her empty stare holding mine as she lifted her hand once more, slamming it against my cheek.

Pain filled my mind, knowing they'd tried to fuck with my head. They might have succeeded if my creature hadn't forced me into a sex dream with Knox and our doppelgangers. My body was a mass of welts and bruises and a few cuts here and there. I'd survive the pain because whatever lived within me, she'd gone ten times harder against Knox, and we'd survived. A fist lifted, slamming against my nose, causing lights to explode in my vision.

I dropped my head back, laughing softly until it bubbled up in my chest, escaping louder until the witches stopped assaulting me. They stood quietly, watching what they assumed was a nervous breakdown unfolding.

"You thought you could pass by our land without offering tribute to us?" one witch snarled, and I turned my attention toward her, laughing harder at her narrowing glare.

"Couldn't get past the crystals," I admitted, letting the laughter subside.

"What are you talking about?" she demanded through blackened teeth, threatened to disintegrate if she ground them together too hard.

"I couldn't get into the castle to murder you because your wards and protection spell prevented it. So, what's a girl to do? I let you assume you'd captured me so I could gain entry," I laughed, yanking on the rope that held me, inhaling the scent of fire as it burned the ropes that secured me to the ceiling.

I smiled coldly, watching the panic igniting within their eyes, and laughed soundlessly. These witches screwed up and walked me through the front door, and I was about to bring their house down on their fucking heads.

Chapter Nine

Black magic rushed toward me, but I sent it right back at them by simply lifting my hands. I stretched my arms, cracked my neck, and smiled at their horrified looks as my teeth slid free, along with razor-sharp claws. I watched the witches slowly backing away, prowling closer, I smiled coldly.

"Sometimes, you just have to play a damsel to create some distress. Anywho, you've been charged, judged, and I'm here to execute you all. Who wants to die first?" I asked, watching them tremble as the Hecate insignia glowed brightly on my forehead.

I studied the witches as they ran from me, dark magic sizzling around them as their panicked minds searched for an escape from the monster they'd brought in through the front gates. Their screams never escaped past their lips as my power rushed through them, shattering them, painting the walls in blood. The hallway emptied of living witches, and I smirked, heading toward the potion room, knowing what I needed was within.

Stepping through the entrance, I paused, letting my gaze slide over the potions brewing, sending steam billowing into the air. It smelled of lemongrass and sage, an enticing combination. Tiny round vials filled with glowing liquid piqued my interest. Lifting one bottle to my nose, I inhaled and frowned.

Still holding the bottle, I spun as a single witch entered the room, her dress flowing behind her. She lifted her hand to draw magic, but she wasn't quick enough as mine held hers in check. I tossed the bottle at her, watching the horror play on her face as it slammed against her body. I ducked the moment it struck. The room shook with an explosion, forcing me to lift from my hiding place behind a table. I peered over it through the remainder of magic vials.

"Holy shit." I watched as the witch continued staring at me with a horrified expression as her body melted.

I could see through her stomach to the rest of the wall still behind her. My attention slid from the dying witch to the pile of bottles next to me, carefully stepping further away from them. On the far shelf that lined the back wall were ancient tomes. I moved toward them, ignoring the witch behind me, as she slowly and silently got her goop on with the floor. Talk about a hot mess!

My fingers brushed over the leather spines of the books, and a smile played on my lips. I loved books and the scent of melting witch in the morning. Actually, the witch reeked, causing my eyes to water and my nose to wrinkle at the stench.

"Book of Potions?" I asked the witch, turning to find

her head gone, and her organs slowly bubbling over her hips bones. "Bad day, huh?" I asked the room, frowning as I heard footsteps shuffling above me.

I had no idea how deep into the castle I was, but I could sense enough to realize I was underneath at least one or more floors from the ground level. The decay of earth was rife, and like most potion rooms, this one sat nestled into the soil. Examining the room's contents, I studied the large skulls from unknown creatures marked with runes and other strange carvings.

Stepping closer, I lowered my head to inspect one skull up close, frowning when I felt power pulsing from the inhuman, unproportioned skull. It was yet another gigantic bird or something similar to the skull I found in the village. Apparently, people collected things like these in the Nine Realms.

Another skull caught my attention, sending a shiver down my spine. I moved closer and paused. Swallowing hard against the unease I felt, I placed my hand onto it, frowning as the room spun around me.

I could see images flashing before me of creatures fighting against unseen foes. A man beside me rattled, exposing serrated teeth and claws before the entire world mimicked the sound and a low, eerie purring escaped from those marching toward the dark shadows and mist waiting across the field, preparing for battle.

Blood splattered my face, and I turned, releasing my hold on the skull as a man with turquoise eyes and silver hair stood staring at me. In his hand was the head of a witch whose prone body was on the floor beside me. He stared at me as a rattle echoed from deep within his chest, filling the room as he turned, placing his hand on the skull I'd been inspecting. Grabbing my hand, he held it to the skull, forcing us into the scene I'd just witnessed.

"You are of both lines," the male whispered, his nose pushing against my hair, inhaling as he rattled, which didn't call to me, but strangely enough, it was soothing. It lacked Knox's intensity, but I felt the call to answer him with one of my own.

"Who are you?" I asked, uncertain that I really wanted to know.

"You're not ready for that answer, Little One."

"Are you, my father?" I turned to look at him as his lips twisted into a smirk.

"No," he laughed, and my attention shifted back to the scene playing out before us as magic shot toward the monsters pushing through the witches' ranks on the battlefield.

A moment before they would have clashed in battle, he pulled my hand away and crushed the skull, freeing the magic it had held. He stepped closer to me, watching as I backed up. His lips curved into a smile as he rattled, and mine answered his.

"You're not even asking the right questions yet."

"What is the right question?" I countered, continuing to move backward as he proceeded toward me.

"That's not it either."

"What am I?" I demanded, and his eyes danced with amusement.

"That's closer."

"Fucking answer me!" I hissed, digging in my heels, refusing to allow this man to back me against the wall.

"Such fire in one so young," he laughed, smirking softly as his eyes searched mine. "Yet so much anger for what you don't understand." His other hand lifted, and a portal unlike one I'd ever felt before opened like a mirror into another realm, wavering, before returning to a solid backdrop. "Come with me, Aria. If you're ready to know who and what you are, step into the portal and join me. We are the same, you and me. We have the same eyes, which I'm sure you noticed, but you know not why you were born with silver hair, nor why you rattle and wage war with the fire of a million stars burning within you. All you'd have to do to find those answers is to come with me. Are you ready?" More men stepped into sight. All with similar hair and eyes, waiting for me to join them on the portal's other side.

"The wee little beast is terrified, is she not?" one man asked.

"I am not scared! I am pissed. There's a huge difference," I snapped, hiding the fact that I was indeed terrified.

"I can hear the thunder of your heart and smell the sweat dripping down the back of your neck. My creature is chuckling at your fear, Darling. Come with us. You don't belong here, Aria. You're one of us."

The power of the portal felt different and yet pure. It was something I'd felt once before when Knox had stopped time around me on the cliff when we'd first met. It was as if he'd pulled me from my realm and into another, yet nothing around me had frozen in time. My attention moved around the room, noting that nothing moved, which meant I couldn't know if time had stopped or not.

"Tell me who I am. I cannot fight this war alone and hope to win if I don't even know who and what I am!"

"You're not alone, Wee One. We are with you. When these witches captured you, we came. In the forest, when men sought to harm you, we killed them to protect you. You are one of us, so you are not alone unless we feel you wish it to be so. Come with us and let us show you the truth of who you are and why you are here."

"I can't," I admitted through a lump forming in my throat.

"I told you she was not ready," the warrior I'd first encountered stated, exhaling as a frown creased his brow. "When she is ready, she will find us and come to where she belongs. Maybe once she's scratched her itch, and stops causing us issues with her scent, our time would be otherwise unhindered. Though, I do enjoy the sound of breaking bones when they come from men who would harm an unclaimed female."

"Indeed, it is a beautiful sound, isn't it? Still, she belongs with her people. Not with some king who mistreats her. Our warriors would duel each other if they caught a whiff of her, which admittedly, would offer some sport to the otherwise droll of the day."

"When you're ready, Aria Primrose, find us," the warrior whispered, smiling as he bowed and stepped back, turning to speak to the others as he joined them through the portal.

The world went deafening, forcing my hands to my ears as all sound sucked out of the room. The place where they'd stood shimmered, and then a blinding light cut through the room with a surge of immense power. I held my arm up to protect my eyes as the shockwaves sent red-hot pain slicing through me. The moment I could see again, I peered around the room, finding it empty.

My nose lifted, and I inhaled, noting the subtle scent of sage and lemongrass. Not even a whiff of their scent remained. Swallowing past the unease that knowledge created, I worried my lip, as the sound of footsteps filled the hallway. Hurriedly, I started forward as familiar magic slithered through my body, igniting everything around me.

Corpses filled the hallway leading up the staircase. Whoever that man was, he'd sent his magic through me, clearing my path from witches. I paused, midway up the stairs, noting the carnage. The witches weren't just dead; they were ripped apart and left in mangled heaps of flesh and bone. Snorting, I continued up the stairs until forced to stop, coming face-to-face with a group of black-eyed witches.

"Aren't you pretty?" I asked, unleashing magic on them.

They recoiled, shrieking as I bathed in the chaos that ensued. My hands pulsed with magic, sending it rushing toward those who stood between me and exiting the keep with the books I'd come to retrieve.

I'd watched this place for over a week, unable to gain entry, and during that time, these withes had slaughtered people like they were cattle. I'd tried to get in, to no avail, so I'd made sure I was in a spot well patrolled, and that they'd bring me in through the front door, locking their death warrants soundly into place.

Witches detonated as I dropped my head back, enjoying the sounds of diminishing evil. My house was so freaking dirty that bleach wouldn't cut it. It needed more than just elbow grease to rid the world of the evil that had taken root in the realm of my bloodline's good intentions.

Fire leaped from the candles, rushing toward the curtains that barred the moonlight from entering their dark home. Rolling my head back, I heard Ciara's rendition of *Paint It, Black* in my mind, humming the song as I moved through the witches. I watched them burn to nothing more than ashes as I passed by, the intensity of my flames burning too hot for the naked eye to see until it was too late.

"I see your red door..." I laughed before continuing to hum, pushing my tongue between my teeth. I sent fire sailing toward the strongest witch, watching as she combusted. My arms went wide as I twirled, slowly moving through the castle as my clothes disintegrated, and everything around me caught fire.

The flames danced seductively, echoing with a crackling sound that sung to my soul as my creature rejoiced from within, dancing to the song I sang as the surrounding witches melted. I grinned as she clapped, fueled by the flames that beckoned to us.

"We are like Oz!" My creature purred happily.

"Wait; what? No. Oz was the city... we're the good witch. You know, the wicked witches melt and shit?"

"I want to be Ozzy and eat things."

"Ew, no. Bats are a hard limit for me. Yucky," I spat out before gagging, noting the shadows moving near me. "Time to go. We're off to see the next evil witch on our hit list."

"That didn't rhyme."

"Can you just give me one thing where you're not making fun of me?" I asked.

"Not until I get Knox's dick and make it sick! See, that rhymed."

"No, it did not! Okay, maybe a little, but I'm afraid to ask what you meant by making it sick. It's hot in here," I muttered, staring down to the bones fusing to the floor as it bubbled from the intensity of the heat.

"So, did you enjoy my dream? I thought you would like him to find us and stripping… and things."

"I see what you did there."

"It was a nice touch, right? I even showed you his wee-wee, instead of just Barbie vag and cobwebs."

"What are you? Five years old? Don't ever say wee-wee again, ever. Also, I hate spiders."

"You get pissy when I mention cock. Knox has a nice cock. We like his cock. It hits everywhere! So good. So thick. I crave his dick. Plus, now you know why we need dick… because spiders are bad! You hate spiders, so if you get his dicker, he will eat the spiders and our pussy. It's a win for all of us!"

"I said no Knox's cock!"

"Look at you, growing up and shit. You rhymed! You

either get his dick into our happy pouch, or I'm going to take control, and you're going to wake up choking on his cock. I will unlock my jaw that Lore loves, and you can stay locked on Knox's cock forever!"

"And no more talk of spiders. You're giving me the creeps. Wait, you can do that? Never do that to me! *Ever.* Promise me you won't," I muttered, staring at the flames as a hooded figure stepped out of the darkness, watching me through the inferno. I turned, moving in the opposite direction of the shadow. I wasn't falling for that shit!

My bare feet padded across the floor. I moved into the cool evening air, peering at the dark sky before looking over my shoulder, staring through the flames, noting that something watched me. My heart echoed painfully in my chest, battering against my ribs as I swallowed. I inhaled, smelling only the scent of burning flesh through the blaze.

Exhaling, I shivered as the cold air touched my skin and sizzled, sending steam from my naked body. I forced myself to move into the woods where I'd hidden my clothing and pack before allowing the witches to capture me.

Digging through my pack, I grabbed some fresh clothes and dressed. Lifting my nose to the air, I caught a strange scent. Turning to scan the woods, I slipped my pack on, looking at my feet, then tossing an angry glare at the castle that was now a raging inferno. I whispered a spell for the dead, slowly melting into the darkness.

Strange men had invited me to god knows where. Strange men who claimed to know who and what I was. Should I have gone blindly? No. That was how people ended up on stakes, burning brightly into the night like a bonfire. Plus, I had no idea who or what they were. No one in the Nine Realms was honest, or friendly, so why would I willingly go into a portal with strange, but rather hot men? It was either a recipe for disaster or the start of an orgy, neither of which were on my schedule.

I had felt the men, though; felt them on a level I couldn't understand, but I hadn't caught their scent. It was as if they'd purposely concealed it from me. I stubbed my toe and paused, turning as I felt eyes heavy on my spine. Shadows moved, and I swallowed down the urge to tuck tail and run like a bitch.

My gaze slid into the shadows once more, and my nose lifted, catching the faint trace of Knox in the air. Smiling, I hid behind a tree, listening as feet moved on a road beside the copse of trees where I stood. Pulling my scent in and whispering the spell for invisibility, I hid within the shroud of it, as I moved toward the sound of horse hooves trampling cobblestone. Knox wasn't the only hunter, nor was I the only prey.

Chapter Ten

I entered a town teeming with life. My gaze followed some of the men from Knox's army, who had broken away to go deeper into the village. Men and women danced on the streets, drunk with wine that smelled sour, and not to my liking.

Knox spoke to Brander, who seemed distracted, looking over his shoulder and then spinning on his heel, catcalling to a woman that swayed her hips, licking her lips seductively as she moved toward him.

Knox shook his head and slipped into a building, but I didn't dare follow, sensing the wards around the structure. Instead, I crossed the road carefully, dodging drunken villagers who danced to a flute that someone played deeper in town. Leaning against a wall, I rested my head while searching the windows across the road for any sign of Knox.

A candle lit within one of the many windows, and

then Knox appeared, staring up at the stars as I took in his tired face. A dark-haired woman emerged behind him, and he removed his shirt, turning to sit in a chair. She moved around his back, running ruby-red fingernails over his shoulder before finding one of the ravens that adorned his skin, lowering her mouth to brush against it softly.

Anger pulsed within me, inciting a jealous rage that had my nails digging into the soft flesh of my palm while I fought the urge to enter the building and rip her lips from his body. She reached toward a table, producing a needle she dipped into a clear inkwell, before slowly poking it into his flesh. Knox didn't so much as wince from the bite of her needle.

I watched them together, noting the way she continually touched him when it wasn't warranted. Blood dripped from his raven, but if it pained him, he didn't show it. His head turned, and he looked down at where I stood, noticing my anger. His nostrils flared, and then his eyes lowered to where the woman's hand stroked his arm.

Dismissing Knox, I turned my attention to where Brander, Lore, Killian, and Greer sat outside the building, smiling at their antics. Lore was balancing himself on a chair, and Brander sat in another, holding a blonde on his lap, nuzzling her neck. The woman who thought to entertain Lore was failing miserably, and that caused me to chuckle. Giving up, she walked away with a stern frown, either from something he'd said, or her inability to lure him to her.

Greer spoke to a male who had his hair pulled back in braids, secured in a bun that would make many women jealous over its beauty. Killian, well, ever watchful Killian studied the drunken crowd of people who milled about, slopping ale over the stone street.

My eyes slid around the square, and it reminded me of Bourbon Street in New Orleans during Mardi Gras, the streets reeking of alcohol and spirits. Women were topless, but they weren't requesting beads to see their tits.

Men hooted and grabbed for them, but the women denied their advances, holding out their hands instead, wanting money for their services. It was dark out, and yet the moon offered enough light, along with the torches, that I clearly saw my surroundings. The more I studied the crowd, the more I noticed the lack of clothing worn and the lewd, sexual acts taking place in public.

Down the street, a woman danced to the music playing. Her body swayed, hips adorned with chains rattling soothingly, adding to the song. Further down the road, another woman with dark kohl around her eyes and henna over her body was giving a lap dance to a warrior who watched her with lust burning in his eyes.

Intrigued by the dance, I lowered my gaze to her nether region, realizing it wasn't a dance after all. Smiling at my naivety, I looked away from the couple and saw a girl with sad eyes following a boy.

They moved through the crowd, picking the pockets of drunken villagers before vanishing into a dark alleyway. Frowning, I noticed more children doing the same, each working in pairs, before sliding off into the shadows to disappear. Turning my attention back to Knox, I found the candle extinguished and the window empty.

I studied the other rooms, watching as a light appeared within another. Knox moved into view with the now very naked woman who ran her hands over his chest as he watched. A wicked smile curved his lips as my heart thundered in my chest. His hand slid around her side, creeping up her spine until he threaded his fingers into her hair, entangling them. Hot tears pricked my eyes, and I knew I should have looked away as he turned her from the window, lowering his head to the skin of her neck.

The room went dark, and I fought the emotion that burned through me. Bile pushed against my throat as denial and anger fought with my need to enter the protected building, ripping him away from her, and claiming him in a way that would leave no mistake of whom he belonged.

Instead, I pushed away from the wall, noting that Lore, Brander, Killian, and Greer were no longer there. I shook off the rage and emotion at seeing him with another woman, moving through the crowd still cloaked in invisibility, quickly draining my power.

I dodged couples, darting through them as I made my way to the center of town. Sensing that someone was watching me, I stepped into a dark alleyway, taking in my surroundings. On the opposite side of the road stood a man with silver hair and eyes of the clearest seas.

I moved toward him and stopped when I caught Knox's scent and frowned. He appeared in the opposite direction from where he'd been, weaving through the people dancing in the square. Inhaling, I picked up another familiar scent and swung my attention to Brander, who was walking in the opposite direction of Knox, each one of them scanning the crowd. I started forward, rushing to the silver-haired male, but he vanished the moment I reached him.

Spinning around, I watched Knox's men as they closed in on me. Stepping back, I forced my magic to hold the thin barrier keeping me from their sight. Crows squawked above me, and I tilted my head to the sky, seeing it filled with them. Panicked, I ran toward the buildings' shadows, seeking refuge in the darkened alleyway where the children had disappeared as screams filled the night.

Pausing at the mouth of the alley, I saw misty fog filling the streets. My heart thundered in my chest as gray, twisting figures emerged among the mist's edge, snapping razor-sharp teeth and claws. I started forward, before stopping moments before the fog reached the first of the villagers, watching in horror as gray husks resembling corpses grabbed a shrieking woman and pulled her into the mist.

Dread entered my bloodstream as the putrid scent of death struck my nose, forcing my hand to cover it as more screams filled the square. My eyes burned from the stench, watering. I went to where the woman entered the mist. The sound of nails scraping the cobblestone filled the air, along with inhuman hisses and a chorus of unholy voices slithering through the night.

My heart thundered against my ribs at the gruesome scene, failing to register as the woman emerged from the mist. I fought the bile burning the back of my throat. I stared at the husk that was once a beautiful woman, now nothing more than a skinned corpse that stared sightlessly at the moon.

The dark magic filling the square pulsed to a heady beat, holding everyone in place. The villagers could not escape the deadly monsters that continually pulled victims into their grasps. I turned as something scraped and pierced my skin, staring down at the husked hand that dug talons into my ankle, yanking me toward the mist.

A glowing blade struck the hand, and then someone shoved me behind a large body. Turquoise eyes peered back at me over a broad shoulder, telling me without words to stay close. I placed my hand on the man's shoulder as we stepped backward, watching as he struck the creatures down, one at a time, within the mist. Suddenly, I froze in place, unable to move.

Taking in my bleeding ankle, I noticed black lines creeping up my legs, as another hand grabbed my wounded skin. Before I could pull away, the hand glowed, and the black lines were sucked from my skin, vanishing. My body unfroze, and I gasped as someone grabbed me while Knox screamed my name.

We turned, staring at Knox, his eyes narrowing to slits as he observed silver-haired men surrounding me. Howling erupted from the mist, and I spun, lowering my hands and calling forth my magic. The dark mist recoiled from the light of my magic, but it didn't dissipate. I frowned, calling forth more magic as a hand grabbed mine, and then the other.

The silver-haired men with matching turquoise eyes smirked at Knox, dismissing him as they chanted, and the shadowy, putrid mist receded. I swallowed, feeling the familiarity of their magic. Combining my magic to theirs, we continued to push the mist away, denying the creatures their prey, noting the husk-like corpses left in their wake. I smiled with victory until all at once, gruesome, hollow faces appeared in the mist as it lurched forward, and screams filled the air as one of the silver-haired men shoved me behind him.

"Run, Aria!" the man screamed, and I slowly stepped back. "You're not immortal. Fucking run, Little One," he hissed, and I turned, rushing toward the edge of town, turning to see them wield blades of glowing flames, fighting against the mist. A twig snapped beside me, and I yelped as Knox and his men surrounded me. I struggled to calm the anger that the sight of him erupted within me.

"Making new friends?"

"Funny, you should ask. You smell like well-used pussy, asshole," I sneered, slowly walking backward toward the woods.

"Jealous?" Knox countered, canting his head as I directed my attention to the men who had just saved my life.

"Hardly. Do you want that? Have at it, but don't think you get to have me afterward," I laughed soundlessly, watching the silver-haired men in the village push the mist further back with their glowing blades.

Reaching into my pack, I tossed some quartz on the ground around me, as Knox's eyes narrowed. Inhaling, I stopped. The smell of the tattoo artist's stank on his skin offended everything within me. I wanted to run my nails over his chest, shredding him and ruining every inch of flesh she touched. His eyes dared me to do it, but I wouldn't waste my energy.

"You think I fucked that woman while you watched?" Snorting, he studied my narrowed eyes as he continued. "Of course, I knew you were watching. No matter how hard you fight to hide that scent of yours, it's still in the air, taunting me, woman. I knew you leaned against the wall across the street, same as the men who watched you from where they rested. Isn't that right?" he asked, causing Brander and Lore to smirk.

My eyes slid from them to the sliver-haired men that had protected me. They had vanished once again. I frowned, chewing my lip as I scanned the streets, finding them emptied of people. It appeared as if everyone had scattered, retreating into their homes, closing their doors against the evil the night had sprung from the mist.

"Remove the quartz, Aria. The night isn't safe. The revenants are starving for souls in which to feast. Whether or not you like it, you're coming with me."

"I've made other arrangements for the evening, and they don't involve the smell of rank pussy," I stated, watching Knox's lips curve into a sinful smile.

He opened his mouth to speak, but the air filled with magic and violence. His men drew their swords, holding them at the ready, surrounding us. Tilting his head, Knox listened to the wind, trying to sense whatever they'd heard as the air thickened.

"It seems your other arrangements have arrived." Knox's smile became cruel. Turning his back on me, he drew his swords as the silver haired-men formed a circle around him and his men, weapons drawn and glowing with eerie flames.

Violence danced in the air, and I shook my head at my saviors. Knox's men moved into defensive poses, and I watched as everyone prepared to attack.

"No," I whispered, noting the silver-haired men tensed, and they nodded slowly, if a little begrudgingly, before stepping back, bowing their heads to me. Knox spun on me, narrowing his eyes.

As quickly as they appeared, my saviors vanished as if they were one with the shadows. Knox's eyes filled with rage as he canted his head.

"Who the fuck was that?" he demanded.

"I don't know," I whispered, shaking my head. "That's the second time they've saved me tonight."

"Drop the fucking protection barrier, woman. I won't tell you again."

"You aren't my boss, asshole. Besides, I got castles to destroy, and villages to pillage and plunder. See you soon?" His fierce gaze dropped to where my bloodied toe had drawn a portal onto the ground.

"Enough running, Aria," he hissed vehemently. "You're going to end up hurt or worse if you keep ignoring the dangers of the Nine Realms. You're wasting my fucking time chasing you instead of doing the job required of me."

"So stop chasing me and go handle your shit. I didn't ask you to stalk me, asshole. Besides, the next time you see me, I will be beyond your reach, and you will watch me reign down hell upon the world, unlike anything you've seen before."

"Never going to happen," he seethed, letting his angry stare settle on my lips before his tongue snaked out, tracing his.

"Eventually, you're going to tire of watching my ass walking away from you."

"Not possible. I enjoy your tight ass, and actually like watching it," he returned, trying to keep me close by, distracting me. I snorted, drinking in the sight and smell of Knox before I exhaled and stepped away from him, tossing him the bird over my shoulder.

Chapter Eleven

I entered the portal to my sanctuary, positioned outside of Hecate's tomb before Knox could respond. The books I'd come for were securely in my pack, and they held all the information I needed to accomplish my task. It was time to put my money where my mouth was. The only thing I needed to do first was alert the others that I would be silent for a few weeks, gaining power and strength to do what was required.

It was time to prepare for the rising of a new House of Magic and put down roots in this cold, dismal land where even the fog would freaking kill you. So far, I'd seen shit that most horror shows couldn't even dream up, learning that I'm stronger and more resourceful than I thought. Still, I needed to be cautious as I'd felt something wicked watching me often from within the shadows since arriving in the Nine Realms, observing my weaknesses and strengths, learning me.

I spent months figuring out the location for the next

fight, and now it was time to gather my strength and power within the sanctuary where no one could track or reach me. It would give Knox a sense of nothingness once I vanished within my refuge, but it would allow me to sleep and prepare for what was coming next.

If I actually survived the next battle, I'd be stronger and more equipped to face him as well. I would do what no witch had ever done before and lived to tell it. Swallowing unease, I smiled as arms wrapped around me from behind.

"My Sweetest Girl," Aurora whispered, kissing my cheek. "How I have missed you. Did you find the books?"

I turned, smiling. "Of course I did. You taught me well."

"Then, let's prepare for battle, shall we?" she asked, and I swallowed hard.

"This is my fight, and mine alone. You can come once I have obtained what we need. I can't focus on the battle if I am worried about you and the others, Aurora. Knox will be on my trail the moment I step out of this sanctuary and back into the Nine Realms.

"I also have another problem. I allowed myself to be taken into a keep to bypass their warding spell. As I was laying siege from within, I found an odd skull and touched it. I believe it was once a phoenix or something similar. It projected me into the memory of a battle. Then, a silver-haired man with eyes the color of mine appeared, saving me from the witches that tried to harm me as I was locked in a vision of the past. Others like him appeared later in the village. They came through some form of teleport or portal that opened directly into a realm of magic. After leaving the keep, I followed Knox into a town where a mist filled with decay and husks from the dead entered the village, pulling victims into the fog and spit their rapidly decomposing bodies back out."

"It was not a mist. It was revenants of the dead who cannot rest. It would appear to an unknown victim as a mist or fog, but it's the souls of the damned, unable to rest until the spell holding them to the Nine Realms has run its course or the caster of such an evil spell is destroyed."

"That's terrifying because the moment the revenants touched my leg, I froze. I couldn't move or even think past the fear sliding through me. I'd be added to their victim pool if my silver-haired saviors hadn't spared me. He held magic, Aurora, identical to mine. Knox found me, and he and his men surrounded me, but the men from the other realm surrounded them all, almost as if they intended to fight Knox to protect me."

"You need to stay away from them, Aria."

"Who are they?" I asked, her expression filled with worry. "You know who they are, don't you?"

"No, but there are many within the Nine Realms who have similar coloring to you," she whispered, pulling back to study my face. "If they ask you to come with them, you must never go. Do you understand me? They're not who you think they are, Aria Primrose."

"Who are they?" I insisted.

"Monsters. They're monsters. You're not like them,

not even a little. If you go with them, that will change, Aria. If you go with them, everything will change. You can't trust them. Do you hear me? You cannot trust anyone in this world." She pushed the stray strands of my hair away from my face, frowning as tears swam in her eyes.

"What are they then?"

"I just told you."

"No, you said they were monsters. Which kind of monster are they?" I demanded. "Is it so bad that you cannot put it into words?"

"The first people were a murderous, magical race that rattled, and made similar noises to what you and Knox create when you're around one another. I think you're the daughter of one of them, but which I could not say. Once, as a child, my mother told me about them and what the Nine Realms looked like when they ruled it. The realms were uninhabitable because of the fiery flames and the death they unleashed unto anyone who came here. They were a murderous race that delivered horrific deaths to anyone they didn't allow in their lands.

"So, my mother, well, she unleashed her darkest magic, that of a goddess to rid the land of these monsters. It took her hundreds of years and nearly drained her of the magic within her soul. I've told you of the legends, and the fortune the other gods delivered unto her, sealing the fates of that race and all the creatures who lived when they drew breath in the Nine Realms." She swallowed hard, searching my eyes.

"But what were they? Why won't anyone just tell me what I am?" I countered softly. Worrying my lip, my gaze narrowed on Aurora's concerned expression.

"Because within you, there is another being," Aurora explained carefully, taking a step back. "It's essential that she discovers who and what she is on her own. If I told you what I thought you were, and she heard, deciding to become that creature, it would end badly for both of you. One day, something will set her off, and she'll evolve and reveal her true nature to protect you both from death. Monsters transcend into being, and she will, too, when the time is right.

"All I know is this, Aria. Your father walked among men and lay with your mother to create you. It wasn't by accident that you're here. Knox's race is also from the first creatures of the Nine Realms, which is why he is a worthy adversary. It also explains how you both sense each other on a deeper level. That much is certain. The attraction may be of the flesh, but the connection you both feel lives within your souls. The monsters that live within each of you are the same, and I fear they created you to either lure Knox to his death or rule the Nine Realms at his side."

"That's two extremes with no middle ground. What if I wasn't meant to be his?"

"If you weren't created to take down a king or to show him that not all witches are vile, murderous beings, well, then you were born to bring the entirety of the Nine Realms to its knees. If that's the case, then, gods save us all, because you're almost strong enough to accomplish it now."

"I'm not stronger than Knox, Aurora. I also can't bring myself to hurt him."

"Yet, Aria Hecate," she whispered, thick with emotion. "You've chosen a path you intend to walk alone. The things you plan to do will only add to your power. You will walk beside him one way or another, how you choose to remain there is only your choice to make."

"How will I know which to choose?" I swallowed, fighting against the anxiety rushing through me, causing me to fidget with my dress.

"You'll follow your heart, and you will do what is right for the greater good because of it. You're smart, beautiful, and you're good, Aria Primrose. You deserve happiness and to know the love of a good man. I made sacrifices in my life to assure that you wouldn't have to. You will know when the time comes to choose, and you'll do what is right within your heart. I taught you to fight for the weak and be strong in the face of defeat and insurmountable odds."

"I think you assume I am something I am not. I am not strong enough to choose a path right now, not when Knox is standing in front of me. I can barely remember my name when that asshole is near."

Aurora laughed, smiling as sparkles of amusement danced in her gaze. "You're the closest thing I have to a daughter, Sweet Girl. In my heart, you're mine. I taught you well. You're a red-blooded woman with needs. Sate the hunger, and if he is yours by right, everything that is supposed to happen will fall into place. None of the best love stories were easy. Come, it will take us days to prepare you for the journey you're about to take, and I have missed your laugh these last few months."

"I have missed you too." I rested my head on her shoulder as we moved deeper into the sanctuary we'd begun to build.

Inside, the keep was nothing more than an altar surrounded by burning candles. Crystal's hiding my position, scent, and location formed a powerful grid, enhanced with long crystal quartz amplifying each stone it touched. Swallowing the worry, I walked to the grid and slipped off my dress as Dimitri entered with my sisters. His eyes slid down my naked body with a hunger that was worrisome.

"Once you awaken, we will prepare you for war," Aurora whispered.

"Up you go," Dimitri said, grasping around my waist before he lifted me onto the altar, kissing my cheek before sliding his fingers over my abdomen, longing burning in his dark blue eyes. "Rest well, Sweet One."

I looked around the room, staring at the faces of my sisters before I leaned back. The cold iciness of the altar bit at my back and the heavy scent of sage flooded my senses moments before chanting started. My eyes closed, and I relaxed, letting the familiar voices of my family soothe me. I could feel Dimitri's heavy gaze on my body and heard his disgruntled yelp as Aurora whapped him.

"Stop drooling over Aria and go be useful standing guard. No one enters this keep while she readies herself for her next task, boy. Her life depends on us preparing her, and her ability to accept the strength we are giving."

"I can hear you," I muttered, smiling softly before opening my eyes, watching something pass in Dimitri's gaze as he looked away and left the room.

Chapter Twelve

Two weeks later, back in the Nine Realms

I stood outside the witch's stronghold I had watched for the past two days, preparing myself for the fight to take their keep and claim the prize they were guarding. My eyes shifted from the castle to a large war party, slowly making their way down the long, winding trail leading them deep into the valley. They marched in four, single-file lines, moving like a well-oiled machine on the road that would eventually reach my line of defenses.

Taking a deep breath to calm my nerves, I scanned the oncoming army. Knox led his men, sitting confidently on his midnight-colored stallion, exuding dominance that demanded your undivided, full attention. He was a sight to see dressed in his war uniform, and I sighed, noting how sexy he looked in his dark, wickedly designed armor. The man knew how to intimidate and plunder your senses.

The sound of men marching, horse hooves stomping on gravel, and the war drums, all bounced off the gorge's high cliff walls, echoing like music flowing through the valley in warning. Combined, they were intimidating, sending a chill rushing down my spine with a foreboding that I couldn't shake.

Large horses, some with two heads and unlike anything I had ever seen, pulled huge machinery behind them. Enormous, terrifying birds with fiery red and orange feathers flew above, shrieking as they flapped their vast, beautiful wings.

The baying of dogs, or something similar, joined the other cacophony of sounds, forcing my attention to the back of the army. There, housed in enormous cages, were dog-like creatures with large, pointed ears and tails resembling a bird's tail feathers, pacing anxiously as they howled to be released.

Knox had brought creatures of legends and myths to wage war against this speed-bump of a keep. His numbers weren't as impressive as what I'd seen when I'd followed him days ago, which meant the rest of the army camped some place near to here. The single fact that he'd not brought his entire army eased my anxiety a bit, but not entirely. The man knew how to make an entrance, creating inner doubt and turmoil in those who entertained the thought of waging war against him.

My gaze settled back on the King of Norvalla, seeing him clearer now that he was closer. Halting his army's progression, Knox placed a helmet and mask combination on his head, the same one he previously used to obscure his identity. He righted himself on his horse as he signaled for the army to proceed. The black skeletal mask was the shit of nightmares, mine, mainly. Of course, he'd chased me down in it and tried to choke me to death while wearing it, so there was a legit reason for those dreams that haunted me.

Knox sat tall on the largest warhorse, watching the keep nestled up against the high cliff walls surrounding it. It wasn't a strategic location in the least bit. It was a bold statement, indicating that the witches living there feared nothing and no one.

Lifting my eyes to the startling blue, clear sky, I closed them, silently praying to Hecate that I made it through this fight without ending up in Knox's bed by nightfall. As much as my body wanted him to punish it, soothing the dark lust and desire he created, I wasn't ready for that to happen. I'd barely slipped out of the sanctuary before Knox could find it since the crystals' power had diminished. Luckily, my sisters and aunt had left soon after, placing the protection wards, leaving Dimitri there alone to guard me in the event I was disturbed.

Knox, though, he'd been relentless in his need to reach and claim me. It was becoming impossible to remain ahead of him. Knox didn't need rest, nor did he tire of pursuing me, as if the chase exhilarated and renewed his energy. The stones upon the ground trembled as the war party entered the valley, closing the distance between us.

I stood in a sea of witches I had recently gathered and turned, silently observing the approaching warriors. All of us wore white silk cloaks splattered in blood, adorned with a red Hecate insignia stitched on the hood and back. Knox approached the barrier that protected us, and I smirked, watching as he swiftly dismounted and strode toward it with purpose. A moment before he would have walked through the warded shield, he paused. My breath caught in my throat as he swung his gaze directly to where I stood, concealed under the hood of my cloak.

My chest tightened, and my heart sped up, clenching with anticipation and need, thundering against my ribs, threatening to give me away. Heat slid through me, pooling in my stomach as Knox's pretty blue eyes lifted to the silent keep behind me. I'd fought the relentless heat and need, my body becoming a solid ache that never eased. My hands balled into tight fists as I closed my eyes, slowly exhaling to calm the army of butterflies assaulting my insides.

A handful of witches that examined the barrier joined Knox, shaking their heads at whatever he'd just said. Angry eyes slid through our ranks as he turned to speak to Brander. One witch grabbed his gloved hand, flirting shamelessly with him. She was brazen and uncaring of the eyes watching them together. Knox didn't acknowledge her touch, not at first. The dark-haired witch's hand touched his chest plate, and his hand lifted, holding hers to his armor.

Anger sliced through me without warning. My blood pounded in my ears, while magic grew dangerous and sharp through the air between us. Knox's eyes slid back through our numbers, slowly narrowing, searching for me. Had he felt my anger?

My heart thundered with unease. I forced the anger down, willing myself to calm, knowing that overthinking things was my super-power. Being alone in a strange world, you learned a lot about yourself. Mostly, you learned your flaws and strengths in the worst ways imaginable, usually figuring it out at the most inopportune times possible.

Knox continued touching the witch beside him as my power rushed to the forefront, driven by jealousy that shouldn't even exist. Slowly, I released it and exhaled, calming my reaction to them. The man was infuriating. He confused me, and yet every part of my body heated for him. This wasn't the first time the sight of Knox with another woman had made me a little unhinged.

My creature perked up, noting his presence. Her attention focused on the hand touching Knox, and I fought against the rattle that threatened to explode from my chest. Closing my eyes to prevent her from going bat-shit-crazy, I shoved the noise she wanted us to make in warning, down. Managing her was hard enough without Knox nearby. We wanted to murder in him in one breath and ride him like a pony in the next. It was part of my bipolar sparkling personality I was cursed to bear.

"Not cursed, blessed! Knox was blessed with a nice cock and the skill to wield it perfectly!" my creature crooned. *"Remember the cobwebs and spiders? We don't want that, do we?"*

"Cursed! You are random as fuck, Creature. We also talked about spiders and the fact that we never talk about spiders, remember?"

"He touches her again; we eat her face! He only touches us! He is ours."

"Quiet, Creature. Knox doesn't know we're here yet. Let's keep it that way."

"I am hungry and horny, and he is right there. He fucks good. We need a good fuck, Aria. Let's fuck him

and then eat him! It's a win, Aria. Feed me his dick!" She was excited, vivaciously so, at the idea of being so close to that arrogant prick. She did not understand how toxic he was or how deadly he could be.

"He also wants our head, which he'd probably take while he fucked us. He doesn't need our head attached to our body to use us. Remember? It's a perfect head, Creature! We like our head, and we need it to keep breathing. Therefore, Knox is bad, very bad for our health and life expectancy."

"He's done bad things to our body that felt good, but he's not always smart. We will rock his cock, and he will want to keep our head so we can breathe. Then we can ride that glorious cock whenever we want. He's so dreamy, and I want to feel his cock pulsing within us… please, Aria? Just one quick rut, then you can fight him!" she sighed, and I cringed inwardly, which only made her laugh.

"That doesn't even make sense. 'He did bad things, so let's fuck him?' Who thought like that? It's a wonder we're even still alive, Creature." I rolled my eyes, and she snorted from within as if I were slow in the head, which infuriated me. *"Now, stop thinking about our vagina because this is a serious situation!"* She snickered inside my head, and I groaned at the sound.

We'd been at odds for the last couple of weeks. She'd eaten a few of the dark witches we'd come across, and of course, she left me standing holding the dead body part the moment she'd had her fill of their corpses. She'd taken partial control of my body, tripping me repeatedly, trying to get us captured as we ran from Knox. She and I were at war over the need consuming us, and eventually, it was going to end badly for me. She'd be sated, but I'd be his prisoner, which my creature wouldn't mind in the least if it meant a daily diet of Knox.

"He's approaching, and we don't want him alerted that we're here yet. Do try to behave, and I'll promise to let you out to play soon."

"To fuck Knox? I am so horny, and you haven't used our vagina correctly. You might as well have sewn it shut!"

"It's our vagina. It's a shared space, remember? I'm not fucking random cock because you want to... what did you call it?"

"Paint our vagina!"

"Right. Paint our vagina. Again, who thinks like that?"

"We need his scent. He smells so good. Can you smell him? Knox is alpha to his core, which means he needs to be in our vagina. Put him there, or I will find a way to fall onto his dick."

"Are you seriously threatening to get me fucked right now? I'm about to face off with Knox, his army, and a castle full of witches behind us. Can you, I don't know, maybe not worry about getting fucked or painting our pussy right now? Our unused vagina is literally the least of our issues at the moment, Creature."

"Fine, but soon. We are in season, and you run too fast. He's not smart, you know. Maybe trip and let him land in our vagina. Then he will think he caught us, and mmm, I will be happy. You need dick too. You're as frustrated as I am, but you can't admit it because you

have issues, major issues. It's easy. Slip, slide down his dick, and then we eat him. It's a plan!"

"That isn't a plan. It's a recipe for disaster. Stop distracting me. He's approaching."

"Quick, slip..."

"Enough! You do understand that he doesn't intend to give us head. He plans to have it removed, placing it next to my cold-hearted bitch of a mother's, playing with it while he holds court."

"As if he would. He enjoyed his cock in our mouth. You should have seen his eyes rolling to the back of his skull when I swallowed him. We gave good head, and he knows it. He's very large and stupid. Easy fuck, easy snack, and then we can go back to frolicking in the forest, rubbing our devil's doorbell to your heart's desire."

"You're not going to drop this, are you?"

"Either feed me, or get me fucked, and I'll behave. I'm horny and hungry, and you're a stubborn human."

"I'll feed you then. Just shut up for now. I have to control an army, and to do that, you need to behave so I won't fail and end up dead, unable to fuck or feed on anyone."

"Present your lord or lady, now," Knox growled, pacing outside the barrier. His angry eyes slanted as he paused, once more settling his attention on my general location within the witches.

I stepped forward with five witches. Each moved to stand beside me while I stood directly in front of Knox. He watched us silently and then snorted when we didn't remove our hoods. Once we mirrored him and his men's stances, he spoke again.

"Here are my terms. I want your lord or lady on her knees before me. I want the barrier to drop. Your lives will be forfeited while he or she watches you slaughtered by my army. Make me wait until the magic in the barrier fails, and I will torture every fucking one of you for days before your ultimate death."

Ouch! Harsh, Knox!

Did he seriously think that would be met with a resounding, yeah, sure, sounds great?

Chapter Thirteen

Knox let his eyes slide between us before snorting. "I'll know your answer now, you murderous whores. Your barrier has already weakened. The magic you wield is continually draining, unable to maintain its strength. Did you honestly believe it protected you from me?"

"Yes," the entire field of witches replied as one.

Knox's gaze slid through the assembly of witches with unease. "Barrier spells need souls for one to be erected. Tell me how many innocent lives you took to create this one."

"Zero," my army of witches stated in unison, laughing at his thinning glare. "Your terms were heard, and rejected, King Karnavious. Please leave, or you will regret it greatly."

"I'm not leaving here until I have your mistress or master on their knees, and your heads removed to build my walls, evil bitches." Knox snarled, and his army replied with cheers of agreement.

The large firebirds he'd brought with him screeched above the army, flapping their wings. It created an echo in the barrier, and I shivered as magic slithered through the barrier's shield. Knox turned, nodding to the giants pulling the heavy trebuchet to the front of the line. Once in place, they loaded a boulder onto it, immediately firing it in our direction. It sailed through the air with a whistle, shattering against the shield. I smirked, watching as Knox and his witches shook their heads, disbelieving the shield was still in place.

"If your lord or lady is present, why have they not shown themselves?" he asked, placing his hands on his sword's hilt. "Are they afraid to face me?"

"She is here. Would you like to see her?" we all asked at once. Knox sneered, placing his hands on his hips as if he wasn't worried about anything.

"Indeed," he sneered, and I laughed at his irritation, causing the entire assembly of witches to follow my lead. "Present the murderous whore of the keep. I've grown impatient."

"Knox, you're very naughty, aren't you?" I stepped closer, and the witches beside me stepped back in synchronized movements. "You've been a bad, bad boy," I laughed huskily.

Pushing the hood back, I allowed the cloak to slide from my shoulders, revealing my scantily clothed form to his hungry gaze. I'd taken a swath of sheer fabric and created a skirt that hung to my bare feet. The top from two cuts of the same fabric, draped over my shoulders, cinched around my waist to expose the sides of my breasts. My hair was in an intricate updo, secured by silver chains that hung down my naked back.

Knox removed his helmet, glaring at me, but the hunger in his eyes was a burning fire that turned to lust. He slid his smoldering gaze over my body, noting that I'd lost weight, and obviously was short on fabric since it hardly covered me. The chains encircled my arms and waist, hung down my spine. His mouth tightened into a thin, white line, and the vein on his forehead pulsed with anger.

"What the hell are you doing here, Aria?"

"I heard they had a massive BOGO sale on sage here, so I came to check it out. It turns out it was a buy two, get the third one free sale, offering shit sage you could get from the Dollar Store. You?"

"I'm here to slaughter witches. You're in my fucking way, little girl."

"Oh, awkward," I chuckled, and the witches echoed the sound, causing him to frown as he surveyed the witches behind me. "Right? He's a funny boy, isn't he, ladies?"

"Cut the shit, now. This isn't a fucking game. Drop the barrier, and I'll go easy on you for the first few times, Aria. Make me wait until it falls, and I'll show you how much I've missed you as I violently savage your greedy cunt."

"Aww, you missed me?" I asked in a saccharine tone, running my finger over the barrier, smiling as he watched its path.

"I've missed you beneath me, woman." He stepped

closer, smiling darkly as his eyes turned to liquid pools of desire. "Let me show you how much I've missed you."

His presence reminded me of how he felt pressed against me, and my core clenched while I chewed my bottom lip. His tongue snaked out, running over his lips, and I recalled how it felt against my clit, battering against it, sucking the swollen flesh into his heated mouth. He'd made my body into a twisting, heated mess of orgasms as he'd moaned with the taste of me painting his tongue. I swallowed hard, jerking my eyes away from his in surrender.

My arms lifted, forcing the witches behind me to do the same. I leaned against the barrier, studying him. "Knox, don't threaten me with a good time, or promises you might not be able to keep."

"Drop the barrier, and I'll have you screaming for me, Little Monster. Your body requires mine to get off, which means you've neglected your needs. I want to get you off."

My eyes grew hooded, and my body heated as every word he uttered seemed to slither through my sex, running over my clit in perfect rhythm. I slowly licked my lips, staring at his full mouth, remembering the feel of his tongue between my thighs, stroking me to orgasm after earth-shattering orgasm. I moaned, trembling, then shook my head to dispel the sound of my breathing and heartbeat, drowning out everything else around me.

"What is wrong with you, woman?" he demanded, noting how I shivered, rocking my body seductively without the control to stop myself.

I could smell his scent through the barrier, which

wasn't supposed to happen. I'd erected it, intending to ignore his seductive aroma that was the bane of my existence. According to Aurora, I was fighting a losing battle to the creature within, and I felt it acutely every time I was near Knox. His eyes searched mine, thinning, and his nostrils flared as he inhaled my scent.

"You run too slowly, Knox," I croaked, losing my hold on the barrier momentarily, allowing him to catch my scent. His eyes slipped to midnight onyx with embers burning within their depths as his creature peered out from his host.

"Your time is up," he laughed soundlessly. "You're fully in heat, Little Witch. Tell me, how badly do you ache for me right now?"

"It's irrelevant, Knox. It changes nothing."

"It's changed everything, Aria. I am no longer the only thing hunting you down. Your body has declared that you're in season, and your womb is begging to be filled. You're not escaping me anymore. You can't run much longer in your current state. Now, bring down the fucking barrier so I can destroy the witches and fix that issue you're having."

"This is sort of an awkward subject to have, surrounded by our armies," I swallowed, closing my eyes, leaning my head against the barrier, and moaning at the heat rolling through me.

"I'm not fucking asking anymore," Knox snapped harshly, his eyes slowly returning to a vivid blue, showing he'd contained his beast, which was more than I could say about mine.

Of course, my body would pick now to have an episode. That's what I'd started calling the momentary events where my body buckled, and my hand slid between my thighs, fighting the pain that ached there. My creature thought it was hilarious when it happened, singing about me stroking the devil's doorbell. It was something I couldn't prevent, and it tended to happen only when I caught his scent while hunting him.

What else could go wrong?

"I've actually started laying siege to the keep already. Arrows are about to be released on me from the lady inside. So, be a good boy and wait here for a moment, please, and thank you. I have something to do real fast."

I stepped back as the witches removed their cloaks, revealing their bodies' decomposed state. Knox's eyes widened as he looked over my shoulder, his mouth opening and closing. I laughed, enjoying the horror playing out on his and his men's faces at the morbid scene before him, grimacing as the dead witches laughed along with me.

Knox watched my undead army opening their decaying mouths, ready to echo my words. Lifting my arms, I swayed my hips, knowing all the decomposing bodies around me mimicked my movements as I danced for him.

"Aren't we so pretty, Knox?" We all spoke together, the magic growing as I rolled my head on my shoulders, causing them to do the same. "How about an undead orgy? You down?" I laughed mirthlessly, noting his eyes lowered to my midriff with naked hunger.

"What the fuck did you do, Aria?" he demanded the moment he regained focus, pulling his attention from my skin.

"I rattled their world. Your turn will come soon enough. Are you ready for me? I told you I'd handle my house. Can you say the same about yours? Mine isn't the only one dirty in the Nine Realms, now, is it? Your house has enjoyed using us, deflowering us, and then keeping us as pets. Isn't that right?" My gaze slid to the witches within his army, then back to him, anger burning in his gaze.

"Careful pointing fingers," he warned coldly, his jaw hammering. I smirked, knowing I'd hit a sensitive chink in his armor. "You've been in this world for a minute. You have no idea what I'm capable of once you've pissed me off. Don't piss me off. You won't like what happens, Aria."

"I've been here a few months, Knox. I've set siege to four castles and brought them all to their bloody knees. You've been at this for how long? And you've done what? Waged war on me? Oh, no. That's right. You've wrecked my world, killed the evil bitch that birthed me, and her wicked sister. Your people raped and decimated innocent lives that had nothing to do with your war, and you think witches are the only problem in the Nine Realms?"

"Your breed, the Hecate line, is the only one that matters at the moment. Kill the head of the snake, and the rest will fall easily."

"I'm right here, Knox. Come get me if you think you can," I snorted, stepping back as power entered the clearing, and the illusion I'd held in place slipped.

Now visible, were the burning embers of bloody husks and blackened skeletal remains littering the ground beneath our feet. The castle walls were singed and covered in blood and gore where I'd waged a battle against the witch who held the keep in Hecate's name. Fires burned all around me, some from bodies, others from pyres I'd lit to increase the magic fueling the altar where I was about to stand. I'd been here for days, playing with these witches, testing my army against their numbers. I was winning until Knox had crashed the party.

Men were such inconsiderate pricks when they didn't know how to ask a bitch for an invitation. I should be thankful he hadn't just sent me a picture of his cock with a date and time for a fuck-and-duck. Flames exploded from the pyres, and my hand touched the altar as I turned, canting my head to the side, blowing Knox a raspberry.

"I'm waiting, Knox. Come and take it if you can."

Chapter Fourteen

Knox was starting to understand that his terms were null and void. He'd wanted me on my knees, watching as he killed my army, but they were already dead, so that was a moot point.

My house wasn't just dirty; it was filthy. If anything, Knox downplayed the state of affairs inside the Nine Realms. I'd walked into a mess far beyond my imagination.

I'd been captured, beaten, abused, and almost killed by witches. They were the one creature within the Nine Realms that should have welcomed me with open arms. Yes, I'd found some nice ones along the way, and they'd assisted me in slaughtering the army I had now, but my reality check had bounced pretty hard on its way to the bank.

This keep wasn't like the others I'd taken, murdering their witches for being vile. The dark witches filling this castle allowed monsters to force-breed innocent witches. I'd freed most that were pregnant before ever lifting a finger against the stronghold. I'd made damn sure those who raped unwilling witches or had taken their babes, didn't escape my wrath.

Turning away from Knox, I peered up at the battlement where the last of the dark witches stood, flanking their leader. My hand waved, dispelling the image of a sprawling meadow, exposing the burning embers and scorched corpses of the army she'd sent to attack me.

I allowed her to see Knox and his army as well, enjoying the fear that fluttered across her face before she concealed her expression beneath a veneer of malice and betrayal. Like I was the bad guy here, right?

A song from The HU Band, *The Wolf Totem,* started playing in my head. I released the barrier on their side, and the leader of these dark witches leaned over the edge of the stone wall, screaming out orders. My body swayed to the beat, sweat beading on my brow, dripping down my spine as swirls of embers filled the air around me.

The witch screamed for her archers, who rushed forward on the wide battlement. They dipped cloth arrow tips into oil before aiming the fiery missiles toward the skies. Smiling, I laughed at their attempt to thwart me by setting me on fire.

My arms lifted, as did the witches' arms under my control, standing next to me on the field. The moment the archers released their arrows, I sucked power from the ground, slamming our hands down hard, causing the airborne arrows to turn before finding purchase in the archers who had freed them.

The barrels of oil exploded, causing men to fall over the battlement walls or be burned alive by the fire rushing through their ranks. Closing my eyes, I listened to the screams of those burning as my body and my army of witches continued to sway to the music in my head. Lifting my hands, I delicately moved them through the air with the heady beat only I could hear.

Shouting began, and I opened my eyes, thrusting my hands toward the keep. Magic slammed against the castle, causing the far sides of the stone walls to cave, preventing escape through anything other than the main gate.

Men jumped over the edge of the stone wall to engage my army. I pulled arrows from the corpses at my feet, sending them singing through the air, impaling the men, and crashing them into the earth as if they were nothing more than raindrops painting the ground.

I lifted the blood from the earth, each in a single droplet, sending it to extinguish the fire on the battlement. I waited for those still upon the wall, to assume it was safe, only to flick my finger as men surged forward to attack, catching fire with the oiled blood I'd rained down upon them.

Slowly, I moved backward as I felt the army preparing to escape through the gate that creaked open, knowing it would be a long process. Smirking, I turned, swaying my hips as I walked toward Knox, who silently watched me.

"Not bad for a witch from the suburbs, right?" I asked, rolling my neck as he narrowed his eyes, staring over my shoulder.

"You're going to end up hurt, Aria."

"By you? Yes. I'm aware. Not today, though, nor tomorrow. But eventually, it will happen. I'm not sure if I should be excited or worried about what you will do to me once you have me." I swiveled to face the last of the witch's army that had assembled outside the crumbling keep. "On a scale from one to ten, how bad is this thing?"

"What thing?" He pressed his hands against the barrier that should have sent him doubling over in pain. Instead, he looked unbothered by it, which was worrisome. The heat in his eyes told me he knew exactly what 'thing' I was asking about, which made me twist the question.

"This war, of course," I stated aloofly. "What else would I mean?" I whispered huskily, bending over to stop the ache as heat rolled throughout my body. I laughed, sucking my lip between my teeth as I stood straight again, staring into his hungry eyes.

"You won't fight your need for much longer, Aria. It is inevitable, and you can't fight evolution either. Soon, you won't care who takes you, just so long as you've sated your hunger."

"This is the second keep this week that I've seized, as you're aware. I did leave some of their skulls for you as my calling card. The others, well, as you can see," I said, waving my hand behind me, "I needed them in battle." I smiled sweetly at Knox as he grimaced, looking at the witches' decaying bodies under my control.

"I noticed, and you shouldn't have. I enjoy killing

witches. It makes my cock hard when they scream and beg me for mercy," he said huskily. "Now, let's get back to your personal matter because sooner or later, it's going to become too much for you to disregard. You're underfed and over your pretty head, Aria."

"I guess I'll have to find someone who can assist me then. You want my head, and all I want to do is ride that deliciously amazing mouth of yours. I think our idea of 'head' differs, Knox."

"I'll let you ride me for however long you can stand it, woman. I've enjoyed the taste of you, and the wonder lighting those beautifully expressive eyes when you screamed my name, dripping your arousal down my chin as you tried to escape my tongue while your body unraveled in an orgasm. Come fucking ride it. I'm hungry, and you're fucking delicious."

I studied the look of victory sparkling in his eyes and tilted my head. "Hard pass, Knox. I don't think you're worth losing my head." Spinning around, I strutted away, rolling my eyes so hard I was checking out my ass in the process.

The remaining warriors had spread out in front of the keep, each one armed with a variety of weapons. Soundlessly, they started moving forward, and I grinned, lifting my hands, I spun in a circle. I severed the warriors on the front line into two grisly pieces, causing the others to back up, trampling one another to get closer to the castle's stone walls.

"What do you want from us?" a woman screamed, untangling herself from the men who fought to guard her.

"Your fucking soul," I chuckled coldly.

"You're a witch! We will yield to you," she cried.

"There is no yielding to me. You trespassed against the House of Hecate, and for that, you forfeited your lives. Lay down your weapons and surrender, or fight to the death. Those are my terms."

"King Karnavious, we yield to you!" she screamed.

"Oh, you poor, dense woman," I chuckled. "He isn't here to save you, witch. He is here to see you on your knees. It seems to be one of his kinks," I laughed, turning to wink at Knox. "After that, he will slaughter your people, removing their heads. I turned the offer down since I didn't think you or your people deserved mercy. Now, it's time to die," I hissed, pulling their magic from them.

Those without magic began turning to embers, burning to nothing more than skeletal remains as they wafted through the air, drifting past as I walked toward those still living.

"I do love the smell of wicked bitches roasting in the morning!" I laughed, closing my eyes as the embers kissed over my skin before sizzling out.

I stretched my arms behind me, cracking my neck as the witches hissed and cried while watching those beside them burn to nothing.

"Bring down the fucking barrier, now!" Knox demanded, but I ignored him.

"Are you ready?" I whispered inside my head, watching as my fingers blackened. It was something that had begun happening when my creature took over. *"Do not leave me in a compromised position. Knox is bad.*

Say it with me, Creature."

"He gives good dick."

"That's not the answer I'm looking for right now. We had a deal, remember? He doesn't get us anymore. He would murder us, and we enjoy living. You wouldn't be able to feed or fuck if he removed our head."

"I can eat, though? I'm starving!"

"You may, but remember what happened last time I allowed you out to eat?"

"I ate your army," she pouted.

"Yes, and I threw up everywhere. Why was that?"

"Because kidneys are yucky?"

"Very much so, Creature," I snorted and groaned as the change continued. *"What are we not going to do this time?"*

"You'll see, won't you, Aria?" she snickered as she took control, pushing me into the backseat of my mind.

Instead of facing the army that was preparing to attack us with magic, she turned, sniffing the air, drinking in Knox's scent. He zeroed in on the color of our eyes, the sclera no longer white, but turquoise with flecks of gold burning within them. The tips of my hair turned black as streaks of obsidian crawled up my arm from my fingertips.

"That's new," Knox admitted, continuing to stare at us, taking in all the changes.

"He smells delicious," she whined. *"I need a drink of him."*

"Focus on the battle, Creature."

"Can't we swing one quick orgasm?"

"No! Absolutely not!"

"You don't deserve our vagina! It's going to waste! It aches, and he would soothe it, painting it pretty on the inside, making the pain stop, Aria. You kept me awake all night, trying to make it stop on your own. It didn't work!" she stomped her feet, flinging her arms around. The witches under our control slammed into the men surrounding them, throwing them around with magic as she pitched a hissy fit.

"Pay attention to the army that I just threatened!" I warned, and she turned as a male strutted out of the ranks, ripping his clothes off.

He neared us, and she rattled loudly. Knox echoed the sound from behind us, only his was filled with a lethal warning. The male slammed to the ground, grunting as he started rocking his hips, grinding himself against the rocks. My creature released her rattle, watching him with disappointment.

"That was unsatisfactory," she groaned, zipping towards him as something wet splattered our face.

Lifting her hand, she tossed his head over her shoulder before moving back to where we had stood. Another male started toward us, and she smiled, tilting her head as the large, handsome male shed his clothes. He was already pumping his cock in his hand as her smile turned feral. It was a huge, knotted cock that had excitement bubbling up through my creature.

"Do not even think about riding that thing!" I

warned, and she arched her back, parting her hips as she went down to the ground, lifting our ass while Knox snarled angrily behind us. *"Get up! Get off of the ground. This was the last thing we should be doing right now. You're ruining the badass battle I had planned to show off my magic in front of Knox!"* I growled.

The male smirked, slowly walking around us, strutting like a peacock. He lowered himself behind me, and I fought my creature for control. Losing the battle, she started rocking her hips, turning to smirk at the man as she purred huskily. Knox was hissing as he rattled and banged his fists outside the barrier. I shivered at his rage, agreeing with him for once.

My creature moved faster than I could register our movements, leaping over the warrior's back in a swift, effortless move that my body shouldn't have managed. She sunk her teeth into his shoulder, ripping it apart, then her claws cut through his throat, and his head dropped from his body, rolling toward Knox's feet. She turned, rattling at Knox, and he studied us, pride burning in his eyes as blood dripped from our chin.

"Okay, honestly, that was badass," I admitted.

"Did you like that move?" she preened, standing before she turned, wiggling her fingers at Knox, who glared at us. "Hey, fuck-boy. Run faster. I need dick. You have a dick. Aria has wasted our vagina on a hand that doesn't get us off. So, if you caught us, that would be great. I'll even suck you off if you do it soon, deal?"

"I'm right fucking here, Creature. Come get me," Knox challenged, holding his arms out wide.

Chapter Fifteen

Knox lifted his eyes, and my creature turned to see what had drawn his attention. I groaned as she danced happily, clapping and excited at the prospect of more victims as more men rushed forward. Turning back toward Knox, she swayed her hips in a come-hither fashion that had him smirking wickedly, assuming she had accepted his challenge, and returned for him. If that's what she had planned, we were fucked, literally and figuratively.

Suddenly, she lunged backward without warning, zooming between the men approaching us in her inhuman way. She paused to look back as the headless bodies continued rushing forward to drop lifelessly on the field. I forced her to flick our hands, sending the zombie witches into their attack setting, ending the thwarted attempts on our life while my creature danced around covered in blood.

"No fair, I wanted to assemble the army of the

dead!" she groaned, crossing her arms to pout before she stomped her foot on the ground.

"Focus," I urged. *"Do not touch the head witch. We need her alive. You may eat the others, though."*

My creature turned a wicked grin toward the feast I'd offered her and growled so loudly I jumped from within her. I didn't get time to ask what the hell that noise was because Knox and his men echoed the sound, causing the entire valley to fill with inhuman growls.

She lowered our body to the ground, crawling to the crowd of witches and warriors who watched her with unease while she prowled toward them. Maybe it was confusion they felt since she crawled on the ground in my very human-looking body like we were something else. Lifting her head, she rattled until it changed to a purring noise she made when she was furious at me, just before all hell broke loose.

Our body hit a jetstream, sailing through it until she was climbing a giant, tearing through him with teeth and claws until he hit the ground, lifeless. The entire assembly of creatures paused, staring at us before they scattered and ran in every direction to escape my creature.

She let out a deafening rattle that shook through the valley, turning to eye the men watching every move she made. She continued forcing the noise out, and Knox rattled low, smooth, and even, causing her to preen and sway her ass.

I smiled from within, laughing at their horrified expressions as one after another victim fell to her. She was hunting them down based on speed and agility, a natural selection from weakest to strongest. She was fierce in hunting mode, that much was a given. It was when she stopped to eat that I cringed.

Once she made it down to the final few witches, she paused to snack on one of the males she'd ripped apart. I gagged from the mess of meat she consumed, gnawing on an arm and then internal organs as she yawned, stretching her arms. My creature grabbed another handful of the male and turned to peek at Knox, winking at him.

"I'm good now. It's your turn. Remember, Aria, let him catch us, or I will fuck him soon. No more grunting all night. I need sleep! I'm a growing girl. In case you needed a reminder of what one looks like, I left a little something for you since it's been so long since you've seen one," she laughed.

"No!" I growled, but it was too late.

The taste of raw, grizzled meat hit my senses, causing me to gag. I peered down at my hands, realizing I held a dick in which she'd just bitten off a huge chunk. Tossing it away from me, I gagged again, standing as I retched uncontrollably.

"You bitch! It was in my mouth!" I threw up what little food I'd eaten. Raw pieces of creatures and dick splattered the ground. "Oh, gods, that was so gross! You nasty bitch! You get back out here and clean us up! You made me eat a dick!" I gagged again.

"Next time, I'll eat more dicks if you don't get one into my vagina!" she chirped in a singsong voice. *"He's right there… in case you hadn't noticed. Alpha dick, Aria. Our alpha dick, or more limp dicks get added to the menu."*

"He's not *our* anything. He's only a dick!" I continued to gag, moving toward the witch with large white eyes, wiping my face on her dress, only to barf all over it. "I'm so sorry, but I think that was some of your friends." I offered, shrugging before I threw up again.

Laughter sounded from the other direction, and I turned, finding Lore bent at the waist, slapping his leg as he laughed uncontrollably.

Greer held up a white cloth, waving it in the air, just out of reach of the barrier. I perked up seeing Greer, but white light rushed at me as Knox howled a warning too late.

Pain shot through me, and I groaned, touching my hands and feet on the ground as the remaining witches attacked in a well-planned magical assault. My ears rang as my heartbeat slowed. I stopped breathing, conserving strength until the assault stopped. They began to cheer, and I smiled coldly, standing as the light dissipated to reveal my unscathed form.

"Mother!" one witch shouted, and I watched as she rushed toward her mom, who turned, staring at me and the mark of Hecate. It covered my forehead, lighting my face with the magic of my bloodline in a silverish glow that caused my hair to float while glowing silverish-blue.

"My turn," I laughed coldly, holding up my hands as the witches began to burn from the invisible flames consuming their flesh, wafting more ashes and embers into the night. The head witch howled, rushing toward her daughter, who was becoming ashes along with the others. "You were judged and found guilty. Your magic will return to the Nine Realms, your souls forever forfeited to the Void of Nothingness. Blessed be, bitches."

My fist closed, and embers shot into the night like fireworks. The witch who allowed monsters to rape and breed innocent women like animals, fired white orbs of magic at me in her grief. Each one slammed into me, but I effortlessly absorbed them and stored the magic while slowly walking toward her, bathed in blood and glowing glyphs of magic covering my arms, belly, and legs.

"Don't make this harder than necessary. I have other castles to visit this week, and you're boring me. Come," I smiled, lifting my hand, dragging her to the altar that rose from the dirt, pushing corpses off to the side onto the ground while candles appeared on the altar, leaping to life.

My other hand rose, and the corpses on the field became nothing more than dust. I was eco-friendly, if nothing else. My army of the dead stood silently, their heads lowered. I clucked my tongue three times, and they dissolved into embers drifting through the air, returning to their corporal forms, hidden behind the keep.

I'd learned a lot about myself since being on my own for months in a strange land. Like the ability to call the dead, and that my magic wasn't just more potent here, it was intensely amplified until it scared me. I'd learned that when evil was present, I needed to remove it, cleaning the land of its presence. It wasn't just something I had said I would do. I had to do it as if compelled by something more profound than I could understand.

The protection barrier around the altar began to glow, exposing the witch's circle the moment I stepped through it. I slammed the witch onto the altar, standing above her crying form as the candles flared, sending flames shooting into the air around us. When I touched her, she went limp, paralyzed.

My eyes lifted to Knox, who studied me silently, his anger palpable. I raised my hand and smiled as the dagger from his sheath landed in my hand. Before he could respond, I sliced through my palm, using the blood to paint the mark of Hecate on the witch's forehead.

"Thank you for your sacrifice," I whispered, slicing through her wrists before hanging them over the edge to feed the protective barrier.

I silently observed her blood pooling over the edges of the altar to fill in the circle surrounding us, touching the crystals as they hummed with magic.

"May the goddess forgive you from your trespass, witch. I sure in the hell won't!" I stated in a singsong voice.

Stepping away from the altar, I walked toward Knox, who watched every single move I made. His eyes slid down my bloody mouth, to the dress covered in crimson, reeking of copper. My nipples pebbled beneath it, hard from both arousal and the wetness of the fabric.

"Did you miss me?"

"Drop the barrier, Little Monster. Let me in," he ordered.

"I don't think so," I whispered. My hands went flat against the barrier, allowing myself a moment to admire him. "Are you ready to see what real magic looks like?" I laughed, tilting my head as Knox lifted his hands, slamming them against mine on the other side of the barrier. I inhaled his scent, running my fingers over his before closing my eyes.

"Enough fucking playing, woman," he hissed, and his eyes turned black, swimming with glowing sparks of heat. "If you are a good girl and do as you're told, I'll only hurt you a little. Make me fucking wait out your magic, and you won't like me."

"Too late, I already don't like you," I grunted with a smile playing on my lips. Slowly turning my back toward the barrier, I rested against it. The blood continued to pour from the witch's body, and my smile faltered as a pang of regret filled me. "I do like your cock, though. Such a waste that it's attached to you, and not someone more... *alpha*," I taunted, knowing it would piss him off.

"Oh, Sweet Girl," he laughed darkly, as I turned to face him. Power sizzled against my flesh, and his scent hit me without warning as he rattled loudly. "I am the biggest fucking alpha in all the realms, and you're mine."

I swallowed against the multitude of sensations his rattling created. Sweat pooled between my breasts, and my hand lifted, rubbing my fingers over my throat as his eyes locked onto the motion. Naked desire burned in his knowing gaze. I moaned, hating that my body heated for him from the noises he made.

"I'm not yours."

"Tell me this," he urged softly. "How much does it hurt you when I rattle? Right now, your pupils have enlarged, and your spine has arched for me. Your nipples have hardened, and those pretty rosebuds need sucking to ease their throbbing, don't they? I've smelled your arousal beckoning me to soothe your body's needs.

Everything inside you, including your creature, has told you to come to me. Hasn't it? Hell, even you want me, and that hasn't changed because you hate it. You're mine. The way you respond to me, and me alone? That's called ownership. All I have to do is wait you out, Aria."

"You suck! You know that, right?" I groaned, peering up at him, noting how his eyes sparkled and danced with silent victory. "You claimed ownership. Why? To use me, to fuck me whenever you want? I'm not a plaything, Knox. I'm unlike anything this world has ever seen, and now I know that too. You're not the only dick in the Nine Realms. My body may want you, hell, my creature wants you. I don't. I control who I fuck, and that won't be you."

"Keep telling yourself that. Hell, you may eventually believe it too, Little Witch. Now, bring down the barrier because the longer I am forced to wait, the longer I intend to hear you scream while I wreck that pretty pink flower of yours."

"That's an incentive not to bring down the barrier," I snorted, crossing my arms over my chest as the witch started crying and whimpering behind me. "Are you ready to watch me rock and rattle the Nine Realms? I'm about to show you what a real witch can do. I'm about to rattle you, Knox. Pay attention. You may learn something."

"You aren't strong enough yet, Little Girl."

Power erupted into the courtyard as I smiled at Knox. I lifted my hand, catching my bag in the air. Slowly, the dress I wore began unraveling, the scraps of fabric decomposing as they dropped outside the circle and onto the ground.

Once I was naked, I turned, allowing Knox's fierce gaze to slide down my bare hip, hearing an angry growl as I stood with my back toward him.

I turned a little more, letting him get a good look at my very erect nipples. I brought my finger to my lips as the witch began screaming, the power of the Nine Realms coursing through her, taking back what no longer belonged to her.

I laughed at the sound of her pleas and screams that mirrored the women I'd saved from her. I should have felt like a monster, but in the months since coming here, I had learned to embrace that I was the monster righting the wrongs of the race, who was supposed to uphold the laws, not abuse them.

Knox rattled, and my spine arched for him. I let my scent linger in the air between us, worrying my lip as I peered over my shoulder at him.

We both knew he was right, and sooner or later I'd have to either go to him or club him over the head and take what I needed. I was leaning on option number two, with him tied to a bed and me riding him whenever the itch arose. It was a very tempting thought, one neither of us would mind in the end.

Chapter Sixteen

I washed the blood from my hair and body before pulling a sheer dress over my head and tying a belt around my waist. Frowning, I winced at the idea of what was to come. Each witch charged with holding land had slivers of power within their bodies removed, returning the magic to the earth.

Tediously, I sliced the witch's arm open, retrieving the fragments of the crystal from her flesh. Her legs, hands, arms, and forehead bled freely as she cried, pleading for her life.

I'd have felt bad for her if she hadn't been a coldhearted, murderous bitch. It seemed to be a common theme for those who ruled to be vile, heartless creatures. Knox was guilty of it too. I could hear him rattling low, and it was soothing even though it shouldn't have been.

Setting the crystal shards into the cauldron, I leaned over the altar, rolling my head on my shoulders as I stretched. I'd gotten little to no sleep lately, with Knox intensifying the hunt when he wasn't out burning down villages and shit. Ever since the silver-haired men started appearing, he'd gotten more brazen, amplifying the search to capture me.

Moving back from the witch on the altar, I flicked my finger, watching as the upside-down cross rose from the earth, and her body floated to it with a wave of my hand.

Sidling closer to the cauldron, I peered over the rim, watching the crystals' slivers as they formed into one shard again. I reached into the boiling water, withdrawing a crystal skull that I cradled in my palm, watching the rainbow hues that danced within it.

Turning toward Knox, I paused, finding his mouth close to his witch's ear, whispering against it. Anger and jealousy rushed through me, causing his blue eyes to slide toward me as they narrowed on the skull.

I closed my fist around it, glaring at him as he pulled her closer against his body. The skull vanished in my palm. I flattened my lips, watching her hands sliding up his chest that was now bare and free of his heavy armor. On her wrist was the exact symbol that adorned the chest plate of his armor. His personal insignia branded onto the inside of her wrist, marking her as one of his witches.

Bastard.

Exhaling the fury, I closed my eyes as the cross vanished, and the witch slammed against the ground. Dismissing Knox and his weak-willed witch, I crept toward the witch in my circle, crawling through the dirt as she tried to escape. Her sobs made my stomach tighten with unease, knowing that I'd murder outside the heat of battle. It sat ill within me.

The moment she crossed the circle's barrier, her body began the slow process of aging and decomposing. Her skin turned leathery, darkening until it stretched wrongly over the bones beneath it.

The stench of death clung to her body, pronouncing her rotten insides had turned putrid. She rolled onto her back, howling as she revealed sunken eye sockets and a rotten tongue liquefying. Lips pulled back as the skin grew taut, and her lungs released the last sigh before her body caught fire.

As I watched, she turned to ashes picked up by the wind and blown through the air, returning her to the land. When we died, our ashes turned into magic particles that returned to our homeland. A newly born witch would inherit her powers if she were born lacking, which added hope to our race.

"Aria," Knox's deep, husky voice disturbed the peace, causing irritation to add to my growing emotional overload. "You need to stop and come to me. Now," he demanded.

"Fuck off," I hissed, fighting the inner turmoil.

"Jealous, Little Monster?"

I snorted, rolling my eyes. "You know what, Knox? If you want that basic bitch, you have my blessing," I growled indignantly, using my fingers to call forth the Keeper of Lightning, the elemental I'd come to collect today.

The sky above me cracked with thunder as lightning

slammed down around me. My hair lifted from the electrical current that rushed through me. I listened to the world howling as lightning began to pulse with the threat of the impending storm.

I leaned against the altar, sensing the presence behind me as it leaned against me, inhaling my scent, bringing its nose to brush against my throat.

Doubt and fear rippled through me.

That moment of clarity where you do something and then instantly regret that you were stupid enough to try it? Yeah, that was rushing through me as something very masculine pushed against my backside, and lips brushed over the scar on my shoulder where Knox had bitten the ever-loving shit out of me. My eyebrows shot to my hairline as raw, unguarded power slithered around me, wrapping against every inch of my body.

"You summoned me?" a multi-layered voice whispered against my ear, while hands cradled my hips precariously.

"I did," I squeaked.

A deadly rattle sounded from behind the barrier as power pushed through it, slamming into me while the being behind me chuckled like he found Knox's warning cute. The creature sensed it, the tension in the air, and the scent of death that clung within it.

I was shoved down hard onto the altar, and an elbow pushed into my spine. I didn't speak, didn't make as much as a whisper of noise while the Keeper of Lightning sniffed me. Fingers slid up my back, curling into my hair as I was yanked up and turned to face him. My mouth opened to explain my reason for summing him, yet no words escaped through my lips.

My breath caught in my lungs, becoming stuck there while my eyes grew large and rounded. I stared into striking violet eyes the color of lightning during a great storm as they scrutinized me.

The male before me had silver hair, pulled back and secured in a ponytail that most men couldn't pull off. However, he had done it splendidly. His chest was bare of clothing, exposing violet light visible beneath his skin as if he contained lightning within his soul. He wore white silk pants, revealing a very thick appendage that the silk outlined right down to the veins of the monstrous cock they failed to hide.

The sight of him and his aroused state caused my body to grow heated, and a heaviness settled on my tongue. Swallowing past the moan that danced on my lips instead of the words I needed to speak, I exhaled a breathy sound of need, which caused his generous mouth to curl into a darkening smile.

My head tilted to the side, and I blinked wide, owl-like eyes before slowly sliding them up the beautiful creature. Wings unfurled at his back, and I shivered, wondering if I'd just really screwed up with my choice to call this being out on his home turf. He was one of five creatures that my bloodline had cursed to remain here for all eternity as Hecate's punishment.

"Blessed be," I swallowed past the dryness of my tongue.

"Blessed be," he echoed, sliding his gaze to the warriors that watched us. Turning, he tilted his head at

Knox, who continued rattling the low, angry warning of death as he watched us. "I unsettle your mate with my proximity to you, woman. I would ask why you'd keep him outside your barrier while calling me within it."

"He isn't my mate," I whispered roughly, fighting the urge to touch the larger-than-life Adonis, who grinned as if he could sense my inner battle. I was losing, which wasn't a good thing considering it wasn't what I wanted or needed from him.

"Good to know," the creature cackled, sending a shiver racing up my spine to wrap around my throat tightly.

He grabbed me without warning, turning me to face Knox as his arms wrapped around my waist. His large silver wings expanded, growing until they created a shadow around us.

His mouth brushed over my mark, causing Knox to slam clawed hands against the barrier in a warning. His eyes turned black, and his teeth elongated as the creature continued holding me. Knox wasn't enjoying the shoe being on the other foot.

"He thinks you belong to him," the male laughed wickedly. His mouth kissed my shoulder, and searing heat slid over my skin as lightning rocked through the bite marks.

A sob exploded from my lips as Knox snarled, slamming against the barrier, watching the creature sear my flesh. Tears burned my eyes, rolling down my cheeks. I opened my mouth, hating that he was removing the mark.

I felt it to my soul, felt the effect that removing it was creating within me. Knox didn't even look human as the sharp features in his face changed, and he rattled loud enough that I felt him. I wanted him to replace it, to mark me as his, the moment the creature had touched it and defiled the scar Knox had left.

To remove it felt horridly wrong, and everything within me felt... *empty*, and broken without it there. Knox turned to his men, screaming orders before he swung back, staring at me as if he had felt that same nothingness. His hands balled into fists at his sides, and his eyes condemned me for removing his mark.

"Stop," I stammered through chattering teeth, trembling as denial rushed through me.

"You *want* his mark? You, a witch, want the mark of a male who wishes to own and end your kind?" the creature asked. "Interesting choice, since you're a daughter of Hecate's womb. Seeing who marked you, you may want to reconsider."

"I know who he is," I swallowed, holding Knox's damning stare that told me he intended to replace his mark, violently.

The male's mouth curved against my shoulder, and Knox stepped back, lowering his head as fiery embers burned in his gaze. I could feel the violence he wished to inflict on the male holding me. His power slithered through me, and I wasn't sure I would survive both men sending power into my body at once.

Even with the male behind me, my eyes refused to leave Knox's gaze, knowing he was the more deadly of the two. The creature's hands lifted, cupping my breasts, his wings enveloping us, and he laughed at the sound of the low, growling purr that exploded through the barrier. His thumbs traced over my erect nipples, sending awareness pulsing between my thighs.

"I didn't call you here for this," I muttered, turning to stare into eyes that reflected lightning within them. "I called you to take the element back, and to remove the curse from your bloodline. I came to free you, and to take the magic from this realm into my soul. Not so you could mess with King Karnavious by fondling me in front of him."

"You've come alone, little one. I cannot give you the power without a coven to ensure you don't die before fully taking it from me. If you failed, my line would die out permanently."

"I will not fail. I am of Hecate's bloodline, and so much more."

"Request denied," he snorted coldly, stepping away from me as if he planned to leave. "You and your kind have been a plague within this world. You've taken and taken until there was no other choice but to do as your whore of a mother demanded of us."

"Grandmother," I corrected icily. "The blood of the firstborn witch resides within me, and something else. My power comes from the Nine Realms, not from other witches. I am strong enough to hold the power alone. The power of the Hecate line is within me to ensure I live to house it, guaranteeing my survival!"

"If you failed, the cost would be your life and that of my children, *child*," he snapped loudly, causing lightning to pulse through the field, his eyes and hair igniting, and his wings vanished as if they'd never truly been there at all. "I won't let you put my people in danger of extinction at the cost of your impending failures."

"I will not fail," I hissed, glaring at him. "You have no choice but to do as I bid! I am of Hecate, born of her daughter. I will take back the magic fueling this world, showing them what this place will be without the magic that holds the balance. I have slaughtered thousands of witches in the little time I've been here. I will undo the evil the witches have created, and I will free this world of their hold. However, I can't do that without the power you and the other Keepers of the Elements, hold."

"You think you are strong enough to hold my power? I am three thousand years old, and I almost failed to house it for Hecate. You're a child, untested and untrained."

"I am Aria Hecate, and I intend to rattle the Nine Realms!" I shouted as the castle beside us began to rebuild from the shambles I'd rendered it into during battle.

The army outside the barrier started floating in the air. All except for Knox, who peered over his shoulder. He turned his angry glare back to me as he lifted a brow with silent question smoldering in his stare.

Chapter Seventeen

The creature looked right, then peered left before he smirked wolfishly, stepping closer, touching my face to brush his thumbs over my lips. I raised my hands, and the entire castle creaked as it lifted from the ground. His lips tipped into a grin, and he grabbed my hands. That would have prevented a normal witch from casting or holding a spell, but it didn't stop me.

The creature narrowed his eyes as he brought my hands to his face, slowly studying them. He pulled me against him, claiming my lips in a sinful kiss, producing a moan that escaped me. When he pulled back, his eyes slid from the castle to the men, still floating in the air.

"You're not of Hecate, Aria. You're of *them*. You're... very special. Your father must be very proud of the little monster he helped create, isn't he?"

"I don't know who my father is," I admitted breathlessly, swallowing hard as heat rolled through me.

Knox's scent was overpowering, pushing the other away, even from outside the barrier. He forced my attention to him. Midnight skies had replaced ocean-colored eyes, and the fires burning within them threatened to consume me. His power wafted over me, bypassing the barrier to carry his scent to me, creating a mass of emotions throbbing through me.

My shoulder pulsed where the mark once was, and I wanted to beg him to replace it, to mark me again. Lips curled into a devilish grin, as if he sensed my need and approved my instinct to be reclaimed by him alone.

"No, but you will soon. Your father is very aware of you, Aria. You weren't just something that he accidentally created. He wanted you. He'd have felt the war coming and designed what the world needed to protect against the destruction coming. Even so, only you can choose the path you will take. It's curious, though, considering who you've allowed to mark your body."

"Choose a path? How am I supposed to know what path to take? I was living a normal life until all hell broke loose, and I ended up here. My mother slept around a lot. I don't think anyone designed me. I think I'm an accident that she wanted to erase, and she tried her best to accomplish that goal."

"Not an accident, Aria Hecate. Your father doesn't make mistakes. He creates solutions for what this world needs in times of crisis. Make no mistake, this world is in crisis, and you're here to be the deciding factor on who will win the war. You are needed. Your choice of lovers, however, may cause you many problems."

"Just because Knox gives good dick doesn't mean

he's anything more than that. King Karnavious tried to murder the only mother I have ever had, and his dick isn't good enough to lose my head over," I muttered, and the male laughed as if I was delusional.

Violet eyes searched mine before he exhaled, sliding his attention to where Knox prowled outside the barrier. His hand slipped around my waist, causing Knox to snarl his annoyance at another male touching me. The creature leaned down, nuzzling his nose against my ear. Knox's scent struck me without warning.

Knox's power echoed through me with a deep, rumbling rattle that filled my ears, calming my response to the male holding and touching me. I frowned, sliding my gaze to Knox, purring huskily for him as his eyes heated, and a knowing smile spread over my lips.

"His mark isn't just for claiming you, Aria. The mark on your shoulder, yes, that was a mark of ownership and a warning to others that you're his and untouchable," he said softly. "He didn't just claim your flesh. He claimed your soul. The mark on your thigh, placed there by his blood magic, is deeply embedded into your soul, not even I can fully remove it."

"I'm aware of the mark on my thigh, very aware of it," I swallowed, unable to look away from Knox or the intensity burning brightly in his eyes. "I'm working to remove it now."

"You can't remove it, woman. No one can, but the one who placed it. Right now, Knox is planning to mark you much deeper than that. He doesn't lose control, but he's fighting for control over his beast because I merely *touched* you. He didn't much like that, or that my lips brushed you, kissing your pretty mouth. Not to mention, I just ripped his mark from your shoulder by force, and you both felt that down to the very fiber of your beings. Let me show you the future, should you sway from the path he created you to take."

"If I agree, will you allow me to take the power of your element?" I asked, watching as he swallowed hard. The tick in his jaw began slowly, and his eyes turned to angry slits as he studied me.

"Yes, but should you die, the world will turn into ashes. Can you live with that? Could you accept that knowing you would be at fault?"

"I'd be dead, so that is a moot point, isn't it? The world is already a place of nightmares. Witches have created slaughterhouses of those who are just trying to survive. Hecate had no business decreeing herself, the Goddess of the Nine Realms. She shouldn't have forced the creatures to bow to a goddess who was selfish, unhinged on her best day, and a monster on her worst."

"You understand that speaking as such is considered treason against the goddess, correct?" he countered, eyes sparkling with mirth. "You do, and yet you don't fear her, which is troubling."

"Speaking the truth shouldn't be considered treason. Are you saying that I am wrong? Correct me if I am, but you're here because Hecate placed a curse on your people to ensure you never rose again to live among the Nine Realms. You didn't bend a knee to the Queen of Witches when demanded you do so, even though you were the king of your realm. You and the others didn't choose this fate, nor was it justified, Taren, King of Gargoyles."

"You know of me?" he asked, smiling as if he found me amusing.

"I made it my business to know who was wronged throughout the history of the Nine Realms by my people. Gargoyles intrigued me greatly. I knew that you were their king, and that Hecate slaughtered those following you. Those who hid in the shadows are still there, or at least those who weren't full-blooded and died of the curse Hecate unleashed upon them and their unborn children. I knew that she cursed you and that it was not right. By taking the magic you were forced to hold, I can free you and your people. I am undoing the wrongs my bloodline has inflicted on others, or I will die trying. Go big or go home, right? I have no home, so I'm going big. Show me what will happen if I fail or stray from the path created for me."

Taren's hands lifted, and his wings wrapped around me once more, clasping my face in his hands as he lowered his forehead against mine.

The world spun around us, changing to darkness before we reappeared in a world of burning embers. Ashes rained down from the sky as blackened ruins covered the meadow. Fields were covered in skeletal remains, and in the distance above the rolling fields stood a castle, built from skulls.

I moved toward it, but Taren grabbed me, pulling me up against him, placing his finger across his lip. His lips brushed my neck as he turned us to follow the knights in armor the color of raven wings with the emblem of a skull, and twin ravens beside it.

Armed knights moved beside us and stopped, tossing

more witches to their knees before dismounting close to where they'd fallen. My heart thundered in my chest, and I tried to step closer to the witches, only to realize they couldn't see us. Arms wrapped around my chest, and Taren forced me to watch as the knights withdrew their swords.

"I didn't use magic!" the witch cried, and I tried to break free, but Taren's hand slid over my mouth as he pulled me backward, hard, holding me against his body as fear rippled through me. "I didn't, please! I didn't cast, nor did she. We've followed the high queen's rules!"

The high queen?

Horse hooves over rotted bones sounded, forcing me to turn and gaze in the direction of the noise. A woman dressed in a black gown and armor molded to her petite form, dismounted. She reached for the sword on her horse's pack. She moved toward the witches; her face covered by the onyx-colored visor of her armor.

The sword swung without warning, and without cause, and tears burned my eyes. She lifted her mask, turning to stare at the knights as the color drained from my face, and my eyes slid to the knights.

"Place their corpses on the wall and collect the heads," *I* stated, exhaling as I wiped my blade off on the woman's dress. "Place their heads inside the palace as a warning to those who oppose me."

What the actual fuck? Was I *fucking evil? How?*

The world spun around me again, and I gasped as my chest tightened. When it finally stopped moving around us, I dropped to my knees, retching onto the green grass of the same meadow. My hand lifted, wiping the bile away from my lips as I gazed at an entirely new scene.

Witches moved about, carrying herbs and cauldrons as the sun dipped behind an extensive, sprawling mountain range. In the distance, I stood with babes dancing around me. I struggled back up to my feet, turning to glare at Taren.

"You couldn't have started with this one? Maybe worked your way up to me being the evil queen?" I snapped.

"You are both, Aria. You house the ability to become either. Which you choose will depend on you and the path you have taken to get here."

"Which path leads to me to becoming evil? I'd like to avoid it at all costs."

"Do you think this world needs a hero? I assure you, it doesn't. It needs a monster, Aria. All the best heroes are villains, after all. If this world only needed a hero, King Karnavious would suffice. His intentions are pure, if not for the ill-planned path to achieve them. The Nine Realms has enough heroes who have tried to save it from destruction. You're not the hero, little one. You're the villain."

"Ouch," I grumbled irritably. "Did Knox pay you to say that by chance?" I queried before turning my attention to the future me, who laughed as she lifted a boy onto her hip.

I studied the dark hair and ocean-colored eyes that smiled up at me with love. My stomach somersaulted, and my heart clenched as the boy's dark head leaned against my arm, placing his tiny hand over my heart. A small girl leaned against my hip, her silver hair and turquoise gaze watching the babe. I adjusted him to run my hand through her silver strands.

Taren watched me gazing at the future version of myself and exhaled. "King Karnavious is a lot of things, but not my friend, I'm afraid. Hence his reaction to my touching the woman in which he has laid claim. I can't tell you which path to choose, Aria. That is something you have to figure out alone. Every direction you've taken since entering the Nine Realms has forged your path toward one of these futures. The pain you will endure. The losses you will survive. The choices you will make in the spur of the moment, or in the heat of a battle, will lead you to one of these two destinies. It is for you to decide. Now, let's get you back so you can choose your path, shall we?"

"I don't want to be a monster," I whispered, shaking my head. My fingers curled into my palms as I balled my hands tightly at my sides. "Unfortunately, I think my path will lead me to the version I don't want."

"No one chooses to become a monster, Aria Hecate. Sometimes the world creates them because it needs one, which doesn't make them bad or wrong. King Karnavious is wounded, and his grief and the promise he made to his wife have turned him down a very dark path. He intends to keep that promise he made to his wife, even though keeping it will destroy the only happiness he's ever truly known."

"He intends to use me against the witches."

"Indeed, and he isn't wrong. There are too many to

stand against without a witch to match their power. You alone can do that. You're needed to win his war. His war leads to one of those outcomes, which one depends on you. Can you sell your soul to the devil and dance beside him, or will you be the end of him?"

"What the fuck does that mean?" I demanded through trembling lips, but the world started spinning around us when Taren touched my arm.

"It means your paths are connected, and you were supposed to meet. How it ends is up to you, and only you, Aria Hecate. One queen will emerge, but the name she chooses to use will decide which side of the war you wage your battle. Choose well, because one ends with you buried in a nameless grave to be reborn, and the other would see you rule the world."

Chapter Eighteen

Taren and I broke apart the instant I could manage to stand on my own. Shaking my head, I shivered as my hands lifted, warming my arms before my attention slid to Knox, the tic in his jaw hammering visibly.

I swallowed hard, sliding my eyes back to Taren, who offered me a crooked grin, noting where my attention had moved to for strength and reassurance. I hadn't even realized I'd looked to Knox for that purpose until Taren grinned, twisting his lips. Lifting his arms, crossing them over his muscular chest, he observed me carefully.

"Are you ready, then? Or do you need a moment to tell your lover goodbye in case you don't survive what happens next?" he asked, studying the way I slid my eyes to Knox once more.

"No. I am ready." I swallowed past the lump in my throat, pushing down the anxiety that threatened to choke me.

Would Knox care if I died?

Would he mourn me?

I doubted it. I'd just be another dead witch he couldn't sleep with anymore. Knowing Knox, he'd miss being unable to cause hell on my libido, but not necessarily miss me. He'd probably place my skull in his bedroom, and skull fuck it to make sure I never fully escaped him.

Taren held out his hands, and I placed mine into his, stepping closer to his body while a frown played on his generous mouth. If I fucked this up, his race was toast.

No pressure.

Right?

Taren's lips twisted as if he was sensing my thoughts, and he tilted his head to the side as he brought me out in front of him, forcing me to face Knox and his lethal gaze.

"You're going to call to the land and ask it for the element of lightning. Then, you'll call the lightning forth, and when it answers, I will push it into your soul. When I disengage, you will need to summon the lightning from the four corners. Contain it, or we die. Do you understand?"

I swallowed past the worry and the lump growing larger in my throat. "Yes." Knox smiled coldly as power continued to slam against the barrier.

My attention slid to the witches beside Knox, adding to his power to break through the barrier that held him at bay. I exhaled, letting my gaze linger for a moment before focusing on Knox's form, letting my hunger-filled eyes slide to lock with his.

Goodbyes were overrated anyway.

Right?

"Knox is impatient to reach you. Considering your body's delicate position, and the scent it is currently releasing; I don't necessarily blame him. Shall we begin?" Lightning crashed beside us, causing the loose strands of hair to float in the air as the rich scent of ozone filled the surrounding barrier.

"I'm ready, Taren."

Lightning lit the field, causing it to turn indigo with the intensity of the power humming around us. Taren threaded his fingers through mine, spreading my arms wide as he chanted softly, the sound swallowed by the hum of energy filling the space. The protection circle pulsed, and crystals shattered as violet-colored bolts slammed into them, sending fragments through the air, pelting my bare legs.

Knox yelled, and my attention slid toward him at the same moment lightning rocked through me. A scream escapes my lips, and my head flew back, exposing my open mouth to the sky as a violet streak of light shot down, moving through me. My body jerked and twisted as pain rushed through every cell.

Screaming filled both sides of the barrier, mine and Knox's pulsing through me as the power slithered around me. Taren held me up, his hands continuing to hold my arms out wide. The pain persisted until my legs threatened to deposit me onto the ground, but the rigid body holding me refused to let me fall.

The moment it ended, Taren released me.

I dropped to my knees, and he stepped away from where I'd crumpled to the ground. My head lifted, locking gazes with Knox, who was on his knees, staring as my body, covered in a violet hue, trembled violently.

It took everything I had to push myself off the ground, my eyes never leaving Knox as he did the same. Power rushed through me, and electrical pulses sizzled over my flesh as I turned my head to the left, holding out my hand, calling for more of the power.

Lightning slammed into me, sending me sailing across the ground as I screamed. Tears slipped free, and my nose popped as everything within me felt torn apart. Sobs escaped, and my eyes closed, reopening to stare down at the ground where blood coated the earth.

Exhaling, I heard screams mixed with the pounding of my blood in my ears. Louder than any battle drum, it hammered deafeningly. I forced my body to rise, slowly moving back to the protection circle.

"Aria," Knox whispered, sounding as if he was inside my head. "Enough. It isn't worth your life, Little Witch. You're killing yourself."

"I will not fail," I mumbled, lifting my hand, turning to stare in the opposite direction. A coppery tang filled my mouth, and I spat blood onto the ground as everything within me demanded I stop. "I can't fail," I implored, speaking to the land more than myself or even Knox.

"This is madness. You aren't strong enough to take what Taren holds. Listen to me! You're going to die if you continue. Let it go. It isn't worth your life."

"You're too late. If Aria stops now, she dies," Taren chuckled darkly, the smile on his face sinister.

"If she continues, she dies, King Oleander. You knew that when she offered to hold the power, didn't you?" Knox accused, his eyes darkening with murderous rage as I swayed on my feet.

"You killed my wife and took my sons away from me, King Karnavious. Did you honestly think I'd allow her to live knowing you marked her for your own? You want her to live? Free my sons from your binding oath, and I'll help her. Refuse me, and you'll watch her die. I'm willing to let my sons and my race die with Aria, rather than them living one more day as a slave."

My attention lifted, locking eyes with Knox, realizing my error. Knox had gargoyles in the library, ones that listened to his every order. Gargoyles were enslaved by a binding oath, or their oaths were given freely as they craved purpose. Very seldom was it the latter.

I wasn't stupid enough to think Taren had willingly helped me. He'd been forced to show my paths because gargoyles helped shape the future, standing sentinel over the living for protection. It was why they guarded churches and homes. They were protectors of the realm. So, what had Taren done to force Knox to murder his wife and take his sons?

My hand lifted, and I called the power of the Nine Realms to me without warning, hearing both men gasp the moment the world answered my call. Pain rocked through me, forcing me to fight against the urge to drop to my knees as the power shattered everything inside of me.

Lifting my eyes, I smiled at Knox as a loud popping noise sounded, and my vision swam. My body began to drop forward, only for a blinding, white light to shoot from the earth, catching me before I could face plant on the ground. The light lifted me, and my body slowly floated above the crimson ground below.

"Impossible," Taren whispered.

"She failed," Knox growled harshly, but I could hear the worry in his tone.

My body spun until I saw the purest blue sky above me. I was suspended in the air by the power of the realm that was rushing through me. My hands dropped toward the earth, hanging beside me as my body bowed in the middle, causing blood to run down my face. Power rippled through the clearing, and I moaned, forcing my eyes to slide to the portal Aurora had just opened.

I slid my eyes to Knox. Worry burned brightly in his gaze as he ignored the others.

His expression said I couldn't die. I wanted to laugh and tell him that I agreed with him for once. There was also somberness in his eyes, and it tugged at my heartstrings. I offered him a sad smile, opening my mouth to speak, but nothing escaped past my lips.

I exhaled a shuddered breath that caused him to wince as more blood rolled from my lips. Warmth rushed over me, along with his scent. He was offering me comfort. I reached a point in my sheer stubbornness to admit I wasn't strong enough to achieve this task.

"Aurora Hecate," Taren said in surprise, but when she turned angry eyes in his direction, he smiled wickedly.

"Still as beautiful as always, Love." He watched her moving toward me, his eyes turning to slits as the smile faltered and vanished from his face. "She failed, which means her life should be forfeited. You knew she would fail this task, yet you allowed a child to face me. Why?"

"You know why," Aurora scoffed, shaking her head as she peered down at me. "Almost, Aria," she whispered, holding her hand above my chest as power shot through me, and my body rejected the crystal shard skull, now filled with violet bolts of lightning. "You took enough to do what was needed. The Nine Realms has found you worthy, and has spared your life, daughter of my heart."

"It hurts so badly," I confessed, releasing a sob before I could prevent it from escaping past my lips. "I'm dying."

I fought against the pain as everything within me felt torn open and rearranged again. It was as if the world was trying to put me back together from the inside out. My eyes moved to Knox, allowing him to anchor me to him, and somehow the pain melted away. He was the last person who should have offered me comfort, and yet he was. His gaze told me I was strong enough to survive, even though everything around me said otherwise.

"We need to take her with us!" Kinvara sobbed, turning her attention to the army over her shoulder. "Jesus, shit-bricks, and sandals," she choked on her words that came out too quickly while she gasped, noting Aurora's lack of panic. She turned back to stare at the men, eyeing the warriors who watched us. "Why aren't they attacking?"

"Aria erected a very powerful barrier with the souls

of the witches she murdered. They'd need a lot more power and magic to get through it to reach us," Aurora frowned, lifting her attention to Taren. "You are free, Taren. Go back to your wife, where you belong, you treacherous swine."

"Are you still angry that I chose Maricela over you? You know I adored you, Aurora, but you didn't put out, nor did you offer me the sons my monarchy needed and demanded I provide. Besides, King Karnavious murdered my sweet, gentle Maricela. He murdered her right before *your* mother placed me into this hell, but you knew what Hecate planned to do to me, didn't you?"

"You were out of control and had gone insane!" Aurora hissed, sending her power rushing through the field in warning, igniting the protection barrier around us.

Kinvara lifted her hand, moving to wipe the blood from my face, but Aurora slapped her hand away before touching me.

"Do not touch her, Kinvara. The power of the Nine Realms holds Aria. If you touch her, she dies. It is healing her because it has found her worthy of its power. You cannot interrupt the process because she *is* dying, and *the realm* is fighting for her life against death." Holding the pulsating stone containing the lightning, Aurora turned to glare at Taren. "Leave now, or you will be returned to that hell as a corpse to meet your dead wife."

"You always did play hard to get, Aurora. I'll see you around, Love. Plan on it," Taren snorted, lifting his hand as a bolt of lightning shot from the sky, and he vanished in the blinding light with a pop, leaving only the scent of thick ozone.

"Aria," Kinvara whispered as she gazed down at me. She ignored the army that watched us, hanging on our every word. "Why are her hands black? Look at her fingertips."

"She murdered witches," Aurora whispered thickly, staring at my fingers that had yet to return to their natural color. "Thousands of witches would be my guess, which caused the markings to appear in warning to others of her intent to gather power." Aurora exhaled, smiling worriedly down at me, softly speaking in the ancient language of witches.

Aurora and Kinvara stood hand-in-hand beside me, right on the edge of the light that shone from the ground, holding me in place. Their whispered chants increased the energy pulsing through me.

I felt even more power from my sisters through the bond we shared as they joined hands, softly chanting together. The mantra would strengthen me to fight against death's icy claws, trying to sink in and pull me under.

I could feel blood trickling from my nose. I watched my family, staring through them to find Knox silently gazing at me, his forehead creased tightly as his witches chanted together with my bloodline. I'd failed my initial plan big time. But I realized now that we hadn't needed to take all the lightning, just enough to fill the skull, leaving a little of the lightning and the power of the realm within me.

Aurora lifted her hand, holding the skull high in the air as power arced into it. The chanting increased in speed and volume, and I realized we needed more than they had to give.

Suddenly, the chanting of hundreds of witches entered my mind, joining those who were here. I gasped, staring at Aurora in wonder, knowing she'd called upon those who still abided our laws, proving there were witches worth fighting to save. Tears rolled from my eyes as she nodded.

"They're out there, Aria. They're waiting for us to come and save them. We're not alone here anymore. Let us help you so we can go together and help them."

"Go," I whispered, barely loud enough to be heard. "You're not safe here. Soon, the barrier will fail, and Knox will catch you. I can only escape him if you're not here anymore when I wake up."

"You can't protect them and us."

"I choose you, than," I stated with conviction, filling my voice. Aurora's eyes filled with unshed tears, her head slowly shaking at my stubbornness. "I choose my family, always. Get into the portal because I will need one to escape. I cannot do that if you're still here. He will find me because I am weakened. Go, I will find you when it is time."

"Aria, you can't fight the world alone," Kinvara shushed.

"Watch me," I smiled sadly. "I love you, but I have to do this. I can't be the reason you or anyone else dies. I can't live with that, so please, just go. I will figure out a way to undo what I allowed to happen," I whispered as pain erupted inside of my head, and everything faded around me but sound.

The pain was visceral and raw, shredding my insides until only guttural cries escaped my lips. The blood stopped running, and white pain pulsed behind my eyes. My entire body trembled, and it felt like tissue was replaced, cells re-situated, before everything seemed to go numb, finally.

"Stand back, Kinvara. Let the world heal her so that we do not lose her. You," she growled harshly at Knox, pointing a finger in his direction. "If you touch her before she has healed, she will die. Do you hear me? To you, she is nothing, but this world thinks she is something special, or it would not have saved her with its powers. Let her be King of Norvalla, or watch her die because she will fight you until her dying breath leaves her lungs to protect the weak from you. You think us murderers, but ask yourself this. Who could be strong enough to push a goddess into her grave, sending her bloodline running in fear? Because that is who sired Aria and created her against all the odds."

"You don't know who sired her, Aurora. She's mine because of that mark on her thigh. No one can question or challenge that. Aria asked me for the mark, and I agreed to give her my name. I protected her when she needed it, and you know that makes her mine now. It's legally binding, and I don't give a shit if you like it or not."

"Neither do you know who sired her, but look at what is happening! The Nine Realms is healing Aria, acknowledging her attempt to do what was right for this world. She was willing to sacrifice her life to protect innocent people. How evil can she be, if she is ready to use her soul to protect them, Knox? Look at her closely because we still may lose her yet. No witch has ever held enough power to take back that which fuels the realms with my mother's powers, but Aria almost did.

"You look at her as if she is a weapon to wield, but she's just a girl who wants to do the right thing. Not everything is black and white, but if you push her, she will unleash hell on those who have endangered those she finds worthy of protecting. She is beautiful and pure. Remember that because unlike you, she's never tasted grief, and when she does, it will be a game-changer. Don't ruin her. She isn't what you hate."

"Oh, but she is because your bloodline runs through her veins. It's all irrelevant because Aria is mine, and I intend to keep her, Aurora. I walked in and took your strongest witch from beneath your fucking nose. You thought you would rise to be queen, but we all knew who held the throne's power. It wasn't you and isn't Aria's sisters. You planned to use her too. You just didn't intend for her to figure that out. Aria is brilliant, and sooner or later, she'll put all the twisted pieces into place, and this world will tremble in her presence." Knox's tone was unforgiving and tense.

"Pray she doesn't, because if she rises, we will all fall, Knox. If she rises, so will the old ones, and that monster that sired her will return to ensure she becomes what she was born to be. A monster with no equal," she hissed, causing my lips to tug into a deep frown. "They're aware that she exists, and they've already tried to get her to go with them willingly. Do you intend to stop her from discovering her truth? Or do you plan to keep her on her knees as your slave? I promise you this; Aria is more than anyone ever expected her to become. She is deadly in her own right, but when she discovers the truth about her parentage, well, goddess protect us all, because Aria will not."

"The old ones will only rise when the true king chooses to return to the Nine Realms. He hasn't been seen or heard from in over five thousand years. You have no idea of who is chasing her, any more than I do. They won't save her from me, and neither will you, witch."

I cried out, causing both sets of eyes to turn toward me. Sharp pain sliced through me, and then my body when tight with searing heat as my lips parted, expelling a soft cry of agony through the dryness of my mouth.

I felt weightless, listening as Aurora gave Knox a tongue lashing, and had I not been motionless, I'd have applauded. But I couldn't. I couldn't move, and pain continually ripped through me as the realm repaired me from within.

I sensed the portal closing and heard the silence of the clearing as the power lessened. I remained within the air as something rolled down my face, tears I hoped, and not blood. All at once, the pain stopped, and I hit the ground hard as everything went black, and consciousness slipped from me.

Chapter Nineteen

Soraya

My eyes slid over the chaos raining down on the keep. The King of Norvalla stood on one side of a barrier with his army, and on the other side was a witch, suspended in the air by Nine Realms' magic. She dropped to the earth, and I studied the form on the ground, exhaling as her chest rose and fell, proof that she hadn't died.

She'd done the impossible. There wouldn't be a single witch who hadn't felt the magic removed from the Nine Realms. That in itself was an impossible feat, but when she'd failed to house it, the realms themselves had reached up and healed her.

My heart thundered in my ears, deafening Ilsa's call while I watched the woman's dark lashes fluttering while an older Hecate witch argued with the King of Norvalla. Large blue eyes narrowed into angry lines while her fists balled up, and she held one out toward him. I stepped closer, craving to hear what they said.

Magic slithered over my skin in warning, and I shivered past the vileness of Ilsa's summons. Stepping back into the shadows, I drew the runes for the portal, slipping through it, back into the Palace of Magic.

"When I summon you, you come!" Ilsa demanded, spittle flying from her rancid mouth as the vile rotten-egg scent hit me full force.

My stomach roiled, rebelling against the scent of death and rot that clung heavily in the chamber.

"I couldn't escape without giving my presence away. Forgive me, My Queen," I dutifully answered in a subdued tone.

"What was that I just felt?" she demanded. "The world just trembled and shook with a power imbalance! No one is strong enough to cause that, and yet I felt it," Ilsa scolded, her eyes fully obsidian with the oily taint of magic.

"A witch just took the power from the Keeper of Lightning," I admitted, somehow managing to keep the wonder and awe out of my tone.

"Impossible! Hecate herself safeguarded the power of the elements so only her bloodline could remove them to awaken her from slumber. No one is strong enough to house that much power, and no coven alive would dare to trespass against us!"

"Yet I just watched it with my own eyes," I countered, flinching as her hand sailed toward my face, sending my head back as pain burned my cheek. "I would not lie to you, My Queen."

"That power would kill anyone stupid enough to try to remove it! Upon their death, it would unleash the power into the Nine Realms, and yet I can grasp no power, Soraya! Tell me, how is that possible?"

"The young woman, she didn't die. She didn't take all the power, though, just some. Another witch appeared from a portal and healed her. A call went out far and wide to heal the woman who had taken the lightning from King Oleander. I believe she is one of the Hecate bloodline witches who entered the Nine Realms."

"Where did she go?" Ilsa demanded, her rotting lips pulling back tautly over her decaying teeth.

I schooled my features as her lip tore at the corner, and black sludge-like blood dripped from her mouth. Bile fought for purchase in my throat, and my stomach flipped as a shiver raced up my spine. The scent of rotting organs and chamber pots slammed into me all at once, as Ilsa forgot to cover her smell amid her anger.

"Nowhere," I admitted. "The witch didn't get up. The King of Norvalla was with her, and I believe he sought to destroy her," I announced, barely keeping the tears from falling as her scent burned my eyes, causing them to water.

I didn't look away from Ilsa. I wouldn't ever give this monster my back, not without wanting her dagger sunk into it. Her head canted to the side and then turned toward the dark corner of the room.

Ilsa's body turned weirdly, slowly moving toward the wide-opened window before she rested her hands against the windowsill.

Wailing started outside, indicating they had added more witches to the grid. I silently prayed that they'd find a painless death before placed among the others. Every time I returned, I prayed my sister Julia wasn't the newest addition to the grid that pulsed with unimaginable power.

"If the King of Norvalla is after this witch, then her days are numbered. Is she the same one who set siege to the keeps?" Ilsa asked, and I exhaled.

"Indeed, it is she. She taunts the King of Norvalla and plays with him. She is powerful, and yet young and naïve in so many ways. I believe that he will capture her, and either keep her on a leash or end her existence. Either way, you will be unaffected by his choice. She won't be your problem should he catch and null her powers," I explained, watching Ilsa's eyes sliding to the room's dark shadows.

A shiver rushed down my spine as I peered into the shadows, sensing nothing there. Ilsa nodded, forcing my stomach to churn with unease. Her skin was taut over bones, and yet in places, it had lost all elasticity and hung loosely. She slithered over toward me, staring into my eyes before lifting her hand, and I stifled the urge to recoil from her touch.

"You will go infiltrate the King of Norvalla's ranks," she stated, and I dropped my composure.

"That is suicide. He knows when a witch holds darkness," I exclaimed.

"And yet you have not allowed it in, which I have ignored. You can infiltrate his camp and get close to this witch, or you can accept the darkness, Soraya. Choose,"

Ilsa sneered, her eyes filling with color that looked glossy and lifeless.

"I will learn what I can for you, My Queen."

"Excellent. I know he won't allow you to leave once you're established as one of his many whores, or camp followers. There are other means of communication that we will use. If you get caught, you die. There will be no one who comes to save you. You're not worth wasting my resources."

I swallowed, nodding slowly before I calmed the emotion her words sent churning through me. I wasn't stupid enough to assume she'd even care if I died. To her, we were nothing more than tools in her armory that forged her true weapons.

"Go! You'll need time to figure out how to let them capture you and become a whore to one of his men. I suggest you lose the air of superiority you hold in my presence. The King of Norvalla would crush and enjoy the sound of your supple skin, tearing as he ripped you apart." She smiled, dragging her blackened fingertips against my lips. "Such pretty skin, wasted on you and your kind. It will land you in some worthless male's bed, on your backs where bitches like you belong. Do not fail me, or Julia will end up in the grid, left alive to be a slave to me forever, Soraya." My eyes widened, and she smiled coldly, her glassy, dull eyes lighting with mirth. "Of course, I knew which line you both belonged. I am the fucking High Queen of the Witches, after all."

"I will not fail you."

"I know you won't, Soraya. Julia is all you have left, and she belongs to me now. If you bring me back the head of this witch or the King of Norvalla's, I would willingly allow you both to live freely under my rule."

There was no freedom under Ilsa's rule. The chances of her freeing us were zero, and we all knew it. Her version of freedom was to be added to her grid, feeding her power. I won't let her add my baby sister or me to that grid.

My eyes slid toward Julia, who continued silently screaming in her mind, stuck in the darkness that fed on her soul. Tears pricked my eyes as I moved past her, not stopping to say goodbye, because if I did or if I showed an ounce of weakness, Ilsa would use it against me.

I made it outside the doors of the palace before I emptied my stomach onto the debris-covered road. People moved around me, turning to glare at where I retched until nothing but bile escaped my lips.

Wiping my mouth, I turned to the miles of tombs spread through the hillside's expanse that peered out beyond the palace. It was a morbid reminder that we were nothing more than fodder for Ilsa to wield against her enemies, of which there were many.

I'd escape this place with Julia one way or another, even if I had to bring Ilsa the heads of her enemies. Staring out over the endless killing fields, where bodies waited to fuel the grid, I shivered with the reality that we may all end up part of the grid fueling the evil bitch.

Chapter Twenty

Aria

Something touched my fingers, and I groaned. Prying my heavy lids open, I peered up into startling blue eyes that threatened to drown me in their churning sea-colored depths. I smiled sleepily, sliding my fingers through Knox's, pulling him closer. He hissed, and I yawned as sleep slowly slipped from my mind, releasing me.

"Morning, Knox," I said thickly, noting the aches and pains of my body. "Ouch," I muttered groggily. His fingertips ran against mine again, and I laughed softly as it tickled.

"Good morning, Little Lamb," he smirked devilishly. I tugged on my hand, watching his eyes sparkling with amusement as his touch sent heat rocking through me. I lifted my spine, arching, focusing his attention to move hungrily down my body.

I rolled onto my side as he pulled my hand closer toward him. His scent offered me comfort and created the familiar twinge between my thighs, clenching my stomach. He rattled the moment my eyes closed, forcing a soft smile to curve on my lips. I purred softly, and a groan escaped him.

"Move closer to me," he urged, and I lifted my eyes to him, wincing at the pain that flitted through me. "Come here, sweet girl, and let me hold you," he whispered, tugging my arm again.

"It's coming down now," a feminine voice announced, causing my attention to lift toward the witches who stood a few feet from us, casting a spell to bring down the weakened barrier.

I stared up at the sky, noting it was no longer night, and the sun was beating down on my face. My eyelashes dusted against my cheek as I swallowed past the dryness of my mouth. I yanked on my hand, struggling to pull it away from his hold.

Turning onto my knees, I whimpered, lifting my eyes to lock with his. I pulled back, crying out as pain rocked through me. Knox's eyes narrowed, lowering to where my other hand clutched my stomach. Slowly, his gaze came back to rest on mine.

"What's wrong, Aria?" Knox demanded, his tone laced with worry that wasn't like him.

"I failed," I said breathlessly. "Failing comes with consequences."

"You lived. What you attempted to do was suicide. You knew you could die, yet you still did it regardless of the cost," Knox growled, his eyes vying between blue and obsidian.

I rolled without warning, crying out as pain rocked through me again. I felt the shield beginning to drop and groaned, holding my stomach. Standing up, I eyed Knox as he followed my lead, pacing like a caged beast.

I reached down, grabbing my pack, and spun around, walking toward the keep. I rushed inside before shedding the dress I wore, entering the courtyard in nothing more than my panties.

Inside, I tossed the dress into the first room I found and ran down a long, winding hallway. At the end of the hall, I skipped up the steps and made my way quickly to the next floor, pausing as I felt the barrier fall, dropping with a loud popping noise.

I slipped my arms into my pack, running faster as the footsteps entering the keep echoed through the empty halls.

Entering a large room, I moved to the wall, drawing the portal before I sliced through my palm, holding my hand out to slap it against the stone barrier.

The portal shimmered as shouting sounded below. I stepped closer, holding my hand against the wall as nausea swirled through me, forcing me to wait precious moments before the portal would be ready.

"Find her! She's here," Knox's deep baritone slid over me as footsteps sounded near the door. The handle moved, and I closed the distance, slipping through the portal to stare as Knox entered the room, finding me already on the other side. "You've weakened, and in no condition to be on your own, Aria. You're not even hiding your scent right now. You allowed Taren to remove my mark, which was a mistake. Without that mark, you are free game to any male who wants you."

"I didn't want him to do that," I admitted softly, hating the pain that entered my voice as the truth rushed from me.

"Let me replace it, Aria. Come here, and I'll make certain no one hurts you, or tries to place their mark on you," he encouraged, holding out his hand while studying the way I swayed.

I wavered on my feet as he slowly stepped forward. Turning my head, I gazed at the people on the busy street behind me where the portal had opened. When I slid my attention back to Knox, I found him inches from me, a wicked smile playing across his lips.

"If you run, I'll catch you. You're unmated, unclaimed, and out-manned, Aria. I don't even need to use the mark on your pretty thigh to bring you to heel. You'll come to me, because everything within you wants the biggest, baddest monster in the realm, and that's me."

I caught sight of the dark-haired witch behind Knox, and I lifted my hands as he lunged, slamming against the portal as it closed. Spinning around, I searched the signs on the buildings along the busy street before finding a dressmaker. I rushed through the crowds of people who had stopped to gape at the portal magic, moved aside to let me pass. There was no need to flash my mark for them to gauge who or what I was, which was sort of cool.

Entering the shop, the metal keys on the door jingled like a wind chime or a medieval burglar alarm. I closed the door and turned, staring at the women inside who gaped in horror at me.

I could feel the blood crusted to my face and hair and didn't need a mirror to realize that I was rocking with my tits out since I was standing here in nothing but my panties. That explained the people gawking, which admittedly made me feel a lot less badass.

"Witch!" a woman shrieked, and I groaned before I brought my hands up, freezing them in place.

I exhaled slowly, inhaling even slower. I fought the pain still holding me in its thrall. I looked around the room, walking to the window, and peering out behind one dress on display. I forced my body to ignore the throbbing aches, spinning back to look at the women in the store.

"I am a witch, but I'm not bad. I am not here to harm you. I have an asshole chasing me, and he sort of wants to make me *his* bitch. I need your help. You know, female power and all that jazz?" Tears slipped free from their eyes, causing my brows to crease in irritation. "Let's try this again. You help me, you live? It's a win for everyone. All you have to do is wear my dirty laundry! Not so bad, right?"

I unfroze them, and they looked at one another before nodding. Tears aside, I wasn't evil. Taren was evil, so maybe his vision wasn't real. A female moved to run, and I slammed my hand down, slowly lifting her to hover in the air with the point of my finger.

"You forgot to change your clothes before leaving." I winced at the horror in her eyes. "Maybe I am the evil queen, but really, is she so bad? Normally they're just misunderstood, right?"

A stammering woman shook her head, her teeth chattering as she whispered, "They're bad, because, well, they're just bad."

"Thanks, I was having a personal conversation with myself here. I wasn't actually asking you!" I stomped my foot, frowning as she recoiled from me like I'd intended to slaughter her over her opinion. "I'm sorry. I didn't mean to snap. I've killed thousands of witches in the last few months, being chased all over the Nine Realms by an alpha asshole who thinks he can just caveman my ass over his shoulder and walk off into the sunset! That isn't how it works, right?"

"Generally speaking, that is how it works," a blonde woman said sheepishly, her eyes darting toward the others who nodded their agreement. "My husband claimed me in the middle of the street, bred, and placed his mark on me. I am his now."

"Oyo, the state of things in this place is a mess. So, each of you takes a dress and puts it on. When you get outside, scatter, running in different directions from one another. That's all I need from you. The moment you are away from the store, you're free to live a normal... somewhat terrifyingly submissive life."

"That's all you want us to do?" a raven-haired woman asked. "That's it, and we can leave?"

"Yes, I just need my scent to go every which way except in the direction that I will go. So, chop-chop," I said, clapping my hands together quickly. "Everyone grab a dress and change, please," I held my bag open for them to take my dirty dresses, which was a little disgusting, but desperate times left me few choices.

After the women left the shop, I grabbed one of the light blue dresses from the rack and slipped it on, moving toward the dressmaker who had yet to move. He assumed I hadn't noticed him behind the counter.

I smiled. The man's white bushy eyebrows shot to his frizzy, silver hair, and his hands lifted into the air as if he thought I intended to rob him.

"I don't intend to harm you, sir," I stated, smiling tightly.

I pulled jewels from my bag, placing them onto the counter. His eyes widened as I turned, pulling dresses from a rack, protected in plastic covers to guard them against dust.

The shopkeeper observed me silently, nodding when I slid my gaze to him to see if he would object. His old, gnarled hands reached up, accepting the jewels while I pushed the few simple dresses into my bag. My attention returned to him, and he flinched.

"I don't have any shoes, sir. I lost mine when I slaughtered a castle of evil witches and woke up later than I intended. The man I'm running from almost caught me, so I had to grab my bag and go, leaving my shoes in the castle and me without them. He's making it rather difficult for me to keep clothing and shoes on my person." Looking around the shop, I felt a twinge of regret for the old shopkeeper. "I hate pilfering from drying lines, and I hope the jewels help repay your loss of sells from me coming in unannounced, running off all your paying customers, for which I apologize."

"May I see your foot?" he asked, and I smiled before lifting it for his inspection.

He pushed his brows together but nodded, bending down beneath the counter to grab something. I tensed, slipping my attention to the women waiting by the door for my cue right outside of the shop doors, held there by magic.

The old dressmaker cleared his throat, and I turned back, staring down at the slippers he held up. Frowning, I accepted them and offered him a quick awkwardly worded thanks, smiling briefly before moving toward the door as power rippled through the shop.

Chapter Twenty-One

Opening the door, I watched the women rush in all different directions away from the shop when I dropped the magical confinement holding them. I slid into the shadows, carrying the shoes. I whispered a spell to become hidden within the darkness. I crept deeper into the alley, allowing myself to exhale against the fear of being prematurely captured. I knew it would happen eventually, but it couldn't be today.

Inside the alleyway, I watched as Knox rushed toward one woman, grabbing her as she released a shrill scream of panic. He glared at the woman, grabbing her dress, and taking a long sniff of the material.

A smile played on his lips as Knox lifted his head, peering around the crowd as my scent rushed in every direction. He found several more women, each having made it only a few feet away from the shop before he'd captured them, creating panic within them all.

I stepped back as his eyes slid to where I stood. Knox's head lowered, tilting as he listened for something. Too late, I realized he easily heard my rapid heartbeat. I saw him inhale deeply before starting in my direction in long, angry strides of his powerful legs.

I turned, rushing into the passageway as heavy footfalls followed. Rounding a corner, I paused, noting several direction choices before me, choosing the darkest path available as I rushed forward.

Knox's rattle sounded through the alleyway, triggering my body to pulse and tighten, forcing me to lean against a wall until the wave of heat passed. A dark-haired woman surveyed me, smirking knowingly as her attention moved to the mouth of the alley where the sound of heavy footsteps approached.

"You want to live, witch? Follow me," she offered begrudgingly, her violet eyes studying me, noting I glanced between her and the sound coming closer by the moment.

Freaking cheater.

The rattling was straight up unfair, and Knox knew it!

The woman opened a portal, and I narrowed my eyes on her as she turned, glaring at me like I was slow in the head. Apprehension slithered down my spine. I moved toward her, unhurriedly deciding my fate. I had only encountered bad people in the Nine Realms, which meant I was probably walking into a trap, weakened.

"You don't trust me, which means you're smart enough to live. That's the King of Norvalla chasing your dainty-ass down, Silver. So, either stay and donate your skull to his throne, or come with me, and live. It's a rather simple choice to make unless you get off on pain."

I rushed forward, deciding to take my chances with the woman. Even weak, I was stronger than most witches in this realm. Knox's scent hit me, and my body went tight like a bowstring as the woman reached forward, grabbing and pulling me through the portal.

Stepping through to the other side, she slapped her hand against the portal, and we both sank to our knees in the dirty refuge alley in a place I didn't recognize.

"Welcome to the end of the world, where everyone is an asshole. What's your name?" she asked, her brows wrinkling her forehead.

"Aria. Yours?"

"Esmerelda. My friends call me Esme, though."

"It's nice to meet you, Esme."

"We're not friends, Aria. You can call me, Esmerelda."

"Noted," I snorted, my lips curving into a smile. "You're an asshole. I can respect that," I snickered while a smile tugged at Esme's lips.

Neither one of us moved to rise from where we kneeled on the cobblestone alleyway. I didn't even try because I couldn't yet. My core clenched and released several times with the need to go back through the portal and clobber Knox over the head and ride him. Esme didn't move, probably because Knox's rattle was enough to make a sane person go insane with fear.

"What did you do to catch his attention?" she asked, pushing herself up using the dirty building side to gain her footing.

"I pissed on his party, ruining his plans for the week," I muttered, forcing my legs to work to follow her.

We moved from the alley into a bustling city that looked like the underbelly of a much larger city. People walked in rags through the street, pushing carts toward a large mine opening at the mouth of the town. A black, oily substance covered hands, clothes, and the rags that covered the faces of those traveling toward the mine.

The scent of rotting meat offended my nose, forcing my arm to move against it to stop the stench. My eyes burned from the fumes and smell of rotten food and something else. Women stood beside buildings in dirty dresses, calling to men who pushed larger carts toward the mine's mouth. My gaze slid over their outfits, or what remained of them. Some women hadn't bothered to cover their chests, allowing their tits to be bare, catching the attention of many men.

"This way, Aria," Esme said, as we walked on a road lined with huts.

I skipped toward her, rushing past some of the women who called out, offering to ease the needs of males and females alike. My eyes lifted to a single dwelling that looked out over the town like an oversight building.

"This is us." Esme nodded to a hut that was barely standing. I followed her inside, pausing as chubby faces came into view from the shadows of the room, peeking up over makeshift boxes shaped like a couch.

"It's nice," I lied, causing her to snort it reply.

"The urchins were here when I moved in, and I didn't have the stomach to kick them out into the street. They don't bite, but they eat a ton. It's not much, but it's our home. There's no bed, but we have room for one more witch in hiding."

"Hiding?" I asked cautiously.

"That's how you don't end up with your head on the King of Norvalla's wall or throne. It's been like that for the past two hundred years. Where are you from?" she asked, eyeing me skeptically.

"Far, far away," I exhaled, shaking my head. "Thank you for saving me."

"Don't thank me yet. We're all just trying to survive. Something made me save you. I didn't want to do it, but when the world tells you to do something, you listen. If it were up to me, I'd have left your ass on that street and not even batted an eyelash in your direction." Still eyeing me, Esme walked to the makeshift couch and rubbed the head of a child peeking out from a dirty hole-infested blanket. "I have enough mouths to feed, so you'll either pull your weight, or you must leave. Rumor has it that the Hecate witches have returned to the Nine Realms. So, now we're all just waiting to see where they fall into the scheme of things, or on which side they end up."

"You think they won't choose the witches?" I countered.

"I think they'll do whatever the hell they need to do to save their self-serving asses. They abandoned us to our fates once already. I'm not holding my breath for them anymore. Not after they put that evil bitch on the throne and left us at her mercy."

"They might just surprise you, Esme," I smirked, watching her eyes narrowing to slits.

"I hope you're right, Aria. I just don't think they're aware of the monster leading the rebellion, and once they meet him, they'll bow as everyone else does before the King of Norvalla."

I smiled tightly, turning my gaze to the urchins who looked underfed and dirty. Settling in the corner, I dropped my bag and slid down the wall, ignoring the aching in my bones and twisting in my stomach as my body protested.

Lifting my hand to my chest, I noted that although Aurora had taken the shard skull, I still held some lightning and magic I'd taken from the Nine Realms. It wasn't as much magic and power as I had hoped to gain, but it's enough to do what I needed.

The vision of me as the evil queen replayed in my mind while Taren's words echoed through my head. Maybe he was right. Perhaps not all monsters were evil. Maybe the world needed one strong enough to stand against the monster currently waging war against us. Perhaps I could change Knox's mind, or maybe I'd end up as another skull on his wall.

Noises sounded outside, and Esme moved to the window, peering out through the torn, russet-colored curtains, groaning. Her finger lifted to her lips, telling me to stay silent. She dug through her pockets, withdrawing a few chains before slipping to the door, opening it just enough to hold out her arm, dropping the chains into a clawed hand.

"You're short again. One more time, you and those brats are gone, witch."

"I'll make it up to him. I always do, don't I?" Esme replied, swallowing back the repulsive glare that danced in her eyes.

"On your back? Tristan is done waiting, girl. One more time and you pay him in pussy, or you will vacate the house. Those bloody little bastards you're protecting will end up in the mines, finding more crystals to sell."

"Understood. Guess I best not be late with the payment then, right?"

"Please, do. I've been waiting to see you on your back pleasuring the lord. I want to watch that haughty look in your eyes fade as he ruins that cunt. I bet you squeal like a pig when you're getting fucked. I'll be back tomorrow to collect the rest, witch."

Esme closed the door, sliding a weak wooden bolt that looked homemade into place. Her eyes met mine, and she shrugged. "Pick-pocketing isn't one of my strong suits. I used to sell potions, but now it's too dangerous to peddle them. The witches either catch wind you're selling in their territory, or the army shows up to take your head."

"We do what we have to do to survive." I swallowed and watched her shoulders slumping in defeat.

"Pray to the goddess that the Hecate witches choose us, right?" Esme frowned, her brows pushing together as she gazed at the children.

I could have said who I was, but I didn't trust her yet. Also, my suicidal action from the day had weakened me. I hadn't had enough time to rest and heal. I needed sleep, food, and enough time to regain my strength before I did anything, or told anyone about myself.

Things went downhill in the Nine Realms within a blink of an eye, and I didn't want to end up captured or on my back unless it was with Knox above me.

I touched my bare shoulder, and it burned as if my entire soul felt the loss of his claim. Hot tears pricked the back of my eyes, but I shoved them away.

Smiling, I recalled the look of intrigue burning in Knox's eyes when he'd figured out I had other women dressed in my clothes to send him searching for me in all the wrong places. A child moved to me, kneeling, as her grubby hand touched mine, and I smiled at her.

"To bed with you both," Esme snapped, glaring at the child who slid past without touching her, rushing into the other room. "I don't know if you're here to save us, or to curse us, Aria. I hope it's not the latter, or you'll regret it immensely. I may not look like much, but I am distantly related to the Hecate royal bloodline."

"Indeed, you are." I could feel her, which meant she had more magic than she thought, running through her veins.

I smiled as my eyes slid shut, and her resounding snort echoed in the tiny room. The single light in the home extinguished, bathing the room in shadows and darkness. Leaning my head back, I closed my eyes, drifting between sleep and consciousness.

My body grew weightless, and before I could stop the spell, I closed my eyes, succumbing to sleep. I felt like I was falling and unable to stop myself. Opening my eyes, I peered down at the warrior on a fur-covered, makeshift bed, frowning at the sight of him without his armor or clothes.

I'd forgotten about the spell I'd used before laying siege to the castle. It was an experiment I hadn't figured would even work. I'd just projected my image in a semi-corporal form inside Knox's tent, bypassing the barriers and protection spell.

Interesting…

Chapter Twenty-Two

I touched my face, slowly acknowledging how real my body felt in this state. My eyes never left Knox's slumbering form, noting that in sleep, and unguarded, he looked younger, but still just as intense.

Dark lashes dusted against the tops of his cheeks, his brows furrowing as his lips formed silent words. My gaze slid to his tattoo-covered chest, marveling at its chiseled perfection as it rose and fell with each breath he took.

The man was sex incarnate, and my fingers itched to trace every inch of his body. Relaxing a bit, I smiled, continuing to admire the sexiness of his muscular form, which he'd left on display for my inspection.

Easing closer, I noticed a white piece of parchment resting loosely in his right hand, bending closer still, trying to see what it held.

This spell I'd used was new. I'd been experimenting

with it to find a way to visit my family without placing them in danger. I'd wanted to test it on Knox and had swallowed the potion needed to enhance the spell. Then I realized he was marching to the same keep I'd been battling to accomplish my first task; to take the lightning. As far as I knew, I couldn't be hurt while using the spell.

I'd been testing my magic ever since arriving in the Nine Realms because time was something I had in abundance here. Idle magic was like hands. It needed something to do, or it would become a problem. I had failures and wins that made me bolder with the spells I used, or cast, like now, for instance.

Leaning over Knox to pilfer the scrap of paper from his grasp, I placed my knee on the bed, hovering over him. My fingers nearly pinched the paper important enough that he'd held it in his sleep, only for him to grab me, rolling me beneath him with his elbow against my throat. The rattle in his chest sounded low, deadly, and I mirrored the noise without thought or effort.

"Aria?" he asked sleepily, his hair wild from sleep. He blinked down at me in surprise and unease. "What the hell? How did you get in here past the guards?" His voice was thick and raspy from sleep, causing my body to respond to the sound as it scraped over my nipples.

Knox's eyes searched mine, and I smiled, lifting my lips to touch against his. He pulled back as I rested my head against the pillow where he'd placed me. Raising my legs, I ran my feet against his thighs, purring loudly as he blinked in confusion. Arching slightly, I rubbed my body against his, feeling him rising against me to answer my needs. I loved that the slightest contact between us created a response of carnal, visceral, red-hot need that demanded precedence over our emotions.

"Hello, Knox."

"What the fuck, Aria?" he rasped huskily.

"Shut up, and fucking kiss me, asshole," I laughed huskily, lifting my mouth to his again. He removed his elbow, crushing his lips against mine, kissing me until wickedly dark desire lit within me.

His kiss was toe-curling, causing a moan to build in my lungs, only to be captured by his hungry mouth. He rocked his hard arousal against my needy core, growling against my mouth as he devoured my moans, lifting his hand to hold my jaw in place when I moved to get air into my burning lungs.

I whimpered as his erection slid against my clit, sending a red-hot rush of need echoing through me violently. He chuckled at my response, biting my bottom lip as he rocked his body, knowing my need was absolute, and he was the cure that would end the ache I was enduring.

"Gods damn, woman. You're so fucking hot when you're beneath me," he snarled, pulling back, forcing me to chase his lips to claim them. He held me against his form before lifting me with him as he sat on his haunches.

My legs wrapped around his waist, and my fingers slid through his hair to hold him where I wanted him. I devoured his lips like a starving creature that only desired the taste of him, and would die without it. He laughed darkly against my mouth, breaking the kiss as he yanked the dress over my head, shucking it aside. Fingers bit into my flesh, rocking my hips against the bulge in his sweatpants as heat swelled within me.

It was good to know he wore his sweatpants when I wasn't around too. I was convinced they were purely there to make my life a living hell from refusing him. Knox's hands slowly slid up my sides, threading his fingers through my hair before he dragged it back, exposing my throat to his ravenous mouth. His nose rubbed against the thundering pulse at the base of my neck, slowly rocking his hips against where my body rubbed wantonly.

The simple action of his touch sent a gathering of heat through me, causing butterflies to erupt into flight within my belly. I moaned the moment his mouth kissed my pulse, sucking the flesh between his teeth and lips as he growled hungrily. He pushed me down onto the bed without warning, crushing me against it with the weight of his lengthy frame.

A storm played in the ocean-blue depths of his gaze. He easily secured my hands above my head, dropping his mouth to the valley between my breasts, peppering me with frenzied kisses. His knees pushed my legs apart, uncaring that the simple lace panties still prevented his entrance. His fiery mouth trailed over my sides, slowly tracing my tattoos with his tongue. I'd imagined doing the same to his ravens a thousand times before.

"I knew you'd come to me." He lifted his smoldering eyes to lock with mine, smiling wickedly hot, before clamping his teeth over one nipple, sucking it between his teeth, and I hissed as they scraped against my delicate flesh. "Fucking hell, you melt for me so perfectly, woman. You're so responsive to my touch."

"You're cocky, Knox," I whispered, arching into his mouth, parting my legs to feel his steel against my softness.

His teeth nipped, and I gasped, trembling against the raw desire he created in my system. Knox was a storm that grew and unleashed devastation in its wake. The man could make you feel like the most treasured thing in his world one moment, and nothing in the next.

He chuckled low, lifting while tightening his hold on my wrists to rake his hungry eyes down my body, leaving a fiery trail in their wake.

"You've been a naughty girl, Aria. I should turn you over and spank your pretty ass. I don't know what I want to do more right now. Fuck you, or mark you. I guess it's a good thing that I can multitask," he said huskily, lowering his mouth to pull at my bottom lip with his teeth.

I claimed his mouth, smiling against it as he groaned with need deep in his chest, mirroring my own. He rose, and before I knew his intention, he flipped me over on the bed, onto my stomach with my hands held against the small of my back, leaving my core exposed.

Teeth brushed against my shoulder, pausing, and a tentative smile played on my lips as my eyes slid to the portrait he'd held in his hands, just moments ago. A blonde woman nuzzled a babe in her arms, a smile curving her generous mouth while eyes sparkled with love at whoever was taking the photo. Teeth slid through my shoulder, and Knox paused, pulling back as he shoved me down, turning my body over to stare into my eyes.

"Witchcraft," he snapped, watching my mouth curve

into a soft smirk as I lifted my hips, wiggling them with invitation.

"Did you honestly think I'd come to you willingly?" I asked, lifting one brow higher than the other.

"Can you feel what I am doing to you right now?" The dark look smoldering in his eyes seemed to burn out, and anger took precedence, sending a shiver rushing through me.

"Everything," I admitted. Grinning, Knox leaned closer, kissing my throat before his mouth brushed against my shoulder. "I need you, Knox," I whispered huskily, pushing my fingers through his hair. If I were lucky, the dream walk would be enough to quell the ache in my loins.

"Good," he growled against my shoulder before teeth sank into my flesh, scraping bone. A scream bubbled up, escaping through my lips as tears filled my eyes.

White-hot pain shuddered through me as he laughed wickedly. The scream ripped through me, escaping past my lips as I bucked against him. It was debilitating agony, forcing my body to tremble as the scream continued.

The hand holding my throat moved to my mouth, smothering my cries as he kept biting me without mercy. He didn't stop biting, moving over the shoulder blade to sink elongated teeth into my collarbone.

He savaged my shoulder, biting me repeatedly until my screams subsided and turned to whimpering sobs. I absently moved against him, mindlessly unable to do anything else. I pushed against his mouth with my hand, moaning through the pain he was inflicting. Knox pulled back, his mouth dripped with blood as he watched me trying to turn over and crawl away from him.

Standing, he pushed his fingers through his hair, noting my blood soaking into his bed. Not that it would stay; it would vanish with me, as would the pain he had inflicted. Finally, managing to slide onto my stomach, I dropped my face to the bed, staring into his family's image, now splattered with my blood.

It was symbolic, all things considered. I was Knox's enemy, and his family was the driving factor for his hatred toward my bloodline. The bed moved with his weight, and before I could even gather the strength to slide away from him, he retrieved the photo, pushing it away from me. His thumb pressed into the wound on my shoulder, causing another scream to escape me.

"Do not ever fucking use your magic on me again, Aria."

"Fuck you," I groaned, hating that I was helpless to do anything until the spell ended.

"No, Aria. But when I catch you, I'll fucking mark you so deeply that no one can erase it from your flesh, ever again. Now get the fuck out of here so I can start hunting you down."

He pushed his thumb further into the wound, causing me to scream until everything within me rebelled against the pain. His other hand wrapped around my neck, baring it as he laughed huskily against my throat. I felt his teeth brushing against it, pushing into it as everything inside me went silent. The pain stopped, and the feeling of weightlessness took hold.

Hands slapped at me, shaking me awake. I gasped while sitting up, slamming my hands against the offender attacking me. My hand flew to my throat, and then my shoulder, finding both smooth and unmarked.

Knox's scent clung to me heavily, and the echo of pain as well. I swallowed the sobs, uncertain if I were relieved that the spell had worked, or worried that I'd trespassed against him with magic. He hadn't been receptive to the intrusion, that much was certain. Knox had responded poorly to me reaching him through the spell, and it had ended in violence.

"Who the fuck *are* you?" Esme demanded, glaring at me.

Chapter Twenty-Three

Esme held a dagger in her hand while standing in a defensive pose, ready to strike if the need arose. The tension rolling from her was thick and filled with mistrust. I didn't blame her, since I could smell the magic thickening in the room, mingling with Knox's scent that clung to me from the spell.

"I asked you who the fuck you really are," Esme hissed coldly, narrowing her eyes while she studied me through angry slits.

"Aria," I growled thickly.

I continued holding my hand against my throat, where Knox had been biting me. Phantom pain persisted, alerting me that while I was out of the dream on my end, he was probably ripping me apart on his. My core clenched, and my eyes widened, shaking it off. I considered what he was probably doing to my dream vagina. Couldn't he have started the torture with that?

"Aria, *what*?" Esme snarled, stepping back, pulling magic around her. "Glamouring yourself into someone else's reality isn't a simple spell. You were attacked, were you not? Yet you couldn't wake up. That means you used magic to project yourself to a different location. You cast a very powerful and dangerous spell that can be traced back to the source by any novice witch."

"So it is," I muttered.

"That type of spell is something only the most powerful witches can achieve in casting, and only after they've reached a certain age. You're not old enough to have accomplished that spell, let alone understand the consequences of using it, idiot. I could smell him on your flesh, girl. I'm going to ask you one more time, and then I'm going to slit your fucking throat if you don't tell me the truth."

Pounding started, startling us both as Esme swung her attention toward the front door. I shot to my feet, mere seconds before a large man forcefully kicked it in, joining several others that barged into the hut.

I smirked at their stupidity, lifting my fingers. I whispered a spell that liquefied them and turned them into puddles on the floor. Esme's violet eyes slid back to me, and I smiled coldly.

"I suggest you collect the children, and any other witches you deem are worth saving. I think the lord you owe money has grown impatient to fuck you and decided not to extend your deadline. It looks like he's ready to collect on his payment." My body arched with power, and the mark of Hecate glowed brightly upon my forehead as Esme took a step away from me. "Open a portal to the Kerrigan Keep, and seek shelter beneath it in the lower rooms, Esme."

"A vicious witch who enjoys slaughtering her kind owns that castle!" she snapped without tearing her eyes from the mark on my forehead. "We would all die if we dared trespass against her."

"That was true, but she's no more than ashes now. I slaughtered her and her entire following when they tried to eat another witch's children. You see, I am Aria Hecate, and I intend to protect and save those who are deserving of it. You're going to help me, Esmerelda. You're wrong about me, you know. I've met the King of Norvalla, and I don't intend to bow to him, ever. I am here to save you and the others who have not turned to darkness."

"I saved *you* though because you were *weak*!" Esme pointed out, slowly pushing her dagger into a leather holster on her thigh before yanking on her hair in frustration. "If you're supposed to be our savior, we're fucked! The universe is mental for making me save you! Now there's goo all over my floor, and I am going to end up on my back for years in servitude to protect the urchins from working in that poisonous mine!" Esme's face was red from anger as she inhaled, gearing up to say more.

"I *was* weakened. I had just attempted to take power from the Keeper of Lightning and failed, but I never intended to take it all." I let her see the lightning as it lit within my eyes. "I'm not captain-save-a-hoe either. I am here to help you fight, to help prevent your head from becoming a wall fixture. I've been here for months, and I've only needed saving once!" I huffed, and she frowned, narrowing her gaze on me.

"Where is your coven hiding?" she asked softly, her hair floating as power slithered through the room.

"I don't need one," I shrugged. "But I am building one. You're the first witch I have encountered who didn't try to murder me, Esme. I guess, for now, you're it. Congratulations."

"You're alone here? I thought there were more of you?" Esme's head canted to the side, peering at me through calculating slits. I glared back, wondering if she intended to turn me in to save her neck. Her lips tugged into a frown, and her eyes lifted to the patched ceiling filled with holes. "You are alone."

"The King of Norvalla marked me," I admitted, watching her lips tighten with my truth laid bare. "I was inside the human realm, in Haven Falls, when I met him. I was naïve when I experienced my first heat cycle. The elders sent him to our town, or so he'd made us believe. He said the mark would protect me, when in reality, it was a beacon for him to find me. It means I can't be near my sisters or aunt, not without bringing the head of the rebellion right to them. I chose to be on my own to protect them from my mistake. So, you will take care of the witches I save, and I will make sure you have what is needed. That's my offer. I expect loyalty. I want your word that you will help those needlessly persecuted for the blood in their veins. I, in turn, will handle the leader of the rebellion, who seeks to end all witches, removing us from this world."

"You make it sound so simple."

"Have you met that man? Nothing is simple with Knox. He wants to own me, and worse, the monster inside of me, she wants him to own us viscerally, which is why I can't be around my family."

"We all have our demons."

I snorted and then laughed as my head shook. "No, I literally have one inside of me. She pops up every once in a while. If my teeth grow, and my fingers turn into talons, just slowly nod and smile while backing away. Hell, you may even like her. Although, she's pretty driven by the need to eat, fuck, and fight. Luckily, she thinks Knox is one-stop-shopping for all of her needs."

"I don't even know what the hell to say to that," Esme scoffed, her lips twitching as she watched me.

"I'm learning to embrace my creature's chaos. I have it on good authority that this world requires a monster to match the one trying to bring it to its knees. I just happen to have King Norvalla's match within me, and I'm hoping I can change his perspective views on witches in general."

"You're planning on taking him on, even though you're aware of whom he is?"

"Absolutely," I said with conviction.

"I was wrong," Esme snorted while searching my face. "You're not smart. You're a psycho."

I smirked before shrugging my sore shoulders. "Sometimes, you have to be a little insane to play with monsters. It's not like I'm planning to take Knox on alone. I have a creature he can't get enough of, and she intends to help me. Most people say they have made peace with their inner demons. I haven't, not even come close. I do, however, intend to let my demon out to play with his, and then I'm going to bring him to his knees. Once he is there, I'll change his narrative on who is leaving and staying in this world. I can't do that and save those who are deserving of it while protecting them during the process. Join me, and I will protect you. You have my word."

Shouting sounded outside the hut, and I turned, moving toward the screams. "Save those you know are good and get to the keep. Beneath the upper levels are several tunnels. Once you're there, keep going through the water until you reach the platforms. Hidden, there is enough supplies and food to feed an army. Don't speak to the dead; they're mine. They'll be joining us for the coming war against those wishing to oppress us."

"Holy shit, you're serious. Aren't you?"

I smiled at the door, turning to wink at her over my shoulder. "I'm afraid I am. I am raising the House of Magic, and I intend to do it as Knox watches, helpless to stop me from accomplishing my goals. You're either on my side, Esme, or in my way. I suggest you choose which one you prefer, quickly. Knox is on his way, arriving within the hour, and I don't intend to be here."

"I'm with you, Aria Hecate. Just don't let me down."

"It's a deal." I stepped outside, noting the witches exiting other small shacks along the road as they watched. Power erupted within me, and the mark on my forehead glowed, my hair turning silver and violet. I smiled reassuringly at them. "Run," I ordered, hearing Esme yell instructions over the men shouting warnings.

Turning toward the men, I studied their stances, cracked my neck, and lifted my hands into the air, forcing their bodies to hover above the ground. Necks snapped, crunching loudly, and the witches whispered in hushed tones, while the lifeless forms dropped to the ground. My head turned in their direction while I wiggled my brows and hiked a thumb toward where Esme was heading off in the opposite way.

"I'd follow her if you want to live. King Karnavious is marching this way with his army at his back. Go now, or stay and fight. That choice is yours to make."

"Aria, don't die," Esme snapped, the dirty orphans holding her hands tightly.

"I can't be killed, and he won't take my head. He intends to wield me as a weapon, and he can't do that without a trigger to pull, which he will never find. I know what I am dealing with, and he's a loaded weapon too. Go. Get everyone out while I entertain the lord of the village. I think he needs a reminder why keeping a witch as a pet isn't a good idea."

"Urchins, come!" Esme grabbed a bag and started hazardously stuffing things into the pockets. "Aria, be careful. Tristan isn't a normal creature. He's enhanced by the crystals we harvest from the mines."

I studied Esme's posture, watching as she hefted the bag over her shoulder and slowly turned to face me. The sound of horse hooves rushing toward us captured my attention. Esme moved quickly into the shadows with the kids, noting how I walked in the opposite direction, muttering a spell under my breath.

Men and women walked toward her, but she passed by them until she reached the safety of a dark alley. Her wide, violet eyes slid to where I now stood, and she seemed surprised at my location, but nodded her dark head once before disappearing into the shadows with the children.

Esme was a fighter with a mouth on her, which I could use. I knew I was in over my head without people who knew the Nine Realms better than I did. I'd been here a moment, which Knox kept reminding me. I agreed with him on that, but I would need witches I could trust to help me wage this war.

Esme would be a good start, and more would come as I made my way through the other realms and places I needed to go. For now, I needed to prepare to face off against Knox, since he was probably still upset about my uninvited visit last night.

Men rushed toward me, and I smiled, cracking my neck, readying myself for battle. I would buy Esme enough time to get the others out of town since I couldn't say who would win. Knox was almost upon this location.

I could scent his anger driving him toward me relentlessly. Soldiers moved down the street in my direction, and I whistled *Gods & Monsters* by Lana Del Rey while walking forward, swinging my hips with a pep in my step.

Chapter Twenty-Four

I stood among the slaughtered men as the slumlord, Tristan, moved into the narrow streets he controlled. His guards studied me, sliding their worried gazes between their lord and me as I softly whistled to the music in my head. My body swayed while I listened to my creature as she sang the words, laughing while I danced for her. The moment the men moved forward, I paused, giving them my attention.

I brushed my knuckles on my shirt, stepping closer to the man in charge as his men closed ranks. Smirking, I winked at one of the men before pausing mere feet from the slumlord who glared at me with something disturbing in his eyes.

"You dared to trespass against me? Do you have any idea who I am?" he demanded, causing spittle to escape past his yellowing teeth.

His hair was slicked back with a days' worth of oil

coating each slimy strand. His shirt was open to the waist, revealing a large, protruding belly covered in dark hair. Tristan, the slumlord of the End of the World as Esme had called it, was an overweight, middle-aged male who enjoyed raping witches.

I could see lust burning in his eyes as he took in my dress, now bathed in blood. The sheer material clung to my body, exposing my curves to his beady eyes. Tristan's pants tented, proving he was interested in me even though I'd dispatched his soldiers onto the next life, removing their heads to make sure I'd driven home my point.

"I have an idea who you are. You're a slumlord. A horrible person who enjoys dominating the weaker sex, and you need a toothbrush, stat." I smiled as rage filled his face, turning it red as he glared at me.

Men grabbed me from behind, holding my arms as I continued smiling. Esme hiding in the shadows caught my eye, and I worked to keep the smile in place as worry entered my mind. What the hell was she still doing here? The men shoved me to my knees as warriors entered the street. My gaze slid toward them, brightening a twinge at the sight of the enraged male who glared at me.

Knox dismounted swiftly, moving through a crowd of onlookers to stand in front of me. He inhaled deeply, smiling coldly as he removed his gauntlets and brushed the back of his knuckles against my cheek. Knox's attention slid to the men who held me down with swords aimed at my neck.

"Get your fucking swords away from her throat," he hissed. "Now, or mine will be at yours before you fucking blink."

Knox grabbed me, pulling me up to my feet. His fingers pushed the dress from my shoulder as he continued holding my stare, only moving the fabric to check for damage. Looking to see if he had marked me in my dream, or maybe he was worried someone else had savaged it? His fingers slid over the unmarred skin as heat burned in his oceanic depths.

"Fancy meeting you here, Knox," I purred, letting the noise vibrate through me as his eyes narrowed to angry slits. "I hope you had a pleasant dream last night?"

"No, but I will have one tonight with you, Aria. I may even do a repeat to make sure you understood the seriousness of your slight against me."

"Is that right?" I smiled demurely as he scrutinized me.

"Indeed, it is. I'm pleased to smell you've hidden your need better, witch. It still isn't enough that I cannot scent your heat, Little One. Move, we're leaving now."

I deliberately stepped closer to Knox, feeling the lord's anger, realizing that Knox planned to march me right out of town with no repercussions for my actions.

It was curious that Knox had found the slum's location so easily, as if he'd known it was here all along. Or, Esme had been right, and he'd found another witch to connect the dots for him. Swallowing, my gaze slid to the hiding place, finding Esme still concealed within the shadows, watching everything unfold.

"She slaughtered my men, My King. I am owed reparations for what she has done here. It is the law. Is it not? Or does the law only apply to those who are in your favor these days?" This idiot man jutted his chin forward, challenging Knox. He must have a death wish.

"I am the fucking law, Tristan," Knox growled, peering over his shoulder at the middle-aged, bulging-belly slumlord. "Do you question my right to take this witch from here?"

"I want to be repaid for the men she slaughtered. I cannot maintain control without them," Tristan whined. "I am owed compensation for what she has done to my army!"

Lore grunted, peering around at the bodies of soldiers littering the ground in a tangled mess of limbs and positions. Some lost their heads, had broken necks and missing limbs. I cut the others into pieces; their organs hung about the cobblestone street among the refuse and trash. Lore's gaze slid to me, his lips twitching with mirth, and I winced, slowly taking in the carnage.

"You should have hired better men to guard your shitty little town," Brander snorted, glaring at me as his eyes slid down my body. "One tiny little witch kicked your ass and took down your warriors? I'd almost be embarrassed to admit that out loud."

"Kill her!" Tristan demanded, and I gasped as a blade pushed through my chest.

All hell broke loose. Knox rattled violence, slicing through the guards that stood beside him before I'd even processed he'd moved. Brander's sword was out with lightning speed, and with one swift twist of his body, Tristan's head went sailing toward a building, bouncing off the window, leaving a spider web in the glass. Knox rushed toward me, his eyes lowering to the blade still protruding from my chest as the man behind me slowly withdrew it.

I turned, shoving my hand through the guard's chest, and he squealed as blood exploded from his lips. "Didn't your momma ever teach you not to stab a lady?" I scoffed, withdrawing my hand, holding his still-beating heart, causing me to gag as I dropped the useless bloodied mess. I turned to wipe my hand on the other guard as something sailed past me. His head, I realized. "Gross!"

Spinning around, I glared at Knox, who dropped his gaze to my unbloodied chest, lowering the blade he'd used to remove the guard's head. He stepped closer, pulling me against him, inhaling deeply. His lips brushed mine, and then he pushed me away as his eyes studied me, touching me as he examined the cut in the dress I wore.

"What the fuck, Aria?" he demanded.

"Oh, this is awkward. I'm not actually here, Knox. I wasn't ready to tip my hand, showing that I had perfected my spell to work outside the dream state, but here we are," I smirked, studying the anger in his eyes. "Don't look at me like that. Tristan was abusing power and raping witches for rent. He was a *really* bad guy. The world won't miss him."

"He was a lord under my rule!" he shouted, anger pulsing through him as the tic in his jaw hammered visibly.

"Pot, meet kettle. Stick out your spout, and I'll lick it for you, big boy," I offered, wiggling my brows while letting my tongue trace over my lips. "I guess I'm not the only one with a dirty house, am I?"

"This is getting old, Aria."

"I told you I wouldn't be easy to catch, didn't I? I could have sworn that I did." My hands touched against his chest as his men moved closer with their weapons at the ready.

"It's only a matter of time before I catch you, and when I do, you're not escaping me again, Little Monster. I'm closer to finding your family, and when I have them at my disposal, you'll be a good girl and do as I say, or you'll watch them die one by one. There are only so many places for them to hide within the Nine Realms that wouldn't cause a stir. You're going to look so pretty on your knees, waiting for my orders. If you're really good, I'll even fuck you and make you come for me."

"You think we didn't account for that? I've been here for five months, and I have already brought houses to their knees. I have barely scratched the surface. You won't find my family, and if you do, I will protect them at all costs, Knox. I don't care if I have to sell my soul to the devil to keep them alive, I will."

"I know. I'm counting on it." He smiled cruelly as he stepped closer, whispering against my ear. "If you ever make me murder anyone else for you, last night will seem like pleasantries between lovers compared to what I will do to you. Do you understand me, woman? If you were anyone else, you'd be dead already for what you did last night and today. I will not warn you again."

"Are you saying you want me alive?" I whispered raspingly, brushing my cheek against his while my fingers slid over his armor, lifting to his cheek. "I like you too, Knox. Although, I think I prefer you mute and beneath me. Unfortunately, I got to fly. See you soon?" I asked, stepping back as he watched me through narrowed eyes.

My body-double dissipated as ravens flew through the air, rushing to where I knelt on the edge of a cliff. Knox's eyes followed the ravens' flight as they reached me, once more becoming tattoos covering my flesh.

I stood slowly, building up the rattle before releasing it loudly, watching the men with him respond to the sound, forced to bow, even though they fought the command. The world around me rattled with the sound, fearing my beast as lightning struck the earth behind me.

Knox peered at his men, his eyes darkening to obsidian as he returned the battle cry, causing my back to arch as I frowned, hating that my legs weakened. Before I could stop myself, I went down hard on my knees, glaring down at Knox as everything within me screamed to go to him.

Knox's rattle was absolute, without question.

Mine had been loud and cute compared to his.

Like a child imitating something an adult had done.

My body heard the rattling call and answered his, bending softly, intending to be freaking mounted. I purred huskily in response. I could not prevent the noise from slipping free as his rattle lessened, and he purred to relieve the pulsing ache he'd knowingly created within me. I didn't move. I couldn't. I sat there, holding his victorious gaze as my body calmed, and everything within me slowly returned to normal.

"See you soon, Little Monster," he whispered, and yet his words floated to me from my perch on the high cliffside that gazed down over the shitty town below as if he were right beside me. "You smell fucking delicious. Next time you rattle, make sure yours is the biggest, baddest one in the area because I won't hesitate to answer your call, proving who the fucking alpha really is, little girl."

I lay upon the ground, drawing the marking for a portal, slicing my hand through the palm before I opened it, and rolled through. The moment I had, Kinvara stared down at me, smiling as she knelt, pushing my hair out of my face. Her wide, blue eyes smiled as they slid down my body, scrunching her nose absently.

"You look exhausted." She smiled softly, tapping my forehead.

"What the freaking hell are you two doing here?" I demanded, groaning. I sat up, staring at Dimitri, who pulled me up to my feet, sniffing me as he muttered beneath his breath.

"Gods damn, girl," he said, growling low in his throat, his eyes like glowing sapphires. "You smell... good. I'm willing to clean the mess I smell with my tongue." His lips kissed my shoulder, and I glared.

"Puppy, you try to bite me, and I'll personally pull out every tooth you have until you eat puppy chow from a straw. One alpha hunting and harassing me is enough."

"Calm your tiny tits, Aria. Just making a statement and an offer," he said, lifting his hands in the air in surrender as he stepped back. "Besides, someone is going to need to help you out sooner or later. You are reaching your limit, and won't be able to fight it much longer, nor will you care that I'm not Knox when fucking your tight pussy."

"That's my problem, not yours. Why are you here? Knox is right behind me!" I seethed worriedly. "You need to go, now. He had his witches hiding around the corner from where I just used the cloning spell."

"Aurora found information after you took the power from Taren. We think we know where the next fragment is, but there's more. She thinks we can break the curse on us, but we have to break them all to do that. Also, if this plan works, we will have a way to raise the House of Magic earlier than anticipated, which means we can escape that dusty tomb. You wouldn't have to keep running, and we could protect the witches who still follow Hecate without you having to do it alone."

"I'm listening," I said, pulling magic to me in the event Knox's witch could open a portal into the area before Kinvara and Dimitri escaped. "Tell me what Aurora found, and the details of this plan. You have five minutes, and then you're both out of here. Open a portal, just in case. He's rather angry with me at the moment."

"What did you do to piss him off this time?" Kinvara asked, smirking.

"I made him kill one of his... lords. In fact, I'm not even sure what you would call that disgusting prick."

"You did *what*?" she asked, her mouth opening and closing while she blinked.

"It's not as if the man was a saint. He was forcing witches to sleep with him to make their rent. I'm pretty sure they will not miss their lord. Knox can't be one-sided. His house is dirty too, and if we're cleaning the Nine Realms, I'm cleaning all the houses."

"You're going to push him too far, and when you do, this plan will be dead in the water, Aria." Dimitri pushed his fingers through his hair while studying my face. "He's their King. He can't slaughter his lords, or he'll lose control of all his subjects. If Knox loses control, someone who can't be reasoned with will take his place, and then Aurora's plan will fail."

"You mean someone I can't seduce, Dimitri. You guys assume he wants me. Last night I used the dream potion, the one Aurora suggested I try to see if it worked to contact you assholes. He hurt me while I was with him. He meant to do so. Knox wants to use me as a weapon; that much is clear. If he wants me for something more, it is still up for question. You have four minutes now. I suggest you use them wisely. His witch hasn't cast magic today, which means they can open five portals before tiring, and I'm exhausted from running for months to stay ahead of him. Let's hear the plan."

"You will not like it," she warned.

"I kind of figured that one out on my own," I snorted, leaning my head against her shoulder. "Talk. I'm listening."

"I hate that you're so exhausted, and out here alone." Her hand came up to hug my head closer. "I wish you would allow us to help you."

"You are, Kinny. By staying safe, I don't have to worry about Knox catching or finding you to use against me. Three minutes."

"Here it is…"

Chapter Twenty-Five

I entered the keep through a portal, strutting in like I owned the place. Technically, I guess I did. I'd come in through the front, noting the skulls of the dead I'd left littered upon the ground. Moss and ivy had taken root on the castle's walls, making it appear abandoned. I'd added an enhancement spell to expedite the growth, but what had occurred was far beyond my hope.

The castle was half-destroyed, the front of which blown wide-open to discourage others from seeking the safety it would have otherwise offered. The high battlement's metal railing hung from a ruined pathway, thick wood splintered beneath it, some of which had collapsed to the ground to be hidden by flowery sage.

Inside the crumbling keep were several pathways that moved to different locations in the bowels of the castle. The protection crystals I'd placed before leaving had stood to ward off anyone that didn't belong.

I put my fingers on the rainbow tip of the largest one, and light shot out to expose a wide barrier. Whispering a spell beneath my breath, I charged each crystal, knowing I wouldn't be back for a while, and what was to come during my absence.

Once completed, I entered the first hall, turning left, continuing down a long winding hallway. To anyone that got past the crystals, it would look like a dead end. It took me twenty minutes to get through the wards below, placed to keep everything and everyone out.

Kinvara had access to enter through the bottom level, bypassing all the high-level security I'd added to the castle. She and Dimitri had a way in for when I was gone. I'd seen to their needs, knowing they were now under my care and my responsibility.

My feet didn't make a sound as I entered the large room, sliding into the shadows to observe the people Esme had chosen to bring with her. Women moved around with large baskets of the cloth and material taken from other keeps I'd destroyed. Some sat around tables, kneading dough with their knuckles. At another table, witches bound thread around small sticks of sage, ready for smudging.

It looked like a scene from a medieval movie was playing out before my eyes. Men entered the large room, silently placing shields and armor into large stacks. My eyes settled on the crest containing a skull with twin ravens adorning one shield's face before scanning the others. There were several adorned with Knox's crest, along with chest plates of armor. Swords were tested, sharpened, and then added to the growing stack.

Children milled about, kicking what looked to be a leather ball. Some moved together, while others observed warily. Exhaling past the unease those stares provoked, I noted the potions the witches were creating with alchemy.

If I had ever doubted that Esme was the wrong woman to help me, that was no longer the case. She watched with a close eye, noting the men until they vanished into the hallway that led out into the fields behind this castle. It was probably where they were collecting the armor. Esme went back to her task when they were gone, and the children moved into another room to continue their game.

I stepped out of the shadows and walked toward her. Esme was helping a child into a dress, and she paused, lifting her head. Violet-colored eyes locked with mine, and she shooed the child away, rushing to me with purpose.

"You're not a witch!" she hissed in a hushed tone, noting the smirk that played on my lips. "You're a lot more than that. You need to explain, now. How am I supposed to get people here with the guise of saving them if things are happening that I don't understand myself?" she demanded, her eyes studying the witches close to us.

"I told you I was more than just a witch. Does this mean I still cannot call you Esme, Esmerelda?" I countered, sliding my attention to the group of witches she'd collected, that were now watching us.

At least she had done as I'd asked while enjoying the show. I'd feared she would change her mind after watching me sink to my knees from Knox's rattle, but let's be real, who wouldn't? Even his men had gone to their knees as he'd reminded the world he was the ultimate alpha caveman.

"Yeah, but you're like him."

"We're something similar, yes. It doesn't change who I am, no matter what I carry within me. I am Hecate's granddaughter, and I intend to protect the witches who have not run amuck through the Nine Realms, rather than destroying it for their ill-gains. Our children do not deserve to be slaughtered, persecuted, or turned into slaves due to their genetics when they have done nothing wrong. Fueled by grief, Knox is prejudiced against us for the wrong-doings of the past. I plan to change that and make him see we can easily be on the same side."

"The King of Norvalla isn't wrong, though. The High Queen has allowed her followers to destroy anyone who doesn't yield to Hecate's reign. You haven't been here, and suddenly you show up like some white knight that's come to save a bitch. Why do you even care? We're nothing to you. What stops you from joining his side, or worse, the high queen's?" she asked as we moved toward a bench away from the others.

I sat down, staring up at Esme, considering my answer carefully. "When I was a child, I was told my grandmother was a saint, and that everything she did, she did for the greater good of the Nine Realms. In school, they taught us to worship her. The other races, too, and no one spoke about any of the Nine Realms' shifters or other creatures. Why? What made our line so special that everyone had to learn about Hecate and all the things she'd accomplished while the other races had also done amazing things? Frequently, those made into saints are merely sinners, who crafted their stories to fit a narrative that made them appear good.

"I didn't buy it. The shit our teachers were selling felt wrong. It felt forced, scripted, and contrived to turn people away from the fact that Hecate took control of a realm that wasn't hers to take. Take Norvalla, for instance. They refused to bow to a false queen when Hecate wore the crown, demanding that every king and queen bowed to her alone. They wouldn't adhere to her laws, and so bad things started happening to them. Their crops failed without cause, leaving the entire realm of Norvalla starving, forcing them into a trade market with other realms in which they didn't have relationships. Joining the trade market opened their borders for the other realms and forced them to adhere to Hecate's laws. That permitted outside influences and politics to occur that they'd refused to allow into their realm until Hecate forced them to obey her. However, the King of Norvalla found other resources and began trading with the King of Unwanted Beasts, another ruler who had refused to bow to Hecate.

"The summit of kings and queens turned into a slaughter. The opposing rulers, who had refused to bow to an unwelcomed, self-imposed queen, died, murdered on their departure to return to their homelands after still refusing Hecate's rule. It's not a coincidence that only those opposing her were murdered."

"Hecate was slumbering during that time," Esme pointed out, her brows wrinkling skeptically.

"So the legend goes. Who could prove that, though? Her witches or her own daughters? Daughters she murdered when they spoke against her? Sure, because that makes perfect sense. Let me tell you the story of Hecate, as told by my aunt. Hecate had three groups of children. The first group of daughters became jealous of one another and killed each other off. Seeing this, Hecate invoked the Laws of Magic, creating a failsafe that would deter her next born daughters from the same outcome. If one sibling moved to harm their sister or her offspring, they would suffer the same fate. Now, Hecate didn't bother to tell her daughters about this restriction, so when Hecate favored one of her four daughters more than the others, they plotted that sister's demise, killing themselves the moment she took her last breath. Learning from her mistakes, Hecate told her final set of daughters the stories of their lost siblings, ensuring they would survive and also that they would never speak or work against Hecate themselves for fear that there was another secret failsafe in place.

"That's a great story and all, but I call bullshit. The Laws of Magic invoke only if a mother kills her daughter, and Hecate isn't immune from it. I believe she cast the spell that led to her daughters growing jealous enough of the other, resulting in their deaths before they could testify to the elders that Hecate wasn't in slumber. I think the *failsafe* resulted from Hecate's actions against her daughters, and she just told my mother and her sisters about it to keep them in line. Hecate's daughters said she was evil, fueled by a need to rule over others, and turn the world into her personal idealist playground. Hell, she'd taken control of the Nine Realms once before, slaughtering the old ones because they refused her when she first showed up."

"You think she murdered those kings and queens to ensure that the walls between realms remained open?"

"I think she wanted to rule everyone and did whatever it took to accomplish that goal. Her laws, to do no harm to others, and to rule justly, were supposedly for the betterment of the realms. But I don't buy into that theory. Hecate was an evil, selfish cow who craved power and control, humping her way to the top. So why would she enact laws for the 'betterment' of the realms, when she clearly only cared about herself?

"Hecate did go to ground, but she did so because something stronger than her showed up. Whoever that was, they forced her to sleep, and the moment she went to slumber, someone murdered her. Now, why am I here? Because we didn't leave by choice, Esme," I scoffed, watching her lips tugging in the corner as her frown deepened. "I was conceived in the Nine Realms, but born in the Tenth Realm, or as you know it, the Failed Realm since the Nine Realms could not procure it. I had no choice regarding where I wanted to live. When my sister, Amara, went missing, we went to Haven Falls to find her, only to come face to face with Knox the moment we arrived."

I smiled at the memory, which felt as if it were years ago, instead of close to only one year now. "I was changing when we arrived, and something about my proximity to Knox woke the creature within me. His scent, or maybe the sound of his rattle, I'm not sure which, but I know it was Knox that caused my change to occur. Once I heard his rattle, I started evolving much faster and couldn't slow it down. The House of Magic in the Tenth Realm was unprotected because someone destroyed its shield, leading my sisters and me to stay in Knox's mansion. I lost my virginity to him when a spell called for hymen blood of a pure Hecate witch to erect the barrier around

231

the house, igniting the power once more."

The blood drained from her face as Esme opened and closed her mouth several times. I snorted, watching her, trying to place everything I had told her into her mind.

"Holy shit," she whispered in shocked horror that matched her worried expression.

"That's one way to state it."

"The King of Norvalla, he's your lover? He's the son of a bitch trying to kill us!" Esme watched the slow nod of my head, dropping her eyes to my lips that curled into a smirk.

"So he is, but I don't intend to allow him to achieve his goal," I announced.

"We're all in danger if he can trace you here!"

I nodded slowly. "Which is exactly why I won't be staying here very long," I grunted. Something crashed on the floor beside us, and I swung my head toward it.

"I don't even know what to say right now."

"So don't." I watched the coloring return to her face. "There is more too, which I'm sure will go over like a whore going down on a priest giving a sermon in Sunday church."

"What could possibly be worse than you fucking our sworn enemy?"

I smiled, watching her eyes filling with worry.

"Shit."

Chapter Twenty-Six

I stared at Esme while she counted out loud, fighting for calm at everything I kept dropping into her lap. I didn't blame her, and admittedly, I should have warned Esme before bringing her and the others here to hide. It wasn't as if we'd had much choice, though, and it was a safe place for them to hide for now.

"You are his lover." she repeated, standing up to pace slowly in front of me. "You're sleeping with the enemy!" She wasn't going to let that one go.

"I was, yes. Knox protected me up until he saved me from my sister before she could sacrifice me to her father-in-law. I was supposed to die so that Amara could prove her loyalties to the King of Unwanted Beasts. Knox came to save me, or so I thought. Instead, he took me as his prisoner, exchanging one jail for another. Then, he told me to remain silent as he moved to assassinate my aunt, who is the only real mother I have ever known. I refused, opening a portal outside the House of Magic, and we escaped. I destroyed any chance we had of ever returning by smashing my grandfather's skull, ensuring no one could ever go back. I sealed our fate, and now I have to fix that by erecting a new safe haven. A new House of Magic has to rise in the Nine Realms."

"Why?"

"I destroyed the skull and the House of Magic, along with any chance of returning for a few reasons. One, we would wage an immortal war among the humans, and they're not a part of this world. I didn't want that. Not because humans are innocent, but because they'd want all of us dead, and we'd strived to keep our existence secret. But also, it is our responsibility to hide the discovery of the Nine Realms from outsiders. Had we waged war amongst ourselves, they'd have noticed. I took steps to protect my family from him and his people by igniting a spell to hide the House of Magic from the naked eye, but that wasn't enough. When it became apparent that we would have to return to the Nine Realms, I had to destroy the house and the portal into that realm to protect the humans, preventing us from ever returning. Now I am going to raise a stronger, more powerful House of Magic here, and I intend to bring Knox and his creature to their knees."

"The King of Norvalla is purging the Nine Realms of the evil that has spread throughout them, Aria. I stand with him on that account, but he is mostly blaming the witches, and we're not all bad. He accepts witches into his army, but they must be pure of heart and minds, which some of us aren't. Some of us had to do whatever it took to survive in this world, and he removes our heads because of those choices."

"I don't disagree with him either. I differ with the fact that it isn't his mess to clean. It's ours, Esme. The Hecate bloodline failed, and in doing so, others have suffered greatly. I have already slaughtered thousands of witches who sought to murder me because of whom I am. You've seen my army, haven't you?" I asked, noting the color was draining from her face. "I thought so," I laughed soundlessly.

"It's hard to ignore them when they groan or make noises beneath our feet," she pointed out, and I nodded in understanding, before rubbing my temples to ease an oncoming headache.

"They're the witches who tried to hurt me or ones I found harming others. No good witches were harmed in the making of this army," I boasted, smirking as she winced at the smile playing on my lips. "Anyway, I'm here to prepare and place protections around the castle because I won't be back for a while."

"You just got here," she pointed out crossly, folding her arms over her chest, staring meaningfully at me.

"I have a mark on my thigh that allows King Karnavious to hunt me down no matter where I am. I can't stay anywhere long, or he shows up and tries to caveman my ass over his shoulder."

"What kind of mark? Did he mark you as one of his witches?"

"I'm not one of his witches. This mark is different. It's the kind that is so deep into my flesh that I can't remove it, not even with magic. When I went into heat the first time, it happened in his home. He offered a way to protect me from the alphas by placing a mark on my flesh. I just hadn't understood exactly what it would mean, but he did. I was naïve enough to think it would remain for a limited amount of time."

"Do you know the type of magic he used to create the mark?" Esme asked, frowning, already knowing the answer.

"Blood magic, which in hindsight should have clued me in on his intentions at the time. I just wasn't aware anyone would actually want to be connected to me, especially Knox. We didn't hit it off or even like each other when he did the marking, so it was easy to assume he didn't want that connection for any length of time. I was horribly wrong, considering he wants to use me as a weapon."

"Every male within the Nine Realms craves to control a Hecate witch, Aria. You're the shit of legends, and we've not had one with a strong link to the bloodline for some time now. You are more than a weapon, and considering the show you gave us the other night, I'm assuming you're not looking for a coven. You are a coven worth of power in this tiny little silver package."

"No, I don't need a coven. However, the House of Magic does. I don't even wield the same magic as you. It's more primal and rawer, which I'm sure you felt when I cast to protect you and the others from Tristan's soldiers." Shaking my head, I waved my hands in front of me, "We're off track, and Knox is currently chasing me, so we need to cut this short. My sister, Kinvara, will bring more witches to you, as well as supplies. I enhanced the castle with a barrier, I'm sure you've noticed. That will keep enemies out and still allow you to go out if you choose. You'll earn your keep, or you'll have to go," I said, smirking as I fed her words back to her. "Prove to me you're worth keeping. More witches will be joining you, but I need someone tough enough to do what is required. I think you're that person. You're powerful, which means you can enforce the rules. If you see someone who doesn't belong or grow suspicious of them, don't take any chances, kill them."

"What are the rules?"

"First rule? Don't be an asshole, Esme," I snorted, watching her lips twitching in response. "Also, you have some serious resting bitch face when you're thinking."

"That may be harder to fix. My sparkling personality and resting bitch face makes people assume that I'm much colder than I am. How many witches are you planning to hide in here?"

"Here? Only a few more, for now, I think. There's a larger castle that will soon be vacant. I think it will be a better fit for us."

"Castles don't go vacant."

"No, but if you murder the dark coven currently in residence, they tend to be open for new ownership," I said, shrugging as I stood to stretch.

"You'd need an army," Esme scoffed, eyeing me.

"Oh, you sweet summer child. I am a fucking army. Esmerelda, this goes without saying, but to be sure you understand, if you cross me, I will burn you from the inside out. I will make sure you feel every moment of the pain until your flesh begins to sizzle, separating from your bones until your eyes pop out of your fucking skull. Then, and only then, will I remove your head and leave it for Knox to find. I'll instruct him to place it on the seat of his throne, so you're nothing more than a fucking chair for his surprisingly firm, very nice ass. My family is the only thing I really care about, and this plan ensures them and the witches within the Nine Realms who aren't evil as fuck, live. If you work out, I think you and I will make great friends. If not, I do enjoy barbeque."

"I don't know if I should be terrified or have a serious girl crush right now. I can't say I trust you yet, Aria, but I can say that if you're serious about helping us, I'm your girl. I am all in with you. I don't want to die, and I don't want to bury more headless bodies. I worked in the killing fields, and I can't do that again."

"What killing fields?" Esme swallowed and shook her head. "Show me."

"It's not safe there."

"We won't stay long, and if they find us, I'll kill every last one of them to ensure we escape, Esme." She nodded, moving her attention to the girl and boy I'd not noticed. "Hello, urchins," I whispered, smirking as they slowly moved closer.

"Little traitors," she grumbled, opening the portal. "I'll remember that."

"Do they have names?" I asked, smothering a laugh.

"Yeah, it's urchin one and urchin two. They don't speak. Tristan removed their tongues after murdering their mother once her usefulness had expired."

Nausea swirled through me as I stared down at the children that held my hands. "How could he be so cruel?" I asked.

"Tristan was their father. He planned to breed the evil out of us with his seed, or he had, up until you murdered him. Now I guess he won't be breeding anything, will he?" She turned her attention to the children and nodded toward an older woman. "Go see old Agnes and ask her for some sweet cakes. She's hiding them in the larder room. Stick out what's left of your tongues at her. She's a softy for a sad tale."

"That's kind of fucked up," I muttered, watching the two children rush toward a witch who didn't look any older than thirty. Old Agnes wasn't that old if you were to judge her by her appearance. Unlike humans, though, we didn't age past thirty, so as far as I knew, she could be ten thousand or so.

"Barbeque? What is that?" Esme snorted, stepping through the portal as I followed behind her.

"It's something you eat after you cook it over open flames."

"But if you cooked me from within, wouldn't I be something other than barbeque?" she questioned, tilting her head.

I exhaled at the rows of sticks fashioned into awkward crosses covering the ground as far as the eye could see. It wasn't a typical graveyard with headstones and tomb markers; this was a sea of nameless graves that stretched on for miles and miles. My breath caught in my throat, and I swallowed, turning to look at Esme, who stared out over the field.

"Who are they?" I whispered.

"Witches, monsters, men, and women," she said

thickly. "My mother is here, and several of my sisters. This is where we bury the dead. Some are headless thanks to your boyfriend, while others weren't smart enough to bow to the high queen and ended up here one way or another. This is a glimpse at the future of the Nine Realms if the war continues to ravish through them."

Chapter Twenty-Seven

I moved toward the hillside with Esme, peering out over the men who endlessly dug graves. Chains clanked around their feet, and I turned, peering at Esme in question.

"They're prisoners of the realms," she swallowed loudly. "Once charged, they work until they expire and succumb to exhaustion. Some aren't immortal, so those will work until death or until the wounds fester on their backs, and they are too weak to work. Once that happens, they're added into the graves alive."

I took in the thick mist that rolled through the clearing, and a chill ran up my spine as the putrid scent of revenants got closer to us. My eyes burned, and I covered my mouth to suppress a cough, noticing Esme's panicked expression.

"No noise when it comes," she whispered barely above a breath.

Esme grabbed me just as their shrieks began. We rushed over the field covered in graves, Esme pulling me down with her when she tripped. I turned, staring over my shoulder where the revenant mist was moving quickly toward us.

I shoved up from the ground, grabbing Esme as we once against took off to the forest that was a little over a football field away. My lungs burned by the time we reached the thick woods, turning to see the gray, husk-like creatures as they stepped from the mist, rushing toward us.

I turned, pulling magic to me, sending it slamming into them at the same moment that Esme cried out. Spinning, I stared at the horrified look on her face before swinging my stare back to the creatures that had paused, growing before my eyes.

"Well, shit," I muttered.

"Come," Esme groaned, grabbing my arm as she yanked me through a portal she'd just opened.

We fell through it, barely escaping the poisonous claws that reached inside, grasping for us. I stood, resting my hand on my knees as I caught my breath. Lifting, I peered at the large stronghold that sat on the horizon.

Guards surrounded it, their power echoing outward, and a large wall wrapped around the complex, moving through the winding countryside beyond what my eyesight could see.

"What is this place?" I asked carefully, shivering at the power coming from the castle, humming through me.

"That's the head of the snake, per se. That is the

palace. Do you see that tallest tower in the middle?" I nodded silently. "That's the heart of the palace, and no one gets inside. Therefore, no one knows what it holds. Dark magic protects it, which I'm sure you can feel. People go into the keep, but they're not the same when they come out of that place. Something inside that stronghold changes them, and it isn't for the better."

"Is the high queen inside of it?" I asked, watching the guards move as someone approached.

A man appeared, screaming and shaking his hands in anger toward the palace. The guards moved into action, lifting their hands without a care for the man as mist billowed from the ground. Their hands shifted, tossing him toward the fog, and my stomach clenched with unease as he was pulled into the mist by the creatures we'd just escaped. I stared in shock as his bones were tossed out by a gray husk of a hand.

"And that is what happens when you get close to the gate without an invitation," Esme whispered so softly that I wasn't certain she'd even spoken.

"Someone controls that mist," I muttered, my tone lower than hers as she nodded.

Esme tugged on my arm and started through the forest. I trailed after her, stopping to watch her climb a sheer rock-faced cliff. Once she was up far enough, I unsheathed my claws and followed until we stood on a hill that overlooked a winding valley.

The same mist filled the valley below, shielding something from view. I silently moved closer, crouching to peer through where the fog was the thickest, but it was no use.

Scanning the area, I noted people moving around inside the outskirts of the mist without harm. Beyond, where the fog had cleared, sat a quiet town that sent a chill rushing down my spine.

"What is that place?" I asked.

"That used to be my home. It used to be Dark Hills, but then the palace was built beside it, and everyone fled when the mist came. Only a few of us made it out before revenants pulled them into the mist. A couple of my sisters died when the fog first appeared. The others were spared, but some of the dark witches eventually took them. Two went into the palace, but the one that came out wasn't my sister anymore. My mother went to find help, but she never returned for us. We sent word to the high queen, but to no avail."

"She didn't care they were murdering witches beneath her rule?" I couldn't believe that the high queen wouldn't want to stop whoever was murdering her witches.

"Ilsa isn't a queen, Aria. She's a horrid being who hasn't lifted a finger in hundreds of years for anyone unless it was for her benefit. We've had to fend for ourselves. In fact, my entire life I have lived with your boyfriend hunting us down, and the one thing that kept him from reaching us was my mother, and whoever helped watch over our town. Then the mist came, and the palace went up seemingly overnight. All hell broke loose, and thousands died within the first few hours of the mists' arrival. I watched my family, neighbors, and friends sucked into that stench, only to have their bones spat out."

"I'm sorry," I frowned, unable to stop the sadness that I knew showed on my face.

"You weren't even here. Come, I want to show you something," Esme stated, holding out her hand.

"No offense, but I won't hold your hand through any portal," I snorted as her lips curled into a smirk, and her eyes sparkled.

"Bitch," she replied.

"Hooker," I retorted.

"Nope, thanks to you, that isn't one of the jobs I have ever done, or will," she laughed, using her bloodied palm to open a new portal. "Not all of my friends are witches, and sometimes I forget when I am around others like us. It's not often I find a witch that hasn't caved and turned to the vile bitch ruling us."

"Noted, but let's hope there are enough of us left to make a change." I stepped through the portal she'd made and paused.

The streets were in chaos as soldiers grabbed women and children, throwing them to the ground. Screams filled the area, and the scent of copper hung heavy in the air. I watched Esme rushing toward a soldier who lifted a blade, intending to harm a child. Calling my magic to me, I slammed him back through the crowd of men.

"Enough!" I screamed, the sound of my voice coming out in layers, giving pause to the warriors.

The witches, or at least I assumed that they were witches, gathered the little ones, and moved them away from the men who turned on me. I snorted, glaring at the warriors who had been picking on helpless women and children. Blood bathed the ground as I walked through the path, flinging my arm toward the men while my magic shoved them away from the women.

"Get back," I demanded.

"You stupid bitch! We are here under the order of the Queen of Nymphs," a soldier seethed.

"And?" I asked while one brow lifted with the question.

"By Her Majesty's orders, all unmarked witches are to be slaughtered. Do you think to stop us? You will fail the same as all the others," he growled, letting his eyes slide down my body with heat.

"Nymphs? Seriously? I thought you guys were supposed to be hot and seductive? My sisters are, and yet you're... lacking in looks."

"You think we care about your opinion?"

"I don't think you *think* at all," I snorted, smirking at the anger my words had caused him. "If you did, you'd have ran from me by now."

A witch accompanying the guards stepped forward, removing her hood to expose a weak insignia on her forehead. Her eyes held mine as if she expected me to have balked from her mark. Her hands lifted, and more witches stepped into the line, adding to her power. I exhaled, igniting my symbol, causing her to pause and step back.

"It cannot be!" she whispered.

"I assure you, it can," I smiled tightly. "You have

two options here. Either you run or you die. Choose wisely," I said, watching them through narrowing slits.

The warriors lifted their weapons, and I unleashed my magic. Slowly, I walked through the space beneath them as they hovered in the air above me. Weapons dropped to the ground, clunking against the earth as they landed.

I raised my other hand, twisting, and the soldiers and dark witches exploded, raining blood everywhere. Blinking, I wiped the blood away from my eyes before turning to look at the witches I'd just saved. They stood silently, staring at me with their mouths hanging open.

"Ew," I whined, spitting pieces out on the ground. "It's in my mouth!"

"Yeah, and you have something..." Esme stated, indicating all of me. "There."

"You don't say?" I asked, laughing. "Here?" I pointed to my dress, and then my face, before plucking a blood-covered braid from my head.

"Yup," Esme laughed, turning to look out over the bloodied field. She lifted her hand, and more unmarked witches stepped forward, adding to her magic as the blood vanished. "Let's get you cleaned up."

Inside a cottage, I pushed a brush made of bone through my hair while watching the children, who sat wide-eyed, staring at me. There were wooden stars placed on the wall, held together with leather twine, hanging beside crystals. Sighing, I decided I needed to go outside to where the unmarked witches waited for me.

Esme moved forward, motioning toward a lattice-covered garden, and I followed, pausing when I got to the gate and looked at the earth embedded with miniature stars. Crystals surrounded each of them, carrying a single use. I took in the hundred or more stars, smiling at Esme, who nodded in agreement.

"Good, unmarked witches," I swallowed, watching her dark head continue to nod as tears shone in her eyes.

A witch stepped forward, placing her hand on a large quartz tower. "Prove to us you are of the light, Aria Hecate. I will not allow a dark witch to lead us to our death. Nor a weak one," she continued, exhaling. "You too, Esme. You know the drill."

Esme smirked, rolling her eyes as she stepped forward. Her finger lifted and pricked on the tip of the quartz, and the star below it began to glow with a soft pulsing hum of magic. I noted Esme held her power back, but it was enough to please the witch who smiled at her softly.

I stepped forward, pricking my finger on the quartz tip, just as Esme had done, before standing back as power rushed through the garden while the crystals exploded with light. The witches whispered excitedly around me.

The entire garden lit up around us. The candles exploded with flames, while the lanterns glowed from the crystals within them. More crystals hung from trees, looking like something out of a fantasy as my power ignited them. Water that held crystals beneath the surface began to glow a bright, deep cerulean hue, illuminating the fish in the pond beside us. All around, magic ignited flames and crystals as the little ones danced around me.

I chewed my bottom lip as Esme bumped my hip.

"Show off."

"You're a true descendant of the Hecate bloodline," the witch whispered in awe. "The rumors are true then; you've returned to save us?"

"I intend to do my best to protect you all and stop the evil happening within the Nine Realms."

"There's only one of you?" she countered, and I puffed out an irritated breath. "I meant no disrespect, Princess Hecate. I only hoped there would be more of you."

"There are," I assured her. "I'm actually on my way to join them. Esme thought I should see what I am fighting to protect. She is wise, but also a wise-ass."

Esme snorted, shaking her head as she rolled her eyes. I let my gaze linger over the assembly of unmarked witches before I swallowed the worry that came with an offering of protection.

"I have a shelter prepared for you all," I admitted softly. "You can't stay here now. The Nymph Queen will come to see why her warriors have not reported back. It isn't much yet, but eventually, my family and I will have a House of Magic set up, and we intend to invite those who have not turned to the darkness or served the high queen in her quest to be a selfish bitch.

"Esme will be there with you, and she could use some strong witches to help reinforce the keep that I claimed from a dark coven. I'm about to do something seriously stupid, which means I may be away for a while. My family will check in on you and ensure that you're all safe and protected. There are enough food and supplies to last through an apocalypse, and it's safe. That's all I can promise you for now."

"She's lying," Esme snorted, causing me to stiffen. "It's more than you have, and more than anyone has ever offered us. It's not just safe; it's a fortified keep held beneath Hecate bloodline power. I have never felt safer within it, not even beneath the watchful eye of my mother. Aria has made room for over one hundred witches to join her there. You will have beds to rest your weary bodies, food for your bellies, and protection against the evil, vile queen that rules us." The witches all stared at Esme, frowning. "Oh, and I've collected incubus males for women to use, too."

"We're in," the witch chortled. "You should have started with that, Esme."

I smiled, turning to look at Esme, who rubbed her hand down her face in relief.

"Witches," we said at the same time, snorting while we watched them collect their belongings.

"You slaughtered nymphs today. Neven will not let it go unchallenged," Esme stated.

"Neven is the Queen of Nymphs?"

"Indeed. Neven is a powerful nymph, and if I were you, I'd be cautious with her. You're making very powerful enemies, Aria Hecate."

"I didn't come here to make friends. I came here to change the world, and that isn't going to make me a lot of friends."

"You are something else, Aria. You are more than I

expected when I saw you running into that alleyway. I didn't think in my wildest dreams that a Hecate Princess would come running toward me or offer me protection. Honestly, I thought we were going to go extinct, and that would be it. There would be no more good witches or those who clung to the old ways with the hope that you and your line would return. I also thought you'd be a lot bigger. I guess beggars can't be choosers, right?"

"I thought we were having a moment there, and then you went and ruined it. You're a smartass. You know that, right? You're lucky your mother didn't swallow you," I grinned.

"I'm lucky yours didn't swallow you!"

I snorted softly as a smile spread across my face. At the sound of feet crunching against the gardens' rocks, we turned, staring into the faces of the witches we'd invited to the keep. Frowning as a tiny hand slipped into mine, I stared down into beautiful turquoise eyes and smiled brightly.

"I really hope you know what you're doing," Esme whispered, swallowing past the emotion we both felt at seeing those who depended on us, looking as if we held all the answers of the world.

"I have no idea what the hell I am doing. I'm winging it. But so far, so good. Let's hope everything goes well when I meet up with my family, and this plan we developed will work in our favor. If not, they'll lead you. If anything happens to me, they'll continue helping you to help others. I have a feeling that once Knox catches me, it will be quite some time before I can return to you. Continue collecting witches, but devise a way to ensure that they are good and belong with us. The only way that the keep falls is from within, and I fear there aren't many of us, so everyone counts."

Chapter Twenty-Eight

My eyes slowly scanned the army that had amassed in front of us. My brow creased, and I narrowed my eyes, studying the largest warrior on the ground below. Turning in the saddle on the large, beautiful warhorse, I glared at up at my sisters.

The animal sensed my unease, tossing his head and stomping its feet onto the earth. I didn't know how everyone else made it look so easy since the horse refused to hold still for me. Scanning the battlement, I found Kinvara watching everything happening below with keen interest.

This was the worst plan in the history of the Nine Realms. And if by some miracle it went off without a hitch, I'd be stuck apologizing to my sisters until I was too old to remember their names. That might have been the only win in that equation.

My attention went back to the male, slowly making

his way to the front of the warriors who all looked ready to eat our faces. Knox's eyes locked with mine, narrowing, before sliding over to Asil's, the dark witch currently calling all the shots of this keep. Of course, I kept pronouncing her name asshole. It was a choice preference.

Asil made me want to word-vomit profanities more often than not when I was in her presence. Or shove something very sharp down her over-opinionated throat, violently. She was one of the worst people I'd encountered since coming to the Nine Realms.

She was a self-appointed expert on every topic, not to mention the most self-righteous bitch who felt the need to shove her opinions down everyone's throats. Those who disagreed, she murdered or tortured with her droll nonsense until they wanted to die to escape her.

I was pretty sure my play on her name was correct. Asil was an intolerable asshole. Her newest hobby was to point out how often I'd said her name incorrectly, which I did on purpose, just to piss her off.

I also found it funny to watch her cringe when I used words like moist and flesh, so of course, I used them together as often as I could, even though her high, nasally voice grated my nerves when she corrected me, like nails dragging across a chalkboard.

I dismissed Asil, letting my attention slide through the murderous gazes of the army before me. Knox wasn't messing around this time and had brought many more troops than he'd brought to the last speed bump of a keep where we'd previously faced off.

These soldiers were rougher; their hard, merciless

stares promised death the moment they broke through the weak barrier holding them at bay.

Nervousness rushed through me, causing sweat to bead on the back of my neck. My horse danced sideways beneath Knox's murderous glare that was holding mine captive.

No one spoke, and my body flooded with apprehension beneath his rage-filled eyes. The knowledge that I was sitting on the opposing side with a murderous bitch made *me* feel ill.

The damnation burning in Knox's eyes, mingled with judgment, filled me with the need to tell him that it wasn't what it looked like, and yet if I did that, I'd ruin the plan and the entire reason we were here.

Warriors pulled huge machines to the front of the line, setting them up as the army stood motionless, watching, waiting for the order to attack. Looking out over the field, I took in the impressive army, strategically spread as far as the eye could see, out over the gorge.

It had taken Knox three days to reach us, and I'd known he would come with a formidable force once he'd realized I hid within the stronghold. The entire time we'd been here, I'd witnessed things playing out in front of me that turned my stomach upside down.

The only reason we hadn't slaughtered these witches earlier in the week was that the moon had to reach its zenith in the sky for the spell I'd crafted to be powerful enough to work correctly, if it worked at all.

I felt Knox's stern gaze studying me, noting the nervousness that I couldn't manage to hide. The horse

I was on danced sideways again, sensing my discomfort while I tried to keep it still without unseating me.

Fear was running rampant through me, making everything seem more intense. My heartbeat pounded louder than the war drums of Knox's army. It sounded in my ears, mirroring the drum solo at a rock concert, echoing through me, creating so much unease that I knew Knox could sense it.

I wasn't worried about my life. I could get myself out of this if I was alone, but my sisters and aunt were in the same vicinity, and I could not abandon them. Their being here complicated everything, and yet I couldn't do this without them. I understood the necessity of allowing others to help when needed, but the cost of failure would be more than I was willing to pay. Not that I hadn't enjoyed spending time with my family.

Over the last week, I'd gotten to hug and visit with all my sisters and aunt, listening to news and plans about the new House of Magic, and discussing everything we still needed to procure. It was blissful to see them without fear trickling down my spine, worrying about Knox finding us and capturing them.

The only downside was Asil. She had almost ruined it by implementing herself in the middle of everything we'd done. I hadn't slept more than an hour or two at a time since we were camped inside this murdering bitch's stronghold, sleeping with one eye open among our enemies.

Now Knox was here, and that would end our time together. Too much was on the line now.

No pressure...

Just breathe and remember who the fuck you are, Aria.

Right?

Sit straight, show no fear, and be a rock in a storm; unmovable and unbreakable.

"King Karnavious," Asil sneered.

Her lips pulled back as she spoke, revealing blackening teeth. Evil had a cost, and this bitch was deep into her payment. Her blonde hair was graying, something that wouldn't have happened had she not used the dark magic she wielded. Her yellowing skin looked jaundiced and taut on her bones.

"Asil, are you prepared to surrender? How many more innocent lives have you ended this month to pay for that magic you use so freely?" Knox asked coldly, sliding accusing eyes to mine before slowly dragging them down my scantily dressed body.

Knox rattled low, letting the sound ease out of him, watching me with a knowing grin. My core tightened, and my nipples grew into perky peaks as his lips twisted into a wicked smirk. Slowly dismissing me, his attention slid back to Asil.

"I have the high queen endorsing my hold to this land. You dare march an army against me?" Asil growled as her power slithered through the clearing, pushing through the thin barrier. "You will be punished greatly for this, King Karnavious. I knew we should have moved on you sooner. You're lucky our hands were tied, or you'd be secured to a post and used for nothing more than pleasure when I wanted it."

I turned my narrowing eyes toward Asil. Like hell, she'd use him for pleasure. That dick was mine, even if I didn't plan to use it anytime soon.

Knox rattled again, low in his chest, forcing my eyes to close against the sound. Silently praying he would stop before he gave me away. My head bowed while I squirmed on the horse, silently pleading for him to stop, but he continued, and the vibrations sent heat rushing through me, causing my body to work against me.

What the hell was he thinking? This wasn't the time to beat his chest, not with armies waiting to clash together in a bloody battle. Yet, I had no disillusion that his rattle had meant to arch my spine, creating a throbbing pain that forced me to adjust on the saddle, attempting to clench my thighs.

He stopped when my horse reared up, trying to deposit me onto the ground. I patted its head, cooing to calm it. I peered down at Knox through my dark lashes as he walked toward the barrier, watching me as he silently approached, turning to glare at Asil at the last moment.

"I see you are aware of the little witch I have with me." Asil stated, her cold, dead eyes slipping to me as I stared forward and away from Knox, feeling her questioning gaze moving between him and me. "King Karnavious, meet Aria. Isn't she beautiful? My men think she's exquisite."

"That little witch isn't here to protect you, though. Or is she? No, that's right. Aria's still hiding from me. Aren't you?" His tone was low and deadly as it slithered through me, scratching at my heart.

I looked at Asil, and her eyes narrowed to angry

slits. Swallowing past the lump in my throat, I turned in the saddle, peering at Kinvara on the upper battlements. She hid behind another barrier of magic that shielded the witches from sight.

Kinvara shook her head, and I exhaled, righting myself on my horse, studying the army behind Knox. My sisters and Aurora worked the spell, but until I made more sacrifices, it wouldn't uproot the magic we fought to remove.

A shiver of agitation rushed through me as I considered every way this could go. I mostly envisioned it going sideways and me on my knees as Knox's plaything before today's setting sun. That was the best-case scenario if shit went wrong.

My eyes closed, and I struggled to calm the war within me, exhaling the worry before I opened them, finding Knox studying me. He searched my face, lifting his stare to the battlements before settling it back on me.

"Something wrong, Aria?" he asked, and I swallowed, shaking my head.

"You know each other?" Asil asked icily, her eyes sliding between us with a calculating look burning in them.

It was the first flicker of life I'd seen within Asil all week, other than the madness that consumed her when she murdered an innocent soul.

"No. I have never met this man before today. I think I would remember him if I had," I lied, staring right at Knox, who observed me through heated eyes. "I'm merely nervous, as I've never faced off against an army before."

Knox chose that moment to remind me of how well we knew each other, replaying every wicked thing he'd ever done to my body in vivid detail within his mind.

I swallowed past the heat it created in my core, causing my body to tighten with need while he watched me. Once he was certain he had filled me with angst from his heated stare, he smirked roguishly, then narrowed his eyes to slits before sliding them toward Asil to answer her.

"Indeed, she would remember me. Most women fidget or get nervous when this many men move toward them. She senses defeat thickening in the air and knows soon she'll be beneath me tonight. After all, battles, more often than naught, do lead to pillaging, and my favorite, plundering. Tell me, Aria, would you enjoy being plundered deeply?"

"Do not answer him, girl. He seeks to bait you with the promise of seduction. He enjoys witches beneath him, but most end up headless when he's finished using them. State your terms, King Karnavious," Asil demanded, lifting her nose in the air like Knox was beneath her.

"I want Aria Hecate on her knees with a promise of her surrender, and everyone else here dead," Knox said without missing a beat.

I blinked at the fluidity of his request before sputtering, "Hell no, asshole." I shook my head, even as a shiver of fear slid up my spine. His lips tipped into a smile, heat burning in his eyes as he watched me. In his mind, I was on my knees with my hands behind my back, doing devious things with my lips.

Bastard.

"I'm the lady of this keep, and only I can decline his terms, girl." Her eyes studied the glare in mine while I stared Knox down. "I do, however, find it most curious that you wish for Aria to be on her knees, King Karnavious. She's been here for an entire week, and yet she hasn't opened her cunt to a single male within my keep. I'm sure if you wanted it, I could find a witch more willing to service you, if that is what you've come seeking."

"That's because they're all weak as shit and basically have vaginas for mouths." I frowned, realizing no one had spoken to me.

Lore spat out the drink he'd taken and started coughing violently as Brander patted his back. My attention swung to Asil, who glared at me before facing Knox once more. I gave him a warning look, but he didn't seem to catch it.

"Aria doesn't put out? That's strange. I have it on good authority that she's a rather volatile lover when fucked. In fact, I'm pretty sure Aria fucking purrs when she comes, and rumor has it that the little bitch screams like a banshee when she's fucked hard enough."

"Why, it almost sounds as if you speak from *experience*, King Karnavious. We all know you like to fuck weak-minded witches, but Aria's not weak, is she? So, why her? Why not one of the other Hecate witches?"

My eyes slipped back to Kinvara, who held up her two fingers, indicating they were close to completing the spell. My heart raced painfully against my ribs, and sweat coated my palms from the death grip I held on the horse's leather reins. My attention moved back to Knox as he opened his mouth to speak.

"You're worried about something, aren't you?" He slid his eyes up to the battlements, finding nothing there.

"Answer the question, King Karnavious," Asil demanded vehemently.

"She's a powerful Hecate witch. Who wouldn't want her? She's also beautiful, and I do enjoy fucking my witches, after all."

"They're all here. So why would you only ask for Aria specifically, why not any of the others?" Asil growled, and my eyes closed as she announced my family presence.

"That's what's wrong," he chuckled, sliding his eyes to the battlements, searching it for any sign of my family. "Oh, Aria. You're all in one place? That's rather convenient for me and thoughtful of you."

"You'll never reach them, Knox," I whispered, grabbing onto the sidesaddle to withdraw a raincoat. Pulling it free, I slipped my arms into it, adjusting the hood, lifting my eyes to peer through the barrier at him. "It looks like it's about to rain, don't you agree, King Karnavious?" I smirked, placing a facade of bravado I didn't feel over the panic rushing through me.

"Is that a dick on your head?" Asil asked. Her eyes were mere slits as she studied my raincoat. "There's not a cloud in the entire sky," she snorted, peering up as everyone else did the same, all except for Knox, who stared at me victoriously.

The second wave of magic rushed through us, and

I studied Knox with an angry frown as he peered up at the battlement. I swung around, seeing everything before I turned back, frowning at the barrier. If one had come down already, it was only a matter of time before the other followed.

"That thing upon your head isn't right," Asil said, fixated on my horn.

"It's not a dick. It's a unicorn horn." I looked from her to Knox, who fought the twitching of his lips while he took in the rainbow-colored raincoat and unicorn horn hood I wore. "Terms?" I asked, shaking off the way he made my breath catch when he smiled. I was so going to smack Kinvara upside her head for the fashion statement gear she'd chosen to pack for me.

"They are the same as previously stated, Aria." Knox grinned, sensing my unease as the barrier weakened. "Come to me, and I will let your family live for now. Fight me, and they die while you watch. You have one chance to take this offer, or you will watch their demise from beside me, on your knees."

"We don't accept your terms, King Karnavious," Asil announced sharply, turning her horse. "Come, Aria, we prepare for battle while your family feeds us their power." I winked at Knox, who glared murderously at me.

Breathe in and out, Aria.

He can't reach them if you stay his hand and hold the barrier.

Everything's going to plan.

"Seize her!" Asil yelled. "Give the signal to the

men above to kill the Hecate witches on the battlements, along with their pet dog." She chuckled, looking me up and down as she shook her head, "If I had a man like that waiting for me, I wouldn't want the peasants here either, traitor. Seize her and secure her to the pole. Once we've killed King Karnavious and his army, we'll have some fun with her. Would you like that? I bet the men would love to eat the flesh from your thighs. Tell me, Aria. Have you ever had the flesh removed from your body while still alive?" she cackled, her skin pulling taut against her bones, blackness moving beneath its surface as if poison rushed through her veins.

Well, shit! So, that didn't work out!

Chapter Twenty-Nine

I jumped from the horse quickly, slapping it on its hindquarter to send it away. One of Asil's warrior witches rushed toward me, and I paused, turning to face him. My foot kicked out as I dropped to the ground, slicing my hands upward as my razor-sharp claws removed his head, sending it flying toward Knox and his army.

Magic rippled through the clearing, and I hissed, realizing I was its target, igniting my magic barely in time to deflect the attack as her entire army of witches turned on me with the sole intent to murder.

"Hey, Creature! Now would be an ideal time for you to come out and eat some faces. Like now, before we die," I encouraged while I dodged blades. Somehow, I managed to recall a tactical spell used in hand-to-hand combat.

Whispering it quickly, I was able to see every move the witch would make before she'd swing her deadly sword toward my body, in skilled, precise movements.

"Anybody home? Look, Knox has his dick out!"

The blade sliced the air beside me as I side-stepped, spinning out of her reach as she lunged, swinging wildly defined moves. Magic controlled my body, noting each signal her arms gave to foretell her lunges and parries.

We danced together as her arm rose, and my claws shot forward, slicing through the artery in her throat as death entered her stare. Her head tilted oddly to the side, and I swung my body, adding weight to the move, sending her head sailing toward Knox, accumulating a pile of heads at his feet.

He watched intently as I fought in a manner in which I was ill-prepared. I wasn't a fighter, but I didn't have time to pull more magic to me as Asil's army attacked in mass, pushing me back to the male who waited for me on the other side of the failing barrier. Maybe if I threw myself at Knox, he'd leave without hunting down my sisters. But that wouldn't get them safely out of this murderous witch's grasp.

Asil was slowly backing toward the others, pulling power to her, which was a huge problem. She was a lot stronger than the other witches I'd fought. She could draw power from the High Queen of Witches, who apparently was fond of the murderous whore.

One of Asil's warriors stepped forward, and I jumped, using my feet against his shoulders as my nails rounded his neck, pulling his head from his body with his spine still attached.

I gagged as I held it, dropping the useless appendage,

gagging several more times. War was so gross and hard on the fingernails. I turned as magic shot forward, and I fell flat against the ground, seeing magic rush toward the barrier. The spell slammed against it, and I whimpered as a tremor of pain went through me.

Something large and round sailed from the other side of the barrier, and I watched, covering my face with my hands as it, too, struck the barrier, before then crumbling to the earth. Kicking off the ground, I glared at Knox's back as he issued orders to the men loading the trebuchets.

His men packed large wooden arrows with metal tips into the machines, releasing them. I stared as they struck the barrier, one after another, and I flinched each time as Knox's sea-colored depths observed with intrigue.

His eyes narrowed as I dropped to the ground, rolling away from the attacks, pelting the land where I had lain. The deflection spell finally kicked in, throwing me around like a rag doll. I hissed in pain, flying over sharp rocks and branches protruding through the ground while arrows peppered my trail, never catching up to me.

Peering up at the battlement, I watched my sisters combine their magic to attack the archers, shooting them backward toward the edge of the wall. Launching myself to my feet, I rushed toward the smiling witch, whose raised hands were covered with thick, black lines running through her veins.

Asil aimed magic at me, and I frowned, noting the others surrounding her had gathered power as I'd fought the witches wielding weapons. The moment she let loose of her hold, I dropped backward, bending my legs as my body went flat against the ground, seconds before her power swept over me. Pain sliced through me, but I hopped up, leveling her with a cold look. I whispered a spell, calling fire as her dress caught and those around her bellowed in pain.

The witches behind Asil called upon their magic, and one of the more powerful witches moved to stand in front of Asil's burning form as she began to chant. Power entered her body, and she smirked, staring at me through blackened eyes while the others echoed her.

I felt my teeth elongating, and I opened my mouth, screaming as power sliced through the witches, their bodies shredding into tiny slices as if sent through a paper shredder. My arms moved as I turned, slamming my power where they'd stood, and blood splashed from the ground. My coat was splattered in it, painted red from the bloodied, disintegrating bodies.

So, maybe I had needed the raincoat after all. Since my last debacle, when slaughtering the nymphs, I hadn't wanted to run around bathed in blood. It was sticky and not particularly good for the complexion.

My breathing came out in labored breaths, and I fought to gain control of it. I bent, resting my hands on my knees until the sound of heavy footfalls echoed from the other side of the castle wall. Righting myself, I paused as the largest male warrior rounded the corner with a broadsword held in his hands. He shouted, the sound coming out in a high-pitched tone that made me quake with laughter.

"I'll kill you!" he squealed, his voice sounding as if he'd inhaled helium.

"Stop talking," I snorted, holding up my hand as peals of laughter rushed through me. He screamed again, and I laughed harder. "Stop talking, vagina mouth!"

"Stupid bitch!" he shouted, and I laughed once more.

The warrior rushed forward, and I lifted my hand, his body bursting into tiny pieces that slammed into me, proving even further that I'd needed my coat. I flinched from the entrails covering me as I turned to see Kinvara screaming a warning. Knox's men flooded into the clearing, past the second barrier, only to bounce off the last, and I groaned.

"Seriously?" Frowning, I scrunched up my nose while gathering my strength. Fighting was exhausting, even after being chased around the Nine Realms and forced into shape, I was quickly tiring.

"Drop the fucking barrier, Aria!" Knox shouted, causing my spine to straighten. I lifted an irritated brow, glaring pointedly at him.

Knox's men moved forward with weapons held ready to dispatch me, but magic rushed toward them as Kinvara and Reign cast on them from above. My sisters held the men in place. I lifted my hands, palms to the sky, summoning my dead army.

I heard my sisters horrified gasps the moment the dead began to crawl their way through the earth, grabbing the legs of the men who thought to attack me.

Reign clapped, and Def Leppard's *Pour Some Sugar on Me* started playing in my head as I smiled, peering up at them. I chanced a peek at Knox and his men, all staring at my army of grotesque corpses. I shook my head but knew what the creature inside of me wanted. Eventually, my army backed off, leaving a few men alive.

I captured the arms of these warriors with magic, threading through them as I worked the spell to control their bodies. Lowering their hands, they grabbed at their armor, removing it, tossing it aside as they danced to the catcalls from the girls above. I turned toward Knox, watching the heat fill his eyes. I removed my bloodied raincoat and lifted the hem of the skirt, the last remaining men from Asil's army, mimicking the moves.

Kinvara clapped, shouting from above, "Take it off, baby, take it off! Momma needs to see what lies beneath!"

I lost it, laughing as I fought to control the warriors moving to a slow dance that didn't fit the song playing in my head. My lips moved, singing the lyrics, Knox's eyes never leaving my body while heat banked in their smoldering depths. I didn't strip, and the more the men moved behind me, the closer they got.

I felt one of the men breaking from the spell, somehow slipping the thrall as his blade rushed toward me. Reign yelled to duck, and I dodged, bending back, twisting my body at an awkward angle. The sword came down beside my head, and I flipped again, landing on my hands and feet, crouched in a tackle pose.

Wind slid over my scantily clad backside. I watched one of the undead lunging toward the man that had broken free, biting into his throat. Blood squirted from his neck, and a scream tore from his lips as he went down.

I turned, pushing the skirt away from my face to find Knox and his men staring at my backside that was only obscured by lace panties. Standing upright, I stifled a blush as Reign and Kinvara laughed at my expense.

My hand lifted, and slowly dropped as the undead pulled the living into the ground, tearing through their flesh in the process, adding them to my growing numbers.

"Surrender, and I'll go easy on you, Little Witch," Knox growled, causing me to turn and smile.

"Hard pass," I smirked, making my way toward the gate at the front of the castle.

Using my magic to open the gates, I paused, lifting my finger to twist the skulls from the corpses that had remained. Setting them on fire, I sent the flaming skulls sailing through the air toward Knox's army, as a parting gift for their efforts.

Slipping inside, I closed the gate with magic, sliding the heavy bolt in place as I rushed for the battlements.

Reaching the top, I paused, staring down at Knox as he continued to direct his army to attack the barrier. Somehow, it was managing to remain in place. Moving to the cauldron in the center of the clearing, I smiled with the knowledge that we were about to pull this crazy plan off. Suddenly, blinding light ripped from within the cauldron, slamming into my body, throwing me backward as a scream escaped my lips.

On the battlement, flat on my back, I stared at the sky above. My body trembled violently in pain as something rushed through me. I swallowed past the taste of copper, opening and closing my mouth. Dimitri grabbed my hand, pulling me up. I cried out, staring at the others who were slowly getting to their feet.

"What the hell was that?" I asked, horrified that

we'd just kicked our own asses.

"It worked, that's what that was!" Aurora announced, standing as my sisters cheered. "Aria, we did it!"

I nodded as relief rushed through me. My sisters cheered and hugged one another while I frowned, doing a general check of my body for damage. Whatever had happened, it was fast and violent. I spat out the blood that filled my mouth, wiping my lips with the back of my hand.

I eased to the wall, peering over the edge to find Knox stripping out of his armor. I sent my senses to test the barrier, which had weakened from the assault he was waging. My eyes slid down his body as he hefted the shirt over his head, chucking it to the ground.

My gaze hungrily caressed him, and my mouth opened with a throaty purr that I could no longer suppress. Heat throbbed in my core, and a naughty grin slipped onto my lips while I feasted on his muscular form.

Knox lifted his head, hearing the sultriness of my purr that reached him through the barrier. His eyes found me as his lips mirrored mine, his rattle slithering through me, causing my eyes to grow hooded with desire.

"You eye-fuck him any damn harder, and I'm going to have an orgasm!" Kinvara teased from beside me, shaking me out of the stupor that Knox's bare chest had created.

"That's not funny." I bit my lip as my attention slid back to the male, watching me like a predator marking his prey for a kill. "Damn, that man is made for sinning, and I'm just a sinner wanting to indulge."

I caressed his abs with my eyes, inhaling his scent as it wafted through the weakened barrier, and my eyes bulged as it collapsed with a pop.

"What was that?" Reign asked, turning to look at Aurora for an answer.

"Go now!" I shouted as Aurora started to draw a portal. She wasn't doing it fast enough, so I lifted my hands, pulling a portal open, using the spell I'd reserved for myself to keep out of Knox's grasp. "Go! Get through the portal. The barrier is down!"

"Come with us!" Kinny urged, and Reign agreed, nodding her head as they started through the portal.

"Come on, Aria," Callista encouraged.

"I can't. Knox has witches who have learned the signature of my portals, and they will follow you if you don't go before they get here. I'll be okay. Kinny, you guard that stronghold you promised me you would keep safe. I mean it! Now go!" I snapped, watching as one by one, they slipped through to the other side.

I didn't release the breath I was holding until the portal closed behind them. I bent at the waist, exhaling deeply, thankful that my family had escaped safely.

I heard something scrape against the side of the castle wall, and I stepped back, narrowing my eyes as hands reached over the edge, followed by a very masculine body as it came over the stone wall.

Ocean eyes locked with mine as we stood face-to-face, taking each other in slowly. I lifted my hand to wipe the blood trickling from a cut on the side of my face.

Instantly, I realized my error. If Knox had any reservations about whether I was real or just another projected body-double, they vanished at the sight of my blood.

Knox smiled cruelly, and I shook my head. He didn't move, didn't twinge as he waited for me to realize just how much I was fucked. He was a lethal predator, knowing it was only a matter of time before he caught his prey. Unfortunately, I was that prey.

I eased back slowly as he prowled forward, a smile curving his lips. His muscles tensed, preparing to chase me as my heartbeat echoed in my ears with every step I took away from him. The world around us went silent, other than our heavy breathing, and the sound of gravel crunching under our footsteps as we continued our dance.

"You're trapped, woman. On your knees," he demanded huskily.

"That's not happening," I laughed nervously, as he continued to stalk toward me.

"I told you that you would be on your knees for me by the end of the night. The moon is rising, Little One. You aren't escaping me this time. You kissed another man."

"So, I did." Swallowing, I stepped back once more, watching him take another step forward.

"You let another man touch what belongs to me," he growled, and anger mixed with desire flared to life in his eyes.

"Only a little," I countered, smiling at the heat burning in his gaze.

"That's a little too much for me, woman."

"What the fuck are you going to do about it?" I asked, noting the way his eyes slid over my shoulder.

"I'm going to reinforce my claim, and remind you who the fuck you belong to, witch. If I were you, I'd make it easier on myself and kneel like a good girl."

"You'll have to catch me first." I took one last step backward, rushing toward the far edge of the battlement as Knox gave chase. The sound of his feet hitting the rough stone, filled my ears as I jumped onto the wall and leaped over the edge without looking, relieved to find a river below me.

"Aria!"

His scream of frustration caused a laugh to bubble within my chest until I glanced up to see him fly over the edge to follow me.

Well, shit.

Chapter Thirty

I hit the water hard, breaking its icy-cold surface with a gasped cry. I sank into the murky depths, my feet touching the slimy bottom before I sprung forward and shot up toward the light. I sucked in air greedily when I crested the surface.

Knox entered the water behind me, bubbles exploding around his form as he sank into the depths. Long, fast strokes took me toward the bank, and I crawled quickly from the frigid water, looking back to see how far Knox was from me. I swallowed past the cold, standing to stare at where he'd entered the river.

He didn't emerge, so I sent my magic to find him. It only took moments to sense the issue. The magic I sent rushing toward the water caused heads to lift from the shimmering surface.

Blonde hair skimmed the top of the water before eerie, green eyes rose to stare coldly at me. I frowned, still waiting for Knox to emerge from the depths, and then sensed a bigger issue.

Still, he didn't surface from its icy grasp, holding him beneath its watery grave. I watched in silence as a female head lifted from the water, spitting out liquid while coldness filled her eyes.

"The Queen of Nymphs sends her regards, witch. Did you think she would allow your insult to go unanswered?" Her clear aqua-blue eyes smiled, watching me. "He is ours now as payment to the queen for your trespass against her."

"Oh, I don't think so!" I growled, taking in the creatures below the surface.

Stepping toward the river, I watched flesh becoming visible to my eyes. More nymphs swam just below the dark surface, and I groaned. I marched into the frigid water, and a nymph bared serrated teeth at me as I prepared to dive into the depths.

"Stupid Knox, jumping off the stupid battlement. Who does shit like that! That dick is mine! And it's attached to him, which makes him mine by default. Stupid hussies, get your own caveman!" I roared, inhaling deeply before diving into the water.

I shot toward the first female nymph that was fighting Knox, who was slowly drowning. My claws extended, and I tore through her skin, grabbing her and shoving her away from him. He was tearing into another female who was running her hands down his torso.

I fought off a third that came up behind me. My teeth tore through her hand as she tried to remove my head, failing to notice the sharp, elongated teeth I'd allowed to break free from my gums. My other hand shot into her chest, ripping her apart easily.

The fighting exhausted my air, and my lungs burned from a lack of oxygen. Shooting toward the surface, I gulped air into my lungs before diving under once more, reaching for the nymph who was readying her siren's call to use against Knox.

My hand pushed through her chest, withdrawing her lungs as her corpse began to sink to the river floor. Knox glared at me through the crimson water as I swam closer. I grabbed his face between my hands, claiming his lips, feeding air into his starved lungs.

Once I was certain he wouldn't drown, I dove lower to the roots of the plants that had wrapped around his legs while he watched. My claws shredded them easily, freeing him, and we both swam toward the surface for more air.

Arms wrapped around me, and I turned to peer over my shoulder. We sank toward the murky bottom, and fear rushed through me as my oxygen depleted. Knox smirked wickedly with bubbles escaping his lips. He held me beneath the water, and my eyes widened with panic, fire burning within my lungs from the need to inhale air. Knox realized the problem and pushed us off the river's bottom, bringing us to the surface where we gulped in air together.

"You should have kept running while you had the chance. I'm not letting you go now, woman," he laughed, turning me in his arms as I continued to suck in air greedily. His hands held me tightly, running the tips of his fingers over my midriff, keeping me above water.

"I wasn't just going to leave you to die, asshole," I seethed, coughing as water splashed into my face. "The water's filled with magic, and you would have drowned. I may not like you, Knox, but I don't want you to die, either."

Now that my panicked thoughts had quieted, I remembered that Knox had magic too, which meant he could have escaped if he'd chosen to do so. Stupidly, I realized he waited for me to jump in, thinking to save him. I hadn't been thinking clearly because I hadn't expected him to follow me over the wall.

He was a king, and I was pretty confident they weren't supposed to do life defying moves, but then, he was Knox. He'd known what was on the other side of that wall and hadn't hesitated to jump in right behind me. Then, he'd stayed beneath the water's surface, testing me because he knew I wouldn't leave him to die. I was the biggest idiot!

Knox pulled me tightly against his body while holding my gaze captive. His mouth lowered, kissing me hungrily until a groan of need left my lips, only to be captured by his kiss. He held me securely, uncaring that the river was dragging us further downstream toward the current of oncoming rapids.

His tongue dueled with mine, demanding I cave to the need rushing through me. His hands tangled through my hair, devouring me like a starving beast that was denied food for far too long. Everything was tangled while we kissed. Our legs. Our tongues. Our thoughts. We were tangled together, the need to get closer, driving us past reason.

Knox growled against my kiss, rattling his approval of the need exploding from me for this carnal beast that promised to consume me whole. His mouth ignited a fire within me, doing more than his hands had ever sought to do as he kissed me like I was everything he wanted or needed. Knox breathed fire into my soul, fanning embers of longing, and showing me what true passion was, all while somehow holding us both above the waters' surface.

I lifted my hand when he started to pull away, yanking him back as his touch created a heat that throbbed within me. My sole focus became the feel of him against my lips, drinking him in as everything around us faded away. Chuckling darkly against my lips, he kept us afloat as my legs wrapped around his waist, securing him to me.

All coherent thought slid to the back of my mind, replaced with the desire he'd promised to deliver. Knox rubbed against my core, showing me exactly how that promise would feel. His mouth brushed against mine, nipping my bottom lip while a deep, husky growl escaped his throat.

"There are only three things in this world I wish to do right now, Aria. They all include you. I want to touch you, to trace every curve of your body with my fingertips explicitly. I want to taste every part of you until you're nothing more than a quivering, trembling mess that begs me to stop, and yet I won't. I want to bury myself so fucking deep inside your tight body that you ache, yet never ask me to withdraw because I'm burrowed within the very being of your center, and you can't think without me there." His eyes studied the heat burning within mine.

I leaned closer, intending to beg him to do just that, but a horrifying sound grew louder around us, pulling me from my thoughts, forcing us to break apart.

Knox reached out and grasped my arm, holding me even tighter against his body, if at all possible. Our eyes slid to the white-water rapids we were about to enter.

Huge, sharp rocks cropped out from the water, exposing our perilous situation. Knox turned us, staring toward the shore, realizing the water had changed while we were lost in the heat of our kiss. The river had grown wider, placing the shore on either side of us out of reach.

"Bloody hell," he groaned while spitting out water. "Hold onto me, Aria," he urged, his hands and arms tightening around me protectively.

The water slammed us against the rocks, and Knox grunted. It was the only indication he'd felt the stone against his back. He prevented me from smashing against several larger rocks, holding onto me as we fought to stay above the rapids threatening to suck us to the bottom of the river. I coughed violently as water filled my mouth.

Knox did the same as the rapids sucked us below. His powerful legs touched the bottom, pushing us back up to the surface as we slammed into more rocks, both of us being tossed upon them while the water swirled in eddies with white kissing the tops of the waves. Knox spun us, and we slammed against another set of rocks, and then another. His body took each blow as the rushing rapids tossed us around.

The water's sound grew deafeningly loud, and I sucked air in. I saw the clear water swirling like a cyclone into the deep. My heart stopped, and the color drained from my face while I wrapped my legs around Knox, who was still protecting me from the deadly rocks with his body. His eyes turned and widened in horror to where the water was rushing us toward.

"Knox!" I shrieked in panic, burying my face against his shoulder, pretending we weren't about to die as the whirlpool grew louder the closer we got.

"Breathe in now, Aria!" he shouted above the thundering water, drawing in air before the water sucked us into the vortex.

We were pulled into the whirlpool, thrown around in a wide circle as we clung to one another tightly. My lungs burned, even as Knox pulled me against him, pushing air into my lungs from his without care that his lungs were starving for it as well. For being such a prick, he certainly was fighting to keep me alive and unharmed from my own stupidity.

I was jerked hard by debris, and something slammed into Knox, forcing us apart as the water ripped me out of his hold. I was sucked down violently and was dizzy from being twirled in the tornado of water. I exhaled, fighting the dizziness, and blackness started to envelop me as water filled my lungs.

Knox's scream echoed in my mind as if coming through a tunnel, forcing me to open my eyes as I coughed up water. The whirlpool had released its hold, and we were in a dark cavern with green glowing crystals that offered a dim light.

"Aria!" Knox screamed, urgency filling his tone as I coughed violently.

"Knox?" I whispered, throwing up copious amounts of water as my chest lessened with pressure. Exhausted, I leaned back, floating, noting the cave grew lighter as the water's sound seemed to get louder.

"Swim to me, now!" he demanded, and I rolled my eyes, bobbing in the water. I turned toward his voice, moving my arms and legs to go deeper into the dark tunnel.

I caught sight of Knox, watching the relief play in his eyes until he looked over my shoulder. He shot forward, rushing to me with long, powerful strokes of his arms as the water pulled me away from him.

My arms burned, and my legs stopped kicking. I turned, staring at the light at the end of the cave. The water vanished over the rim as if it just dropped off.

My mind caught on to the problem, and I screamed. My body fought to get to Knox, knowing that he was my best shot at survival.

I didn't make it to him before water rushed us toward the mouth of the cave and shot us over a waterfall that made Niagara Falls look like a kiddie pool. I screeched as I free fell in the air, staring up as Knox dove headfirst toward me with his arms outstretched, as if he intended to catch me midair.

Screeching sounded, and I swung my head toward the noise, shouting out in horror as a large, black, three-headed bird-like creature flew toward me. It looked like something straight out of a *Stephen King* book of nightmares.

The moment it got close, I flipped my body, kicking

it hard in one head. It recoiled briefly, flapping giant black and orange wings tipped with fiery crimson-colored feathers.

The three heads opened their jaws of long, needle-like teeth that snapped toward me. The moment it would have caught me, Knox landed on its back, slicing through the three necks in one swift, well-placed strike of his deadly claws.

I fought the tears that escaped from the relief I felt that he'd saved me from death by the horrid creature's teeth.

Knox held out his hand, and I reached for him as I peered down at the water we were about to hit.

His fingertips touched mine, and I tilted my body, slowing my fall as he dove close enough to grab me. He pulled me against his chest, holding my trembling form before he purred softly, searching my face for injury.

"This is going to hurt a lot," he muttered. He stared at me before peering between our bodies at the fast-approaching water.

When he lifted his head, I closed the space between us, nipping his lip softly before his hand cupped my neck, kissing me hard and fast, ending it abruptly.

"Brace for impact," he warned, forcing his body lower so that he would shoot through the surface first. I held on to him, hugging my arms around his neck as I inhaled.

"This is insane!" I shouted, gulping in air moments before we hit the waters' surface. I felt no pain, as if his body cut a path for mine through the water, protecting mine once again.

Chapter Thirty-One

The moment we were in the water, I pushed away from Knox, shooting my body toward the shoreline. I didn't wait to see if he followed since I could see the bubbles beside me, and the evidence of another whirlpool fighting to suck us into its deadly grasp. I knew he'd follow me since he was Knox, and he made everything look freaking easy.

Crawling onto the shore, I coughed up more water. Flipping onto my back, I watched the male who had just protected me from certain death, taking powerful strokes to reach the shore where I laid.

I flipped onto my stomach, moving to my knees while fighting to stand through the exhaustion. My body burned from misuse and screamed in protest. I fought the skirt I wore, heavy with water as it clung to my hips in danger of sliding off them.

When I finally gained my footing, I rushed toward

the next cliff edge, leaping over it onto black slate rocks. My bare feet protested against the rock's surface, and yet I kept moving.

I progressed down a few tiers, pausing once I'd placed enough distance between myself and the beast hunting me. I could hear the shouts of his men above us as Knox silently stalked me, his eyes smiling with victory, even though he hadn't caught me yet.

I bent at the waist, placing my hands on my knees, staring up at him. Knox smiled wolfishly while closing the distance between us without showing a single ounce of the exhaustion I felt coursing through me.

My muscles burned, rebelling against more movement. He paused and slowly knelt, studying me while he allowed me to catch my breath. He stood, letting his stare drop to my exposed belly.

"You could just give up," I offered as his eyes moved back to hold mine with challenge burning in them.

"You could be a good girl and get on your knees for me."

"I prefer being bad," I smirked, and his eyes lowered to my mouth. I licked my lips, noting the smoldering heat that filled his. "See something you like?" I taunted.

"I was thinking of how I intend to fuck that bratty mouth of yours. I bet you'd stop arguing if it was busy, wouldn't you?"

"My mouth isn't planning to do *anything* to your dick, Knox," I snorted, standing to glare at him with a fire burning in my eyes. I hated that my body reacted to his words, uncaring that he was a murderous prick who wanted me on my knees in eternal servitude.

"That's a waste of your pretty lips and very talented tongue, woman. I personally enjoy what that mouth does immensely."

"That's too bad, isn't it?" I whispered, fighting the heat that pulsed in my belly, clenching with need.

I turned from him, jumping over a few more of the flat-surfaced rocks. I noted the noise they made as they creaked and groaned beneath my slight weight. Pausing, I turned to tease him, only to find him one stone away from me. My heart hammered in my ears as adrenaline and need clashed together.

I hadn't even heard Knox moving, and yet he'd closed the distance between us. He looked at me, calculating. He enjoyed hunting me down. His muscles clenched while he watched me, enjoying the look of worry burning in my eyes.

I didn't jump, not wanting to move blindly as he examined me, lowering his gaze to peer over the edge to gauge the distance of the fall. Slowly, his eyes slid back to me before I stepped toward the edge, dropping down to the next tier, using his distraction to my advantage.

"You're going to be on your knees for me the moment I catch you," he promised as he once again closed the space between us. "You could end this now, and I'll go easy on you. Make me chase you much longer, and I'll make you wish you'd ended it much sooner."

"Are you going to hurt me, Knox?" I asked huskily, watching the cocky smirk playing on his full mouth.

"Only a little, but then you do enjoy being hurt, don't

you?" he countered, causing my nipples to harden from the deep, rich sound of his voice sliding through me.

"Not happening, asshole."

I shook my head, watching how his body tensed while he prepared to close the distance between us. I stepped back, intending to move until a sickening crack sounded from beneath me.

My heart stopped, and the smile dropped from my lips, sending what blood was inside my veins coursing through my ears in a deafening roar as the rock broke.

A scream ripped past my lips as I began to fall. Knox dove forward without thought of himself, grabbing my hand. I cried out, dangling thousands of feet from the ground.

Staring down at the earth below me, I watched the rock slam against others, causing an avalanche of deadly rocks to rush down the cliff, crashing onto the ground, sending a dust cloud into the air. My body trembled, and tears slipped from my eyes while panic rushed through me blindingly.

"Look at me, Aria. Don't look down," Knox demanded, grabbing my wrist with his other hand. I dangled from the precarious height, unable to step onto anything since I was out further than the rocks beneath me.

"Knox," I whispered through trembling lips, forcing my stare to meet his as I prepared to fall to my death.

"Just breathe," he growled, and I wasn't certain if he spoke to himself or me in the urgency filled tone.

He shook his head, worry flashing in his eyes as he yanked me up, holding me against his shaking body as he slowly exhaled, running his hands over my arms as I trembled.

"I have you," he whispered, kissing my forehead.

Another cracking noise filled the air, and I gasped as we both started free falling. I dropped through the air, my body slamming painfully against one slab of rock, only to be tossed onto another before I stopped moving. I stared at the cloudless sky above me, inhaling past the pain that erupted in my back. I sat up, staring around.

"Knox? *Knox!*" I screamed thickly. I stood slowly, leaning over the edge of my rock to watch others crashing down the cliff, slammed into the earth, shattering. "Knox!" I shrieked as tears pricked my eyes, burning them. My hands reached for my hair, pulling on it as pain ripped through my heart. Denial that he'd fallen to his death ripped through me. "*Knox!* Don't be dead! Please, don't be dead, you stupid asshole," I sobbed, wrapping my arms around my middle to stop the pain rocking through me.

"Careful, Aria, I may start to think you actually care about me," a deep voice chuckled from above me.

I peered up, exhaling with relief as he studied my reaction. Tears slid from my eyes, and I dropped my head backward, closing them.

"That would be a stupid thing to assume," I whispered thickly, still fighting the tears in my throat. I opened my eyes, allowing him to see the relief burning in my gaze.

We stared at one another, both checking for any visible injuries from the fall. It was several moments of silence before we were satisfied that the other was okay. I started to speak, but the rock I stood on made a loud cracking sound.

Knox shouted for me to move, and I spun around, jumping to the next one, and then the next as the sound of rocks cracking followed me. I felt him behind me, following me over the rocks that threatened to give way beneath our weight. Neither of us spoke as we made our way down the deadly mountainside, racing against the rocks that cracked with every jump we made.

The moment I reached solid earth, I rushed forward, forcing my burning legs to move to the next cliff's edge. I leaped into the air when I was close enough to go over the edge, but Knox grabbed the back of my shirt, stopping my movement and throwing me backward. I rolled across the earth several times before coming to a stop on my stomach.

My eyes lifted, watching Knox's men as they walked toward us. I rolled to my back, jumping to my feet, staring at Knox. I fought to get air into my lungs while my body rebelled. Knox smiled, victory burning in his oceanic depths while he watched me.

"Submit, Aria," he demanded as his muscles strained, anticipating a fight.

I moved, and he mirrored the action, blocking my way while he tensed and prepared to advance. His scent was rushing through me, causing my already tense body to tremble with need.

"Never going to happen," I whispered breathlessly,

crouching low to swing up at him the moment he moved closer to me.

Chapter Thirty-Two

Knox dodged me easily, sliding to the right to capture my arm midair. He held my wrist as I hissed. I kicked my foot out, which he easily stepped over as he noted the sluggish movements of my attack. We both knew I was losing this fight, but I didn't intend to make it easy.

I swung my other hand and pulled back before he could grab that one too. I closed my eyes, taking a step back as he yanked my body against his solid form, and a moan escaped my lips. Knox took me to the ground, hard.

Silently, he stared into my eyes, and I searched his face as the fight left me. Both of us fought to regain control of our breathing, and the moment I had, he growled huskily. His mouth crushed against mine, claiming my lips in an earth-shattering kiss that caused everything around me to vanish but him and what he made me feel as he claimed ownership of my mouth.

I moaned against him, letting the heat of his body warm mine. His hand continued pinning mine above my head as he ground his body against me.

The rattle within him echoed through me as he pulled away, watching me chase his mouth, needing more. His lips curled into a cocky smile as I lifted, writhing against him as everything within me demanded he destroy me.

"Knox," I whispered huskily, unable to fight the urgency I felt for him with his scent rushing through me, matching mine in red-hot need that threatened violence. My body shuddered fiercely, and his eyes smoldered with knowing heat.

He smirked devilishly, lowering his mouth to my throat, which I bared for him. Warm lips kissed my racing pulse, and his tongue escaped the heat of his mouth as he brushed it over the wildly beating pulse at the hollow column of my throat. I whimpered, feeling his need against my belly, begging to give me what we both craved.

Everything within me demanded he claim my throat. I needed his teeth against my vein like some suicidal idiot wanting to be sacrificed to the beast. Knox dragged his lips across my throat to my shoulder, growling as he kissed the curve of my neck, nipping gently as a violent shudder of desire shot through me.

He growled louder, rubbing his erection against my apex that prepared for his large cock. His nostrils flared as if he scented my need, and then he groaned loudly, teeth scraping over flesh as he gave a silent warning by biting softly against my shoulder, without breaking the skin.

"Submit to me, Aria."

He craved my willing submission as much. I wanted his domination and to take me by force. I lifted my hips, purring huskily while he turned his head, rubbing his nose against my cheek.

"Give me your submission. The monster inside of me hungers for you, woman. Say the words and I'll give us what we both crave."

"No," I replied in a gasping tone, even though I wanted to beg him to put his mark on me again, needing it against my flesh.

I'd felt lost without his mark after it Taren removed it, violently. I desperately wanted it back, but I would not submit. His hand tightened on mine, staring at me through hooded eyes.

He chuckled against my shoulder as pain erupted, only to become an unbearable pleasure, and I cried out while it ripped me apart. My entire body vibrated with the claiming bite and softly murmured his name, barely above a whisper as the pressure of his bite gathered in my core, clenching hungrily for him to satisfy that need too.

His hand released mine as he pulled back, staring down at me with my blood painting his lips. Knox rolled his hips, watching my reaction to his thickening cock, and the pressure he applied to my clenching sex.

"Knox, please," I whimpered through the pain created by my desire, rocking my apex against him with wild abandonment.

I couldn't stop my body from moving, the bite

forcing me past the brink of sanity and into the haze of everything I'd fought for months. I struggled with the urge unsuccessfully, rocking my body against Knox and the ground, and his eyes grew hooded. He lowered his mouth, brushing against mine before lifting his head.

Covering my mouth, he pushed his elbow on the ground to lift his body. He grabbed the hem of my skirt, lifting it on my hips, glancing briefly at his men, then back to me.

Slowly, he slid his fingers through my core, and I moaned against his hand. He growled, running his fingers against my opening teasingly. I cried out the moment his finger entered my body, finding it wet with need. He groaned, clenching his teeth audibly while he pushed another finger into my body.

"That's my good girl, come for me," he urged huskily, rubbing his thumb against my clitoris, eliciting a throaty moan against his hand, still muffling my cries. Knox's eyes burned with fire, smoldering until my body combusted from his touch.

The slight penetration, and two more circles of his large thumb, and I exploded violently. Pleasure ripped through me, and I arched my spine into his touch as his nostrils flared with my release. Stars burst in my line of sight, and my legs dropped apart, lifting for him to give me more.

I wanted all of him, every single inch of him, buried so deeply into my body that I became the temple he worshiped. My eyes widened with the force of the orgasm. He continued to rub my clit, tears leaking from my eyes with the intensity as pleasure rolled through me nonstop.

"Good girl, Aria," he crooned, lowering to rest his forehead against mine without removing his hand from either location. He peered into my opened soul he'd bared to his heady gaze, grinning, "You're so fucking wet that I want to bury my face in that magical cunt of yours and drink it until you beg me to stop."

Fingers slid through the slick arousal, pushing against my naked flesh. Knox closed his eyes, fighting for control. His jaw clenched with the effort it took to gather the will to win the battle he waged.

His hand moved, and his mouth crushed against mine, capturing the loud growl escaping his lungs with my lips. I slid my hands through his hair, holding his mouth against mine, kissing him with a need that we both felt as the world faded to background noise and melted away.

It was a kiss that left me boneless, sending the butterflies within my belly into flight. His hand lowered, pulling my skirt down even as he pushed my thigh up to rub his thumb over the sensitive inside.

His thick cock pressed against the sensitive nub, and he growled against my lips at the sound of my moan that exploded, captured by his greedy lips. Knox pulled his mouth from mine, smiling. I cried out at the loss of his heat when he lifted back, staring down at me through hooded eyes.

"I missed you too, Little Monster," he whispered raspingly. His words were coated in thick gravel that grated on my nerves, pinching my nipples until they throbbed for him to suck their swollen tips between his teeth. "But I'm so going to punish you for making us both wait for what we crave. You also kissed other men, and that isn't something I will allow to continue. I can smell that mutt on you, Aria."

I didn't speak, not even when crunching sounded all around us. Knox peered up, watching his men surrounding us as he still held me on the ground in submission. Knox lifted my hands above my head once more, staring into my eyes as someone grabbed my wrists, applying something metal and cold around each one.

I shivered as my strength weakened, and something shot through me, something… *wrong*. It was as if they'd splashed ice water over my face, waking me from the haze Knox had induced when he'd marked my shoulder.

I gasped, fighting for air as he studied me, even as worry flashed in his eyes. I exhaled a shuddering breath, and he mirrored it before glaring down at me, as if he, too, was awakening.

"You could have fucking died, woman," Knox whispered, helping me to my feet before turning me to stare up the cliff we'd come down. Before I could say anything in my defense about our suicidal romp down the sheer rock face, he walked me toward the cliff he'd prevented me from jumping over, and grabbed the back of my hair, holding me over it. I screamed. My hands lifted to his hold on my hair, forcing myself back toward his massive body. "If you are ever that reckless with your life again, I will chain you up and throw away the fucking key. Do you understand me?" he demanded harshly. "I expect a fucking answer, Aria!"

"I understand, Knox," I swallowed past the chattering

of my teeth as what had almost happened hit me.

Over the edge of the cliff was a sheer drop that continued down to blackened earth below. There was nothing to break my fall if I'd gone over, and I would have if he hadn't caught me and thrown me back before I'd succeeded. I trembled as the reality of my stupidity hit me.

I hadn't expected to have to run this far, because I hadn't expected him to jump off a battlement blindly, or follow me down a slate cliff to catch me.

He was a fucking king, and they didn't follow bitches over perilous jumps or into raging rapids. It was like law, or some shit that they had to remain protected!

Knox turned me toward him with anger etched in his tone, but there was something in his eyes that tugged at my heart. He was worried at how reckless I'd been with my life, and that I'd almost died trying to escape him.

I nodded silently, watching as he slowly released the anger, pulling me against him while he cupped my cheeks, and fought past whatever was happening within him.

He shook his head the moment he released my face, turning to speak to Brander. "Find us a way up that fucking cliff that doesn't end with us dying."

"There's no way up, other than to climb. Not unless we go up the falls, but that only works if someone above knows we're down here and tosses us a rope. No one knows we're down here, not since we followed you, and you followed her. She, on the other hand, was the first idiot over the edge." I would have snorted, but I hated that he had a valid point.

"I guess we're going back up the way we came down," Knox muttered, turning to stare at me before a devious smile played on his lips. "Do you have rope in one of the packs?"

"Of course," Brander stated, eyeing Knox curiously.

"Get it out," Knox stated. "You're going to secure my little runaway to me. She's going up with me. I don't trust her not to try something stupid to escape me again."

"You're joking, right?" I asked sputtering, turning to stare up the cliff, noting that it wasn't slate at all. It was obsidian, polished by the elements into a glassy finish. "What the hell is that?"

"It's an unknown anomaly. Whether naturally made by the Nine Realms or man, no one knows." He watched me as I shivered, fear pinching my face. I could feel power pulsing from it and wasn't sure if they could feel it too. "Don't worry; I won't let you die. I have so many things planned for you. It would be such a waste to lose you so soon after catching you."

"I can't wait to see what that includes," I grumbled, unable to look away from the obsidian covering the entire cliffside, mirroring a fortress.

We started forward, and I winced as a shard of glass cut into my foot. I bent, pulling it out, and I stood, crying out in surprise as Knox lifted me into his arms, staring pointedly at my bare feet.

"I lost my slippers in the water, saving your ass." My lips tugged into a pout, hating that I felt precious in his arms as he smiled, placing his mouth close to my forehead while the men moved ahead of us.

"Don't worry. You won't need them when you're on your knees at my feet, Aria."

And there went the moment.

The man knew right where to aim to bring me down from ever thinking he could care about me. It was like he had some secret map to every part of me. The moment his fingers touched me, they moved as though he could sense every thought and knew my deepest, darkest desires.

I felt him to the very center of my being, like he snapped the cords of my restraints, unleashing something primal within me. When I'd relented to the desire and feelings toward him, he'd open his mouth and say something to fuck it all up.

"I'm not getting on my knees for you."

"Everyone has a breaking point." His lips curled into a smile as my frown deepened. "You don't want me to break you because I know your weaknesses and your strengths. I know your fears and your desires. I know what drives you and what can destroy you."

"Are you planning to destroy me, Knox?" I asked. His smile dropped, and he worried his lip with his teeth before the smile returned, and steel entered his eyes.

"You're my enemy," he admitted without looking at me, as if doing so would break the steel he erected around him once more. "And considering how easily you just submitted to my will, you'll give us both what we crave soon enough." He stopped at the edge of the cliff as Brander approached, and Knox set me on my feet. "Wrap your legs around my waist and don't move. Tie Aria to me, Brander, and let's get back to the army. I need to get her into a tent and mark her with my scent. Based on how she smells, I'm surprised the entirety of the Nine Realms isn't hunting her sweet scent down like rabid beasts."

"Isn't that why you keep biting me? Oh, but someone did remove your ownership tag, didn't they?" I asked, watching as he lowered his head, securing my bound hands over his neck as he gripped my hips roughly, helping me settle my legs around his waist. His smile turned wolfish, promising to draw blood. "I don't care how I smell. You're not touching me. Your mark will have to do, at least until I can have someone else replace it. Dimitri offered, and honestly, I think he's more akin to my needs."

"You're mine, Aria. I'm going to fuck you so hard, and sink so fucking deep inside of you, that you'll never be able to work me out from under your skin, ever." I swallowed, studying the conviction burning in his eyes.

His hand lifted, capturing my jaw, and he applied pressure until my mouth opened, tipping it up and forcing my stare to lock with his in a silent battle.

"I am not yours!" I snapped, shuddering violently with need. His eyes sparkled with the knowledge that my body was a spring preparing to uncoil violently.

"You. *Are*. Mine. And by the time I am finished marking you, you won't want me to ever leave your body. That's the difference between that mutt and me. When I claim something, I mark it on a level so deeply embedded within the soul, that no one could erase it."

Knox leaned forward, biting my bottom lip before he growled, smiling as he pulled back with victory shining in his eyes. "That's the difference between a monster and a man. I mark to kill or own, and I want to fucking own you, Little Creature. You and I both know you were built to be savaged by me and me alone. Now, be a good girl for me and shut that bratty mouth before I fuck it to silence your taunts."

Chapter Thirty-Three

Brander tied the rope around my thighs, and then around Knox, securing it onto us like a harness, forcing my body flush against the male who was enjoying the situation entirely too much. Brander finished his task while Knox held me up, rubbing small circles into the back of my thighs, listening to his men while studying me carefully.

Done with his task, Brander joined the other men and started ascending the cliff. Knox waited, watching their path up the cliff as they chose the safest route to the top. His attention slid back to me, and I swallowed, noting the heat burning in his eyes, my body tightening with an awareness of just how exposed I was to him. His devilish grin told me he had realized the same, as he stepped closer to the cliff face, resting my rear on a rock.

"If you do anything to hinder the climb, I'll push your perky ass against the nearest rock and fuck you into submission. Do you understand me?" he asked, dropping his stare to my tongue, which had darted out, wetting my lips.

"Perfectly," I whispered, hating that his scent was rendering me stupid.

I understood I wasn't human, but responding to Knox's enticingly male scent how I did, was for the birds. Everything within me wanted him, and while I realized it was my basic instincts working against me, I knew that if we started, we wouldn't stop anytime soon. My body rubbed his, and I closed my eyes against the feel of his warmth heating me.

Hands cradled my face moments before soft lips brushed against mine, forcing my eyes to open. Knox stared into my eyes before lifting his head to the men scaling the cliff. I could feel his need against my apex. His thickness pulsed as his scent drifted to me, removing all reasonable thought from my mind.

"The moment we get inside a tent, I'm fixing that issue you're having. You'll end up forcing me to fight my entire army with your scent."

"Excuse me?"

"I'm fucking you, end of discussion."

"That isn't happening," I argued, glaring at him as he grinned like it was cute, and as though I didn't have an opinion. "I'm not sleeping with you, Knox. End of discussion."

"You want me, woman."

"I'd be lying if I said I didn't, but it changes nothing. I am your enemy, and you're mine. We're not lovers.

We're not even friends. I'm your hostage, which means my vagina is out of your coverage area."

"Out of my coverage area?" he asked, narrowing his eyes as they sparkled with amusement.

"Yes, exactly." I nodded, glaring at him as his lips curved further, revealing his sexy-as-fuck dimple that pissed me off. "If I were a map, I'd be the spot marked out of boundaries for you. Consider it unobtainable territories, and so far beyond your reach, you can never conquer it. If I were a palace, you'd never breach its walls, or get through its gates."

"You seem to forget, Little Monster. I've already laid siege to your borders, scaled your walls, and planted my sword into the queen's heart."

"That's a horrible analogy!" I snorted, and he smiled wickedly.

"I took your virgin lands and claimed them for my own. I set your borders on fire and battered past the wall no other had penetrated before me, woman. Tell me I didn't." he challenged, fire smoldering in his stare.

Peering up the cliff, Knox checked his men's status and location, still making their way to the top. My fingers slid over the rigid muscles on his neck, and I tensed, knowing I was losing the fight I held over my control as his scent continued to slither through me. Knox's attention swung back to me as my hands continued their slow perusal of his muscles.

When he opened his mouth to speak, I lost the fight, pulling him against mine. I ravished his lips, pushing my tongue past them the moment he allowed it. I moaned huskily against his lips as he returned the kiss. Lifting his hand to my neck, he tilted my face to permit better access as his tongue moved against mine.

It was a demanding kiss—the type of kiss you never wanted to end. When Knox finally pulled his mouth from mine, he searched my expression before our eyes locked.

"How's that battle going, Aria?" he whispered thickly, pulling me tighter to his hard arousal that I rubbed against, rocking my hips as an orgasm threatened to consume me. "Yeah, I'm about to fuck you like a castle in which I'm setting siege. I am going to pound against your defenses, set fire to your bailey, and then I'm going to plunder every ounce of pleasure you have while pillaging until you beg for mercy, of which you know I have none. You're not out of my coverage area. You're mine, and if you're not careful, you're about to snap what little control I have."

"You don't lose control, bastard," I pointed out, hating that I couldn't put distance between us while tied to him. My arms around his neck left his lips too close to have control over my brain.

His laughter was dark as he studied my face, peering lower at my erect nipples. He grumbled in irritation, finding hard pebbles begging that he taste them. Ignoring their plea, Knox lowered his hands to my legs and fixed my dress's skirt to assure it didn't hinder his climb.

Sliding his hands between the ropes and my dress bunched between my legs, he freed the fabric but kept his hands in place. Rubbing his thumb along the inside of my thigh, he forced my eyes to his, and we stared intently at one another. Then, slowly, he pushed his fingertips against my sex, finding the swollen nub with ease, as if he had some direct link to its location and how to work it perfectly.

"Everyone loses control, Aria. Your scent would make a saint sin. If I were you, I'd fight harder to conceal it because everything within me is demanding I bury my cock into your tight cunt, and mark it with my scent so that no one else tries to touch you. So, be a good girl and hold on tight so I can get us up this cliff and satisfy that need."

"This climb is suicide, and you know it," I whispered, fighting the urge to call him out, to see if he would lose control. I was sick and tired of being the only one with control issues.

"Who the fuck climbed down the cliff in the first place?" he asked, grabbing my legs as he stepped back, preparing to jump to the first set of outcropping rocks.

"Who's the idiot that followed me over the edge?" I stammered, shivering when his scent assaulted me as if he were purposely projecting it to fuck with me.

"I did. If I hadn't, you'd be dead right now."

"You don't know that. I could have saved myself; you know?" That was a lie, and we both knew it. Had Knox not stopped me from jumping off that last edge, I'd have fallen to my death. Not to mention that he'd given me air in the water funnel, preventing me from drowning, and he saved me from impaling myself on all the rocks in the rapids. But who was counting?

"You'd have fucking died, and we both know it. You'd have never made it to that cliff alive in the first place. I should spank your ass to punish you, but you'd enjoy that, wouldn't you?" he chuckled, dropping his stare to lock with mine.

"I doubt it, asshole." Ignoring him, I turned my attention to his men moving up the cliff, and Knox still didn't start climbing.

Knox dismissed me, gazing up at the men before he pushed me against the rock, brushing his hand over the arousal wetting my panties, amused that my eyes grew hooded from his simple touch. He used one hand to pull my panties aside and slid two fingers into my body.

I moaned loudly, rolling my hips against his hand as it slammed firmly against my sex, his fingers pumping into my body twice. Suddenly, he growled, withdrawing them, pushing his fingers into his mouth to suck them clean while I watched, my core throbbing, wanting release.

"Remember that control issue?" he asked, his tone etched with lust. "It's snapping."

I crushed my mouth against his without warning or thought. I moaned against the softness of his lips, trembling with a need that rushed through me like a wildfire hitting a dry field in August.

My hands pulled him closer as he shoved me against the slate, devouring my mouth like he was going to war against it, conquering it with no mercy offered. I rocked against him, purring loudly as what little control I'd held snapped along with his.

A rattle built in Knox's chest, swallowed by my mouth, and I refused to cease my attack. Everything within me desired and wanted him to take away the clenching need that consumed all coherent thought. Arousal coated my pussy, enticing him to take what I offered. His tongue captured mine, dominating it easily until I was moaning against his kiss, wiggling my hips with a silent invitation.

Coughing sounded above us, and Knox slowed the kiss as his hands brushed over my thighs. Pulling back, he pushed the hair from my face. I shivered, and my lips trembled for more, my teeth catching my bottom lip to hide the quiver of need from his triumphant, smug expression.

"Careful, Aria," he warned. He moved his hands from my legs and crouched, jumping to grasp onto the first outcrop of rocks. We hung there for a moment, and he smiled wickedly at me before pulling us up easily. "You kiss me like that again, and I'll assume it's an invitation."

"It would be stupid on your part to assume it was anything other than hormones."

"Keep lying to yourself, and you might actually start believing what's coming out of your mouth. I sure in the fuck won't," Knox growled, crouching, and shooting us onto the next outcrop of rocks. "Scared, Little Lamb?" he teased softly, peering up as he continued to scale the cliffside.

Every sinewy muscle in Knox's body pulsed with the climb, taking us higher and higher as fear thundered through me. I didn't dare close my eyes, even though I wanted to do just that. My heartbeat mirrored the sound of his war drums pounding in my ears.

"Terrified," I admitted, holding him tightly, fighting the urge to close my eyes.

"Good, because you're in my world now," he warned. "We're playing by my terms, Aria. You may beg me for mercy, but remember, I don't plan to give you any." I didn't respond to his taunts. I didn't need to since they didn't deserve a response.

Knox's body was sleek and predatory as it climbed skillfully up the rocks. The air grew thinner the higher we went, and I lowered my head as my heart raced, and fear filled my mind. I was utterly powerless against him, and worse, I was powerless to do anything right now, and that sat ill with me.

I didn't have magic. The cuffs on my wrists had ensured that, and if we fell, that was it. We'd simply become a splash of color against the earth. I turned against the curve of Knox's neck, and he stopped, slamming me against the rocks as a lethal rattle built in his throat, and I yelped in surprise.

"Keep your fucking teeth away from my throat, woman," he hissed coldly, his eyes black as night.

"I wasn't going to bite you." My brows pinched together in a frown while I searched his face. "I don't understand why you think I would do that at this height, considering you're holding my life in your hands," I admitted, and then cried out as the thundering sound of rocks sliding against others exploded above us.

Knox shoved my body beneath him, holding me tightly as rocks rained down from above. They slammed against stones on either side of us, sending more rocks down the mountain in an avalanche of deadly debris that crashed loudly against the ground below.

I shivered against the realization that I may very well die before we made it to the top. Purring started, and I realized in embarrassment that I was crying and choking Knox out as he held me tightly beneath him.

He'd used his body to shield me from the rocks and was now fighting to calm my fears. My lips brushed against his softly, thanking him for understanding that I was losing my shit.

After a few more moments had passed, he stepped back, jumping to the next tier of rocks, and then the next. He climbed as if created to do this from birth.

Every time we'd catch up to the others, he'd pause again, purring softly as he noted my reaction. His purr was a sedative, calming everything within me. I purred in response, replicating his.

Knox jumped to the next rock, and I screamed as it gave way, sending us crashing down the cliffside. I held onto to him tightly, while he reached blindly for anything to stop our fall. Shouting sounded from above, and I breathed him in, remaining perfectly still as he fought to save us from death.

His legs hit something solid, and he pushed up, forcing me back against a jagged rock that bit into my flesh. Pain coursed through me, and I gasped as he cradled me, turning us so I wouldn't crash into the rocks.

"Aria," he whispered, using his fingers to lift my chin to see my face, which I'd buried against his chest. His purr sounded again, filling my body and calming my racing nerves and pounding heartbeat echoing in my ears.

"I'm okay," I admitted, ignoring the pain in my side.

After a moment of catching his breath, Knox stared upward and then back at me. "Hold on tight. I'm getting us the fuck up this cliff before it ends both our lives."

Knox didn't wait to see if I did as he'd asked. His muscles bunched, and his scent increased until I could not stop myself from rubbing against him, heat blooming in my cheeks. If he noticed, he kept it and his taunts to himself until finally, Brander helped us up the climb's last crest.

"She's bleeding," Brander pointed out, touching my side. I jolted and tightened my hold against Knox's throat, which didn't go unnoticed.

"You're safe, Little Monster," Knox hissed. I noted his men behind him, watching cautiously as Brander sliced through the rope holding me to him.

"The rock scratched up your back, but it's nothing that won't heal on its own," a warrior stated, glaring at me. I lowered my legs to stand on firm ground. "There's a trail ahead. Luckily, it's not as lethal as the last."

"Walk, woman," Knox demanded, ignoring Brander, who stared at the blood painting my dress. "Run ahead, Brander. Have our men ready to move when we reach them. It's time to leave this cesspool and head toward the mountains. Have Aria's cage readied as well."

A cage? I turned, glaring at him as he smiled.

"Don't worry. If you're a good girl, I'll take you out often and play with you."

Knox's men laughed as angry tears pricked my eyes. I glared at him, his eyes narrowing on me as if he didn't like the flash of pain he saw. Dismissing him, I walked past, uncaring that my sensitive feet were sore and that every inch of my body ached in pain and need.

The sooner we reached Norvalla, the sooner I'd be able to put distance between us again. This man made my brain turn to mush, and everything within me wanted him, except, well, me. One minute I wanted to rip off his cock, and the next, I wanted to ride it.

I couldn't make my creature realize the error of belonging to Knox, or that he didn't really want me other than for what I was and what I could do for him. I was his weapon, one he intended to use against my people. And for the moment, I was helpless to do anything since he had placed magic nulling cuffs on me. On top of that, I'd expelled the magic I held to save my family from ending up beside me in cages.

Chapter Thirty-Four

I started up the narrow trail that followed the river, leading us back to the castle. I pushed past Knox, who insisted that I move faster, his men grunting in agreement. Several hours later, we reached the top of the plateau, and I could see the castle. My feet ached, and my legs burned from the hike.

Once we reached the castle gates, Knox pushed me to my knees, turning to issue orders to the men surrounding us. My ears perked, and I tilted my head toward the castle, hearing voices behind its walls.

"Knox," I called, but he ignored me. My heart leaped into my throat, pounding harder as horror entered my mind. "Knox, answer me!" I screamed in a dead panicked tone, echoing as he turned, flashing irritation at me. "Are there people in the castle?" He narrowed his eyes, smiling, before noting the horror on my face, and his gaze slid over my head. "Undo me now!"

"No," he growled, focusing on the castle where I could hear his men inside.

"Undo me, or your men will die! It's all going to come down. It was part of the spell we crafted. Dammit, undo me!" I demanded, and he grabbed the cuffs that bound my magic to remove them. I lifted my unbound hands at the same time the castle groaned and started to crumble.

Magic rushed through me, and I watched in horror, realizing it wasn't going to be enough to stop the castle from falling onto the men inside. I turned toward Knox's witches, who stood absently talking to one another, staring at the castle.

"Help me!" I cried. Their eyes slid to Knox, asking permission, and he growled, swearing loudly at them.

Their hands grabbed mine, and I began chanting. Magic was the only thing holding the castle up as men flooded out the front gate. Knox's hands touched my side. I sagged, holding me up while pushing power into my body. He took a step back, watching as more and more of his men escaped from the castle that continued collapsing, even as I fought to hold it up.

Lore exited the gate, looking worried. Seeing the fear on my face and hearing my chant, he turned back toward the castle, screaming for those still inside to exit quickly. Magic was leaking from my pores. Sweat beaded on my brow as men rushed from the stronghold carrying chests and other items. Lore remained by the large, wooden gates, and then exhaled, nodding to me as the last man ran free of the destruction.

I dropped the hold on the witch's magic, staring

at Lore as Asil's stronghold collapsed completely, crumbling to the ground.

Everything went still around me, and I dropped to the earth, screaming in pain. It had taken every drop of magic I had to prevent Knox's men from being crushed to death.

Knox kneeled beside me, touching my face as he stared at me. "What the hell is wrong with her?"

I couldn't even blink, and yet I felt nothing but pure pain ripping through me. I screamed, calling for help, but no one replied. They continued talking as if they couldn't hear my screams. I sobbed inwardly, stuck inside my head, realizing no one could hear me crying for help.

"My guess?" one woman said as she leaned over, smiling down at me. "She just used up all of her magic and is stuck inside her head because she's drained herself to the brink of death."

"Can she live like that without being in pain?" Knox asked, and she nodded, still smiling at me as her eyes turned cruel.

Lying bitch.

I was being ripped apart from the inside out.

My eyes stared sightlessly at the sky as my wails continued to go unheard. I was dying a witch's worst nightmare, trapped in a shell without the magic to escape.

It was the one thing you didn't do as a witch, no matter what happened. You never drained your last amount of magic because to do so was a fate worse than death. I'd thought it was a myth, and now here I was stuck inside my mind.

"No. You're wrong. She is in hell right now," another witch admitted, causing the other to snort. "She is in the worst pain you can imagine, and without help, she will stay that way until death finally claims her."

"Goddess be damned, you're such a stupid bitch, Siobhan. She is our enemy. Aria Hecate is an enemy to *our* King!"

"No, Bekkah, she isn't. If you leave her like that, My King, she will die. She is stuck in her mind, slowly being ripped apart because she used every ounce of magic she had to save your men from dying. Allow me to help her."

"Save her life, Siobhan. She is not to suffer such a fate, especially since she saved my men."

"As you wish, My King." Siobhan turned to look at Bekkah. "Help me."

"No. She's my enemy," the dark-haired woman hissed.

Knox touched my cheek, staring down at me as he nodded. "Do it, Bekkah. Lore, bring Aria's cage so she can rest as we travel. We leave here within the hour."

I felt Siobhan touching me, her magic pushing through my soul as she helped ease the pain. I still couldn't move, couldn't speak as what bit of magic she gave me wasn't enough, considering the power I typically held in reserve.

My eyes closed on their own as powerful arms lifted me, holding me closely before placing me onto blankets. I sighed, hearing the metal lock clink closed, knowing it sealed me into my cage like a pet.

I fought against the overwhelming panic that rushed through me, wrapping around my throat, cutting off my air supply. The blackness that came with my panic saved me, enveloping me as I faded into unconsciousness.

Chapter Thirty-Five

Soraya

Sweat beaded on my brow, the night stiflingly hot while I watched the large army below the cliffs I hid upon, preparing to ride out. They had placed the silver-haired witch into a cage, and her body was limp from expelling too much magic to protect the King of Norvalla's men, who would have died, crushed beneath the massive castle.

I'd been studying the witch for a few weeks, and nothing she did, made any sense, other than destroying keeps that belonged to the weaker witches. She had started with the lesser keeps, moving through them easily. Then, without reason, she'd come to a stronghold and Asil herself admitted her and several others she had with her.

It was the first time she hadn't been alone, and those accompanying her looked closer than just a coven. They had laughed and acted like a family.

I had intended to rush off to Ilsa and report that they were all inside one of her strongholds together, but the sight of Esme on the battlements peering down into the sprawling courtyard stopped me. She'd hidden within the veil, moving freely around the castle as if she, too, was tracking the silver-haired witch.

No battle drums sounded as the army started up the curved trail that led away from the crumbling stronghold. There was no celebration of victory that normally clung to an army from setting siege on a fortress and leaving victorious.

Of course, the army themselves hadn't had to lift a single finger to bring the stronghold to its knees. The witch had done that alone. The others with her had stood on the battlements, working a spell that had exploded away from the castle, spreading through the air until I'd felt my body jerk with the intensity of it moving through me. It had spread across the land, something Ilsa would have felt, and would expect answers.

I slipped into the shadows, watching the impressive king and his men as they led the army at the forefront. My stare slid over the men at his side. They were strong, hungry-looking men that made my body heat with need that had gone unsated since the day Julia had returned home with black, deadened eyes, turning my life upside-down.

I'd once earned a lucrative income by selling tonics, creating spells, and entertaining visitors from across the seas and lands of the Nine Realms. Countless people had come to our town to procure my remedies, to ease ailments, or remove curses, and yet that had stopped the day they built the palace.

Ilsa coming to town had run away my clientele, and then disaster had struck down against the village as darkness flooded into the souls of the weak. Those not inflicted, or that had willingly succumbed to the darkness escaped, leaving their homes behind.

Some of us didn't get that choice before the men of Ilsa's army sought to slake their needs, to rape, and take women brutally. Broken women were easier to control. I was away that day, seeking passage for myself and Julia on a ship in Dorcha to escape the palace and the Kingdom of Vãkya.

I'd returned to find my sister raped by a group of men, her arms and legs bound to her bed, beaten brutally. Julia's vacant eyes had leaked tears, and yet she'd never spoken or whispered a word about what happened in my absence. I'd screamed and yelled at her to get up, fight the darkness I could sense entering her, and instead, she'd let it in to quiet the pain.

My eyes slid over the men, and I swallowed down the nervousness at letting them get too close while stuck in my memories. Slipping further into the shadows, I watched sharp sapphire eyes slide to where I hid within the shadows, outside of where they could sense my presence.

The cage moved closer, and I winced at the pain etched on the silver-haired witch's face. Even with her eyes closed, agony etched her delicate features in a pinched tightness. Almost as if within her mind, she was living inside a nightmare.

I knew that pain intimately. I'd sold my soul to stay close to my sister. My body was used viciously by cold-bastards who got off on hurting us for fun. Whatever it took, right?

I felt a connection to this woman's pain, and I hated her for it. I hated that I felt anything for the woman since her life could release Julia's from the nightmare she lived at Ilsa's bidding.

The man with sapphire eyes paused, canting his head on his large warhorse, peering right at me. Swallowing past the lump in my throat, I fought the sudden thundering of my heart as it thumped wildly in my chest. Eyes that bespoke of fire slid over my body, and I went completely still, staring into their promise of passion and power.

Someone up the line spoke, and he turned back toward the male with platinum hair and amber eyes, who slid his golden gaze toward me and frowned. The larger of the two males nudged his mount forward, and something touched my shoulder.

Spinning toward the hand, I frowned at finding Esme there, watching me. I vanished without warning, unwilling to deal with her or her group of rebellion leaders today. I appeared outside the palace on the rolling hill filled with crumbling graves and crude gravestones.

"You're not making it to the palace to tell your master what happened," Esme snapped, appearing before me.

"Get out of my way," I warned, pulling power toward me.

"You fire at me, and I'll be done with you, Soraya. I know you think Ilsa will allow Julia to escape, but she won't ever allow her to go free. You and I both know that. Come with us and help us. We can make a difference together!"

"By doing what? Pretending what I do fucking matters? You and I both know that unless you find someone much stronger than Ilsa, you're only stalling the inevitable from happening."

"I found someone stronger," Esme argued, lowering her voice as guards passed by the road above us.

"Like the last one? Or maybe like the one before her? The corpses of your so called hero's now swing from the walls inside the palace, Esme. I know because I pass their rotten bodies every day. I enter that blasted place to see my sister, who remains trapped in her body filled with darkness."

"I know you think Julia is in there, but even if she was, you can't remove the darkness. No one can! Julia is gone, and you need to face that fact! You and I both know that she's lost, Soraya. You can't save her any more than I can save my sisters. Once they succumb to the darkness, they're gone. You know what Julia went through, and why she took that darkness. She was sweet and pretty and didn't stand a chance in this world. They never allow those types of girls to live long. The smart ones got out and hid, and yet you couldn't let her go. It's understandable to want to save our bloodlines, but think about this, there's a reason they're rotting within their bodies. They're already dead."

I lunged, slamming my fist into Esme's nose before she could deflect it. The crunch of bone meeting fist was satisfying, and yet the pain her words created within me caused hot tears to prick my eyes.

"I will do whatever it takes to free my sister. Unlike you, mine didn't get out in time."

Esme snorted, her violet eyes flashing with the pain we both felt at reliving the memories of the first few weeks of Ilsa moving into this place. Her dark head shook silently.

"I lost my mother, and both brothers, Soraya. I lived the same horrors. Ilsa's soldiers held me down and raped me until I *wanted* to die. Do you know how many men can fit into one woman's body? I do, vividly. I watched them slit my mother open from her throat to her pubic bone, withdrawing her organs while her children watched. They spared me what came next because I was busy entertaining five men in the bedroom. Five men, for what felt like days, who all took turns raping me until I wanted to consume the darkness within the jar they held in front of my face. They left me for dead after they'd beaten me to nothing more than a pulp. So, don't come at me with your accusation for leaving you and Julia behind. You escaped the worst of it by searching for a way to get her out. I am sorry for what happened to Julia. But she knew what would happen when she consumed that vile magic. You won't want to hear this, but she is free from the agony. She does not feel or remember the pain she endured while they brutalized her. I relieve it every day."

"I'm not betraying Ilsa without a way to get Julia out of her fucking presence."

"I'm not asking you to betray Ilsa. I'm asking you to keep what you know about Aria Hecate to yourself,"

Esme snorted, wiping the blood from her nose.

"Who the fuck is that?" I countered, narrowing angry eyes on the blood dripping from her nose. At least I knew she wasn't dark or one of Ilsa's spies yet, which the red blood proved.

"The silver-haired witch you've been stalking," Esme snipped, her eyes rolling at the question. I opened my mouth to argue that I hadn't been stalking her when she lifted her hand, shaking her head. "Don't even, Soraya Waterford. I have been stalking you while you've spied on Aria. Do you know what she's done?"

"I've watched her taking down weak keeps, if that is what you're asking me."

"Asil's keep was weak? Because I'm pretty certain Aria just leveled a stronghold by herself. I watched her dream walk into the King of Norvalla's head. Tell me, how many witches do you know with enough power to do that? Many have tried, but none have even come close to breaching the walls in that man's head."

"None. But that means nothing," I argued, knowing damn well it was a huge accomplishment.

"The same day, within hours of doing that, Aria cloned herself. She fucking *cloned* herself and stood against Tristan and his men, then faced off against that same monster that has her now. She stood in her cloned form before Knox Karnavious, and he couldn't tell it wasn't her. That isn't just power, Soraya. That's Hecate bloodline power mixed with something else. She's unlike anything I have ever seen before."

"So she's powerful? Who fucking cares? It changes

nothing."

"You're wrong. It changes everything. Think about it, Soraya. If Aria can remove Ilsa from power, she could rule the Nine Realms. She could stop the King of Norvalla from hunting witches and slaughtering us, one witch at a time!"

"You think she's strong, but right now, she's in a cage, being taken to goddess knows where!" I argued, hating that her words had caused hope to glimmer in my chest.

"I think she's our only hope of winning against Ilsa, even if she can't overpower King Karnavious, yet. I think we'd be stupid to let this chance slip through our fingers."

"You thought the same thing about the last two saviors, Esme. Look at them now! They're nothing more than rotten corpses preserved to remind us of what happens when we step against Ilsa. Thousands of witches died when you tried a plan like this last time. What is going to stop it from happening again? Who is going to protect those who cannot protect themselves?"

"Aria will. She has vowed not to stop until she's removed those who have trespassed against Hecate's laws. She hasn't been here for very long, but in that time, she's rained down hell on this realm. You know she has because Ilsa sent you out to deal with her! You're the only one who can get into that camp, and we all know it."

"Can she win?" I asked, noting the look that took root in Esme's stare. Hope. That single word that had ended countless lives and left our entire race scrambling into the shadows, filled her violet depths.

"Honestly? I think we shouldn't underestimate Aria. She's sleeping with our enemy and plans to bring him to his knees. I think any witch that is suicidal enough to be riding the cock of the King of Norvalla, shouldn't be underestimated, Soraya. I don't know, but she's more powerful than Ilsa. She's a purebred witch of the Hecate bloodline, and something else. She's something frighteningly close to that murderous bastard who hunts us down and takes our heads. I watched her fighting men like they were child's play, ending lives without blinking while she slaughtered them, dancing around the street like she was merely playing. So, again, I ask you, what other witch has done these things?"

"None," I admitted, considering what she was saying.

I studied Esme's eyes, noting she didn't back down. If this Aria was that powerful, could she kill Ilsa? Or would she end up dead like all the others who had tried and come before her?

"Stop that shit," Esme snorted. "Stop thinking she's like the others. How many have taken in witches? How many have brought keeps held by Ilsa to their knees, single-handedly? Aria has and continues to do so. I know because I didn't trust Aria either, so I followed her. She's strong, Soraya. She's so fucking strong that I have never seen or met anyone like her before. If Aria Hecate combines her magic with the King of Norvalla, and together they go against Ilsa," Esme paused, whistling with a smile burning in her eyes, "it's a sure win. I guarantee you that together they will change the world, but they're fighting each other. We need to change their focus and move some parts together."

"And do what together?" I snapped, glaring at her. "My sister is still inside the palace, and if I fuck up, Ilsa will add Julia to that grid. And your girl is currently the King of Norvalla's newest fucking pet witch. If I were her, I'd stomp his ass and end it."

"So don't fuck up, Soraya. Do as that evil bitch instructed you, but don't give her information to harm the one bitch who may be our savior. If she's not, we'll know soon enough. I have to get back to the castle, but find us if you need someplace to hide. Aria has gathered enough of us to start a small rebellion, and she put me in charge of collecting witches worth saving."

"Aria may be smarter than she looked. She faced off against King Oleander," I muttered.

"What?" Esme gasped.

"Yeah, your girl took the lightning magic into her soul, and she lived."

"I can't believe she would do something so stupid!"

I snorted, studying the look of worry in Esme's eyes as she sucked her plumped lip between her teeth. "If you don't believe in her, then why should we?"

"I do believe in Aria, but I also don't know her well. She challenged the Queen of Nymphs and slaughtered the warriors sent to remove the unmarked witches from their land when I took her there. She made them float and then splattered them while standing beneath them. Nymphs are no joke, and Aria *popped* them. Of course, she also showered in their entrails, which was disgustingly cool."

"And then abandoned the witches to their fate? She sounds like a *great* savior." I tapped my fingers on my thigh, watching the guards moving through the terrain toward the palace.

"No, she took them to her sanctuary and has gathered those who aren't evil as shit. Tell me any of the others we trusted who did that? Aria's new here, that much is a given. She's so strong and powerful. She stood up against the King of Norvalla, to his freaking nose, and smiled in his face. I've seen no one with enough balls to do that, ever. She's fearless. I think she's backed by her family as well, or at least some of them."

I slid my eyes to the palace where Julia would bathe in the black tar to renew the darkness within her. I could believe Esme, and risk my sister's life by rolling the dice with Aria, or I could tell Ilsa where Aria was, and who had possession of her.

"If Aria took the power of the land, then she might also be able to pull the darkness from people," Esme mused, chewing her lip before her eyes locked with mine. "If she can do that, she's not our savior. She's the monster we need on our side to battle against the ones slaughtering our kind without prejudice or reason."

Twigs snapped behind us, and we vanished, disappearing into the veil between worlds before escaping through separate portals. If Aria was what this world needed, then she'd need to prove it to me.

I wouldn't chance my sister's life on the mere fact that a Hecate witch had finally shown up to the party. They'd been gone far too long, abandoning us to the evil growing within the land. It was time to put up or shut up.

My one goal in life had always been to protect my baby sister, and I'd failed. Making my choice, I appeared in front of the palace. The guards raised their weapons until they caught sight of me.

"The high queen isn't seeing her slaves today," the guard snorted, spittle painting my face.

"Tell Ilsa that I know where Aria Hecate is, and who holds her."

"There are no Hecate witches left within the land," he snorted, his pig nose making gross noises while he looked down my body. "You smell nice, girl. Ever had a hog fuck you before?" he asked, and I swallowed bile, shaking my head.

"Tell the high queen that the King of Norvalla has Aria Hecate. Tell her I'm going in to get closer to Aria, and I'll bring back her head. Tell the queen that when I come back, I hope she keeps our agreement to release my sister in exchange for the Hecate witch."

"I'll tell her, but I doubt she will care for your lies."

"She'll care because Aria Hecate just removed Lady Asil from power and took down an entire stronghold by herself. I know she felt it and will want to know immediately. She'll probably reward the one who tells her greatly."

The guards watched me, studying my lifeless eyes while they looked from me to where the interior gate was closing. Once the gate closed, it would seal for the entire night. Both of them rushed away at once, fighting amongst one another while they ran toward the high queen's quarters, leaving the main entrance unguarded.

The moment Ilsa discovered their failure, she'd slaughter them both.

Whistling, I started away from the palace. If Aria Hecate's head was the price of Julia's freedom, I'd pay it tenfold. Esme had searched for saviors endlessly, never finding one who could stand up against Ilsa and her power.

I doubted Aria Hecate was our newest hope, even if she'd done impossible things. Who said she was any better than Ilsa? We didn't need to replace Ilsa. We needed a witch who didn't care about the bloody throne.

We needed a witch who wanted to end the deaths of the innocent beings and would stand against all tyranny we'd faced in the last five hundred years.

That wasn't a Hecate-born bloodline witch. They only hoped to rule over our kind without bothering to help. No, we needed someone strong enough to square off against evil, while never needing the darkness to fuel their light.

Chapter Thirty-Six

Aria

My fingers touched metal, and a violent shiver rushed through my body. The sound of men speaking in low muttered voices forced my eyes open, but my vision wouldn't gain focus. My heart thumped rapidly against my chest, and sweat coated my palms.

My skin grew clammy, covering in goosebumps as the chilled air fanned against the sweat layering my body. A terrified scream began building deep in my throat at the memory of my last cage, where hands had pushed my legs apart, groping my body painfully.

I groaned, trying to escape their touch, escape the pain of them exploring my body roughly. The horrifying noise of their dark laughter caused my blood to turn to ice in my veins.

They held my mouth open, pushing something inside, even as my head shook to dispel the object as they shoved it deeper into the back of my throat, holding my mouth closed around it. Teeth pushed from my gums and howls of pain erupted as something slammed against my head. My body jolted as more pain assaulted me until finally, it abated all at once.

The sound of hooves moving over gravel filled my ears, and I yelled, a blood-curdling howl of fear mixed with remnants of pain. My vision blurred through the hot tears that pricked my eyes. I screamed and cried while my body convulsed.

Everything within me fought to live, fought to get out of the cell where death awaited me. Sobs rocked my chest. I begged for Garrett to stop hurting me, and for Amara to stop him.

The scream ripped from my throat, filling the cell as his inhuman cock aimed for my flesh. I sat up, pulling magic to me, and yet nothing came. My only defense was gone, just as it had been in the dungeon cell.

"Aria," Knox's deep, rich baritone filled my mind while I continually begged for them to stop hurting me. Shadows rushed around, touching my flesh. I sobbed unabashedly, begging to be freed and allowed to live. "Aria, you're safe," Knox's voice whispered before his purr slithered over my body.

My eyes regained some focus, and I peered out of the bars, staring into oceanic eyes that sent soothing waves rushing through me. My sobs lessened, and I looked at my surroundings, noting Lore, Brander, and Killian were close, and staring at me with pity.

"It was just a nightmare," Knox growled, holding my stare, locked in silent comfort. His jaw clenched like he knew exactly what I'd dreamed, and whom I'd tried to escape.

"Yes. I dreamed I was with you again. It turns out, some monsters are real, and don't leave when the dream vanishes." I pushed the sweat-drenched hair away from my face and fought the deeply sated fear that wrapped around my throat. I stared through the cage bars, hating that I was as helpless now. I'd been in the Kingdom of Unwanted Beasts.

I pulled the blanket tighter around my body, closing my eyes, and I chanted inside my head, while I rocked. I did this often when the nightmares visited. I told myself Garrett couldn't reach me anymore, that I was safe from him.

Amara was dead and couldn't gift me to her husband or father-in-law to be raped and murdered. I lied to myself, telling my sub-conscious that nothing could hurt me again, and yet here I was, in a new cage, with a man who wanted to do just that.

Technically, Knox only wanted to destroy me in a deliciously enticing way, and then use me against my people. I didn't fear rape with him because Knox knew he only had to outwait my hormones to get what he wanted. What worried me was how he intended to break me while forcing me to wield my magic against my people.

I couldn't escape the memories of the cell in the Kingdom of Unwanted Beasts. My nose inhaled decay and the scent of rotting flesh as it fell from the bones of the dead or dying. My body trembled violently, and no matter how much I tried to stop it or dispel the images playing out in my mind, I couldn't.

My knuckles were white from holding the blanket tightly as my body rocked faster, trying to escape the memories.

Other images and memories I must have suppressed were surfacing in my mind, haunting my sleep, creatures that had been with Garrett when he hurt me. I wasn't sure if I'd conjured them from my imagination or if they had actually been there, partaking in his exploration of my body within that cell.

I silently took in the sprawling forest in which we moved. The marching army was daunting, but they were silent, the sound almost hypnotic. It was as if they were waiting for something to attack, or for something to happen.

The hair on my neck rose, and my heart continually thundered, consumed by the hopelessness of the cage, and my vulnerability during an attack with me stuck inside.

"Cold?" Knox asked, frowning as my head shook in response. "Then why are you trembling?"

"Just remembering the last cage that held me," I admitted through chattering teeth, fighting to calm my body from the turbulence rushing through it. "Just another monster who wanted to hurt and use me."

Leaning back, I dismissed Knox to gaze at Lore. He nudged his horse closer to the wagon that my cage sat within, removing his cloak, and pushing it through the bars. Accepting the much thicker covering, I brought it to my nose, inhaling Lore's masculine scent, and my body heated from it alone.

I dropped the thin blanket and wrapped my body in the dark cloak, pulling the comforting, fragrant smell to my nose while studying the surrounding area.

Knox reached through the bars without warning, ripping the cloak from my body before tossing it back at a chuckling Lore. Knox removed his thick cloak and pushed it through the bars, his eyes narrowing to angry slits when I refused to accept his offering.

"Put it on, woman," he demanded, frowning as thunder clapped above us.

"I prefer Lore's scent to yours, Knox." Blue eyes narrowed as he turned to Brander.

"Get her out of the cage and hand her to me. Now!" Knox snapped, glaring murderously at Lore, whose amber eyes danced with mischief.

"I prefer the cage to you as well," I grumbled, glaring at Knox.

"I didn't ask what you wanted, Aria," he hissed. Brander dismounted, and the entire procession stopped their forward march, waiting for him to retrieve me from the cage at Knox's bidding.

Pulling me gently from the cage, Brander handed me to Knox, who righted my legs astride the giant warhorse. One arm slipped beneath my bound arms to pull my body against his, and I sank into the heat he offered.

The sky chose that moment to release a downpour, forcing me to curl closer to Knox for what warmth I could get, trembling as the nightmare's remnants mixed with the chill in the air from the storm.

"You're freezing. Bloody hell, Aria, next time say something," he snapped, turning to Lore. "Send a team out to scout the area. We'll camp here for the night before moving deeper into the mountains."

Lore nodded, nudging his mount toward the front of Knox's efficiently moving army. I silently watched as men broke from the large assembly, rushing toward the meadow ahead of us to secure a perimeter. Fires lit around the edges of the clearing, and people started dismounting. Knox handed me down to Brander, then dismounted his horse. He pulled me to where a small table sat under a tent, to protect us from the rain and elements.

I'd assumed Knox would sit me beside him, but he didn't. Instead, he pulled me into his lap, and before I could argue, pushed a drink of warm whiskey into my hands. I lifted it in my bound hands to my nose, inhaling the woodsy scent.

Tipping the cup back, I downed the fragrant liquid in one solid swig to warm my insides. Brander chuckled, refilling my glass while Knox slowly ran his nose over the back of my neck. His heated breath offered some relief from the chill of the night.

I drank the second glass of whiskey slower while my aching body grew pliant in Knox's arms. I curiously watched as they erected the camp without a problem. The rain relented and became a light shower instead. If the weather bothered anyone, they kept it to themselves.

Women moved with the men, assisting them to get a sea of leather tents assembled to stave off the rest of the rain. Blankets were handed out or placed into tents while everyone moved to secure the area, building a small village in the meadow.

Fires lit the perimeter of camp even with the rain thwarting their efforts. I watched as several fires glowed, offering some light against the darkening night. Narrowing my eyes, I noted all the witches were eyeing me as I sat with Knox. They all wore Knox's insignia on their wrists and didn't seem unwelcome by the people within the camp. Knox brushed his fingers over my thigh, forcing my gaze to turn to him.

It intrigued me that with this many creatures together, they effortlessly built a village as if they'd done it a million times. Maybe they had, and perhaps that wasn't a good thing either. My army of corpses probably couldn't erect a tent against the rain without losing an arm or another body part in the progress.

I knew I was in over my head. I wasn't stupid, but I also wasn't going to give up. I'd find my footing, and I'd rattle this man until he felt me in his bones.

Brander approached, nodding toward a giant tent, constructed by several of his men completing the last stages of its preparation. It was huge, almost like an army command center, set up in the middle of the field with all the other tents surrounding it.

"They'll have your quarters ready within a few minutes. There's no food to prepare tonight, but I'll have some dried venison brought to the tent. The men are already noticing Aria's scent, and even some of the women warriors seem enticed. I'll be right back," Brander grunted as a growling male started toward us, coming to a stop when he heard Brander rattle a warning. The man's hooded eyes slid over me before he slowly stepped back, glaring hungrily as he moved deeper into camp, away from where we sat.

I looked around, noting that everyone did their best to ignore us for the most part. Knox rattled against the back of my neck, causing my spine to arch as his breath tickled my hairline. Knox's legs parted mine, allowing him access.

His hand slid beneath my bottom while his fingers slowly pushed against my core. Heat entered my belly, along with a throbbing ache in my sex. I moaned softly, unable to prevent the sound from escaping.

"Shhh, if you moan, I'll be forced to divert into the woods, and show you why running from me wasn't such a good idea."

"Stop touching me then," I hissed.

"Why? Because you liked it?" he laughed darkly as his other hand slipped around my belly.

Knox pulled me back, wrapping his enticingly scented cloak over my lap. I anxiously watched his men moving around us. Knox pulled me further against his body, once again using his legs to spread mine apart wide, his cloak preventing others from seeing.

Heat flushed my cheeks as his men paused, glancing at where he held me tightly, his cloak the only thing protecting them from witnessing where his hand was touching me.

Chapter Thirty-Seven

I could hear the soldiers muttered comments about their king's ability to tame even the vilest of creatures. Women also paused, glaring toward us, their displeasure evident at the thought of Knox touching me or even being close to me.

His breath lingered against the back of my neck as his fingers entered my core, and I stifled the moan building in my lungs.

Knox's husky laughter rushed over my skin while his mouth kissed the red mark he'd left on my shoulder. Knuckles skimmed my clit, and I closed my eyes to hide the heaviness of lust burning within them. His heated kisses moved from my shoulder to my neck and back.

My body rocked against the need he created, riding his fingers, uncaring who watched us. Teeth skimmed my shoulder, and I gasped as my cunt clenched hungrily against his fingers, causing him to groan with need.

Knox withdrew, sucking the juices from them loudly, to be sure I hadn't missed what he was doing.

"You're fucking delicious, Aria," he rumbled, the silken voice wrapping around every nerve ending in my body.

Knox worked small circles on the inside of my thigh, his breath fanning my neck, and I groaned as a male passed by, stopping to stare at me. I rattled in warning, and Knox chuckled behind me.

The next male paused, peering down as if he intended to watch, but Knox growled, his rattle low and deadly, vibrating through him, and slithering over my body.

Brander approached with a stern look in his sapphire stare. He stopped, nodding toward the large tent, finally completed. "You may want to get Aria inside since her scent is about to start a fucking riot. I'm too fucking exhausted from chasing the two of you through the water, and then down that bloody cliff to relish fighting an entire army for her."

"They'll know to whom she belongs soon enough. I intend to remedy that problem tonight."

"I don't have a problem," I argued in exhaustion, standing with Knox behind me.

"Look around, Aria. You see every male here staring at you? They can scent your need, and they know you're unmated. Unclaimed pussy within the Nine Realms is fair game to anyone who wants it and is willing to fight to take it by force. It's either them or me tonight," Knox stated with heat banked in his eyes.

"Brander," I whispered, swallowing hard.

"Come again?" Brander choked out, lowering the whiskey he'd been drinking, wiping his mouth clean of the liquid he'd just spat out everywhere.

"No, that's the problem. You didn't come last time. You can fuck me tonight. Problem solved." I crossed my arms, only to fight the cuffs until I gave up, placing a hand on my hip, glaring at Brander.

"That isn't fucking happening," Knox laughed coldly.

"Why not? Are you worried that I may come harder for Brander than I did for you?" I smirked at Brander, wiggling my brows. He swallowed audibly before sliding his attention toward Knox with a '*help me,*' look in his eyes. "Come on, big fellow. I say you and I give it a real go this time. Let's go wreck my vagina!"

Brander's mouth opened and closed before his gaze dropped to my aching sex. His hand lifted, scrubbing over his face as he groaned.

Knox stepped out from behind me, looking at Brander, brow raised, crossing his arms over his chest as Brander shook his head, scowling at me. Apparently, Brander was on his own to get out of fucking me tonight.

"Sorry, Aria," Brander snickered. "You have Knox's mark on your shoulder, and that means no one else can fuck you without challenging him for that right. He may say he'd allow it, but I assure you, he'd fight for the right to fuck you tonight. I don't plan to fight my brother for you, no matter how fucking enchanting you smell. You may find it barbaric, but that is the law within the Nine Realms. You're not in your world anymore, little girl. You're in ours."

"That's the law in Norvalla or the entire Nine Realms?" I questioned carefully, as Knox's lips curved into a dark, wicked smile. "If anyone wants me, they have to fight Knox to get me, just because he bit my shoulder?" I frowned, my brow creasing. I studied the dark look burning in Knox's eyes while I added up what Brander had just disclosed.

"The Nine Realms all share laws," Brander confirmed. "Once someone has claimed you, the only way to remove the claim would be to challenge the one who placed it there. Unlike the other men in this camp, I know what happens when you challenge Knox, trying to take what he's already claimed. I'm not willing to fight my brother for you, no matter how tempting you are. If you're smart, and I know you are, you'll allow Knox to place his scent on you so you have more than just his mark. You'll have his protection. Let him protect you, Aria. He's willing, and your body is willing too, or it wouldn't smell so fucking delicious, causing a disruption within the camp of warriors."

"Pass," I muttered.

"It isn't a pass tonight, Aria. You're going to allow me to place my scent on you, or I'll put you inside a tent and let you take your chances with whoever among them wins the right to mark you. You see, I won't fight my army for you. Not when this is a simple thing to fix."

"You said that about the tattoo, and that shit worked out smashingly for you, Knox. It didn't work out so well for me, though, now did it?"

"It worked out rather well for me, didn't it? That was me as an evil prick. I saw something I wanted and took it by any means necessary. This is to protect you, and yeah, I can't say I won't fucking enjoy it. If you're a good girl, and I know you can be so fucking good for me, I'll let you come too, Little Witch."

"How kind of you," I muttered, jerking forward as he grabbed the cuffs and pulled me toward his tent.

The tent's inside was impressive and included a large, opulent, white fur blanket over a feather mattress with large pillows placed at the head. A dark-gray fur sat at the foot of the bed, and I marveled at its softness. I ran my fingers over it while Knox watched.

A table sat in the tent's far corner, and upon it was a decanter of whiskey and two glasses. Rugs covered the floor, made from the same soft gray fur, soothing my weary toes as they dug into them, uncaring that Knox studied my reaction to his belongings.

A brazier lit the tent before we entered, expelling soft heat that warded off the chill. I moved toward it as Knox stared, snorting when I dismissed him, adjusting the cuffs on my wrists that were chaffing the skin raw.

The chain between the cuffs was roughly three-foot-long, giving me a little room to move. I held my hands up to the flame, groaning as the welcoming heat soaked into my bones, warming me.

Brander entered the tent with another man carrying a large chest that they set at the end of the bed. He let his gaze slid down my body, smiling at the angry glare I aimed at him.

Chicken.

His smile turned dark and sinful. He nodded to

Knox, who watched our brief interaction before clearing his throat, dismissing Brander as he nodded toward the tent's opening.

"Right," Brander said, clearing his throat. "I stationed guards around the tent and camp's edges. We cleared the woods. There is no trace of magic within fifteen miles in each direction of our camp. The women are currently placing crystals around the perimeter to add an extra layer of protection for the night, in the event someone tries to rescue our little witch. Unless you need something else, you're all set, and I'll retire to my tent for the night."

"Thank you, brother." Knox lifted his glass, watching me from where he stood beside the table. "Take off your wet clothes, Aria."

"I have nothing else to wear," I pointed out.

"You don't need clothes for what we're about to do." When I just stared at him blankly, he exhaled. "Sit down and have a drink. You're going to need it tonight." Swallowing the last of his drink, he took his seat across from where I stood, letting his eyes slowly slide down my frame, noting each bruise and scrape I'd endured running from him today. "You can strip once you've had a drink to settle your nerves." he offered, pouring himself another glass, not bothering to hide the heat pooling in his eyes.

"If you're trying to get me drunk, you should know that there isn't enough alcohol in this entire camp to achieve that goal, jerk."

"If I wanted you drunk, you'd be drunk already. I'm trying to calm your nervous trembling, and allow you a moment to gain your composure, woman," he snapped, daring me to argue more.

Sighing in defeat, I moved to the table and sat in front of Knox, frowning. I considered how screwed I was at that moment. It couldn't get much worse than being stuck in a tent with my enemy, could it? It could. It so fucking could. I was stuck inside a tent with an enemy that I craved and wanted to do very bad things with, even though I wouldn't.

He didn't deserve to have me or use my body for pleasure. There were ways around doing what he wanted or what I craved. We'd just have to get creative, which shouldn't be a problem.

Right?

Right.

Chapter Thirty-Eight

I studied Knox over the rim of the glass I held between my bound hands, his lips turning down slightly into a frown. The glow from fires burning within the camp cast shadows about the tent, making them seem more daunting and larger than what had cast them.

I could hear the muffled moans of women finding pleasure amongst the men surrounding our tent.

My cheeks blushed with embarrassment as the noises grew louder and more urgent. Knox smiled, finding it funny that I was uncomfortable hearing the sounds of the couples screaming their release unabashedly.

Knox stared at me, and then at the dress I wore, still damp and ripped in several places from our daunting climb down and back up the cliff. He stood abruptly, and my eyes narrowed in apprehension, following his movements toward the large chest the men had previously carried into the tent.

Slowly, he undid the belt at his waist, releasing his scabbard and sword, setting it aside. He removed the armor that he had replaced after chasing me through the water and over rocky terrain. My heartbeat increased as Knox bent to retrieve a few items from the chest. I swallowed hard, hating that his enticing scent was playing havoc on every nerve in my body.

Dismissing him, or trying to, I sipped the whiskey, moaning as it exploded on my taste buds. At the sound, he tensed, giving me a dark look over his shoulder before he returned his attention to the trunk, removing his shirt.

I tried not to stare, but I lost the battle, mesmerized by the hard, tapered muscles along his back, caressing each one with my hungry gaze. Tightening my grip on the glass, I fought against the urge to trace the ravens that adorned his side, moving up his spine to his shoulder blade.

His back muscles were amazingly toned, and each curve begged me to explore them with my fingertips, to learn every single edge of his body in explicit detail. His pants hugged his hips low, exposing the globes of his firm ass to my stare, and I caught myself licking my lips absently, recalling the feel of it beneath my hands.

Knox spun, catching me off guard before I could look away. A seductive grin spread across his face as he slowly unbuttoned his pants, shoving them past his hips, and stepping out of them to reveal that he wore nothing beneath. I stopped breathing, greedily staring at the V-line of his abs that led to dark curls cradling his enormous cock. Even soft, it was large and hung proudly between his legs.

I licked my lips again, slowly sliding my gaze over his sinewy abs that tensed at my leisurely examination of his form. Air slowly expelled from my lungs before I lifted my attention to his face, discovering him smiling at my blatant gawking over his body's exquisitely carved perfection.

"See something you want?" he asked huskily, slowly moving toward me.

"This whiskey's really good," I whispered, jerking my eyes from his to stare at the glass like it held all the answers to the universe.

Dark laughter filled the tent as he pulled on a pair of sweatpants, which were the bane of my existence. I watched him from beneath my lashes as he sat across from me, setting his elbows on the table before he uncorked the whiskey and held it up to his nose.

He leaned the bottle toward me, offering to top off my glass, and I extended my shaking hands, holding his gaze as he refilled my cup until it threatened to spill over the rim.

"It's aged one-thousand years," he admitted, and my eyes widened, moving from the glass, then back to him in surprise.

"How do you know that?" I inquired, studying the way his lips twitched while his eyes sparkled with amusement.

"Because I made it myself." His admission caused my mouth to open and close several times before I clamped it shut, narrowing my eyes on him, waiting for his laugh or some sign that he was joking.

"You're one-thousand years old?" I questioned, aghast that he could be that old.

"Older, actually," he chuckled as my eyes bulged, and I shook my head, sitting back in my chair, peering down at the amber-colored whiskey.

"Wow, this relationship just took an inappropriate turn." His forehead creased, and his fingers ran over the bottle's rim before his attention lifted to me.

"What relationship would that be, witch? The one where you're the prisoner of the opposing king or the one we don't fucking have?" His jaw clenched, and something cold entered his stare.

I glared at him, anger sliding through me at his words. I wasn't even sure why it bothered me, but it burned to hear him state it more than anything. I snorted, downing the drink before leveling him with an icy glare.

"Go fuck yourself, Knox," I growled, standing to move to the brazier, letting the heat it offered soak into my bones.

I studied the coals that glowed red like the anger rushing through me. I lifted my eyes to where the smoke swirled up, exiting through the top of the tent.

The smoke was scented, I noticed. It smelled of soft sandalwood and eucalyptus, which was soothing and calming. Inhaling the scent into my lungs, I gasped as Knox slid his arms around me, pulling me against his body's heat.

"Let me go," I whispered, barely loud enough to be heard.

"Never, woman," he growled, kissing my exposed shoulder that carried his mark.

"I said, let me go."

Knox didn't listen, choosing to grab the chain that connected the cuffs to my wrists. He hefted it up, placing it over his neck, forcing my arms to lift, and my back went flush against his chest. My toes danced on the rug's fur, and my breathing hitched in my lungs as he growled huskily against my ear, kissing my neck where it met my shoulder.

I watched as he shredded the dress I wore until it pooled at my feet in a tattered heap of fabric. His hands caressed my stomach, lifting to cup and gently squeeze my breasts as a gasp expelled from my lungs.

My breathing hitched as his thumbs ran over the pink tips, and my heartbeat rapidly spiked as a pulse thrummed in my belly, causing my body to heat. Butterflies erupted, fighting for space with the ravens that took flight, creating a multitude of sensations from his simple touch.

"You are mine now, Aria. You're my prisoner. I am the king on the opposing side of this war. I don't intend to let you ever escape me, not when I have you at my mercy." His hands lifted, slowly unbinding my hair until it was free from the bands and silver jewels that he tossed aside. My hair slid down my sides, stopping at my waist before he brought his nose closer, inhaling my scent greedily.

Knox's hands slid around my body, running down my sides as goosebumps spread over my flesh. His fiery breath fanned the side of my neck as his mouth peppered me with soft, gentle kisses. Fingers slid down my abdomen, pushing past my panties until they rubbed against my clit in slow, leisurely strokes that caused my head to roll back as a soft moan escaped my lips.

One hand lifted, cupping my breast, and I cried out, gasping as he growled hungrily against my throat. He dragged his fingers through the arousal of my sex, dipping them into my opening. I felt him growing hard against my spine. He pinched my nipple and clit at the same time, causing me to buck against the sensation that threatened to consume me and make me combust into flames.

The only sound in the tent was the fire and my muffled noises while Knox slowly brought my body to a teetering edge. He refused to let me reach the precipice of pleasure that danced right beyond my reach.

Walking me to the bed, he lifted my leg to place my foot against the soft mattress, giving himself more access to my body as he prepared me to accommodate his thickening cock.

"You're so fucking hot, woman," he hissed, nicking my shoulder with his sharp teeth. He ignored my panties, pushing them aside as he plunged two fingers into my body until I was clenching against the pain and pleasure they created. "I want to throw you down, and bury my cock so deep within you, that you feel me in your soul."

"No," I replied, fighting the fog of lust he'd forced into me.

"No?" he laughed darkly against my throat, kissing his way down it as he lifted my arms from over his head, pushing me forward onto the bed.

He followed, watching as I struggled to get upright only to grab my legs, parting them as he settled behind me. He kissed my hip, and purring sounded from him, slowing my rapid pulse as if he sensed my unease, and instinctively sought to calm me.

I whimpered, balancing on my elbows as he grabbed the edges of my panties, ripping them from my body as a scream escaped my lips.

"I said, no!" I turned to look at him, falling on my side with tears threatening to spill.

"Shall I wake Brander and tell him you prefer whoever wins the use of your tight cunt tonight?" Standing, Knox walked to the table to pour another shot of whiskey.

"No, but I am not fucking you either, Knox. Find another way to get your scent into my body. You're not fucking me tonight or ever again, asshole."

He sat, staring at my naked body with heat and anger burning in his eyes. I sat up, glaring at him in defiance. He lowered his gaze to the tight, hard nipples that were begging to be kissed and tasted. Arousal coated my apex, glistening from the light of the brazier as a small flame burned. In the soft glow, his eyes narrowed to slits of anger as he snorted.

"I'm the fucking King, Aria."

"I don't give a shit that you are the king, Knox. Unless you intend to force me and rape me, you're not fucking me. I said no."

"I could easily make you want me."

"It wouldn't matter how you achieved it," I whispered thickly, fighting angry tears. "I said no, and I meant it. No matter what my body does, I don't want to fuck you." I wasn't ready to have sex with anyone, not even him.

"You're not leaving this tent without my scent on your flesh. You are in a breeding cycle, and every male within fifty miles of you can smell your dripping cunt screaming its need to fuck. The only way to prevent you from *being* raped *is* to place my scent on your flesh." His eyes searched mine, and he grunted, slowly taking a long drink of the whiskey before placing it on the table, steepling his fingers in front of him. "I'm trying to prevent someone else from forcing you to do what your body willingly wants to do to sate its needs. I'm trying to protect you, Aria."

"Can you just tell them I'm not some feral bitch in heat? Tell them you forbid them from raping me like one! You are, after all, the fucking King, aren't you?"

"You *are* a feral bitch in heat. Every man here is under my protection. I am their king and have vowed them my protection. You, on the other hand, are a prisoner of war. One I have not offered to protect from my men, nor will I offer it. Not unless you're mine in all aspects of the word."

"Then find another way to make it happen, Knox," I whispered, standing to move to the cup he'd refilled.

His heated stare slid down my naked body, feasting on every inch before sliding back to my face. I moved to the table, lifting the mug between my hands to drink as he observed me. The intensity in his gaze sent my ravens soaring into flight. Every part of my soul wanted to cave to the baser needs his smoldering look promised—all of me except for, of course, my heart.

"You think it is that easy?"

"You just need your come to be inside me, right?" His eyes lifted from my exposed body to lock with mine, and he nodded. "Then use your fucking hand and make it happen."

"I'm not using my fist to protect you from your own stubborn ass, Aria. You want it, take it from me," he snorted, sitting back in the chair as a sardonic smirk played on his lips, and challenge flashed in his eyes. His arms rose, folding behind his head while he stared at me in challenge.

I licked my lips, drawing his attention. I chugged the last of my whiskey before standing and moving back to the brazier, frowning. Exhaling slowly, I rubbed the back of my neck, which forced my other hand to my shoulder, brushing my fingers over the raised scar his teeth had left there.

His mark offered comfort, and that wouldn't change no matter what I told myself. I'd given Knox my back, dismissing him before I said something stupid or made him angrier. My eyes closed, realizing my mistake. I fought for strength, preparing to face the heat in his eyes again.

Spinning around, I found him standing directly behind me, which caused me to take a step backward. He grabbed me by the waist, yanking me against his body, preventing me from backing up into the brazier's open flame and knocking it over.

His ocean eyes held a storm of emotion in their angry depths, threatening to drown me. I walked to the bed when his hands released me, but he grabbed my neck with one hand, pulling me back as his mouth crushed against mine. His other hand cradled my chin, making it impossible to escape his soul-crushing lips.

Knox didn't just kiss.

He devoured me like a delicacy he would never taste again. His tongue parted my lips, and he kissed me as if he might die if he didn't. I moaned against his mouth, placing my hands against his chest.

I lifted on tiptoes, unable to fight the assault of his mouth as he took me to heaven with the way his tongue dominated mine, demanding obedience as it dueled for ownership. His hands held me confidently, as if he had every right to hold me in this place and time.

When Knox kissed me, the world quieted around us. The sounds of our breathing echoed through us. It became the only sound that mattered in a world filled with screams.

He made my body heat with need, desire rushing to the forefront, dispelling all coherent thought. I felt the corner of his mouth tilting into a grin, and I knew he was aware of his effect on me.

He lifted me against him, never removing his lips from mine as he walked me to the bed and carefully set me down on its edge. He kneeled before me, and I continued kissing him until it became a choice of breathing or continuing to kiss this untamed creature, claiming me with an intensity that excited and created fear within my soul.

I started to pull away, but his hands cupped the back of my head, holding my mouth in place as he growled deliciously against my lips. When Knox finally managed to break the kiss, it was to search my eyes for any signs that I was willing to give in to the need we both felt. His thumb traced over my kiss-swollen lips, staring at them as they parted, sucking it between them. I slid from the bed to kneel before him as he stood.

Knox didn't speak right away. He just stared at me on my knees, gazing at my lips that were closed around his thumb. "You look so fucking pretty on your knees, woman," he growled and then smiled as my teeth sank into his flesh. If he felt pain, he ignored it smiling down into the defiance burning in my eyes. My tongue slid around his thumb as his jaw tensed, clenching with need while he watched me suck on his wounded thumb.

The coppery tang of his blood danced on my tongue as he withdrew his thumb, tracing it over my lips. I licked them clean of his blood, glaring at him as his smile turned cold. Freeing his cock, he pushed against my lips, demanding I open for him.

"You bite my cock, and it will be the last thing you ever do, Aria," he warned, and then hissed as my tongue snaked out, drawing small circles on the velvety tip, moaning as the taste of his pre-cum hit my taste buds.

My hands wrapped around his thickness, lifting it against his belly, allowing me to kiss the underside's sensitive ridge. His lips parted, and he moaned, watching me lavish his cock with attention. I kissed my way down his shaft, licking the delicate edge while locked in his heavily hooded stare.

Smoldering heat banked his depths, and he studied my lips as my tongue jutted out, lapping against the bead of cum, causing something animalistic to flare within me. My lips wrapped around his cock, taking him into my mouth.

He watched, pushing loose silver strands of hair away from my face, brushing his knuckles over the hollowed portion of my cheek. I sucked against the saltiness of him. I moaned around him, and he smiled darkly at my reaction to the taste of his need.

He grabbed the chain that held my cuffs, lifting them over my head to rest on my back, forcing me to teeter on my knees. He slid his hands through my hair to the back of my head. I continued working him deeper, slowly. Holding my head firm, he pushed into my throat hard, watching as my eyes widened from his thrust's savage. Knox didn't stop, forcing me to relax my muscles to accommodate more of him in my throat's tight channel.

"Come on, Aria, you can do better than that," he taunted, closing his eyes, and he forced more of his cock into my throat, swallowing around him. "Good girl. Such a greedy little thing, aren't you?" He shoved in deeper, and I gasped around him.

I cried out, gagging, and he smirked darkly as he went further, deeper into my throat while water trailed from my eyes. He wasn't gentle about it, and I wasn't sure if I cared either.

The sounds escaping his lips made me want to hear more of them, to hear his weakness. I brought him to his knees with my mouth, enjoying his pleasure. Each moan sent him deeper until finally, he withdrew, and I wiped the drool he'd caused away with my arm.

Lifting me to the bed, he stared at my body with a carnal look of ownership, creating a mass of emotions that slid straight to my clenching core. Before I knew his intentions, he yanked the chain around my wrists beneath my belly and shoved me onto the bed with my ass up and fully exposed.

I tensed, which didn't go unnoticed. I started to move away, but he stopped me. Panic slowly rose, threatening a scream to rip from my lungs. Then he purred, and I calmed.

"I won't fuck you unless you tell me to do so," he growled, sensing the problem. "But I'm going to make this pussy sing for me. I want to taste you dripping down my face as you come on my tongue, woman."

He spread my legs slowly, exposing my needy core to his hungry stare. His fingers brushed against my opening, slowly dancing over the arousal he'd created. Two pushed into my body, and I cried out at the fullness they created.

My body clenched against them hungrily, hearing his pained groan as I took what I needed from him. I felt his heated gaze on where my body greedily accepted what he offered.

Knox pushed another finger into my core, and I slowed my movements, adjusting to the fullness of it. His other hand moved to my clit, slowly rubbing soft circles against the swollen nub. My head rested on the bed, smothering my cries into the fur covering it while he stretched me full.

My legs spread further apart, and I moved faster while he turned his fingers to go deeper into my cunt. His thumb and forefinger pinched my clit, and my head lifted as a soft cry of pleasure ripped from my throat.

He withdrew his fingers from my core, and I felt his heated mouth before his tongue slid against my pussy. When he tasted my arousal, the noise he made was almost enough to send me sailing through the heavens. Knox lifted my legs as he settled behind me, savaging my cunt without mercy as he devoured me. His tongue slid from one end to the other, slowly lapping against my pussy until I was gasping and crying out as he used his tongue to fuck me.

I was stuck, helpless to escape what he did, my arms pinned beneath my belly. He held my legs apart, devouring my aching need until I screamed, unable to stop coming as his throaty laughter rumbled against my pussy.

Knox didn't stop. Instead, he went harder against my opening, pushing his fingers into my body. I moaned, and took what he gave me. Finally, his assault lessened, and he turned me over, licking my arousal from his lips and fingers.

"I don't know what I love more, Aria. The sound you make when you come, or the pleasure I find when making you come." He smirked as I opened my mouth, but only a moan slipped free from my throat.

Kneeling on the bed, he lifted me and dropped me onto the pillows. He sat back, slowly stroking his cock with one hand and parting my legs with the other. He pushed my knees up as his smoldering stare dropped to the sleekness of my flesh, smiling as he found me soaked from his mouth and fingers.

Settling between my spread legs, he leaned over, staring at my body as it twisted to touch his. He touched my cheek, and his mouth brushed mine as he growled hungrily. I chased his kiss as he pulled back, watching me try to reclaim his hungry mouth.

He secured the chain connected to my wrists in his hand, holding my arms above my head. Knox lowered his mouth, nipping my bottom lip between his teeth. His other hand slid down my body slowly, pausing at my breast to tweak the hard peak between his fingers, rolling it as I panted from the pain and pleasure.

He pulled back, staring down between us as he adjusted himself to rub his cock against my center. The friction sent pleasure rushing through me. We locked eyes at the sound of my sultry gasp, feeling every pass over my clit as his cock rubbed against it, uncaring that he knew how turned on he had made me.

His forehead rested against mine briefly before lifting back. I started to bring my legs together, but he stopped me by pushing them apart. Knox lowered his mouth to the inside of my thigh, brushing his lips over the sensitive flesh with feather-soft kisses.

Knox teased and taunted me as he moved his hungry mouth around my sex while leaving it neglected. His heated breath teased my aching cunt as he refused to go where I needed him most. His hand held both of mine by the chain, using it to secure them against my stomach. I tried to direct his mouth where I wanted him. Dark, husky laughter vibrated against my thigh.

"Knox," I whimpered, rolling my hips.

His eyes lifted to hold mine, lowering his mouth, and slowly dragging his tongue through the arousal coating my sex. I cried out loudly. When he reached my clit, he sucked on it, pulling his teeth over the sensitive nub threateningly. My body was already begging for another orgasm, needing him to give it what it wanted savagely.

He was slow, calculated, and everything I didn't want. I needed him to lose control, to release whatever control he held to become the animal that I craved. I wanted him to release his beast and devour me until I came undone against his heated mouth.

Knox didn't. Instead, he played with me, running the tips of his fingers against my opening. Slowly, he pushed their tips inside me before withdrawing them, teasing me until I was crying out with the need to come.

Knox slowly leaned back, freeing my hands as he grabbed his cock. I slid my hands down to my core, rubbing against the place I wanted to feel him the most. Leaning my head back, I closed my eyes to the sensation, pushing my fingers into my core.

Suddenly, Knox grabbed my hands, pressing them against my stomach, before slapping my clit as I cried out in surprise.

"You fucking look at me when you touch your greedy cunt. Understand me? If you look away from me or break eye contact, you won't come again tonight." I shivered, letting the dominance in his tone slither through me as I nodded. He slapped my flesh again, smiling as my eyes grew hooded as he rubbed my clit to lessen the pain. "You answer me when I speak to you, Aria," he warned.

"Yes," I whispered thickly, rubbing my need against his fingers, and his attention diverted to the arousal he had created.

"You like it when I'm rough, don't you?" I nodded, dropping my legs open, inviting him to punish me more, daring him to continue, while I remained silent. "Bloody hell," he groaned, dragging his hand over his mouth as he watched me lift into a sitting position.

"Lay down, Knox," I ordered in a sexy tone, covered in a layer of need.

His eyes flashed as if he'd never been given an order or had anyone tell him what to do. His abdomen muscles tensed, and I lifted my brow as he continued to stare at me. Smiling, I leaned forward, grabbing his cock while holding his gaze, slowly stroking it as he tensed, never breaking eye contact. I tried to wrap my fingers around his girth but failed.

"Lay the fuck down, King Karnavious, so I can help you come for me."

Chapter Thirty-Nine

Knox swallowed hard, causing his jaw to tense, narrowing his eyes to slits as he canted his head to the side. Glaring, he moved to the bed, laying on his back and placing his hands behind his head, daring me to follow through on my taunt.

Silently, I took in the sheer beauty of his hard, perfectly sculpted body. My fingers slid over his powerful thighs while his attention remained on my face.

The man was all muscle and toned flesh. My hand slid to his cock, wrapping my fingers around it, kissing the underside as his body tensed, locking eyes with mine as heat pooled in their depths.

I held it up, using my knees to push myself forward to lick the tip of him, and he gasped, studying me with an undiscernible look burning in his eyes. I took him in my throat, moaning as his salty pre-cum danced over my tongue. My hands stroked his need while my mouth worked the tip until he groaned, giving me more power than he realized.

Pushing up from the bed, I stepped over him, smiling down at the look of hunger in his expression. Knox didn't move. He didn't offer to help me lower my body from the precarious height. I slowly straddled his hips, setting my core against his silken cock.

I shivered visibly at the desire in his eyes as he dragged his needy gaze down my body to where my pussy stretched against the tip of his hardened cock.

"You could just drop your hips and let me fill your needy cunt full, and give us what we both need and want." The tone of his voice was a sexy mix of lust and dark desire that echoed through me. I slowly began moving my hips. He hissed, dropping his gaze to my pussy that was caressing his cock and painting him with my arousal.

"I could, but I won't," I whispered huskily, moaning as his cock repeatedly rubbed against my clit.

I lifted my hands, playing with my breasts, and my eyes closed, pretending it was his hands caressing me. My body moved slowly, teasing while pleasuring us both. Every rock of my hips caused his cock to brush against my clit, taking me closer to the edge I was trying to send us both over.

My hands lowered, moving down my stomach, and my eyes opened, finding his locked onto the path my hand took, watching as my fingers found the swollen nub and his eyes lifted, finding mine locked with his. He growled his approval, removing his hands from behind his head to touch me.

He gripped my hips, watching my face while he controlled the speed of my body until I was trembling, grinding against him, and holding his stare brazenly.

Knox rattled, and my body drenched with arousal that he used, sliding my pussy faster against his cock until the orgasm threatened to consume me. He laughed the moment I would have reached a climax, smiling at the way my body trembled from the denial. Knox's hands stalled, watching my fingers smooth down his chest, tracing the tattoos that moved with his breathing.

I leaned over, bracing my hands on his abdomen, placing soft kisses against his stomach that tensed beneath my lips. Slowly, my tongue tasted his flesh, kissing each raven on his chest until I reached his nipple. Lifting my eyes, I watched him studying my tongue, enjoying the way it felt against his flesh. I was his softness, and he was the silent strength allowing me to learn his sharp edges.

My tongue traced over his nipple, flicking the puckered flesh before I nipped it hard. I sucked it playfully, slowly rocking my pussy against his cock while his eyes heated further still. He was panting, his mind on nothing else than the path I took to reach his lips.

I enjoyed the hiss that escaped between his teeth, biting his nipple harder, kissing it as his eyes lifted to hold mine once more. I chuckled as his eyes grew heavily hooded with lust. Leaning against him, I pulled on his bottom lip with my teeth before sliding my mouth to the pulse on his throat. Suddenly, he rolled me beneath him, his elbow wedging against my throat as I gasped.

"You keep your fucking teeth away from my throat, woman," he snarled coldly, staring down at me. I gave him a worried look as my throat bobbed against the elbow that held me down. "That's a line that you and I won't be fucking crossing."

"You really don't like your neck kissed, do you?" I asked, sure that my expression conveyed my confusion.

"Just stay the fuck away from it with your teeth, Aria."

His eyes searched mine before he exhaled, leaning back. Pushing my legs apart, Knox angled his body between them, staring at me. His dark head shook as he leaned over, kissing the racing pulse against my throat, nipping against it. I purred, unable to prevent the sound from coming out.

My hands found his silken flesh, pumping it against my core. I used him, rubbing his thickened cock against my clit while he held its base tightly. His neck muscles tensed as I continued stroking him, whimpering louder every time his cock landed against my clit.

Knox took control, and my hands moved to my breast, pinching my nipples as my hips lifted, rubbing my pussy against his cock that continued teasing me. His tip slid against my opening as he purred loudly, pushing the head against it teasingly, but never forcing himself into my body.

Knox lifted, staring at where his hand held his cock against me as he increased the pressure, rubbing it against my clit until I was moaning loudly. His fist worked his cock feverishly, and my legs lifted, dropping wide open as he groaned, closing his eyes, then opening them again to hold mine while his body tensed.

Curling his lips into a pained smile, Knox grunted, and his cock pulsed against my opening, painting my body with his arousal. His fingers slid through his release, pushing his essence into my body until I shook violently.

I went mindless the instant his come entered my body, growling and purring, screaming his name as orgasms ripped me apart painfully.

Knox purred loudly, pushing his fingers further into my pussy to get his scent deep within me. My body tensed, and I clenched tightly, sucking his fingers off as the orgasm continued to course through me, causing him to moan as he watched me come undone.

It was a primal need that ripped through me, shoving all human nature to the back of my mind while the animal within me demanded he give me what I needed.

Knox continued rubbing his scent against my sex. I drifted back to earth, exhaustion sliding through me. My mouth opened as a needy sound escaped, like some feral creature's wail, echoing through the tent.

"Sounds like he fucked that whore good, huh? Stupid slut will know her place is on her knees, serving us before the sun rises in the morning. That's how you break those evil bitches. Feed the cunt, and the mind follows," a guard grunted, and another snorted his agreement.

I couldn't stop my body, not even when angry tears flooded my eyes. I continued rocking my hips, pushing Knox's cock against my opening even as he pulled back to prevent me from taking him wholly within my body. I fought hard to regain control of my mind, forcing the red haze of need to the backseat. I urged the human within me, back to the surface.

"Damn, he's still making that whore come hard. Do you hear her? Fucking beautiful noises; the sounds of a beaten-down witch learning her place beneath us," he chuckled. "No better sound in the world than that."

"Stop moving, or this is going to take an entirely different path than you want, Aria," Knox warned. I pushed against him and then paused as cheers sounded from outside, spiking my anger. "I'm about to lose control, and you've already lost yours, so stop fucking moving." Knox tossed an irritated look toward the front of the tent.

People outside were celebrating Knox conquering me. I felt my heart shattering inside my chest, and pain tightening within it. My anger spiked, and embarrassment flooded through me, pinking my cheeks.

I'd been lost in the pleasure Knox had given me, swept away in the sea of his heated gaze and kisses until I'd crashed against the rocks, only to be left adrift without realizing what had happened.

Knox studied me as I rolled onto my side. Pulling my legs up against my stomach, I listened to the men outside as they continued to speak about whore witches and virile kings. Tears rolled from my eyes as anger erupted within me, causing a sob to build in my chest.

"What the fuck is your problem, woman?" Knox asked as if he couldn't hear the men outside the tent.

"I'm tired," I whispered thickly, hating that I'd been weak enough to get lost in the pleasure his body offered.

"If it's all the same to you, Your Majesty, your whore would like to sleep," I hissed.

Knox sighed heavily, before pulling me against him, adding another cuff to my wrist, attaching it to his.

"Then sleep, witch," he snapped harshly, and yet he hadn't scooted away from me.

"Stop touching me, and I could sleep, asshole," I grumbled.

Ignoring him, I struggled to get comfortable with my hands bound, and my body close to his. I hated that my body automatically sought his out for the comfort it offered. "Are these cuffs really necessary?" I asked after a moment of trying to adjust beside him.

"They're staying. Go to sleep," he growled. The men grew louder outside the tent, and Knox rattled a warning, shutting them up immediately.

Knox flipped me over without warning to face him. He stared into my angry eyes, before he placed my head into the crook of his arm, pulling the covers up and wrapping his other arm around me to hold me.

"You could just put me back into the cage, now that you've tamed your dirty slut of a witch." I stared coldly into his eyes as he searched my face before grunting.

Knox left the bed abruptly, dragging me with him, pausing to hoist me over his shoulder. He took long, angry strides toward the front of the tent, smacking his hand hard against my ass to remind me that I was stark-ass naked.

"Knox, stop!"

"Changed your mind already? You sure you don't prefer the fucking cage? You're wearing my mark and my scent, so if sleeping beside me bothers you so much, you can sleep outside like the rabid little bitch you're acting like," he snapped, and the men outside the tent chuckled.

"I hate you," I seethed, purring low and even.

I was certain the volume of my purr was a warning to him that I was about to attack. His hand landed against my flesh again with a smack, and I yelped. Sinking my nails into his ass cheek, I drew blood, dragging them up his back, causing him to cry out angrily.

He slammed me onto the bed, holding me in place as he wrapped his hand around my throat. He leaned in, closing the distance until our lips brushed together as his angry eyes peered into mine.

"Touch me like that again, and I'll bend you over and let my men hear how you really purr for me, Aria. Now go to fucking sleep before I remind you why I'm the alpha by bowing your fucking spine in submission to me while I rattle."

"I don't bow to you!" I shouted, but Knox rattled low and even until I did just that on the bed.

My spine arched, lifting my ass. I rolled onto my stomach, taking him with me because of our bound hands. Knox landed on my back with my legs spread and my ass pushed against him, a growl of need bubbling up my throat, escaping past my lips.

His rattle didn't stop until I came undone without him fucking or touching me or forcing me to. Everything within me bowed, right down to my will as his rattle vibrated throughout me, establishing his absolute dominance.

"I seriously hate you," I whispered as tears silently flowed.

"Oh, my sweet Aria, you do bow so pretty for me," he taunted, pushing his fingers against my flesh, purring loudly with approval at my submission and response to him. "This lovely flesh knows who owns it, even if you don't."

"I'm going to cut your cock off with a spoon and feed it to you one day, Knox."

"You'll be doing many things to my cock, but that isn't one of them, Little Lamb. Now, I'm going to sleep because some little bitch had me chasing her sexy ass all up and down the countryside, and then exhausted me by draining my balls. Go to sleep, or I'll fuck you until you're too exhausted to do anything else."

"Dick."

Chapter Forty

I woke to an arm resting over my hipbone, and fingers tracing its curve while silently exploring. My mind grasped for who it was learning my curves, and a smile played on my lips.

Heat curled in my belly, tightening it with the memories of Knox's mouth against my sex, and a soft whispered sigh escaped my lips, followed by a breathy moan of his name. The sound of his heart thundering at the whisper made my smile deepen.

Knox lifted his fingers from my hip, pushing the hair away from my face. I whimpered, not ready to give up the only decent sleep I'd had since entering this hellish place. My hands moved toward the source, brushing against his chest, before tucking my head deeper into the crook of his arm, placing a soft kiss against his heart.

He lowered his fingers, touching the raised peak of my nipple before he leaned over, kissing my forehead as my eyes opened. Knox pulled back, peering into my sleepy gaze with something dark passing through his expression.

We stared at one another, neither willing to break the spell or peace of the morning with words. I swallowed, the smile on my lips vanishing. I felt his cock growing hard against my belly. I peered down, finding my leg draped over his hip, and our bodies tangled together. At the sight of his cock, I licked my lips, recalling the way I'd lost control last night.

A blush flooded my cheeks, and my eyes lifted back to his. Knox rolled over, and I blinked, noting that he'd removed the cuff before I'd awoken to him exploring my body. I rolled onto my back, lifting my knees to close them against the tension flowing through my midriff. He groaned, inhaling deeply as he rubbed his eyes and sat up.

I studied his stiff posture as he leaned over the edge of the bed to push his messy hair away from his face. He slowly stood and moved to the table, grabbing a glass of something, and tossing it back. Knox rested his hands on the table's edge, showing off his impressive backside. His back still held visible claw marks, even if the scratches had scabbed.

I smiled with victory, sitting up to pull the covers around me. My hair was a lost cause, and the white fur of the blanket tickled my flesh, causing my lips to tip into a sleepy smile. I yawned, stretching my arms while dispelling the sleepiness from my bones.

Knox turned around, opening his mouth to say something, but paused, staring. He slid his gaze over me, swallowing hard as if he forgot whatever he was preparing to say. Leaning back against the table, he studied me as a soft smile played on his lips.

"Good morning," I whispered past the dryness in my mouth.

"Morning, Aria," he said breathlessly. Scrubbing a hand down his face, he groaned, picking up the discarded sweatpants and pulling them on to hide the scratches I'd left on his ass. "You've slept most the day away, so now we can't move camp until tomorrow morning."

"You could have woken me," I replied, narrowing my eyes on his hungry gaze.

"When's the last time you slept more than a couple hours?" he countered crossly.

I snorted, giving him a pointed look as my brow lifted with laughter dancing in my eyes. "A Neanderthal, who wanted to do rather bad, bad things to me, was chasing me around the Nine Realms. I didn't get much time to sleep on the run, and when I did, it was with one eye open. He was rather relentless and quite the hunter."

Knox's features softened as he smiled, slowly shaking his head as he rested his hands on his hips.

Staring at me briefly, he reached into the chest at the foot of the bed and pulled out a dress, tossing it in my direction. I caught it, dropping the blanket, realizing my mistake as a playful smile flitted over his lips.

"Get dressed. You'll be sitting with the other witches as I meet with one of my dignitaries. Best behavior today, Aria," he warned. I slid to the edge of the bed, staring at the cuffs encasing my wrists.

"Do you intend to free me of the cuffs? How do you expect me to get this dress on exactly?" I held up the garment, and he looked at it, before moving back to the chest, pulling out a white spaghetti-strap dress that looked like it belonged on anyone else but me.

He handed it to me and took a seat in the chair, staring at my bare thighs. I lifted from the bed and stretched before stepping into the dress and pulling it up.

Knox's loud purr caught me off-guard, forcing my attention to him as my body echoed the same sound without thought. I blushed, glaring at him as he rattled, canting his head as mine once more repeated the noise he made.

"Are you enjoying yourself?" I whispered, fighting with the straps that tied onto my shoulders, which wasn't easy since he had bound my hands.

"I am," he admitted, lowering his head as a boyish grin played on his mouth.

He stood, slowly walked to stand behind me, snorting as he moved my hands away from the ties. His fingers captured the laces, tying them tightly. His breath fanned my shoulder as he lowered his mouth, brushing his lips over his mark, reassuring himself it was still there.

He brushed his fingers through my hair and turned me around to face him as his eyes slid over my body, resting on my face. He swallowed, causing his throat to bob and a blush to fill my cheeks under his examination.

"Am I to your liking?" I teased, and he bit into his bottom lip before a sexy grin reached all the way to his eyes.

"You're very beautiful, woman. Especially this morning with your hair matted from last night's pleasure, and your full lips swollen from all the kissing and playing. However, the intensity burning in your eyes from finding release has my balls tightening to see if they sparkle even more once I fuck you."

I swallowed, and he smirked, leaning his head back as if he were counting to gather his control. I inhaled deeply, finding my scent mixed with his musky aroma, covering his body. It made me smile as a rattle of desire escaped my lips. His head lowered, and our eyes locked as a knowing smile spread across his face.

"I smell good on you, woman," Knox laughed, but something worrisome was etching his tone as his throat bobbed.

His attention moved to the chest's lid, and I frowned at the look burning in his eyes, sending a chill racing through me. Knox clenched his jaw, and his eyes lifted to mine with indifference, as if everything else had been for show. His teeth caught his bottom lip as he ran a hand over his mouth and shook his head.

Silently, Knox withdrew a shirt and pants from the chest, staring at it a moment longer before he closed the lid. He didn't bother turning around, forcing me to do so, offering him some sense of modesty. It was more than he had given me, but just because he was an asshole, it didn't mean I had to be one too.

The clang of his sword and scabbard drew my attention, as did the sounds of women talking in low voices, speaking of lovers, and how to ease their aching muscles.

Food burned somewhere within the encampment, and I heard a child cry in the distance. I looked up through the hole in the tent at the brilliant blue sky.

"Come, witch." Knox's voice caused me to jump, spinning around to find he'd snuck up close enough that when I turned, my nose touched his chest.

"You do know that I am not a dog, right?" I countered, following his quick pace that took us outside and a few steps away from the tent.

"If I tell you to sit, you'll fucking sit. If I say jump, you will ask me how high I wish for you to jump, woman. You're my fucking prisoner, not my guest."

"Yeah, how about you hold your breath while you wait for that to happen," I offered angrily, and he swung around, causing me to run into his chest.

I was about to argue more when a scream ripped through the camp, focusing my attention on a woman being dragged between the tents by her hair. A man shook her as tears streamed down her face, and I noted other women pulled behind her in the same fashion.

My heart leaped into my throat, and I turned to see Knox watching the scene with no emotion on his face or in his eyes.

Stepping back, my stomach plummeted to the ground, and I frowned. I watched silently as soldiers brought children and women in dirty dresses into the camp by force, exhaustion marring their faces.

Men in blue armor followed the procession, slapping each other on the back as they pointed out one woman or another.

Knox swore beneath his breath, shouting orders in a foreign language as Greer appeared from thin air, no longer dressed in his butler ensemble, but wearing a light, form-fitting armor.

"Peasant," Greer chuckled, leaning over to kiss my cheeks before pulling back with a bright smile. "You look like shit."

"And you still smell like week-old roadkill. I guess some things never change," I grunted, turning back to the crying, terrified children corralled into a circle in the middle of the camp like livestock.

"Take Aria to Bekkah, and don't let her out of your sight," Knox snorted, giving me a warning look before walking off toward the men entering camp. "Make sure my girls play nice together," he said as an afterthought over his shoulder.

My girls?

My throat tightened, and I snorted as Greer shook his head at my reaction. "What is that about?" I asked, and Greer lifted a brow.

"That isn't your concern. Come with me," he said in a firm tone.

"They're hurting children!"

"Leave it alone, Peasant. It will all get sorted out, eventually."

I followed Greer's stiff back to a group of witches casting magic. Most worked basic spells that even a child should know by their age. Some were younger than twelve, and each one held Knox's insignia on their wrists and wore silver chains with spelled lockets around their necks.

Greer nodded to a chair, dismissing me before he moved to the witch that had told Knox I'd be fine upon expending all my magic. I rolled my eyes at Bekkah's glare, turning to take in the women as Greer moved toward a group of shirtless men.

He was such a hussy!

My attention slid back to the women who continued to cry while trying to reach their children. I watched in horror as a large male slapped one of the tiny women, sending her body to the ground, and blood coursed to my temples as anger erupted.

I turned around as Bekkah shouted at one of the young witches who had cast a spell, missing her mark. I swallowed the unease and rage that rushed through me.

My attention slid to Bekkah, watching her eyes dance with enjoyment as she stood over the girl, swearing at her vehemently while the child apologized profusely. Bekkah backhanded the girl, cutting the young witch's lip wide open with the rings she wore, splattering blood over the other girls.

I inhaled slowly, exhaling as men shouted at other witches in the center of the camp who continued trying to reach their children, fear fueling their overwhelming screams of frustration. The men laughed as they watched, amused to see children taken from their mothers.

I lifted my hands to my ears as my chest rose and fell with the rage burning through me. Fear etched into my mind watching witches die beneath Knox's blade again. Blood coursed through my veins, pounding as it sought an outlet through magic, and finding none. Nausea swirled within me, bile pushing against the back of my throat as Knox's image, covered in the blood of my friends and neighbors, flashed into my vision.

Bekkah turned toward Knox as he watched my reaction to everything happening around me. He nodded to Bekkah, who turned toward me with a stern look in her eyes as she pulled her lips back, revealing blackened gums that fueled the fury within me. He was allowing women, children, and young witches to be hurt knowingly?

Soldiers moved in front of our position, blocking my view of Knox and the others brought into camp. I tried to search for him through the crowd, needing his purr to ease the fury and rage pulsing through me.

Children screamed for help, and women begged for mercy for their children as men called them monsters who deserved to be put down.

The witches near me sobbed in fear, and then it all went silent minus the blood pumping in my ears. I stood, turning to the nearest threat to the witches.

Bekkah slapped the same young witch repeatedly when she tried once more and failed to master the spell. I moved before I could stop myself, using my inhuman speed to attack Bekkah before she could assault the girl any further.

Chapter Forty-One

I balled my hands into fists, and slammed one into Bekkah's face, twisting my body when she fell to the ground, kicking her face as she landed upon it with a sickening cracking noise. My foot moved again, and I smiled at the satisfying crunch of her nose, and I turned in time to see a fist flying toward my face.

Pain ripped through me as the warrior continued his attack, slamming his other fist into the side of my face as the world spun around me. I blinked stars as pain so brutal and debilitating smashed into my head with each punch he landed.

I dropped to my knees, sucking in air as he kicked my stomach, continuing the assault as I fell to the ground, curling into the fetal position. He savaged me, hissing and grunting as he continued landing blows to my body.

If the warrior spoke, I couldn't hear him over the blood pounding in my ears. It wasn't until something slammed into him and then turned to cover my body that I cried out in pain, closing my eyes as some semblance of protection was offered.

"She's not to be touched, by the king's orders!" Greer shouted.

"Fuck that! She needs to learn a lesson!" the warrior snarled.

I didn't move, gasping and wheezing for air as Greer shielded my body. Blood dripped from my face, and I didn't need a mirror to know he had savagely beaten me within an inch of my life. I tensed as heavy footfalls sounded, and Greer lifted from where he'd used his body as a shield to protect me.

"Who fucking started it?" Knox's angry tone echoed through my head.

"The bitch on the ground, Sire," one warrior answered.

Knox grabbed the chain on my arm, dragging me to my feet. He growled, forcing me to run or be dragged behind him as everyone watched. Knox never looked back at me, causing my aching body to move without choice.

Greer rushed after us, staring at me with wide, horrified eyes as Knox hauled me behind him.

"Knox, stop!" Greer demanded.

"Not now, Greer," Knox snarled in warning.

"My King, you need to stop!"

"Go handle the other rabid bitch, Greer," Knox

warned, pushing me into the tent before he spun around to deal with Greer. "Not another fucking word about Aria, or you can join her in her punishment."

I pushed off the floor and crawled onto my knees. I didn't move from where I'd landed, unable to keep my balance, staring at the tent that spun in my vision. Warmth spread down my face, and I noticed the cuffs had cut into my arms when I'd fallen.

My ribs burned, aching to the point of feeling as if they were in danger of pushing through my flesh. Breathing had become increasingly difficult past the swelling in my face, and my lungs refused to expand fully.

"What the hell was that about, Aria?" Knox demanded, and I shook my head, sending black dots swimming in my vision. "Fucking answer me, woman," he ordered coldly from behind me.

"They're children, and you're allowing your men and your witches to hurt them," I whispered, still staring away from him. "They're just babies."

"They're witches," he snorted, dismissing their worth or concern for their safety.

"Oh, my bad! I forgot that's what makes them not worth caring about their mistreatment. What would your wife say about your whores? How would she feel about the abuse of women and children you allow within your camp, at the hands of your men?" I demanded coldly, wanting to hurt him as much as me.

"Careful, Aria," he warned, barely above a whisper.

"How would your son feel about you allowing your

men to harm children for their enjoyment? Do you *allow* them to rape the children as well? Does it make you *feel* better to know they're hurting?"

"That's enough. You don't want to go there," Knox hissed, and his rattle started low in warning as anger pulsated through the tent, stifling the air.

"What would they think about you now? Would they be *proud* of the man you've become, fueled by your grief? Or would they hate you as much as I do for how you treat other beings?"

"Aria, shut the fuck up now!"

"That's right. Your wife and your son wouldn't think *anything* because they're *fucking* dead!" I snarled, turning around as his hand landed against my cheek, sending my body spinning to the ground once more.

Gasping, I blinked past the pain in my face while blood poured from my nose and mouth, covering the carpet of the tent. My shoulder sent pain echoing through my body. I inhaled, unable to do more than gasp for air.

I felt his stare burning into my spine. I gulped greedily for air, unable to get enough into my lungs past the pain ripping through me.

"Get up, now, Aria," he demanded coldly.

It took everything I had to stand back up, and when I did, I refused to face him. My head hung in defeat, and my body screamed in agony as blood dripped from my face, staining the already soiled dress even more.

"Look at me, *witch*," he demanded, and slowly, I turned to face him, watching as his eyes widened in shock at what he found. "What the fuck?" he whispered, staring at the multitude of damage done to my face. "Brander, now!" he shouted, and no sooner had he called for his brother, Brander entered with Lore, Greer, and Killian on his heels.

Every one of them stopped dead in their tracks the moment they caught sight of my damaged face. I could feel it swelling, and knew that Knox had added little to the damage, since he'd pulled back before striking me, yet his anger was what I had wanted. I wanted him to hurt and feel rage like I did for what was happening outside the tent.

"Gods damn. What the fuck, Knox?" Brander whispered, slowly stepping closer to where I stood.

"I barely fucking touched her," Knox stated, still staring at my injuries in horrified shock.

My arm hung limply at my side, dislocated from the warrior's kicks and Knox dragging me behind him during his rage. My face steadily poured blood from my nose and mouth. I could feel the gash in my lip, and multiple lumps forming on my body as Brander moved to stand in front of me, silently gazing at the damage while trying to figure out what part of my body to address first.

They waited for hysterics, which didn't come. It was internal. Fear ripped through me as I realized I could actually fucking die here. I swayed on my feet, staring through them as Brander shook his head.

"Why the fuck didn't you tell me she was hurt, Greer?" Knox snarled, turning his anger on Greer.

"With all due respect, My King, you refused to hear

me. One of your warriors attacked Aria for assaulting Bekkah. She took quite the beating from him before I shielded her with my body to prevent even more injury to her person. So, to answer your fucking question, you weren't hearing me when I told you to stop, adding to her injuries by dragging her through camp."

Knox swallowed audibly, dragging his hand over his mouth before turning to look at me again. "Brander, do something."

"It's too much fucking damage to heal on my own," he stated, lifting his finger to my chin, staring at my injuries. "He crushed her cheekbone and shattered her nose. The veins in her eyes have ruptured, and her arm is dislocated or it's broken. That's just what I can see without knowing her internal damage. I'd need to see her undressed to know about her other injuries. Judging by her shallow breathing, there's something else going on with her lungs we're not seeing."

"Maybe give her some privacy?" Greer asked, but my claws extended, and I used my good arm to drag the dislocated one to the lace strap, severing it and the other tie to let the dress drop to the ground. "Or not. Peasant, we can allow you your dignity."

"I'm a prisoner, not a fucking guest," I stated, wheezing the words out as Brander hissed, staring at the rib pushing through the skin beneath my breast at an odd angle.

"That's not good," Brander groaned, lowering his hand to touch the taut skin. "Lore, grab my med-kit. We need to heal her enough to get her to the village up the mountain. There's a healing pool there," he stated, turning as Knox exhaled, glaring at Brander for even considering using a magical healing pool.

I stared down at the rib protruding from my flesh, pressing against my lung. Using my nail, I sliced through the skin while everyone else stared away from the sight of my naked body, trying to decide how to heal me correctly.

I slid my fingers in around the offending rib bone, gathering my strength before I snapped it off. Crying out, Brander turned around, his mouth falling open as he watched the bone slip through my bloody hand to land on the ground. I grabbed my limp arm, pushing it up forcefully. I ground my teeth together. Screaming past the tears as it burned and ached, popping back into the joint.

Everyone stood, silently gawking at me. I walked carefully to the brazier and grabbed a lump of burning coal with my bare hand, pressing it against my open wound to seal it. The sizzle and scent of burning flesh filled the tent, causing my stomach to churn.

I closed my eyes and swallowed past the scream that sat at the back of my throat, which I refused to allow to escape.

Once composed, I schooled my expression and turned to stare at Brander. He took in my burned flesh, shaking his head, tilting it to the side as he opened his mouth, then clamped it closed, deciding against whatever he was about to say.

He ran his hand over his face, closing his eyes and tilting his head toward the tent's ceiling, staring at the blue sky.

"Gods damn, woman." Brander's startling blue eyes lowered to mine before lifting once more.

"I'm ready," I whispered, gaining enough air to speak clearly.

"Did that just fucking happen? I mean, I *saw* it happen, but I've seen grown men scream like a *bitch* when a bone dislocates! Not Aria, she's like *oh, my bad, let me slide this bitch-ass bone back into place*. Oh, and who the fuck needs ribs, anyway?" Lore snorted, pushing his hands through his hair.

Greer wrapped his cloak over my naked body, slowly easing me down onto the bed. He turned, staring at Knox, who had yet to speak as he stared down at me.

His jaw clenched, grinding together as he turned, staring toward the tent's opening as if intending to bail to avoid looking at my damaged face.

Chapter Forty-Two

"Everyone out now," Knox whispered hoarsely, bending down to pick up my discarded rib. "Killian, prepare a small group of men to travel with us into the mountains. But only the few you trust to remain silent about what we're planning to do. Lore, have the women set out ale and get the camp followers to keep Lord Andres and his men busy for a few hours. Greer, help Brander gather what he needs to prepare Aria for travel through the mountain passes. She won't be able to walk."

"I can walk just fine," I stated, watching his eyes return to mine. "I'm not your fucking damsel, King Karnavious. I'm Aria Hecate. I am not a weak-ass bitch who needs coddling by you or any other man. You must have me confused with your other whore outside, weeping and waiting for you to notice her."

"Out, now." Knox's jaw clenched and unclenched, his eyes burning with rage and unease, a strange combination for him.

The men escaped the tent as if dire wolves were giving chase while Knox stared at me. After a moment, he kneeled directly in front of me.

"You aimed for my throat, Aria, but you missed. You hit my heart. You're not allowed to speak about my deceased wife nor my son, do you understand me?"

"I didn't miss," I stated, glaring at him.

Knox's eyes searched my face, finding the truth of my words. His anger pulsated through the tent, smothering the air with the tension. He rattled, and I answered it, even though it hurt like hell to do so.

His eyes dropped to my chest, and he shook his head, standing to move to the chest, withdrawing a new dress. He pulled me up, causing a cry to escape my lips as he removed the cloak Greer had placed over my shoulders to shield my nudity from the men.

"Some wounds never heal. Some fester, and when you scratch the surface of the scab, you make them ooze poison. Don't do it again. I shouldn't have hit you, but you don't make it easy for me when you use your claws."

"It's not my job to make this easy on you. I'm nothing but a witch who didn't even warrant your protection. I think it is best we identify where the lines are in this arrangement early on, and now we have. I mean nothing to you, and I'm okay with that. You're nothing to me, and now we know where we stand and what we mean to one another. Absolutely fucking nothing," I whispered, wincing at the pain that speaking caused.

"You think you mean nothing to me?" Knox carefully pulled the dress over my head as he studied my face, more than likely unable to judge anything past the swelling.

"I honestly don't give a fuck if I do or don't anymore. I will escape you again and again. I will never be yours, King Karnavious. I won't be a tool you use to harm innocent beings. If you were only against the witches who had unjustly wronged the Nine Realms, I would stand beside you, willing to wage war with you at your side. That isn't what you want, and those children abused by your lord outside of this tent prove that point very clearly."

"Your side didn't care about the loss of innocent life either, Aria. You've been here a moment, but we've endured the witches' tyranny for hundreds of years. Your family abandoned us to the dark witches, leaving those monsters in charge of the Nine Realms, and we have had enough of enduring it."

"I'm twenty-five years old. I have done nothing wrong to you or your people. Those witches who harmed this world are not on my side, either. As I have said, we're fighting toward the same goal, and yet we're not even close to being on the same side." I winced as Knox reached around to replace the cloak I had worn with his own.

"You forget that I have claimed you, and you're also my prisoner. You are here, and we're fighting on the same side because you have no other choice, woman. Not a fucking word when you step outside this tent. Do you understand me?"

"Is the king afraid of his lord?" I scoffed, wincing as he grabbed my arm, releasing it immediately. I gasped, exhaling to hide the pain he'd just caused.

"I am the leader of the rebellion against your people, Aria. You're warming my bed, even if unwillingly on your end. I will not look weak in front of my people. Not even for you," he warned through clenched teeth.

"Does my face make you look weak?" I asked pointedly, forcing him to look at it again. "Don't worry. You look like such a man beating defenseless women and children. Your cock can stand proudly at full mast. It's safe from looking weak in your lord's eyes, with how well you tamed the rabid whore witch last night; he'll be singing your praise. If you like, you can polish your reputation by raping me in front of your army and your guests. I think it's the one thing that you have yet to do to me. I'm sure the murderous bastards out there would enjoy watching you teach this whore a lesson, showing her where her place is by your side. Wouldn't they? Would you like to rape me, King Karnavious? I can scream really well for you to complete the image of obedience."

"You think I wanted to hit or abuse you?" he snarled, stepping closer to me, and I refused to back down. "I will never force you to be with me, Aria. *Never.*"

"I think I'm your enemy, and that you refused me your protection to make a point. You never expected me to come to harm, and yet you knew it could happen. You could have stopped this, but you chose not to. I think you're regretting that choice, but regret comes when failure to act has already happened. It comes too fucking late to matter, which is why it is called regret in the first place."

Coughing sounded from the front of the tent, and Killian entered, lowering his eyes, unable to stand the sight of my face. He met Knox's glare and nodded toward the tent's opening. Knox turned toward it, tilting his head as if listening for something.

"Greer!" Knox called, and Greer entered the tent, staring from me to Knox, before waiting for Knox to speak again.

"Watch Aria. Ensure no one touches her while I'm gone. I will return in a few moments, and then we will escort her to the village to heal the damage. No one gets in or out of this tent," Knox growled, grabbing his scabbard and sword before leaving me with Greer in awkward silence.

"Your face is literally killing me," Greer grunted.

I stared at him, moving to the table in silence to pull the cork out of the whiskey. I struggled to lift the bottle to my lips before Greer grabbed it, pouring a dram into a glass, and handing it to me.

"Thank you," I whispered through the tightening in my chest.

"Next time, aim for his balls, Peasant. Leave his heart alone. It's broken, and when touched, he strikes hard and fast to protect what little of it remains in his chest."

"Knox doesn't have a fucking heart," I snorted, sitting to stare at the tent's opening.

Chapter Forty-Three

Knox

I'd wanted nothing more than to part her thighs and bury my thick cock deep into her tight haven. Instead, I'd watched the little bitch coming undone for me. I'd never seen a woman pleasuring herself or been so fucking turned on in my entire existence than when Aria's clumsy-as-fuck fingers pushed into her tight paradise while she held my stare.

I didn't care who the fuck she was; I'd wanted her. Never in my entire life had I not taken what I wanted. Women begged to fuck me, and most of them regretted it the moment I entered their sheath, stretching it out painfully. I didn't do soft or sweet fucking. I abused vaginas, making them sore because once I'd fucked them, it was over. I didn't go back for more, ever. Not until Aria.

Aria was a savage, like me. She fucked like she waged

war against my cock, and fuck if I didn't enjoy losing for a moment to let her think she held some resemblance of control. Her eyes undid me, growing heavy with lust, banking with a fire that left me burning for her.

She took all of me, and when she got to the end of my cock, she lifted and slammed her pussy home, again and again. I missed that feeling. I missed the feel of her tight cunt clenching down hungrily against my cock, draining my balls.

I'd never had anyone take me on and want more. Aria was the first woman ever to do so without complaint. She fucking rode me hard, and when she finished, she climbed off, patted my chest, and walked out the door like my dick wasn't the best thing she'd ever felt pounding into her cunt. That pissed me off even more.

So fucking what if it was the only cock she'd ever had? The moment she smiled with me buried in her pussy, she'd signed her soul over to the devil in red lipstick with a fucking *'call me'* note on her panties.

"Are we going to talk about what the fuck happened back there?" Brander demanded, and I turned, glaring at him.

"That little bitch aimed for my heart, and she dug it out of my chest. Aria meant to hurt me, and I'd be fucking shocked if she hadn't wanted me to give her that reaction. She's like me. When she hurts, she strikes hard and fast, and she doesn't miss."

"That doesn't excuse putting your hands on her," Killian muttered, his eyes holding mine with unease. "You want her, fine. Take her. Fuck the little bitch out of your system, Knox. Hurting her during a battle is one thing, but putting hands on her because she hurt your fucking feelings isn't something we do."

"She asked me how Liliana and Sven would react to what we had happening in the camp," I admitted, noting their foreheads were creasing. "Then she told me they couldn't react because they were fucking dead. I pulled back, but I never even saw her injuries past my anger. It just wasn't soon enough to stop my hand. If she were anyone else, she'd be dead right now. I barely fucking tapped her. Trust me, assholes; no one is more disappointed in me than I am right now."

I stared up at the cloudless sky, closing my eyes against the rustling wind that cooled the heat of my skin. I'd hurt her, and I hated myself more than I already did because of it. I hadn't meant to touch her in anger, but she'd ignored my warnings to reach for my rage.

I'd spent all night holding her tiny body against mine, unable to ignore how perfectly she fit against me. I'd never allowed a woman to sleep beside me, not until Aria. Fuck, not even my wife had slept beside me through any part of our marriage. I'd been horrified at the idea of harming Liliana with my sheer size, and her weak body hadn't been able to handle me.

Aria didn't cower from me, though, not even my anger. She dug her heels in, and that fire within her burned in challenge. I'd never in my entire life been denied anything until I'd met Aria.

Last night, her cunt dripped down my throat, and it was fucking gloriously delicious. I'd known I could have buried my cock deep into that naked flesh, but I hadn't. I wanted and craved her willingly to want to fuck me.

She was my enemy, and yet I hated the idea of her in pain or hurt. That realization bothered me. However, the more I was around her, the more I understood that Aria was too perfect for me. Everything within her called to me.

I didn't just want sex with her anymore. Yes, I wanted to sexually destroy her pussy and hear those sweet, sensual noises as I stretched that cunt hard, making her feel every single fucking inch of me within her. But I craved her kisses more than I craved her cunt.

I needed the taste of her lips against mine, the pleasure they created as my heartbeat raced like some fucking punk-ass kid learning the taste of a woman for the first time. Aria kissed me, and everything faded to nothing around us.

There was her need and mine, and who the fuck cared about breathing? I couldn't kiss her enough, and as a general rule, I didn't kiss women. I'd barely kissed my wife, and I had never kissed another woman because that insinuated feelings, and I didn't feel women. I fucked them hard and mistreated them because it ended things quickly without a mess left in my wake.

Aria's mouth was heaven against mine. Her mind drew me to her; the way it worked knocked me on my ass. She calculated, contemplated, premeditated a plan, and then she went balls to the wall to see it through. Aria was five steps ahead of her enemies. She'd Trojan-horsed her sexy little ass into a keep and set fire to it from the inside.

She made my cock hard with her battle strategies. Aria gave me pause as an enemy. Knowing with her, I had to be on my fucking game. I loved her mind as much, if not more, than I loved the feel of her body around mine as I savaged that tender center, where I'd written my name.

She wasn't just brilliant; she was a self-taught genius. She's read the *Art of War* and taught herself how to wage a battle, not with strength, but with her mind. She was a dangerous adversary, and that made her intriguing.

"You know how this ends. You have two options, Knox," Brander stated. "Marry her and claim her throne before she rises, or end her life. You can't keep her like this, not even that mark on her thigh, or the one on her shoulder will ensure no one can use her against us."

"I'm not marrying Aria," I spat out, rage filling my vision at the idea of marrying a witch whose line ended my wife's and son's lives. "That isn't an option. Neither is killing her. I can turn Aria against the witches. She's young, brilliant, and her soul is pure. Aria knows Aurora intends to wield her as a weapon, but for what we don't know."

"There are other assholes chasing your girl, dick," Lore snorted. "Well, besides me. You are fully aware that if she ever gives me the green light, I'm going to be all up in that heaven until I'm her baby daddy."

I glared at him, noting the way his eyes sparkled with amusement. "Fuck off, Lore. You couldn't handle Aria in bed. She'd eat you for breakfast and spit you out by lunchtime. That girl took my cock and rode me like she was heading into battle, and fuck if she didn't drain my balls and pat my chest like I was cute."

"It's disturbing how much we talk about you fucking

her, asshole," Brander grunted, shaking his head while Lore started moving around, rocking and thrusting his hips. "What the fuck are you doing?" Brander demanded.

"Exercising my hips, readying myself for Aria for when she tires of Knox's shit," he explained. "If I'm going to make it to lunchtime, guess I better up my pelvic game. I've heard Knox fucking her, and damn, it sounds like baby girl likes for daddy to go deep into the womb. *'Oh, Knox, deeper! You hit those fucking lungs, big boy! You better push that cock up and out of my throat so I can pat it for the good job it's doing before you fill my cunt full of that alpha scent. That's it, fuck me harder!'"*

Everyone stared at Lore before bursting out laughing. Brander held his stomach, shaking his head as I dragged my hand down my face, enjoying the rare moment when everything wasn't life or death.

"You're a fucking idiot," Killian chuckled, wiping away the tears from laughing.

Lore didn't miss a beat, rocking his hips while flipping Killian twin birds. I shook my head, turning to peer at the warriors standing beside us, staring at us in horror. I scanned their hands, finding the man that had hurt my girl as anger ripped through me.

Chapter Forty-Four

Knox

The warrior was easily over six and a half feet tall to Aria's barely over five feet some change of fuck around and find out, she had. He had a good three hundred pounds of muscle on her and sported beefy hands with broken skin on his knuckles from hitting my girl repeatedly.

"That's him," Brander stated as if I needed confirmation.

I moved silently as the men quivered, feeling my anger. The rattle in my chest was raw, angry, and filled with unleashed rage. Standing in front of the warrior, I stared him in the eye, noting how his gaze dropped quickly.

"You can't fucking look me in the eye, but yet you can beat the shit out of a tiny girl?" I snapped coldly, watching his jaw tense beneath my angry glare. "Fucking look at me, asshole. I'm not your fucking friend. I'm your King. I asked you a fucking question. I expect an answer."

"She started a fight with Bekkah, and both are under your protection, My King," he stated, holding his head up while peering through me. Aria had done inside the tent, her face mangled from this asshole's hands that were larger than her entire head.

My hand moved, slamming into his face without warning, sending him to his knees. I gripped his hair, ripping his head back. "Explain to me why you felt the need to hit her more than once, or better yet, at all? Explain to me why after my girl was on the ground, you continued to fucking kick her ass?"

"Bekkah said Aria would spell you if we allowed her to live," he uttered, spitting out teeth. "We cannot allow Aria Hecate to live, Sire. She is too powerful. Our job is to protect you, not some whore who can't learn to listen and obey."

"My girl isn't a whore, you brainless fuck. Aria has known one cock in her entire lifetime. *Mine.* Your whore, however, has fucked the entire camp of warriors more than a few times to see whom she could poison with her cunt."

"With all due respect, you fucked her, too," the warrior sneered.

"No, I didn't. You see, she's not worth fucking to me. Bekkah enjoys power over men, and I can't be subdued by a loose twat that would fuck a minotaur and have room for more than one of his friends in her loose cunt. She played you, and you believed her because she touched your cheek and told you she feared for your life.

Here's the thing, you hurt my fucking girl. I expressly made certain everyone knew not to touch her. She didn't just have my protection, she had my mark on her shoulder, and my scent freshly placed between her legs."

"She will die, either by one of us or by the witches. Aria Hecate betrayed her people by slaughtering them, and she will do it again. Just because you like the feel of her cunt around your cock doesn't make her any less evil, My King."

I kneeled, staring the warrior in the eye as I smiled evilly. "Reach into your fucking chest and give me your third rib bone. Now."

I stepped back, watching the fear playing on his face while he decided if he could manage it or not. His nails sliced through his chest, and a scream tore from his lungs while pathetic tears ran down his face. His trembling hand pushed into his chest, but he paused, unable to pull the rib out. I kicked his shoulder, watching as he howled while falling forward onto his face.

"Put your arm back into the socket and don't make a sound while you manage it." With disinterest, I watched his bloody hand lift to his shoulder as he howled again, screaming like a pussy while he held his arm. "My girl did both, and she barely fucking made a sound as she removed the rib you broke and fixed the arm you dislocated. Right now, she's standing in my tent, absolutely silent and utterly pissed off at me. That little girl you hurt, she has more balls and strength than you will ever have. Do you want to know why? It's because Aria Hecate is a fucking monster, one that I intend to keep at all costs. Get up," I growled, watching the man fighting to get back to his feet, moving slower than it had taken Aria with the damage she'd sustained.

The men waited behind me while the warrior struggled, crying out with every attempt he took to get to his feet. Once he stood, I slammed my fist into his cheek, smiling at the sickening crunch. I hit him again, uncaring that blood splattered the other warriors who had remained silent throughout the ordeal, never looking away from where Killian had told them to look.

When the man went down, I followed him, never stopping as I delivered blow after blow until nothing remained but a flat, useless face that lacked the brains with which he'd been born.

My claws extended, and I slowly removed his head before standing to accept the cloth Lore handed me, smiling deviously with my need for blood.

"Now, you assholes want to tell me why you thought it was a good idea to build a wall for this man? Why you felt it was important to keep me from seeing the damage he inflicted on the woman I told you all was off-limits before she'd ever fucking arrived in our camp?" I asked, watching as they faced forward. No one spoke, and I snorted. "Take their heads if they can't find their tongues," I ordered, watching all three men step forward, claws extending as excitement burned in their gazes.

"My King, we don't know why we moved to build a wall with our bodies. Only that we did, and we couldn't stop it from happening. Not even once you'd pushed through. We stood there until Killian retrieved us to bring us here," Carsen answered, his green eyes never moving from the mark in front of him.

"Which female did you fuck before you felt the urge

to build a fucking wall with your body?" I asked carefully. He swallowed, and I pinched my nose, scrunching up my face.

"Bekkah, she was with us all." The statement had come from another male, who didn't flinch as I settled before him.

"Do you know the punishment for breaking an oath to protect someone beneath my protection?" I asked, watching the slow nod.

"Death," he swallowed hard. "It has been an honor to serve you, King Karnavious. I broke my oath and I'm prepared to die as punishment."

I exhaled, studying his unwavering loyalty. "Stand, all of you." Once they had, I stepped closer, noting they didn't move or back away from the fact I sentenced them to death. "Aria Hecate just saved your fucking lives. You owe her yours now. That *evil* witch you assume is so horrid; she'd stand in front of my blade to save your lives. You're now her personal guards, and you will watch her to ensure nothing like this happens again. Seek Siobhan and tell her Bekkah spelled you, and stay the fuck away from her evil cunt. It's not worth dying over. Not a word about this when you go back. Let this man serve as a warning for any of you who fail to protect Aria from harm."

I watched the relief flowing through each warrior as I turned, staring at my men who looked peeved about not getting to kill. Killian nodded. It was the only indication he was thankful I hadn't slaughtered the warriors he'd spent countless centuries training to serve in our army.

"You let them get off easy," Brander snorted.

"No, because each one of them now knows the moment they allow someone to touch Aria, that is their fate," I nodded toward the corpse.

"Aria made him look like a bitch," Lore replied. "She's something else."

"What's the word from the council?" I asked, watching Brander's jaw clench at the change of topic.

"No one knows who gave the order for Aria to remain alive. I have runners searching through kingdoms, and Gideon has his spies searching the beast kingdoms for any hint of who might have sired her or what she may be. Here's some shit we have to figure out. Aria is in heat, and your scent, while within her, isn't strong enough to stop my need to mount her and mark her for myself. You didn't fuck her last night, brother. It sounded like it, but you didn't paint her needy womb with your scent. She rattled, and she purred. She has magic unlike anything we have seen before. She has men with similar features hunting her down, but whether it is to protect her or harm her is still debatable. When we encountered them, they took orders from her. Aria didn't want us hurt, so they didn't fight us. Everything about her is perfect, but what if she's too perfect?"

"I have thought the same thing, often," Killian grunted.

"We all have," I admitted.

"Not me," Lore snorted, shaking his head. "It's real, her scent. I feel it in my balls. Her noises? I have heard nothing like them, and I can't get enough. I'm not even ashamed to admit that I pulled up a bed roll and slept next to your tent just to hear her sweet-ass noises."

"That's fucking creepy, asshole," Brander stated.

Lore looked around and slowly shook his head at our agreement. "Fuck you guys. I have never heard a female make that sound before Aria. Everything about her calls to me, and I don't understand why. I wasn't alive when our women made those noises, let alone went into heat. I have never smelled anyone like her. Sorry if needing to experience what she is makes me a creep, but I don't fucking care. She's like watching the discovery channel, but with our species on it, ya know?" Lore frowned, sucking his lip between his teeth while crossing his arms over his chest. "And she fucking fought an entire stronghold wearing a unicorn raincoat and rocked the shit out of it too."

I frowned at his response, knowing we were all in the same fucking boat. Aria was something none of us had seen in a very long time. In Lore's case, ever. I hated that she felt right against my body, cradled in my arms. I hated that I enjoyed everything about her, even the snarky comments.

"So she did," I muttered.

"She actually did that shit," Brander snorted, smiling. "Only fucking Aria."

Only fucking Aria.

Only Aria turned me inside out and made me want more.

Only Aria made my heart beat like lightning in an electrical storm with her heated looks and kisses.

Only Aria rattled to my beast, challenging him openly as she bared her pretty, soft throat to him, uncaring that if we crossed that line, she'd be more than mine. She'd be ours. That was a thought that made warmth flood through me, and yet it couldn't happen.

Liliana and Sven deserved justice.

I was leading a fucking rebellion against Aria's people, and even if she wasn't one of them, the only way to stop the high queen from reaching the Hecate witch line was to slaughter them or remove them from the equation permanently.

"Get rid of the body," I ordered. "Meet me at the tent so we can get Aria to that pond. She's in pain, even if she won't admit it."

I bent in the creek, washing the blood from my hands before returning to the tent. Pausing at the entrance for a moment, I listened to the voices inside. Greer spoke, but Aria was silent.

My heart clenched at the thought of her in pain, knowing she wouldn't complain no matter how much she felt it. She barely made a sound when she removed her rib and only screamed slightly when she'd pushed her arm back into the socket.

"Ever heard of twin flames?" Greer asked, and I closed my eyes.

Greer's words from long ago replayed inside my head. Me, drunk and fueled with rage as I'd decided to set the world on fire.

"Why do tragedies like this exist and strike against us?" I'd demanded, on my knees, seated between the tombs of my wife and child.

"Because they made you to rage, and in your grief, you are to unleash it upon the Nine Realms, My King."

"Why am I to unleash my rage? Why does everyone I love get taken from me? I have never wronged this world or any other. I am a good king to the people! My son was loved, as was my queen, Teacher!"

"You are to unleash your rage because you're fueled with grief. Without grief, you would never find the true one who seeks you. This world will never know the truth without her, or you. Someday this will fall away, and a new fire will burn. When you find the twin flame, the other part of your soul, and you become whole again, this grief will no longer consume you."

"You think I will ever love anyone again?" I demanded harshly, rising to my feet to look at the man who had become closer to me than my father. *"I never want to feel this weakness again. I was vulnerable because I loved them and let others see that weakness. I won't ever make that mistake again."*

"Love is never a mistake, Knox. Love is two souls that meet and intertwine and then burn brightly together. When you meet your twin flame, she will challenge everything about you. Your mind, beliefs, needs, and whom you will become will be because you chose her over this rage, trying to consume you. You are destined for her, as much as her destiny is to be yours. You can't see it right now, but someday she's going to walk in and knock you straight on your ass, and by the time you realize who she is, you won't be able to walk away from her. Your attraction will be more intense than either of you will understand. You will fight hard against one another, tearing each other apart to reach the bare bones

that you crave. Your laughter will be intense, as will the pain you will endure."

"I don't fucking want her, or that for myself. I love my wife."

"Loved, as she's dead, Knox," Greer amended, unafraid to speak plainly or guard his words in my presence. If he had been anyone else, I'd have taken him to the courtyard for punishment. *"The hardest part of losing someone isn't saying goodbye. It's learning how to live without them. You will not fill that void growing within you until your twin flame is born, and then you'll become restless without ever knowing why. It will fuel you with the need to find her and claim her as yours. You will unleash this pain upon her because you won't have healed by the time you find her. Her anger won't stay long, but it will be sharp. She will have a warrior's soul and a lover's heart."*

"I have a mate," I snarled, daring him to argue it again.

"So you did*, and she was beautiful, and everything good in the world,"* he stated, but there was a look of unease in his eyes as if he hadn't thought so. *"She was an amazing queen to her people and greatly loved you and your son, My King. At the end of the day, that is all that mattered."*

Killian stood in front of me when I opened my eyes, peering into eyes the same shade of blue as Liliana's. Frowning, I exhaled as Greer exited the tent, turning to me with a tight smile. He nodded to a guard who slid into place at the front of the tent and moved toward me.

Greer didn't speak because we didn't need words.

He did the same thing Aria did, speaking with his eyes; which was another thing I enjoyed about her. I didn't need to tell her what I was thinking. She saw it playing out in my eyes in vivid, delicious details.

Greer, on the other hand, asked if I'd heard their conversation, and the quick nod of my head told him his answer. I didn't drop my gaze, hating that he'd bring this shit back up now when Aria fit every fucking checkbox on my wish list.

I didn't need to tell Greer that Aria wasn't my twin flame.

He didn't need to tell me to wake up and open my fucking eyes and see what was right in front of my face.

I didn't need to tell him to suck a dick.

He didn't need to tell me he would enjoy it immensely.

"Asshole," I snorted.

"If you hurt her too much, you'll lose her beyond anything you can repair. Don't burn out that beautiful flame, because once it is out, that's it. It's gone forever." Greer kicked a rock beneath his foot, which slammed into my knee, a sadistic smile playing on his lips while he tilted his head, shaking it. "You don't fucking deserve her. She's so much better than all of us. We're all just too fucking jaded and fucked up to see it anymore." He shook his head and moved toward the horses with the others, leaving me to retrieve Aria on my own.

I swallowed hard before entering the tent, stifling the wince that came at the sight of her swollen face and dented cheek that no amount of quick healing was going to fix.

"Not a fucking word, woman." I moved to her, watching her slight flinch as I reached for the hood.

Ignoring her reaction, I pulled the hood over her head, hiding her identity while touching my mark that adorned her shoulder.

Frowning, I stepped back, turning on my heels to move out of the camp and past the high queen's spies who continually watched our every move. We led Aria away from the war party she had engaged during her battles at several keeps she'd taken in the last couple of months.

Aria gasped, and my gut tightened, turning to watch her slow movements as she fought to hide the pain she felt. She was a born warrior, but worse, she was born to be a queen, crafted in fire, and built to wage battle against anyone who opposed her. The best part of it all? She was mine.

Chapter Forty-Five

Aria

The moment we stepped from the tent, Knox's men surrounded us until we reached the horses. Knox mounted, holding his arms open to receive me, as Brander grabbed my hips, wincing as I gasped, smothering the cry with my hands. Knox gently grabbed me, helping me onto the horse as he reached for my hands, pulling on the chains until they snapped.

The instant it happened, I brought my hands to my mouth, stifling the scream trying to escape my lungs. Red-hot pain flashed through me as Knox softly purred. Pain from my shoulder and rib mingled with the wrist. Knox forced my body to lean against the large warhorse's neck, allowing me a moment as he held my hips, silently allowing me to give in to the pain for a moment.

Knox carefully pulled me back against his body, cradling his arms gently around me. The horse started forward at an easy gait, but it still caused more pain to fill me. Knox was careful, and even so, my body rebelled against the jerks and bouncing of the horse.

It was over an hour on horseback to where we dismounted as the trail grew narrow, forcing us to walk into the lush greenery that thinned out as we moved into the mountains. Knox passed me to Brander, watching as Brander studied my face as he set me on the ground. He wasn't satisfied with whatever he found, moving to the side to speak to Knox as Greer stood beside me.

"And here I thought having a nose job would improve your overall appearance. I was wrong," he announced.

I laughed soundlessly, turning to look at the worry shining in his eyes, causing another laugh to expel from my swollen lips. Greer studied me as I laughed almost hysterically until tears filled my eyes. The pain dulled as my immortality slowly healed my body, but the magic-nulling cuffs on my wrists seemed to prevent the magic in my blood's ability to heal me fully.

"I'm sorry I wasn't there, Peasant," Greer whispered.

"I'll live. It's not the worst beating I've endured since being born," I admitted after a moment of silence filled the group.

"You're stronger than you look. You'd make a horrible princess. I don't believe you'd be whiney enough for that role, I'm afraid."

"I missed you too, Greer," I whispered through swollen lips, wrapping my arms around his neck as he stood awkwardly. "If you don't hug me back, I'm going to gnaw on your neck." His arms wrapped around me softly, and I pulled back, plugging my nose. "I thought we discussed aftershave and cologne."

"I believe you had a conversation without me agreeing," he chuckled, guiding me toward Knox, who watched us through narrowed eyes.

I passed, ignoring him to follow Greer into the narrowing pathway. The rock cliffs that stretched high into the mountain's side were golden sheen obsidian that glittered in the sun while appearing black in the shadows. It was a naturally occurring crystal formed from the volcanic glass with higher silica content. Though rare compared to regular obsidian, most preferred it for the beauty it offered in the light.

Witches often built around obsidian for balance and used it as an energy shield or for meditation. It made sense that it would be near a healing pool since witches used it to determine when someone needed to heal one's true self.

Greenery covered the rocks, reaching up through the cliffside to find the sun. The higher we climbed, the narrower the path became, until we had to walk in pairs through the slender passageway.

My eyes slid to the golden obsidian, discovering ancient writing, which gave me an excuse to pause. I leaned against the wall, running my fingers over the scrawled lettering. The men remained silent, but a shiver snaked down my spine. The sound of shuffling feet drew my attention as a hand touched my shoulder, causing me to peer into striking azure-blue eyes.

"Hecate's native language," Knox announced.

"I'm aware of what it is," I snapped, turning away from the writing that bespoke of peace and new beginnings.

I felt Knox's irritation at being dismissed as I moved ahead of him. I paused, taking in the cliff's changes, becoming more colorful, the higher we climbed from the multitude of other crystals within them.

This land was created by magic, not naturally formed. I could feel it pulsing, and the need to reach out and run my fingers over the magic within the air was becoming rampant. I balled my hands at my sides, fighting the urge as we climbed higher, and the air grew thinner.

The sound of rushing water exploded around us, and I paused, peering over the cliffside to where the water flowed beneath us. Hundreds of spouts poured water from the mountainside below us, cascading into one large whirlpool that rushed in a cyclone formation down into the earth below. On each spout sat a large, raw crystal rock formation, and the moment the sun touched it through the clouds above, thousands of rainbows glistened over the falling water.

I gasped, leaning over further, even though it caused me pain. Knox grabbed my arm, pulling me back as my footing slipped. He didn't speak, didn't even acknowledge that I'd almost fallen to my death as he shoved me away from the edge and took that side of the trail for himself.

My fingers touched the cliffside, and I smirked as it lit up, sending fluorescent light burning through the narrowed pathway with the single trace of my fingertips against the surface.

The further up the path we moved, the cleaner the air became. No sound followed us, nor filled the space of the trek up the mountain other than the water below. Even that sound diminished as we turned into a cave.

Knox slid his arm around my waist while his other grabbed my hand, touching it to the cave's mouth. His eyes held mine, smirking at the way I shivered from his touch. The entire cave lit with violet hues, causing everything white or lighter within the cave to glow.

The power pulsing inside the cave was stifling, pressing against me as I walked inside, uncaring that my hair glowed brightly. Amethyst clusters covered the cave walls, and the ground under our feet was fire opal, creating an illuminating pathway through the mountain. I paused as it became too much, leaning over to close my eyes while my hands rested on my knees.

Exhaling slowly, I fought the magic that searched for a host. Someone had banked and stored an immense amount of raw magic within this cave.

No one spoke, as if they knew the issue, waiting to see if I had the power to take what this place offered. But I couldn't. It wasn't good magic. It was dark, oily, deadly magic that would usurp the user, turning them evil until the magic ruled the body and the soul, and the host withered and died.

Standing, I hurried forward through the cave only to emerge on the other side to a wooden, moss-covered bridge that precariously swung in the wind. I paused, narrowing my eyes on its rope sides, and then did the worst thing I could do. I peered down into the drop below it. Only you couldn't see where the drop ended because clouds prevented you from finding the bottom.

My gaze slid to Knox, who smirked as he realized the problem. He moved ahead, waiting for me to join him.

"It only holds two people at a time," he explained. "You can hold on to me. I won't let you fall, Aria."

"I'm good," I snorted, watching him turn toward me, pausing as he took in the damage to my face before spinning back around and starting forward over the bridge.

I followed him in silence, my heart pounding painfully against my ribs. My hands slid through the moss, watching as it fell into the clouds below the bridge.

The wind picked up, and Knox slowed his progression, tilting his head like he was ready to turn around and retrieve me if it made the wrong sound. A gust of wind caused the bridge to whine loudly, and my breathing grew labored as panic rushed through me.

My hands tightened on the rope as a burst of wind sailed toward us, sending us rocking as we reached the middle of the long wooden bridge. Panic took control of my mind, and everything within me screamed to run from the bridge. Loud purring sounded when I moved back in the direction we'd come, calming me to an almost subdued state.

"Just breathe, Aria."

"I am breathing," I whispered, as his soothing purr calmed my panic and replaced it with a silent strength.

It took several more moments before we were finally off the bridge, and Knox pointed to a large bounder for me to rest on while the others made their way over. Knox handed me a canister, and I shook my head, but he pushed it into my hands, ignoring me.

Crouching in front of me, he stared up, "Drink. It will help ease the pain. We have a few more miles to go, and you insist on walking it yourself, which I have respected. I won't watch you suffer in pain, not even for your foolish pride, Aria."

I removed the lid, happy to have the chain off the cuffs, even if it now hung and jangled every time I moved my arms. I pushed the canister to my lips and gasped in pain as the whiskey burned the cuts inside my mouth.

I closed my eyes, ignoring the agony, drinking deeply of the smooth whiskey, letting it soak into my bones and soothe my discomfort.

"You're not nothing, Aria," Knox whispered, and I snorted, passing back his fancy canister.

His words burned in my mind, knowing it mattered little what I was or wasn't to him, since I wouldn't be sticking around for long, anyway.

I tore my eyes from his stare, studying the moss while doing my best to pretend he didn't exist. Varying shades of sage and lavender covered the side of the cliff to calm travelers that passed through. It was a nice touch, and something witches did to relax weary people or force their enemies into a false sense of calm before they turned them to ash.

Once all his men crossed the bridge, Knox held out

his hand, and I ignored it, moving past him to start up the trail which was growing wider. We neared another large cave that was more like a tunnel, pausing at its moss-covered mouth. My hand moved to the sign with a mass of symbols announcing a place of sanctuary. It also warned that once you entered, you could not exit along the same path. A shiver snaked down my spine as I turned, staring at the men who watched me silently.

My attention slid to the altar, and I snorted as apprehension filled me. This was a place of sanctuary for wayward witches. It was a place where they came to find blessings and purpose, reclaiming their place among the Hecate ruling high queen.

Moving toward the altar, I opened the ancient stone box, withdrawing sage and a tiny jar of frankincense. I dipped the sage into the jar and then placed it onto the altar, watching as flames leaped to life from the magic.

"Did you just use magic?" Lore asked, causing me to turn and look at him.

"Blessed be, Lore," I whispered, turning back to the altar. "I am of the blood who blessed this land, and I am seeking safe passage through her hand. Blessed be the lost souls, to find the light within the night, they come to thee seeking sanctuary. For those who are lost, and those who need found, blessed be, you're homeward bound."

I turned as the mountain lit up with glowing blue runes, stretching as far as the eye could see. Sage bloomed abundantly, opening up to free the scent while the lavender joined to fill the surrounding air. Knox held out his arm, indicating the entrance into the illuminated tunnel that mirrored the mountain walls.

I marveled at the stairs covered in glowing stones that looked as if someone had placed UV lighting beneath phosphate paint. Moving into the tunnel, I listened as it began singing a sultry, soulful tone that mirrored SVRCINA's *Who Are You* as we slowly walked deeper onto the spiraling stairs that led down into the unknown.

The female singing switched to the song playing in my mind, and I smiled. The men behind me had no idea that the tunnel was listening to my soul, hearing my worries and fears while I moved further into the sanctuary.

As we reached the bottom of the spiral stone steps, I looked back, noting the runes that warned against entering. Someone had destroyed the sanctuary, and someone else had given those coming to it a dark warning of foreboding. Knox turned, staring at the steps as my eyes watered.

"We're not supposed to be here."

"No, they don't like my kind here, Aria. After all, I am the murderer of witches and wicked things," Knox snorted, moving ahead of me.

I swallowed hard, following behind him silently, lost in my thoughts. We stepped out of the tunnel into an abandoned village. The scent of decay filled my senses. Altars sat on the side of an enormous cliff, stretching until the mountain opened up, revealing the endless sky. Sacrificed humans still sat on them, long forgotten with moss covering their bones.

I exhaled, stepping further into the village, watching the torches come to life, exposing the hanging bodies now little more than bones. My heart thundered in my chest as ravens gave flight, filling the sky with their shadows as Knox turned, staring back at me with a dark, sinister smile.

"They don't want you here either, Aria. Interesting, isn't it?" Knox asked, searching my face before he turned, staring at the angry birds who squawked as feathers rained down from their flight. My eyes studied them, noting that they were corpses. Raven corpses. "Welcome to the Valley of the Dead; home to the Hecate witch line, or those who tried to live without their Hecate name to keep them alive. Hiding couldn't even save them from the monsters who wanted them destroyed."

Chapter Forty-Six

We walked through an overgrown meadow flowing with poppy flowers that created a beautiful splash of color to offset the greenery. A deep sense of dread rolled through me, and the altars became fewer, the closer we got to the village. I left the trail without warning, moving toward one altar, needing to know what was on it, and why someone had made it.

I paused before a large, stone slab etched in ancient language around the edges. Pulling the moss away, I studied the symbol for male and firstborn son. My gaze lifted to the petite form that held a decayed babe, molded in place by the moss that had covered him.

Tears pricked my eyes and regret flooded through me. Senseless deaths never felt right. Especially when our grandmother had cursed us because of some fortune told long ago.

"What's it say?" Knox asked, causing me to jump,

his voice catching me off-guard.

"They're male altars, reserved for male children of Hecate witches, but they're all wrong. The poppy seeds keep the dead here, luring them to remain so the altar would be worthless. The sage is common, and it should be Palo Santo, which would purify the spirit. Mixing rosemary and sage would give them masculine energy since they're male. This is just normal sage, which isn't strong enough for the ceremony to send the deceased to another womb able to offer them life."

"There are hundreds of them, witch. Maybe they used them as sacrifices instead of worrying about carrying them into the next life."

"That is blasphemy." I turned, glaring at him as I laughed soundlessly. "You find everything we do evil, don't you?"

"Every single thing," he admitted, a chill filling his tone.

"Am I evil when I'm naked with you?" I asked, slowly stepping forward, taunting him. "Or when I have your cock between my lips, does that too, feel evil? When your blood pumps through your veins and the sweat cools upon our bodies, do you think what we shared was evil?" His eyes dropped to my lips, and a sardonic smile lifted his.

"Do I think when I fuck you, that you could be something evil sent to lure me into a trap? Absolutely Aria," he whispered huskily. "Witches are sexual beings, who often more times than not, lure men to their deaths with the promise of pleasure their magic pussies deliver to us."

"If I am so evil, then end it, King Karnavious. Put us both out of our misery. Come on. Take my head and be done with it. I'm tired of you and your hatred of me."

"Oh, Aria, you don't get to die on me." His jaw clenched at my words, his eyes slowly searching mine as silent tears filled them.

"Someday, you're going to realize that you're the evil one and not me," I swallowed, glaring at him before I snorted softly, moving to the next altar, scraping off the moss, then moving to the next.

I slipped back to the trail, cleaning my hands off before I stopped dead in my tracks at the sign marking the town. Instead of welcoming visitors, it warned to *'get the fuck out of here'* with death runes.

"We're really not supposed to be here," I muttered, groaning before my attention moved to the first house.

Huge claw marks had severed the protection wards written upon the wooden door. The hair on my nape stood as a chill wrapped around me, tightening in my throat as sweat beaded on my brow. I balled my hands into fists and canted my head to the side, reading the warning. Magic was in play; cold, lifeless magic, judging by my reaction to it.

Beware the Forbidden Witch. She, who is of Hecate's womb, is unwanted within this home. Blessed are the forgotten and those that have strayed, for in their darkest day, they found their truest way. May we remain forgotten, may we remain sane, for fear of the mad witch who bathed the realms in its darkest, wicked ways.

"Jesus, fuck! What the hell is this place?" I asked

the door as if it was going to answer me.

"It's the Valley of the Dead, in the Dark Mountains that lay between realms. Your realm and mine, Aria," Knox whispered against my ear, causing me to jump again. "We're in the middle where people came to escape persecution for being together. Couples who had fallen in love or those who wished for a new beginning without the war destroying them," he explained solemnly.

"What the hell? Did you take creeper lessons from Greer? Put a bell on it!" I snapped, hating that he'd scared me right out of my skin. I leveled him with a chilling look, and he laughed softly as I turned back, frowning at the sign. "Who is the Forbidden Witch?" I asked softly as his heated breath fanned my neck.

"That's the million-dollar question, isn't it?" He kissed my neck, forcing me to step away from his lips. Turning to face him, I glared. "What does it say?"

"You can't read it?" I asked, feeling a small sense of victory.

"No. It precedes me."

"It says, beware the prick that plays thy heart, for he is a loser of the lost art. Though his prick is thick, and sometimes it plays nice, it comes too fast, with strings attached, and has a hefty price. Thou shall not let your guard down, for the moment that you do, he'll scare you and won't prepare you for the horrors awaiting you. The man is broken, his grief outspoken, and such a lost cause that his ghosts still haunt his pathetic ass, for only they would welcome his cold, dead heart, blah, blah, blah. Then end."

"Does it indeed? Because that word right there," he said, pointing to the sign, "that's your family name in your native language, isn't it?"

"I thought you couldn't read it?" I countered.

"I can't, but you just confirmed what I thought it was. Should I kiss you as a thank you?" he asked.

"No, does it look like I need a kiss? My face is dented in, asshole," I frowned, moving toward the side of the house to peer in through the window.

I stared at my reflection, wincing at the damage. Exhaling, I caught Knox watching me with an unguarded look in his eyes. He didn't enjoy seeing me hurt. That much was obvious. Although, he hadn't helped the situation or offered to rectify it. Men sucked with their bipolar mood swings that changed faster than the weather in Texas during the spring.

Using my good arm, I rubbed away the dust from the window. Cupping my hands and peering through the ancient glass, I noted an altar, an overturned table, and grimoires that were little more than dust-covered leather bindings now. Whatever happened here, it had happened a long time ago.

I studied the cottages, all built with the same thatched roofs in varying states of decay. There was no scent of rotting food or wood, only the decomposition of bodies and earth. Moss blanketed the roofs and outer walls of the small square cottages.

The silence of the place was deafening, and the deeper we walked into the village, the more profound it became. We were in a site long forgotten. It was an abandoned beauty left in ruins that lay untouched by the world outside the high stone walls.

We passed more doors covered in the thick green moss, and I zeroed in on the warning and claw marks that once again marred the doors. I tilted my head, trying to make out the language etched into them, but came up empty.

"What language is that one?" I asked quietly, trying not to disturb the silence of this place, and yet needing to know what language marked the door on the largest house.

"Mine. Do you want to trade information?" he asked, smirking while he waited for my answer.

"No, it's not worth it. You'd just use what I'd tell you to attack my people."

I stepped closer to the cottage, running my fingers over the design etching into it. I yanked my hand away as it glowed. My head pounded, and I lifted my hand to my forehead. Stepping back, I watched as the other doors started glowing as hidden wards pulsed to life. The pain in my head grew until Knox grabbed my arm, pulling me with him, away from the door while studying my face.

"Careful. Most of these doors are warded to protect from you and your family line, Aria."

Frowning at his warning, I moved to the side of the house and peered in through the thick glass, staring at the upturned furniture. The table had massive cuts in its top, and the depth of the sword marks sent a chill racing down my spine.

It was in the same disarray as the other cottage I'd

seen. They were all ransacked, and those who had lived within them had vanished without a trace.

Chapter Forty-Seven

I turned to look out through the open meadow and gasped. Hundreds of skeletal remains lay around the field, each connecting to the next by either limb or skull. My hands trembled as my heart pounded in my chest. My breathing grew labored as I stepped forward to study the scene. I took in their moth-eaten clothing and what remained from the harsh elements and insects.

"Jesus," I whispered breathlessly.

Everything inside me said to turn and leave, but the table sitting in the middle of the remains drew me forward. My fingers trembled as I reached out, running my fingers over the skull of a toddler who sat cradled in her mother's lap. I fought the tears taking in Hecate's mark that covered the poor thing's skull and peered at the others at the table.

Their clothes were of higher quality, which was discernable even through the rot. This family was in the middle of the dead, posed and left there as if they'd taken a meal while the others lay dying around them.

"Tell me what you see, Aria," Knox asked softly, and I shook my head.

"Evil," I stated, turning to look at him. I whispered it, accusation marring my shaky tone. "Pure evil that thinks it is good."

"Indeed, but who decides what is evil, and what is good? What you see as evil, we see as a right to be unoppressed by our oppressors," he countered, peering over my shoulder toward the family of corpses. "Sometimes, the world needs a villain more than it needs a hero, Aria. Every villain starts out thinking they're doing what is right, or what is needed. The world around them forces them to become the monster. I'm the monster your family created by taking those I loved away from me. You're the monster I am creating because I am threatening to do the very same thing to your family. Which one of us is the hero, and which is the villain? Who decides? It depends on which side you stand, does it not?"

"If we are to kill the children, then let us burn. They are the only innocent beings of war. They could not choose a side or know their mind. They're innocent of crimes, and not wicked of ways. If we are to burn, then let us all burn together. Let us destroy one another, but never the ones who have yet to harm another soul."

"War isn't black and white, Aria. In the Nine Realms, your birth decides your side of a war."

"I don't believe that. Not for one moment would I decide to be evil just because of my parentage. In fact, my mother taught me my most important lessons in life. She showed me that birth doesn't decide who your parents are. I would always choose the side that is fighting to protect innocent lives."

"And yet you refuse to join me because of the side your family is choosing," he stated as his jaw clenched, and I frowned. "This is one of several villages attacked at the start of this fight, Aria. You have yet to see real evil."

"Are the events in this village your doing?" I whispered, turning back to look out over the dead as his words ripped through me. "Did you murder these children?" I pried, turning watery eyes to his.

My family created Knox, the monster he became was because we'd failed to protect him from our people. Now he was returning it tenfold and was planning to force me to help him. Maybe it was karma's way of righting a wrong, but I intended to fight him to prevent him from succeeding.

"This happened a long time ago, Aria."

"I didn't ask you *when* it happened. I asked you *if* you murdered children for your war."

"Leave it alone, witch. You won't like the answers you find here." He turned, leaving me alone with the dead.

I closed my eyes as tears slipped free. Anger rushed through me as the wind picked up, causing the sense of foreboding to slither around me. Grasping my throat, I looked for a higher vantage point.

Silently, careful not to disturb the dead, I moved to

an altar, frowning deeply. I crawled on top, staring down at the deceased. I had to get higher to see the design of the large grid.

I walked to the tallest house and slipped inside, carefully climbing the stairs, fully aware that Knox was once again behind me. He was like a silent shadow, enjoying my horror at what he'd done to the witches of this village.

At the window, I stared down at the circular pattern of bodies spread out through the entire meadow. It was a beautifully morbid display of the dead with colorful flowers blooming through the earth. Some flowers had pushed through the ribcages or mouths of the dead to reach for the sun.

"We are not in Norvalla, right?" I asked.

"We are close enough to it that these people shouldn't have been here," he whispered against my shoulder as if he feared I would retaliate against him for the crimes he'd committed against the witches, and planned to subdue me should I put up a fight.

"She was just a baby. What crime could she have committed against you, King Karnavious?" I murmured, turning to peer up at him.

"They had no right to be this close to Norvalla after what they'd done to the queen and prince," he repeated, as if it explained everything, or should. "They trespassed where they weren't welcome."

"So the big, bad King of Norvalla slaughtered them? Babes included because he feared she was a threat to him and his people," I whispered thickly through the emotions tightening my throat. "We trespass now against the dead. We shouldn't be here. It is forbidden. I can feel the warning."

"So can I, but its close enough to my land that I am still the ruling king here." His eyes searched mine for more argument, and I shook my head, knowing he wouldn't leave no matter what I said.

"Did you place their corpses in this pattern or did the dark witches come here afterward and create the grid?"

"What does it fucking matter? They're dead." Knox stared out the window, noting the pattern I spoke of, and turned, watching me. "It's a grave. Who cares how they were placed after death?"

I frowned, noting the way we studied each other's reactions. It was as if we expected to glimpse some explanation for the body's positions, and their placement on the field. Hundreds of corpses were placed in circular patterns, all touching somehow, except the furthest one that pointed west through the small hole in the cliffside.

In the middle of the design was the family. Their hands, all except the babes, touched together, pointing west? It was a power grid formation, similar to the one I found in the other village, but it normally took living witches to wield the magic.

Plus, there were large, raised altars further out that I hadn't noticed before, and on them were what appeared to be feminine corpses, dressed in purity gowns. Moss had grown over the altars, making them near impossible to see from the ground, unlike the babes on the way into the village.

The walls of the valley weren't walls at all. They were rooms with altars, each one carrying the remains of yet more witches. This wasn't a village. It was a tomb.

Stepping closer to the window, I leaned out, noting the large rocks that adorned the high cliffs that hid the village. Apparently, not good enough if Knox had discovered it and slaughtered them.

I peered up at the sun, noting how it hit the altars, creasing my brow before I turned around, only for the wood beneath me to give way. Knox grabbed me before I could fall, pulling my body against his as we both breathed hard. After a moment of panic, I frowned while sucking my lip between my teeth before releasing it.

"I'm good," I murmured as pain sliced through my chest, where my ribs ached. Stepping away from Knox, I glared at the window ledge that had given out from decades of rot. "You came upon them during sacrifices, I take it?"

"Does it matter? This happened a very long time ago. The dead no longer care, Aria. Leave it alone. You have no idea what it was like back then. War is brutal, and often those who are innocent pay the price for the deeds of the guilty."

I snorted, leaving him standing in the room as power slithered over my flesh. I turned silently on the staircase, staring at Knox, where his eyes glowed with red embers and extinguished so quickly that I wasn't certain I hadn't imagined it.

He stepped toward me, pausing as I dismissed him, slowly starting down the stairs to find a shimmering apparition waiting for me. The temperature in the house dropped, and my breath came out in a cloud in front of me. A chill rushed down my spine, and nausea churned in my stomach.

The ghost wore a purity gown, her wrists and throat dripping blood upon the floor, and yet no blood reached it. I stepped back, finding Knox right behind me, his arms going around me protectively.

Her ghostly eyes lifted to the man behind me as her mouth opened, and a shrill scream escaped from her. The volume of her scream caused me to cover my ears, holding them as she continued shrieking like a banshee.

Knox picked me up and rushed us outside, only to pause as a sea of dead witches stood around the house we'd entered. Knox's men closed in around us as he set me down. My skin ached from the chill in the air, and I shook my head while blinking to keep my eyes from freezing open. It was as if we'd stepped into the Arctic Circle, and yet the sun shone around us but didn't offer heat.

"They're cursed to remain here," I whispered more to myself than to the others. "They'll kill us to keep this place protected."

"How the fuck do you know that?" Knox demanded.

"Look at the markings on their heads. They carry the curse into death, forcing them to remain where their soul last lived. That is why there was so much power in the cave. This place is someone's power source. Someone is siphoning magic from the dead and storing it for something massive. Considering the amount of magic kept in the caves, it's someone very powerful. Possibly the same person creating the power grid in the other village," I pointed out, crossly.

"Let's go," Knox growled, and the witches all let loose ear splitting screams that took us to our knees as pain ripped through us.

"I think that's a no," I groaned, searching through the ghosts for the head witch anchoring the others with her magic. "I told you we shouldn't be here."

"It's unclaimed land, which I added to Norvalla by force."

Knox turned glowing eyes in my direction, and I shook my head. "By all means, King Karnavious, explain that to the dead. I'll just sit here bleeding out of my ears while you make them see reason." He growled as my lips curled into a pained smile. "I'm waiting. Or, you can unbind my magic and let me send them on to the next life, freeing them from this place of death in which you caged them."

Chapter Forty-Eight

Blood dripped from our ears, noses, and eyes while waiting for Knox to choose between death or freeing me. I'd offered to give them a solution, and yet he procrastinated. His warriors were rattling along with him, but no one moved. After another moment had passed, Knox grabbed my arms carefully, his eyes burning with a silent warning.

"One wrong move, and I won't hesitate, witch," he snapped.

The cuffs slipped from my wrists, and I stood, smiling down at him as power rippled around me, sending my hair into the air. Knox stood with me, unfearful of the power slithering over him as I pulled the magic to me. I drank it into my pores as the pain from the beating lessened with the taste of magic that instantly began healing some of the damage.

"Step aside, King Karnavious. This is a job for a

witch, not a warrior. We wouldn't want you to get hurt, now would we?" I hissed, moving past him to face the witches.

The deceased witches continued to howl and shriek with cries. I started through them, moving toward the strongest witch. I rushed forward, expecting to slide through one witch, only to end up shot backward from a jolt of power the moment we collided. Her black gaze turned, lowering to me as her head tilted.

"Well, that was rude," I grumbled, hating that I hadn't expected them to hold *that* much power, let alone be corporal forms.

"You are unwelcomed here," the strongest witch snarled.

"I didn't ask if I was permitted entrance, now, did I?" I snorted, feeling Knox at my back. "You're cursed to remain here, and yet you don't belong here either. You're dead."

She blinked, tilting her head to the side before she scoffed, pulling an alarming amount of power to her. Her mouth opened, and she screamed, forcing Knox and me to our knees. My head throbbed, noting the others with her pausing in confusion.

"Your plan is so much better than mine was, Aria," Knox grumbled.

I lowered my head, collecting the rattle before I screamed back at the witch, forcing my body up from the ground as my creature chuckled. Her power added to mine as she rattled through me to fill the meadow and the village until the golden sheen obsidian cliffside began crumbling as rocks slid free.

The ghost's eyes turned to slits as she continued shrieking louder than any banshee could ever hope to achieve until another rattle joined mine. It was more masculine and absolute power that forced my hips to spread as my back arched.

Knox's hands gripped my hips, pulling me back against him, stilling the storm his rattle held over me, threatening to release and render destruction to my body. One hand slipped around my chest, pulling me back as we continued rattling together until the witch dropped to her knees, her eyes wide with wonder.

The combined noise echoed through the valley, sending rocks cascading from the high cliffs to reveal amethyst points, larger than any skyscraper in New York City could ever dream of reaching.

My rattle lowered, changing octaves as I melted against Knox's heat, turning to gaze into his sea-blue eyes that smiled at me knowingly.

Hell, even I could scent my need this time.

"That was the hottest thing I have ever seen, Peasant!" Greer chortled, forcing my attention to him.

Greer's words struck me stupid. I turned, finding all of Knox's men on their knees along with the apparitions, but where they bowed their head. Knox's men on the other hand, looked perturbed at what we had done.

My nose lifted to the air, inhaling their arousal as Knox's hold tightened on me. He dropped his lips to my shoulder, kissing the mark he'd made as if to remind me I was his. I could scent their aroused states, which called to my creature, making her perk up. Knox growled softly against his mark, and I shuddered.

"My Queen," the dead witch whispered, causing my eyes to narrow.

"Nope. Not your queen!" I laughed nervously, uncomfortable with her words. I needed to figure out if the Nine Realms offered counseling after Taren's little future walk. "I am just a girl trying to do the right thing here." Her head dipped to the ground in a bow without a response, and I turned toward Knox, frowning. "This next part is going to be rather... dark. I have to light the sage and chant, so I'm going to need you not to murder me if it affects your men. I can't shield them and send the witches onto their next path."

"If you so much as whisper a spell to harm them, I'll remove your head."

"You're such a romantic asshole." I swallowed hard, nodding. "Just don't look at my head while you're... you know. Doing *things* if you do end up removing it today," I swallowed, hating that the scent wafting from him was driving me mad with need.

My body clenched minutely, and his eyes dropped to my apex as if he had sensed it tightening. A cocky smile played on his generous mouth before he nodded.

"No promises on that one, Aria."

I shook my head, expelling a slow breath, before moving toward the largest stone altar used to do powerful spells or blessings. Once I reached it, I bent down, retrieving the stone box of herbs probably way past their expiration dates, but I had little options at this point.

I pulled out a few small glass jars, sprinkling the entire contents onto the altar before stepping back, slowly lifting my hands as I summoned fire to ignite the valley's sage.

"Aria," Knox warned, and I turned to peer at a house that began to burn. Obviously, they stored sage within it, or it wouldn't have caught fire.

"Let them burn. This is a tomb that shouldn't be left for others to disturb. If nothing remains, others won't wish to return to it either. I need your blade," I whispered, turning to see his eyes narrowing on me. "Cut my palm then," I offered, holding my hand out to him.

Knox hesitated, staring at the broken skin on my wrist before reaching into his scabbard, withdrawing his sword. Candles erupted around us, sealing the circle we stood within, and Knox glared at me in silent warning.

"It's a protective barrier to guard us against attack since we're exposed and vulnerable during casting, which I'm sure you're aware. Don't worry, King Karnavious. I'll protect you from the monsters," I smirked, watching his lips twitch as I offered to keep him safe.

"Aria, I am the fucking monster."

Knox response sent a shiver rushing through me. Lifting his hand as an invitation for mine, I studied it with a frown of indecision. The moment we touched, sparks tingled, and the witches rose, causing us to turn toward them as they closed in around us. They chanted, their words were ancient and of the First Witch, Hecate. Swallowing hard, I shook my head against their words. Bitches be crazy if they thought I was marrying his ass at their altar!

"What are they saying?" Knox asked, sliding his stare to mine.

"Oh, you know, things like goodbye, and that they're thankful we're here," I offered with a frown, sucking my bottom lip between my teeth while still shaking my head as he studied me with a smoldering look in his eyes.

"Are you planning to marry me on this altar, Aria?" he asked, causing me to sink my teeth into my lip as my eyes turned to slits. Warmth spread through me, and I ignored it, stifling a groan at what it meant.

"Absolutely not," I whispered thickly, uncertain why saying it created an ache in my chest. I started to pull my hand away from his grasp, but he held it tightly. "You know the first language, don't you?"

"I know everything about my enemies, Little Lamb. I make it my business to know every detail about someone before I declare war against them."

I shivered as he brought his sword up, slicing carefully through my palm before releasing my hand. Moving to the altar, I made a fist and grunted as pain slid through me, and the magic grasped for me, uncaring that I was weakened from my last attack.

"Aria?" Knox whispered, standing closer to purr softly beside me.

"I'm fine," I replied, counting the blood droplets before it began flowing too fast.

I swayed on my feet and relaxed against the body that stood behind me. Knox offered me silent strength, which I wasn't sure he intended, and yet I still welcomed it all the same.

"You're not fine. You're already weakened from the beating, removing your rib, and then being stubborn to prove you're not weak. You walked over twelve miles through a mountain pass to reach this village."

"I made it here, didn't I?" I asked irritably, weakening from the blood loss. "Something is wrong," I admitted thickly, turning toward Knox as he grabbed my hand, holding it against his mouth to lick through the wound. "That was just wrong." Knox gazed up at me with black eyes, his mouth opened to reveal serrated teeth as his head tilted, smiling wickedly.

"You taste fucking delicious." He pulled me closer, brushing his lips against my throat. "Who hurt you? I will rip them inside out, and bring you their heart, mate."

"Well, that escalated quickly."

His lips curled against my neck, sending everything within me, screaming for him to continue. My hand lifted, holding his mouth to me as the chanting grew louder around us. My body heated, burning with the need for his claim.

"So willing for me, Little Mate?" he growled huskily.

His teeth brushed against my flesh, and I gasped, turning my mouth toward his as black eyes turned to blue, and Knox watched me. Anger slithered over my skin as he studied me, reacting to his creature.

"He'd destroy you, Aria. He'd savage your pretty little throat and drink your blood as you bled out in his arms. Remember that. Finish the fucking spell and stop acting like a..." he paused, and I stepped back from him shaking off the haze of lust his creature had sent me spiraling into.

"A whore?" I asked, glaring at him.

"Like a feral bitch in heat, because my creature is becoming harder to control where you are concerned," Knox corrected. "I'd hate to wake up to you dead beneath me, soaked in your sweet tasting blood while I fucked your corpse because he took control and murdered you in his need to savage your soft body."

"I'm not even sure what to say to that." I offered, moving back to the altar as he stared at me with a look burning in his eyes that both terrified and intrigued.

Whatever had just happened between us, it had spooked him. Knox had just lost control, and I didn't know how to react to it, or him.

Smoke billowed from the cottages, along with the sage that grew naturally within the valley. I closed my eyes as the blood ignited, and the chanting changed to what was replaying within my mind.

"We do not die. Do not stand at my grave and weep for me, for my soul is now finally free. I am not there. I do not sleep. I rejoice in the freedom that death has granted me. I am now the wind that fills your sails, that echoes through the valley as it wails. I am the glint within the snow. I am the sun that feeds warmth into your blessed soul. I am the rain that grows your crops, for I am everything that feeds the realm and heals your ails. I am not here, nor am I there, for I have moved on to strengthen your air. I am released from curses of flesh. I am released from curses left. I am free of this living realm. Go now to where witches freely dwell. I am the magic that will feed the land. I am she who releases you from this place of sadness where you dwelled. Blessed be, sisters."

I turned, staring at the witches as tears burned my eyes, watching as they turned to ash, carried with the wind that rushed through the valley.

Knox didn't watch them returning to the earth. Instead, he watched me as tears rolled down my cheeks for the dead. His hand grabbed my wrist, carefully replacing the cuff to one before repeating it with the other as candles extinguished around us, and the circle broke.

"You cry for the dead?" he asked carefully, lifting his hands to rub away my tears with his thumbs.

"I cry because they've been here a very long time. I feel their pain and relief that it is finally over for them. They're now free. I did that for them," I said thickly, turning to look at Knox. "And the sage fucking stinks. It's burning my eyes and making them water, asshole."

He smiled before using his hand to hide his grin as he turned away from me. "Come on, woman. Let's get you to the healing pool. I don't enjoy seeing you bruised and hurt."

Knox escorted me through the increasing smoke toward a tunnel built into the amethyst cliffside. The moment we crossed to the other side, I gasped at the sparkling crystal cove filled with a turquoise pool and a sprawling forest that stretched further than my eyes could see.

We entered it silently, moving over a citrine pathway

that time hadn't touched, still shining brilliantly as the sun beat down on the clear yellow stones. Once we reached the pool, I paused, shaking my head at Knox.

"You've got to be fucking kidding me. My vagina is not getting in that pool!" I snapped, glaring at Lore, who laughed outright as Greer choked on air.

"You're getting into that water. We have hundreds of miles to travel before we reach the next place to camp for Beltane celebrations. You're wounded, and I am not watching you continue to endure pain, Aria. Strip and get into the damn pool."

"Beltane too? Damn. You're doubling down on the vagina mojo, huh? That is a fertility pool. You bath in it and then create a life with the blessing of the fertility goddess, and for the record, it isn't Hecate. It's Hora, which I do believe is *your* goddess, is she not?"

"Do you plan to fuck me?" he asked pointedly as he searched my face.

"No, but that isn't the point. Accidents happen!" Growling erupted, and I shivered as shadows slithered out of the woods. "Dire wolves! Are you fucking kidding me right now?" I snapped as Knox pushed me behind his body protectively. "I told you we weren't supposed to be here!"

"I don't do dogs!" Lore snapped, drawing his sword as the others followed his lead.

"Aria, why would they be here?" Knox asked icily.

"Because *we're* not supposed to be, which I keep saying, but what the hell would I know?" I asked, peeking around his shoulder at the pack of dire wolves.

"Fuck me! They're dead, too. Don't kill them again."

"Why the fuck not?" he snarled.

"Because they multiply when they're dead. You can either chant them away or force the dire wolves to heed orders, but you can't cut them! They multiply to increase their power against whoever hurt them," I groaned, dropping my head. "This idea of yours to heal me? It fucking sucks balls, jerk."

Chapter Forty-Nine

I screamed out a warning as one of the dire wolves lunged toward Knox. His blade swung, severing the giant wolf into two large, decayed portions. The other wolves growled, spittle running from their blackened teeth while huge dark eyes tracked our movement.

We all stepped closer to the pool, knowing they couldn't enter because of the magic within it. The drawback to this plan was that the wolves would have the upper hand by trapping us in the pool. That and they wouldn't need to leave *ever*, which left us still having to escape them.

The wolves appeared as rotting corpses with matted hair clinging to their bones. The putrid scent of rotting meat filled the air thickly.

It forced my stomach to roil with the need to expel what little was there. Huge black fangs protruded from their mouths, while dark, deadly magic filled their eyes, slithering through the clearing.

Magic wrapped around us, and I shook my head at the wrongness of it. Dark magic that didn't come from the wolves choked us with the vileness and taint of it on my flesh.

My blood thundered through my veins, pounding loudly in my ears while the wolves prowled closer, slowly lowering their heads while keeping us within sight. They were predators, preparing to savage their prey.

We were that prey.

Just freaking great. Couldn't I get a break for five minutes? Was that really asking too damn much?

Every step they took closer, forced us toward the crystalline blue water. The men held their blades up, taking defensive positions, the wolves prowling forward, uncaring of the threatening swords. Knox turned, glaring at me over his shoulder like I'd conjured them from thin air. I held up my arms, proving I still wore the cuffs on my wrist.

Knox's body rippled with raw, pulsing power, forcing me to step further away from him. He held the sheer authority at the moment as his power in the clearing mixed with the high voltage of his men. It was stifling, sending shivers of unease rushing down my spine.

Knox's men created a crescent moon formation in front of the pool, with Greer and me behind them. I held my breath when Knox swung once more, and the wolves lunged into the air toward the men.

Knox moved fluidly with purpose. Every swing of his blade was like a dance, slicing through the wolves with fluidity and strength. He landed the first blow, severing the bones of three enormous wolves into six pieces.

I shook my head, watching the corpses multiply, rising almost instantly. Sucking my lip between my teeth, I peered down to find Greer holding my hand. My eyes slid to him, and he turned even whiter, if at all possible.

"Really?" I muttered.

"I don't do dead dogs, Peasant."

I expelled a breath and grimaced at the irony of Greer's statement. Frowning, I silently watched the men swinging their swords in deft precision, dismembering the already dead wolves.

Knox and his men refused to hear me or listen to my previous warning, and every wolf they severed in half rose with another at its side.

This was going to suck, big time.

"Knox, free me," I demanded, holding up my wrists.

He spun around, staring at me as a wolf leaped toward his back, but he sent his sword backward, severing it into two pieces without even looking at it.

Knox shook his head with a wicked grin marring his thinning mouth, his eyes flashing with anger as if he blamed me for this. He hissed from between clenched teeth.

"I don't think so, witch," he growled harshly. "Call off your dogs."

"They're not my dogs! They're *dead!*" I snapped

and fought the urge to kick him in his balls for the sheer audacity of his accusation.

"They're fucking dire wolves, which are your family's familiars!"

"They're *Hecate's* familiars, not the bloodline, jackass!"

"Call them off, now!"

"You call them off!" I snarled, crossing my arms over my chest to glare at him.

Knox spun, slicing through the wolves that lunged at his back. His men continued cutting them up, creating a mass of dire wolves that snapped deadly fangs at us. It was pointless because you couldn't kill that which was already dead. We had to send them back to their resting place.

It felt like hours had passed since we'd entered the clearing with the pool, and as I watched, the men continued to slaughter the wolves until hundreds of them were yapping and biting at us. Men were such macho idiots.

Knox spun toward one that got around him, lifting his sword as the wolf turned toward me with hollowed black eyes. He turned back toward Knox, and I smirked.

Hecate bloodline one, Knox, zero.

"I send you now; I send you home. I send you back from which you've come. Heed my call; Heed me now. Return to your rest, for you are not of now." I watched as all the wolves turned to look at me before they continued attacking the men. "You created too freaking many of them!" I accused, watching Knox turn his angry glare toward me. "Oh, screw you. I warned you!"

"I'd be very careful, woman," he growled.

The men moved toward the pool, and I exhaled, clearing my mind. I faced the wolves, watching the angry horde of them that pushed closer, held only away from us by the men's sheer strength and their will to prevail. The men were growing tired, and with every kill, more and more rose to fight against them. Eventually, they'd give in to exhaustion, trapping us in the pool for eternity.

I pushed the cloak off and stepped in front of the men, knowing the wolves couldn't enter the pool, nor could they touch me.

Knox snarled, but I snapped my angry stare at him and snarled right back. His eyes lowered to where the wolves had stepped back the moment I stepped forward, damnation burning in his oceanic glare when they rose, locking eyes with mine until I dismissed him.

"You will hear me!" I screeched, listening to my voice echoing off the high walls of the cove where we stood. It echoed, bouncing around us while I swallowed to ease my tone, to pull forth the voice that would chant at a perfect harmony to their ears.

One lunged at Knox, and I screamed as my hair rose, and magic filled the space between the wolves and me. I lifted my hands, throwing up a shield to protect Knox and his men from becoming puppy chow.

The wolves slammed against the glowing barrier, yipping and snarling when they discovered they could no longer reach their prey. I floated from the ground, turning my hands over with the palms heavenward. The power of my blood ignited, and the wolves sensed it, whining.

"I forbid you from hurting him! You heed my call, you heed my line, and I send you away from this place and time." I hissed as my power erupted, sizzling against my flesh. It was power Knox couldn't touch because it wasn't ours to take.

His heated glare burned into my spine while I stared down the largest wolf. He moved to lung toward Knox once more, and I hissed, rattling until the wolf whined. "I know your pain; I know it well. I release you from this place of hell. He is mine, and mine alone. You cannot have him, for I am *owed*. Find your peace. I bless you now for eternal sleep." My feet touched the ground, and they jerked back from me.

The wolves bowed their heads, slowly backing up. I walked further away from the pool, threatening them with the power that hummed through me. It wasn't my power, but it was that of the blood that pulsed through me, enough that it had overflowed and surpassed whoever had placed their remains here.

There were only a handful of witch lines powerful enough to raise the dead, but to raise a dire wolf from the tomb of Hecate, and place them here to protect the pool? It felt off. It felt like there was something else they were guarding.

I turned, finding Knox's blade poised at my throat. "You have magic, Little Witch," he murmured, studying the way I slowly allowed my hands to lower.

"Not entirely, Knox. I have the blood of the fucking

Goddess of Magic in my veins. That is something that you cannot remove. I can chant, and I can speak. Therefore, I can break curses and enchantments. My magic doesn't come only from my grandmother. It comes from the Nine Realms, as you're well aware. I used good magic to battle evil magic, which just drained me. I warned you we shouldn't be here. You ignored me because you don't trust me. That's fine. But, for the record, I just saved your asses, *twice.* They were protecting the power of the dead witches, and whoever placed them here was *very* powerful. Had you brought any other witch here with you, you'd all be dead. So go ahead, take my head for saving your ass."

"I don't trust you," he snapped harshly, slowly pulling his blade back while I continued walking toward him, daring him to push it through my throat.

"I don't care if you trust me or not. Do you think if I had full access to my magic, that I'd still be here after what your man did to me today? Look at me, Knox!" I snapped, watching his eyes slide over the wounds on my face. "I promise you this: when I do get my magic back, and I will, I won't play prisoner to you anymore. I'll simply vanish into the night without a trace, asshole." Knox lowered his blade, studying how I glared at him, before pushing it back into the scabbard at his waist.

"Get a perimeter set up around us. Make sure no other surprises arise." Ocean-colored eyes watched me precariously, like he wasn't certain he trusted me past where he could see me.

"No more dogs, right, Aria?" Lore asked, stepping out of the pool slowly.

"Don't worry, Lore. I'll protect you from the big, bad, dead dire wolves. You, I actually like," I laughed as he smiled boyishly.

"You like me, Peasant," Greer injected.

"You too, Greer," I snorted, shaking my head while he exhaled, and his usual coloring filled his cheeks again.

Lore turned to the guys, hiking his thumb over his shoulder. "You guys can go, she likes me. I'll tend to her bath and rub her real good. What can I say? It's this pretty smile and amber eyes. They get the ladies every time."

"Go set up a perimeter with the others, asshole," Knox snorted, turning to stare at me as his men fanned out to do as he'd ordered. "Strip and get into the pool, Aria. We've wasted more time than we should have here."

I snorted, rolling my eyes at him.

Chapter Fifty

Frowning, Brander hesitated, searching my wounded face as he set down a large pack. He was about to open his mouth to speak, but a deep rattle stopped him. Sapphire eyes slid over my shoulder to Knox, before slowly coming back to mine. Brander gave up and turned away from me, jogging to catch up with the others, leaving me alone with the overbearing, demanding, obstinate prick.

Lifting my head to the sky, I took in the splashes of vibrant colors signifying the change from day to evening. The sound of heavy armor clanging together as Knox removed it, peaked my awareness that he stood behind me.

I didn't turn to look at him, knowing I'd find him naked or in the process of becoming so. Knox wasn't a spark; he was the entire flame. He drew me to him, and the moment I got too close, he rendered me to nothing more than ashes.

I was about to enter a fertility pool with this man, and I feared it. It was reckless to be here with this dominant creature who exuded masculine intensity, shouting how virile and animalistic he was to every feminine part of me. Knox was everything I craved and wanted, and everything I couldn't have.

When I was with Knox, the world faded away until only we existed. It all just stopped around us, or maybe it went on without us being a part of it for the time we were together. His eyes held mine until he was the only thing I knew or wanted to know. Our eyes spoke the words that our lips could never say out loud.

Together, there was no noise, no people, no thoughts or concerns, no yesterdays, no today, no worries for tomorrow or the day after. With Knox, the world just stopped turning, and we stood where nothing could reach us, within the beauty of it all.

Just him and me, both lost in the silence and stillness together. But when he was absent, when he wasn't touching me, everything fell apart. *I* fell apart like I was missing a piece of myself. The world turned again, and we moved against one another. I didn't like it, but I would live in it and always keep moving toward my goals. It was who I was, and who I needed to remain in this violate world and war.

I craved him, yet that could very well destroy me. Sometimes though, when I was alone, I yearned for the world to stop turning so he could wreck me. I craved the intensity of his stare, the silent conversations our eyes had together, and then I reminded myself that in the end, the world had to turn to go on, and wishing differently was selfish. What I craved was forbidden, and while beautiful, it was wrong. How could something that felt so right be so wrong?

The idea of climbing into the fertility pool with him, even to heal, screamed *'bad fucking idea'*. The pool was fed from the water cascading over crystals embedded within the design, spelled, heated, and filled with essential oils. It was here for healing, yes, but it was so much more.

Couples came here to have their unions blessed, signifying the beginning of their new lives together. The witches had designed the pool for seduction, blessing, healing, and creating life. I was about to strip naked and enter the water with this equally naked male that made my brain turn from brilliant to dense, faster than the speed of light. What could go wrong?

He was a savage who knew how to seduce your senses in all the right ways. Knox's persona screamed, *I'll fuck you while killing you, and I'll do it while making you come undone,* and you'd happily do it, thinking both were your idea.

Knox oozed carnality, brutality, and savagery that called to my creature, telling me we were alike, while also so very different on so many levels. It was surprisingly shocking that he didn't just look at a woman with the smoldering heat burning within him, and she'd wind up pregnant without even having to drop her panties.

I felt his fingers on my shoulders before the dress slid from my body, pooling at my feet, and a gasp escaped my lips as the cool evening air touched my flesh. Turning, I stepped back, swallowing past the tightening in my throat at finding him smiling roguishly.

His gaze lowered slowly, swallowing hard, and his smile faded as he inspected the red mark from where I'd scorched my wound on my abdomen closed earlier today. His blue eyes narrowed, slowly rising to search my face as he took in the rest of the damage.

Dismissing him, I bent over to remove my panties and strolled toward the pool. I let my gaze caress the waterfall, creating soothing noises. The moment I stepped into the water, it changed from crystalline blue to a peaceful, translucent blue-green of the Caribbean Ocean to match Knox's eyes. The pool was reminding me of the male I'd allowed to mark me—*stupid pool*.

When I was deep enough, I dove into the water, trembling as it sent power rushing through me. The water's magic sought the damage to my body and immediately went to work, fixing and repairing it.

Magic slithered over my nerves, soothing the aches and pain that echoed briefly before warmth washed over me. Every inch of my body came alive, heightening my senses and needs until I shot up from the water, peering around to search out Knox's location. I scanned all around me, not finding him.

I touched my ribcage, finding the flesh smooth and unscarred. I could already tell my face had returned to normal, free of damage. My gaze moved across the surface of the water, not locating Knox.

It wasn't until I'd turned in a full circle that he lifted from the water right in front of me, cupping my cheek before his thumb brushed over it softly. He studied the lack of damage with something tender in his gaze that threatened to undo the anger I'd stored up for him.

Knox lowered his mouth, and I turned away before his lips found mine. I felt him glaring at me, knowing I'd just given him the cold shoulder. He deserved it, and so much more. After a moment, I turned back to give him a biting look before sinking into the water once more.

He didn't move, which caused me to open my eyes, realizing my mistake as something very masculine met my stare head-on. I sank toward the bottom, floating there leisurely with my eyes staring upward as Knox peered down, watching as I slowly sunk further into the depths weightlessly.

He didn't join me, choosing to cross his arms over his chest while staring down at me. My hands touched the fire quartz bottom, spelled to supply sexual energy, enhancing virility and sexuality between couples.

I peered up at him, smiling as the magic rushed through me. I slowly righted my body, pushing off of the crystal floor to escape the water as my lungs ached with the need for oxygen.

"Do you intend to watch me bathe, or are you here for more sinister reasons? I can bathe myself, King Karnavious. I'm a big girl, you know?"

"How long do you intend to call me by my formal title?" he asked, glaring at me as I kept a safe distance between us.

"Until I escape you again," I murmured, moving toward the waterfall, only for him to appear in front of me when he'd been several feet away.

Knox hadn't disturbed the water, or so much as created a ripple on the surface as he'd moved. There was no warning to indicate he had moved. He was just suddenly standing before me, blocking my path.

The cocky smirk playing on Knox's lips told me he'd done it on purpose. My breathing hitched in my throat as he gripped my hips, narrowing his eyes.

"You're not escaping me, Aria. I will not allow it to happen." He studied my face, running his fingers over my hipbones.

"That's why we call it escaping. Normally, you're not aware of your prisoner leaving, which is why they *escape* you," I pointed out, smiling at the look of annoyance on his face.

The man wasn't beautiful in a beguiling way. Knox was rugged and masculine, which called to every part of me. He was hard, sinewy muscles that made him appear more unbreakable than he was. His body was composed of hard lines created to lure the eye to leisurely caress the perfection of masculinity he displayed in spades.

His mouth was made for pleasure, with sex dripping from his words the moment they escaped his talented tongue. The V-line of his abdomen could drive a female mad with the need to explore it with her tongue.

The look burning in his heated stare caused me to chew my bottom lip as I fisted my hands at my sides, preventing them from reaching out to explore him carnally.

Releasing the air from my lungs, I lifted my gaze to the sky. The evening turned to night, and galaxies of stars shot across it, filling it with beauty. The rocks within the pool glowed, exposing our naked bodies to one another.

The red veins within the fire quartz created a red tinge of light that screamed romance. Knox wrapped his arms around me, yanking me against his hard body as we silently watched the pool change around us. The moment I tried to move away, he tightened his hold, kissing my shoulder softly.

"Magic has beauty within it, doesn't it, Little One?" he whispered against my shoulder, kissing it softly, sending shocks of need shooting directly to my core.

"It's our ideal fantasy made true. Stolen from our darkest desires and brought to life with magic from the pool. The magic sensed our fantasy and created the perfect place for our coupling to occur."

"Then this must be your fantasy because you alone are mine, Aria," he murmured, causing my throat to tighten with emotion.

"You need to stop saying shit like that," I snapped, spinning around in his arms.

I pushed him, watching as he didn't budge even a whisper of an inch. He swallowed hard, slowly licking his lips before catching his bottom one between his teeth.

"You're beautiful when you're angry. You are beautiful all the time, but more so when the anger ignites within you. Your eyes glow from within, and I need to feel you burning against me when they shine so brightly. When you find something that excites you, you light up with pleasure. History intrigues you, and you love to learn, which helps you adapt to your surroundings surprisingly fast."

"Shut up," I swallowed past the lump growing in my

throat at the pain his words caused.

"Your excitement creates the same feeling within others, even me. When you want fucked, you don't light up. Your spine arches, your pretty eyes narrow on your prey, and your sex exudes this scent making everything within me that is male, need to own every inch of you that is woman. The moment your spine arches, and your hips part for mounting, my heart races. When that happens, I fight against every male urge to prevent me from taking you, because that is a line I won't cross. I won't force you to fuck me. Not even when I know we both want and need it more than the air that fills our lungs."

I swallowed, and tears swam in my vision as I glared at him. "Pretty much all of that goes into the aforementioned shit that you need to stop saying. I am your enemy. One you intend to use as a weapon against my people. You don't get to tell me I am anything but that anymore. You kiss me like I'm worth kissing, and then you turn around and make me feel as if I should be ashamed for the blood that runs in my veins. You confuse me on purpose to disorientate me, and it works because I could fall in love with you, and that would be a fucking disaster because you couldn't ever return that love. I would be your whore. One you fucked when you wanted and then wielded as a weapon in the next moment before the sweat has even cooled from our flesh." I swallowed past the thickness the words created as my throat constricted. He didn't argue it, and I had known he wouldn't. Our relationship wasn't complicated; it was doomed.

"Let's just keep it easy, King Karnavious. You're the king of the army that plans to murder everyone

I love, and I'm the one bitch who intends to stand in your way of accomplishing that feat at any cost. That's much simpler than adding messy emotions into, isn't it? It should be simple for you to remember who and what I am, since you never fail to remind me as a punishment for when you're kind to me."

"You think because I'm your enemy that I don't think you're one of the most beautiful creatures I have ever met? Enemies can be lovers, and they can want one another, Aria. Chemistry doesn't care which side of a war you are on. You and me, we have chemistry in spades. I want you, and I'm not afraid to admit it, not to you or me, and I know you want me. It doesn't need to be complicated."

"No, but when you let your guard down, and you're gentle with me, I get treated like shit because you punish yourself for letting it happen. That isn't my fault, and I don't deserve to be your target when it happens. If we stay enemies, it's so much easier than getting whiplash! Besides, eventually, I will meet someone else. I will fall in love, and this thing between us, it will just fall away and be meaningless."

"It's cute that you think you're ever going to be with anyone else, Aria," Knox growled with a low rattle, causing me to step back while he prowled forward in the water. His jaw clenched, twitching with unstated anger while he hunted me in the pool.

"I'm going to escape you, eventually. You can never love me, and I deserve to know what it feels like to be loved. I deserve to have someone look at me as if I am the moon and sun in their sky. I deserve to have someone willing to look past my flaws and see my strengths and weaknesses, accepting me for who I am." My ass touched against the pool's side, and he leaned over, boxing me in as his hands gripped the edge.

"You won't ever escape, Aria. *Ever.* I will cherish you and protect you, even from your own foolishness, when needed. Do you think any other male will willingly touch you now that I have claimed you? They'd have to first issue a challenge to me, and no one anywhere in this world would dare challenge me openly to battle. I am the fucking alpha they fear. I am absolute power, and I kill without hesitation. Those who have tried to oppose me are dead and have fed my crows with their rotting corpses."

Power sizzled over me, causing my flesh to tingle. It was a warning, and no matter how much I tried to ignore it, Knox wasn't allowing me to. His cerulean-colored eyes studied my reaction to the power he released, smirking as my spine arched, and my eyes grew hooded.

I was so screwed.

It was an outright battle of willpower, and mine was slowly slipping away.

Luckily, every time Knox opened his mouth, he inserted his foot.

It would be the one thing saving me from ending up impaled on his really nice, thick cock.

My creature, she was on his side.

His creature wanted what mine wanted.

Knox wanted me.

I was the odd man out in the situation.

Just freaking great.

Chapter Fifty-One

My gaze slid from Knox's sea-blue depths to the skin on my belly as twin ravens moved around my waist, turning their heads to peer up at me with matching blue eyes. I gasped as they pulled away from my skin, returning to his sides before opening their mouths and spreading their wings wide, posed for flight.

My heart thundered in my chest, staring into Knox's eyes as the reality of their presence sent me reeling. He'd placed his ravens on me without my knowledge. How? When? His lips curved into a cocky grin while he studied the panic rushing through me.

"You were never alone in my world. You think I wasn't aware of when you slept, when you hungered or touched that needy cunt trying to get off. I felt your half-assed efforts to relieve that never-ending ache between your thighs. You weren't alone. I stood over you as you slept one time, pushing the hair away from your pretty face before I kissed your forehead, and you never even realized I was there." He lifted his hand, cupping my breast before his fingers found my hardened nipple, pinching it until I cried out. His other hand snaked around my neck, cradling my head as his fingers twined through my hair, yanking it back to brush his lips against mine.

"You're a bastard," I hissed, unable to move from his hold, and uncertain I wanted to.

"Yeah, I am. I never pretended to be anything other than a cold-hearted bastard from the first moment I met you. Do you know why I was in Haven Falls, Aria? The council sent me, that's true, but I planned to force your line to return, and I waited for you to come to me. The first time I set eyes on you, I couldn't look away. You were the most beautiful thing I'd ever seen in my entire life. I had to force myself to hold up the appearance, and I couldn't manage it because all I wanted to do was get closer to you, and learn you explicitly." His mouth slid over the erratic pulse in my throat, chuckling huskily. His teeth nipped the skin, and I moaned loudly, unable to stop the noise of need that escaped.

"I walked into Haven Falls, knowing that one of the Hecate women would be powerful enough to become the new high queen." His mouth brushed over my ear, nipping at the delicate lobe as he growled roughly. "I found her, except she turned out to be this ethereal, beautiful little spitfire who rattled and purred. Her scent drove me insane with need, and every part of her called to every part of me. It was supposed to be easy. Walk into your life, end it, and force the rest of your family to return so I could murder them on my land. I changed gears after meeting you. I have wanted no one or needed anything as much as I do you, Aria Hecate."

"But I am your enemy."

"But you're my fucking enemy. So the king walked in, and he took their queen. Checkmate," he chuckled, releasing his hold on me to cup my cheeks between his large hands while searching my eyes. "And now she's mine, and I took their strongest weapon for my own needs. Selfish? Absolutely. Does it change the fact that I want you? No, because war doesn't care what we want, or ask what we need. This thing happening here, it's bigger than either one of us. There are too many lives that depend on me to win this war, and I can't allow a pretty face or a beautiful woman to sway me away from my course."

"And when your people kill me? Will you mourn me and add me to your list of ghosts? Or will I just be another dead witch you celebrate? Because that is what is going to happen, and I am not willing to be added to either of those things for you," I snapped harshly, hating that no matter how much I lied to myself, I wanted him too.

I wanted him, and it changed nothing. I felt helpless and lost without him, and yet with him, it still wouldn't change anything. He'd set a course, and he was one hell of a navigator. Nothing we did would change the war or prevent what was coming.

"I gave the order that you weren't to be touched before you ever stepped foot into my camp, Aria. You're mine, and I protect what is mine. The guard who overstepped was punished harshly and relieved of his post. I handled him and made an example of him to ensure you aren't touched again."

"You're delusional and prideful. That order failed, and you weren't there to protect me. You couldn't even see past your anger to notice that they hurt me. You have allowed your grief to consume you. It has painted your vision, blinding you against reality. I almost died, and you didn't even notice me. How long before it happens again? How long before one of your people finally achieves the goal of ending my life?" I demanded.

"It won't happen again, nor will I leave you unguarded."

"You assume I won't escape, but I will. I'm not some weak-minded woman that you can flex your pecs at and melt my brain cells. I *will* escape you, Knox. When I do, I will find someone who loves me and isn't afraid of you. Do you even know what the difference between love and lust is?" I asked. When his eyes searched my face, I laughed before leaning over, pulling him closer to me. I kissed him hungrily, devouring him until his rattle sounded, and mine echoed the noise perfectly. Pulling away, I took in the hunger burning in his stare. "That's me wanting to fuck you," I clarified.

My eyes lowered to his mouth, watching the tight line form. I wrapped my legs around him, pulling him close, brushing my fingertips over his cheeks. I allowed him an unguarded look at me, peering up with my feelings exposed.

"This is the part of me you will never know." I smiled brightly, letting him see me with my shields down before I leaned closer, pressing against his mouth as I gave him everything.

I kissed him so hard and so softly that even I was

lost in the kiss's intensity as my hands slid through his hair. Both of us tried to get closer to one another as he purred, and I echoed the sound with a deep, soothing tone that bespoke of soft kisses and heated embraces. Savoring the last of the kiss, I pushed him away with everything I had left within me.

"That is what I will give to the man I love. See the difference? One is me needing to be fucked. The other is my bare soul, open without fear or needing protection from the man I love, someone who will give me their love in return. There's a huge difference."

I slipped from the rocks, splashing into the pool, as I paddled away from him. He silently watched me; his emotions so violently confused that I couldn't stop the smile that curved my lips. I celebrated the small victory before it dropped, and I turned toward the deadly rattle escaping his chest.

"You kiss anyone else like that, and I'll fuck you on their corpse after I've ripped their spine out through their fucking throat, Aria Primrose." His eyes darkened to black with the warning. I slowly waded backward toward the waterfall.

Knox's expression turned sinister as something deadly studied me through his eyes, awoken by my threat. His gaze slid over my body, raw, naked desire burning in his smoldering depths.

"Get your naughty little ass over here before I remind you who I am, and why I'm the fucking King."

Chapter Fifty-Two

I stared at Knox's outstretched hand as if it were a viper. Frowning, I expelled the air from my lungs as I made my way to him. He watched me, lowering his eyes to the clear water that exposed every single part of me to his heated, ravenous gaze. When I neared him, he turned toward the pool's side, grabbing a bottle out of the bag before meeting me halfway.

"Turn around, woman," he ordered.

I narrowed my eyes at the command in his voice, sliding them to the bottle he held. He waited, watching me decide if I was going to argue or not. I wanted to say that it wasn't smart or something we should do.

The pool's magic was settling in and driving the need to have him inside of me to a painful ache that had my thighs clenching tightly.

A smarter woman would have argued the stupidity of what we were doing, but Knox wouldn't hear anything

I said. He'd used the tone that brokered no argument. I could state the reasons why I shouldn't allow him near me until I was blue in the face, but it wouldn't change his mind.

He started to argue when I refused to turn around, but I rolled my eyes. The man had my heart hammering painfully against my ribcage. The ravens within my belly were fighting for freedom, and the heated look in his stare told me he felt the magic at work.

I opened my mouth to speak, and Knox opened the bottle. A soft smile played on his lips the moment the scent lingered between us. I turned away from him, inhaling the rose-scented shampoo deeply. He lathered his hands before tossing it back toward the bag.

"Did you steal my shampoo, King Karnavious?" I questioned, sucking my bottom lip between my teeth to still the smile that was spreading.

"No. I had some commissioned for when I captured you. I brought it with me, knowing that once I had you, I would want you to smell as you had when we first met. I find the scent soothing and beautiful. I like it on you almost as much as I enjoy your cunt's scent during your heat. Although, together, they make you irresistibility delicious smelling."

I snorted, shaking my head at his reply. He collected my waist-length hair, working the blissful-scented shampoo into it before reaching my scalp. His fingers were heaven, massaging the soap into my hair, forcing me to moan at the skillful way he kneaded my scalp.

He'd done it before, obviously, and that knowledge created an ache in my chest that didn't sit well with me.

"It was a little presumptuous to assume you would catch me, wasn't it?" I asked, and his deep chuckle made my hackles rise. He abruptly shoved me beneath the water, and I shot back up, sputtering. "Dick move," I said, coughing while he inspected my hair for any remaining soap.

"There was no chance of me not capturing you, Aria. Your scent lured me to you, and the idea of you unprotected in a world that enjoys harming pretty things didn't sit well with me or my beast. You're not pretty," he stated, causing my eyes to narrow on him. "You're fucking gorgeous. I won't allow them to alter that beautiful soul or mind of yours, not even a little."

"You think my mind is beautiful?" I countered, studying the way he watched me. He didn't open up about his feelings for me easily or often.

It was several moments before Knox spoke again, and yet he held a guarded look in his eyes when he did. He studied me, sucking on his bottom lip before releasing it, nodding slowly.

"You're highly intelligent where it counts. Naïve on a few things, like being with someone for sex," he pointed out, carefully choosing his words. "You think the act of having sex should mean something deeper, and while it isn't wrong, it is naïve. It's not something people here consider when indulging in the needs of their baser urges or bodies. Your strength is in the way you calculate and plot your battles before you ever engage. That's something rare, and not many can do it and be five steps ahead of their enemies.

"I plan things, knowing every misstep that can

happen along the path I choose. It took me countless losses and over two hundred years to master the precariousness of war, yet you make it look easy. You have a softness for the weak and a need to protect them against what you feel is wrong. They're your weakness, and you make it easy to use them against you because you wear your bleeding heart on your sleeve.

"You know they're your weakness, and so you hide them to protect them while placing your own life on the line instead of theirs. That's because you're intelligent. Your mind takes a puzzle and looks at it from every angle, seeing it from both sides before you process how you feel about the situation. Most men take lifetimes to accomplish that ability, let alone use the findings to create a solution for both sides. You were born to be a queen."

"I won't ever be a queen," I snorted.

"You will be one day, but you will never rule. You will be the face for the people, and I will be the one who rules through you."

"So you'll marry me and rule through me? You'd need my permission because of my bloodline, and that isn't something I'd ever agree to do. Besides, Aria, Queen of Norvalla, and Queen of Vãkya doesn't seem to have the same ring to it, now does it?" I glared at him, studying the way his jaw tensed at the idea of marrying me.

"I won't marry again, Aria. There's also the fact that you could never sit on the throne to Norvalla. I wouldn't allow it."

"I wouldn't want to be your queen anyway," I

supplied thickly, watching the tic in his jaw, pulsing and straining at my words. "Nor will I steal the throne from Aurora. She will sit upon the throne, as is her right as the oldest Hecate witch."

"Aurora wouldn't ascend, Aria. You know it as well as I do, that won't happen. She's weak of mind and too kindhearted ever to rule. She abandoned the Nine Realms once already because of fear of opposition, and she runs when scared. Her siblings are all gone, and Hecate can't rise without a host from a direct descendant. Aurora isn't strong enough for her mother to use. Your sister Sabine, she wants the throne, but she's weak too. The rest are powerful, but they're followers. You were created to lead armies into battle and built to savage those who oppose your path to the throne.

"I wasn't certain it was you who would take the crown at first. At least not until you attacked Bekkah. Three things rule the High Queen of Witches — the need to protect and defend *her* people who are too weak to manage on their own. The ability to lead *her* armies, and the power to destroy realms at *her* discretion and desire," he snorted while studying the way I watched him silently. "You don't need an army, but if you had one, they'd follow your pretty little ass into battle and die to protect you, Aria. You already feel the need to protect those who are weaker than you, and you also took power from the Nine Realms, which required an actual goddess to place it there. The only thing you're missing is your crown and throne."

"And apparently, whatever magic mushrooms you ingested to buy the drivel coming out of your mouth. I've killed more witches than I care to admit since entering this shit-hole you love so much. They've tried to feed me to monsters and drugged me to give to men to breed my bloodline by force. I've been beaten, abused, and chased since the moment I got here. You think I want to rule a place like that? I told you I would clean my house, but once that is done, so am I. I'll slip away, find a charming man who stares at me like I'm the answer to his universe. I'll have a few kids, and live a long, boring life with him while we watch our children grow into nice, respectful adults who don't run a reign of terror onto the Nine Realms."

"You couldn't be boring if you tried, woman. You'd eat a *nice, boring* male for a snack. Hell, you'd probably even eat his young while he watched, just to prove you weren't his bitch."

I opened my mouth before snapping it closed. Knox smiled wickedly while I searched for the words to shoot back at him, knowing he'd just pegged me right in the ass. I bristled as his eyes sparkled with victory.

"Why do you have to piss on my dreams?"

"I'd piss circles around you if it got my point across. You're mine. End of discussion. There's no ending here that doesn't result in you as mine, Aria." He splashed me with water, and I spluttered, lifting my hand and slapping water back at him.

He opened his mouth, smiling, and my lips mirrored his. Knox splashed the water back at me, and I repeated it until I was outright laughing as he did the same. I lifted my hand to do it again, but he vanished.

Peering around, I tried to sense him but couldn't. I closed my eyes, seeing if the little magic I held could pinpoint his location, but a hand touched my face, and I looked up, finding him watching me intently before he took me down into the water.

Sputtering, I came to the surface, looking around for Knox, and when I found him a few feet from me, I zipped with inhuman speed to catch him. Missing Knox completely, I ended up slapping my entire body into the water, coming up choking.

I turned slowly, finding him watching me. I launched myself at him before he could move, and it sent us sailing beneath the waterfall that pelted us with water that felt more like bullets. I yelped, and Knox grabbed me, protecting me as he took us to the other side of the waterfall.

The waterfall hurt a lot more than movies or TV shows ever made it appear. I laughed, touching my head while Knox watched me, smiling as his eyes sparkled with laughter. My breath caught in my lungs at the sight of his unguarded smile that lit his eyes with a playfulness that struck me stupid.

Knox unguarded was dangerous because there was a side to him that was mischievous and playful that called to the woman in me. Yes, his masculinity spoke to my vagina through a direct line, but this side of him disarmed me and left me without defenses.

"Well, that wasn't romantic like the movies play it out to be," I murmured, dispelling the moment that had left me uncertain how to proceed. "I can officially add flirting to the list of things I am not good at."

"Are you trying to flirt with me?" he asked huskily, tilting my chin. Heat pooled in my center at the look shining in his eyes. Knox, vulnerable and playfully sexy, was lethal to my senses. His smile made him appear younger, carefree, and his eyes shone with humor as his mouth lowered to mine, brushing against it softly while still holding my chin.

His kiss was devastating, causing my eyes to close against his assault against my senses. He wrapped his arms around me, lowering them to grab behind my thighs, lifting me against him.

Knox's tongue found mine, and need tore through us. My fingers trailed through his hair, holding him against my mouth while we devoured one another, giving in to the pool's magic.

I felt Knox against my opening and didn't fight him as he pulled away from the kiss, staring at me. He searched my eyes for permission, smiling roguishly when he discovered it. Power ripped through the cave we'd entered, and we turned to take in the rows of skulls that lined the walls.

"Your vacation home?" I swallowed, noting the pentagrams marking their skulls.

"No." Knox growled as he readjusted himself away from my wanton flesh. I shivered and almost argued about him not giving us what we both wanted and needed. "That's a tomb," he disclosed.

"So it is," I agreed, slipping into the water.

"Don't move, woman," he ordered, diving beneath the waterfall.

I let my attention return to the wall of skulls, standing waist-deep in the pool. Power rippled beside me, and I turned, finding a man with silver hair and light turquoise eyes beside me. His eyes were a softer blue than the others I'd met like him.

He swallowed, dropping his gaze the length of my body. Scrubbing his hand down his face, he lifted his fingers to snap them together.

I shivered, peering down at the white dress that appeared on my body, soaked from standing in the healing pool. The man reached down and grabbed my hand as he smiled.

"Can you feel that?" His watchful eyes moved over my face. "You do, little one."

"Who are you?" I asked softly, stepping back as he peered over his shoulder. The man vanished the moment Knox returned, pausing and lifting his nose to scent the air.

I looked down at my naked body, frowning. What the hell? The dress had vanished with the male, and now I was left with a very suspicious Knox. My gaze slid toward the door of the tomb, held closed with magic.

"Do you feel that?" I asked, swallowing the worry that slithered through me, knowing the silver-haired male was still here, watching me. I could feel his gaze heavy on my nape while Knox looked around, as if he, too, sensed the other male.

"Come here." Knox grabbed me, kissing me hard and fast before his lips brushed over the mark on my shoulder, growling before his rattle sounded. My spine arched while his hand snaked around, running his fingers over my belly. Teeth scraped my shoulder, and I moaned at the feel of him pressing against my ass. "Why the fuck do I smell male?"

"Because you're here?" I squeaked and felt the vibration from his laughter.

"I know my scent, and it isn't the one I smell on your flesh, woman. Do you think me stupid?" he asked, sliding his fingers through my hair, turning me toward him.

I felt the flicker of magic and lifted my stare to the door that buzzed with power. Walking closer, I paused in the darkness, noting the glowing blue light illuminating the markings on the skulls and the door.

Glowing runes were carved above the door, written in the language of the elders. Older than any language the world knew or could decipher. I doubted even older-than-dirt Knox could read the runes.

"What the hell is this place?" I whispered into the cavern, feeling Knox at my back as I slowly exited the pool.

He yanked me back toward him, turning me to face him as he placed a soft, delicate blue dress over my body. Knox righted it over my thin frame, then lifted my face to his while he searched my eyes.

"We're not done discussing the dick in this room."

"I only sense one," I smirked, lowering my attention to him pointedly. "Of course, when he's in the room, he's all I sense." I swallowed, blinking at the throaty voice that had escaped.

"Keep it that way, Little Lamb," Knox smirked,

bringing my mouth against his with a hand pressed against the back of my neck. His tongue swiped my lips, demanding access, which I gave, moaning against the dominating male who turned me inside out, uncaring that the other male watched from the shadows.

Knox's hands slid down my back, cupping beneath my knees before he lifted me against him, striding up the stairs that led down into the pool. The moment my feet touched the ground, a hissing noise sounded.

I shivered, spinning to look at the wall of skulls that turned before the jaws opened and the hissing noise grew into an ear-piercing shrill. The door clicked and then slid up into the top of the cave.

Air escaped the door, blowing my hair behind me. Power radiated from the opening, slithering over my flesh until a violent shudder rushed through me. I stepped closer. Fear wrapped around my throat and everything within me said to turn back and leave now. Knox was following me, taking in the freaky skulls that continued hissing until we'd passed through the doorway. My spine snapped to attention at what my eyes told me I was seeing.

"Holy shit," I whispered.

Chapter Fifty-Three

The entire antechamber held hundreds of crystal pillars and crystalline stalagmites. The huge stalactites on the ceiling were shaped like icicles, with colorful drops of liquid dripping from their tips. The droplets collected into a stream of water that rushed through the chamber, moving deeper into the cavern. Well, some of the water did. My eyes followed what appeared like droplets of blood that dripped, only to float in the air before it shot up toward the stalactites and vanished.

Large stalagmites glowed along the path, lighting the way deeper into the cave. The walls were covered in writing, and white-blue words pulsed eerily to a beat that made my blood sing to hear the words. It sounded like a lullaby, seducing me, pulling me further into the cave.

Knox grabbed my arm and then hissed as power rushed through the cave as if it would attack him. I reached for his hand, threading my fingers through his, peering over my shoulder to give him a dreamy smile.

He was so beautiful. My lips curved into a sultry grin, and I turned toward Knox, humming to the music. He narrowed his sea-blue eyes, holding mine captive as his lips moved, yet I couldn't hear words over the cave's song.

I laughed, pulling Knox to me and lifting on my toes to claim his lips as he rattled deep from his chest. My rattle echoed his with approval as I cupped his cock, growling ravenously at finding it erect and ready to destroy me with the euphoria he offered.

"I want to fuck you," I admitted, watching his eyes burn with a matching fire that threatened to consume us to nothing more than ashes.

"You're glowing, woman."

"With the need to be fucked hard, fast, and brutally," I murmured thickly, the words coming out sexy and wantonly. "I want you inside me. I want to feel you in my soul, touching every single piece of me until there is no more me without you." I watched the tic in his jaw, noting his tongue jutting out to swipe over his lips at my words.

I released my scent, watching the muscles of his stomach tense with his own need. I smiled, leaning closer to kiss the words on his ribs, flicking his nipple with my tongue as he hissed loudly. His eyes began glowing with a vibrant color of the high seas amidst a raging storm. I held his erection in my hand, feeling it jerk as my hungry mouth craved to taste the saltiness of his cock against my tongue.

"Something is wrong, Little One." Knox's tone mixed with worry as lust grazed over my flesh, tightening around my nipples to thump against my clit painfully.

"You're not in me. That's what is wrong, My Love," I whispered, watching his attention move from me to slide through the cave. When he didn't free his cock, I pouted, which made his lips curve up at the corners.

"Obviously, something is really wrong, Aria. You're pouting over me, not throwing you onto the ground and fucking that dripping cunt that I can smell luring me. That's not you." Knox grabbed me, pulling me against him as my throat tightened. He pushed my legs apart and moved his hand to the hem of my skirt, lifting it to slide his fingers through the arousal flooding my sex. "Bloody hell, woman," he groaned, finding my core soaked with the need for him to drink me, lapping with his talented tongue against the desire threatening to consume me. "You need to pull it back before I lose control. Do you understand me?" I rolled my eyes, stepping away from him to move deeper into the cavernous underground room.

At the entrance, I turned to look at Knox, watching him suck his fingers clean with a smile on his generous mouth. My pulse spiked before sliding to the midnight-colored eyes that sparkled with fiery embers burning in their depths.

"Do I taste good, Monster?" I whispered, and he smiled around the finger.

"You taste like sin and trouble. I want to eat you until you scream my name, begging me for mercy. I fucking crave you, Little One. I crave the need to wreck you, to taste you when you come against my lips. I crave the sound of your cries as you come so violently on my cock it becomes painful because your body needs me deeper, knowing you don't even understand why. I crave to fuck that fight out of you, to fuck the happiness you felt with us buried deeply within your tight cunt when my creature and me made you a woman."

My body grew flushed with need, and I purred huskily for the beast who stepped forward, sliding his hands over my hips before lifting me against him. I wrapped my legs around his waist and pushed my fingers through his hair until the song stopped, swallowing past the heaviness in my head.

"Can you hear me?" Knox asked, and I nodded while blinking rapidly. "Something is wrong."

"Obviously, but this is sort of hot," I admitted, watching his eyes turn back to the startling blue that indicated he'd tamed his monster for the moment.

"Honestly, so was your dirty mouth telling me how much you wanted me buried inside your tight body. It doesn't change that something is making you ravenously needy, woman."

I swallowed audibly, and the dimple in his cheek appeared. I wanted to kiss his dimple, to memorize it with the look of happiness burning in his pretty oceanic depths that promised to swallow me beneath the storm churning in them.

Instead, I slid down his body, narrowing my eyes on the wall. "It's the sounds creating the song in the cavern. It's a spell of some sort, a lullaby that calls to me. It made me shed my inhibitions and lower my guard. It's dangerous to hear it so close to you," I admitted, dropping my stare from the fire raging in his eyes.

"Why? Because it made you want to fuck me?" he asked softly.

"That's exactly why," I admitted, moving away from him and down a staircase that led into the darkening cave.

The deeper we walked, the more the crystals pulsed on the ceiling and floor of the cave. As the cave grew wider, it forced us to follow a set of narrow stairs that led down until we reached water once more.

The water turned to the same color as the outside pool, sea blue of the deepest, wildest depths that made me think of Knox. Walking through a narrowed passage, we emerged in a large room that held an altar in the middle of a round platform. Around the platform's edges were five female sculptures, each one clutching a colored sphere in a raised hand. The other hand of each statue pointed toward the middle of the platform as if something had once been there.

Each of the five different-colored spheres represented the five elements.

Amethyst for lightning.

Carnelian for fire.

Moss agate for earth.

Aquamarine for water.

White fluorite for air.

Around the edge of the platform was apophyllite that represented the ether.

Swallowing hard, I moved closer to the altar as the stones ignited, and the room came to life. The air was thick with the scent of herbs and sage. I sucked my lip between my teeth, worrying it as I moved onto the platform.

Turning back, I found Knox slamming his hands against a barrier that was glowing an eerie color of blue, preventing him from entering the chamber. His mouth opened and closed, and yet I couldn't make out his words.

I started toward Knox, but scrapping sounded behind me. I stepped back as more silver-haired men leaped onto the platform, observing as it turned, and the crystals sent rainbow prisms onto the floor. The moment each crystal lined up with their correlating statue, the floor opened, and something rose from beneath it.

"I told you she could do it," one of the men snorted.

My eyes lifted to find the male with the softer blue eyes studying me. Unlike the others, there was an intensity in his stare that caused me to become unsettled. His lips tipped up in the corners like he'd felt what his gaze did to me. He was strikingly handsome with a ruggedness that spoke of hard lines and jagged edges. His shirt failed to hide the strength of his body, which held my stare hostage.

He rattled low, and my eyes widened at the sound. My body jerked, and I slowly blinked, lowering my eyes from the power of his rattle while it rushed through me. A louder rattle sounded behind me, forcing my eyes toward Knox and his men.

Knox looked murderous, his eyes staring past me to the man who had rattled. Soft turquoise eyes met and held his in challenge, and I exhaled, moving my attention away from the pissing contest to where a body was revealed.

"That can't be good," I muttered, and then gasped as someone grabbed both of my hands, and the men started chanting. Power rushed through the room, and my body burned from the pressure of it pulsing and throbbing through me.

The magic felt right.

It felt like home. I whimpered, opening my eyes to find the male watching me through heavily hooded eyes. He smiled, exposing razor-sharp fangs that caused my body to clench with anticipation. The magic stopped, and the men supported my weight when my legs threatened to give out.

"Be careful, young one," the man beside me stated, smiling. "It drained your magic to release her from the binding spell."

"You might want to tell the pretty little princess what is about to happen," the male opposite of me said, his eyes still sliding over my face.

I peered at the motionless form before me. The woman had silver hair, brushed to a fine sheen that glittered in the light of the crystals, creating a halo around her head. Her dress was aquamarine and didn't carry a single wrinkle. I moved to get a closer look, but the men held firm, refusing to release their hold.

"Eva is about to wake up, and she's going to attack you," the male beside me announced, as if he'd told me it looked like it would rain soon. "She'll be confused, and since you're the only female present, she will test you. Don't let her win, or your life will be forfeited. If you cannot beat her than your existence is unneeded."

"Excuse me? It sounded like you just said that you made me wake her up, freeing her to kick my ass. So, I must have heard wrong."

"Hecate trapped Eva here, luring her with the song of magic. It made Eva think her true mate was within the tomb, that the other half of her flame burned within it. Once Eva was inside, Hecate drained her power and left her without magic. The fact that you carry both royal bloodlines allowed you to free her from the spell that held her in stasis."

"Yeah, no. Not happening." I peered across from me, watching the male who oozed sexual tension toward me in spades.

"I've watched you, sweet Aria," he said softly. "You're more advanced and stronger than Eva. All you have to do is fight her until she tires, and you'll survive. You can do that. Your father created you for war; to wage it and win. You're an alpha, and you know it. Let your pretty monster out to play. I know she wants to come out."

"You've watched me?" I asked.

"I've watched you do many things." He dragged his stare down my body, which caused an angry rattle to sound behind me. "You are a rarity, and a beauty unmatched comes from within you. Yet you throw it away on a man who can never return that fire. He may see your fire, but he will never taste your flames."

"But, you would?" I snorted. "This is insane. I'm gone. It was so nice for you to lure me here. I'd say it's been fun, but it really wasn't. If you intend to use me as well, do me a favor and fuck off," I growled, moving to leave the platform when a rattle sounded that made the hair on my nape rise.

"Good morning, Eva," the seductive male said, watching the woman rise into a crouching position on the altar. "This is Aria, and I intend to mate with her. Be gentle with Aria, for she is untrained, and stubbornly prideful."

I wasn't sure what horrified me more, that the woman with the matching soft turquoise eyes had zeroed in on me, or that the male had dropped the mate shit like it was already decided. What the hell was it with the men in this hellish world?

The woman rattled again, and everything within me went on high alert. I watched the men move away from Sleeping Beauty, who bared serrated teeth and surprisingly long claws. She crawled to the back of the altar and rattled again.

I felt my mind switching, and yet it didn't fully send me to the backseat as it normally did when my creature took control. I leaped onto the altar, crouching to mirror her pose. My chest vibrated, and my mouth opened, releasing a rattle that sounded through the cavern, echoing off the walls as I arched my spine. I felt twitching within my body as things attached to my spine itched to be freed from my flesh.

"I am Eva," she hissed.

"I am me, and you are threatening my host," the creature snarled, using my lips to speak. "No one touches my Aria. Not without having a really nice cock for me to use."

"You're not even combined fully yet," Eva mused, and when my hand lifted, and the middle digit rose, she snapped. "I'm going to rip your head off," she snarled.

"You can try, but I don't think you have the tits to do it," I shot back, smiling coldly as the female's eyes became solid turquoise. "Shoulders back, tits out, and let's fuck some shit up, Creature."

Chapter Fifty-Four

The woman lunged, and I barely avoided colliding with her. Her body smashed into one figurine, sending the statue and the crystal into the water. My eyes slid to Knox, finding him and his men watching me.

I jumped from the altar, slowly moving around the woman toward them. My creature itched to fight, but she had also done the math of how many men were in the room with us, recognizing that those wanting us alive were on the other side of a barrier.

Eva rattled, and I echoed it. I could feel my creature helping me from within, directing me through the knee-deep water.

She lunged, and I flipped into the air, landing on Eva's shoulders. Slamming my body over hers, I sent her crashing into the barrier that sizzled and popped. Eva howled an ear-piercing scream that had my hands coming up to protect my ears.

I danced away from her and the barrier, noting her charred skin from touching it. Knox, on the other hand, had his hands pressed firmly against it. His eyes studied my movements, but there was anger in his stare that worried me.

He thought I had led him here. Eva moved in at an inhuman speed, sending me sailing across the room to crash against the barrier.

I howled, jerking my skin away to find pieces of it still stuck to the shield. I growled from deep in my chest, slowly moving closer as I silenced the room, homing in on her and only her.

Eva moved again, and I jumped, kicking my leg up into the air with the weight of my body, sending her crashing against another statue. She stood, cracking her neck while staring at me.

"You're one of us," she snarled.

"No, I'm really not," I grunted, watching her head cock to the side while her eyes slid over me.

"Not entirely true. I hate liars," she jeered, zipping forward.

I used the same movement, crashing into her with my claws extended, my creature releasing them to cut through Eva's side before I reappeared on the other side. It was the first time my creature and I worked as one, and it seemed to be successful.

Eva moved again, and I lost her in the jetstream, peering around the cave's emptiness until she appeared before Knox, rattling.

Knox's eyes slid to obsidian, and I rattled, forcing him to peer over her shoulder. He smiled, cocking his head to the side as he purred for Eva. I silently studied the way he flirted, noting that Lore's mouth had dropped open, and Brander seemed just as floored that there were more females like me.

I purred low, deadly, watching as Eva turned just in time for me to hit the jetstream and shove her against the barrier, holding her there. My eyes held Knox's heated stare, and I rattled until his lips tightened, and his men struggled through the call.

Pain ripped through my stomach, and I snarled, slamming Eva against the barrier before I shot back, uncaring that my belly had her nail holes in it.

"You fucking bitch, fighting corpse of a hooker!" I leered, watching her eyes sparkle with amusement while she slowly strode forward.

She didn't attack. Instead, she lifted the dress over her head to reveal nothing beneath. Knox's eyes slid over her body, and I glared at him. She was flawlessly built, with large rounded breasts and hips that gave her the perfect hourglass figure.

Eva bent over, and I watched Knox and his men tilting their heads while they took in the goods. *Pigs.*

Eva lunged, and I slammed into her, punching and ramming nails into her torso, shredding it while she howled and cried out until she dropped to her knees. Instead of removing her head, I backed up until I was far enough away to see an attack coming.

When she flew out of the water, I stepped aside, allowing her momentum to send her body careening into the barrier with the projected force. She turned, glaring at me while I waited for her, calm, collected, and intending to shred her face off so Knox wouldn't think her prettier than me anymore.

Jealousy was a bitch, but then, so was I.

Eva flew at me, and I jumped before she reached me, appearing on the altar. The dress was offending my skin, forcing my attention to where it itched against my flesh. I reached down, lifting it over my head only to come face to face with Eva, whose hands lifted to my face.

"One of us is something more than she thinks." she offered, and I punched her in the stomach, hard. Eva coughed, choking on the dust in her stomach I'd just sent to her lungs. I flung my body up, perching on the statue as I built up a rattle, allowing it to escape until it demanded she bow. "She thinks she's the alpha. You're cute, Aria. I see why Aden wants to breed you. You're strong and fertile. But you're not the alpha to our kind."

"Are we done yet?" I asked, staring her down as my skin itched, and everything within me felt as if it wanted out. My teeth elongated, and my skin turned black at my fingertips, gradually spreading up my arms.

Eva slammed her foot into the statue, and I flipped backward, landing in the water as she landed in front of me, kicking me into the air before I found my footing. Her other foot lifted, smashing into my face before she turned her back, ripping my arm forward and sending me over her shoulder, directly into the barrier.

I slid down it, growling as I shot forward, slamming

my knuckles into her face, enjoying the crunch. I didn't stop hitting her, sending one punch after another until her head jerked back, and she vanished, appearing next to more silver-haired men who'd emerged from thin air.

Eva's bloodied face was still pretty, and Knox wasn't looking at me anymore. His eyes were on the men who helped Eva into a clean dress while I walked toward them.

"Enough. It is finished." Aden kept his eyes trained on my face.

"Because you say it is? You wanted me here to wake Eva up. You said Hecate placed her here. I want to know why."

"You're not ready for that answer."

"I didn't ask if I was or not. I'm tired of everyone knowing who and what I am, while I know nothing!"

Aden smiled, finally letting his eyes slide down my body with a hunger that sucked the air from my lungs. He vanished, and I spun, searching the room for him. Something grabbed me, and before I could argue or fight back, I was dressed, and Aden was standing where he'd been before he'd moved.

"When you're ready to know who you are, you will come to us. I look forward to that day, Aria," Aden said, bowing his head before they all vanished, leaving me standing alone in the cave.

My attention moved to Knox's men, who watched me through narrowed slits. Knox turned the moment Lore spoke, scrubbing his hand down his face at his words.

"I don't know where Eva went, but I want to go there! That was another like Aria. Right? Daddy needs one too! Knox, we have to follow them! She was hot, hot, hot!"

"Yes, she was." Knox held my eyes with something cold and deadly playing in them. "You led me here alone."

"I led you here?" I scoffed.

"You led me to a room filled with men, Aria. Your sweet words and needy flesh forced me to follow you. Who were they?"

"I don't know," I admitted. "They say I'm like them. But they're wrong."

"Are they though?" he asked.

"I'm much more advanced than they are."

The barrier dropped, and Knox's men zipped around the room at an inhuman speed. My heart pounded in my ears, but I remained still. They created wind with their sudden movements, and I knew they searched for the jetstream the others had used to vanish. I tilted my head to the side, brushing my fingers against my neck, feeling the soreness of the fight down to my soul.

I may be more advanced, but I lacked the training Eva had. She hadn't allowed outside influences to interrupt her thoughts, moving fast and without pause. Her hits were brutal and hard. Mine had probably seemed like love taps in comparison, but I'd known her every move. I'd calculated her actions, subtracted her thoughts, and met her head-on.

I sensed power sizzling against my back and felt Knox's fangs before they slid through my shoulder. He wrapped his hand around my stomach, while the other applied slight pressure to my throat as he growled against my flesh. We sank in the water, him marking me, and me unable to stay upright with the sheer pleasure his mouth sent rocking through me.

"You will tell me why they appear around you, Aria. He touched you, and that isn't something I will allow to happen again."

"You eye-fucked Eva, so we're even," I snapped, and he chuckled.

"She was pretty," he stated, and I snorted. "But you're mine, and she isn't. Now, let's get the fuck out of here. You've wasted enough of our time." He stood, pulling me with him to my feet.

"I wasted your time?" I watched his attention move back to me slowly. "I didn't ask you to bring me here. I didn't plan on releasing some magical creature from her stasis, either. You can go to Hell, King Karnavious, and take your ever-changing tone with you."

"Oh, Aria, we're already in Hell. Your family built it, and I'm just the asshole making it crumble to the ground. Funny, you think my tone changes, and yet you were just begging me to fill that tight cunt less than an hour ago," he growled, pushing his fingers against the wounds in my stomach. "Be a good girl and dunk your body under the water so that your wounds heal. It's a long walk back to camp, and I'm about to lick the attitude out of you."

"Lick?" I snorted, turning my head to watch the blood dripping down my shoulder.

"I'm about to eat your pussy until the only thing you can do is scream. Now dunk yourself in the fucking water, woman."

"Screw you," I growled, and a sinful smirk spread on Knox's generous lips.

"Leave us," he announced, prowling toward me.

Knox lowered his gaze down my frame and then nodded at the water. Rolling my eyes in annoyance, I dunked my body where it was scratched or bruised. Once the water touched the damaged tissue, it glowed while healing my body. I stood as his lips twisted into a sinful smirk.

"Sit on that boulder, now," he demanded, and I turned, peering over my shoulder before moving my attention back to him.

Knox was inches from me, causing my heart to thunder in my chest. I gradually stepped back, needing distance between us to think. He didn't allow it. Knox hunted me with an inferno burning in his gaze. He looked angry, yet there was something else in his eyes that swam just below the surface.

My legs bumped against something cold, and he caged my body in by placing his hands on either side of me. His mouth lowered, brushing against my throat while his silence unnerved me. His heated mouth moved over my throat, nipping the flesh as a soft moan escaped my lips.

Knox lifted me without warning, staring at me while something dark and dangerous passed behind his eyes. *Possessiveness*. His eyes promised me he fully intended to possess me and make sure I knew to whom I belonged.

"You looked at another man," he accused, pushing my legs apart before he settled between them.

"You did the same thing with Eva," I shot back.

"You think I want her, Aria?"

I swallowed, hating the tightening in my stomach at the idea of Knox wanting anyone else. I may not want him, but I didn't want him with anyone else, either. It was selfish and pathetic, but it was how I felt. His eyes searched mine, and the smile that spread over his face pissed me off.

"I hate you," I swallowed, gasping as his hands tightened on my thighs in warning.

"That's not nice, now is it?" Knox chuckled, his lips closing the distance between mine. "Now I'm going to have to torture you, Little Lamb. It seems you need reminding of whom you belong to."

Chapter Fifty-Five

Knox

Aria's eyes studied me while I drove her to a heightened state of fear and need. The subtle line between them was so thinly drawn that it was hard to decipher one from the other. Her eyes grew hooded, and I hadn't even fucking teased her yet.

My hand snaked up, wrapping around her throat to anchor her on the stone. When she reached up and touched it, her pretty blue eyes closed as a gasp of pleasure escaped her pouty lips that I wanted to taste.

Fuck if I didn't crave those lips against mine or around my cock. I enjoyed watching Aria's eyes fill with heat while I fucked that welcoming throat. Aria may be naïve in many things, but she knew what I liked, and she used it against me.

Her knowing tongue would draw swirls against my cock while that throat cradled the head, and within moments, she'd drain me and have me purring like a bitch. Not that I'd ever told her the effect it had on me when she'd done it in the mansion's basement in Haven Falls. No, Aria felt my pleasure and used it as a weapon to bring me to my knees, and fuck if I hadn't lost it and come in her tight canal while she drank me down.

My hand tightened, and her pupils dilated with pleasure. For something so delicate, she enjoyed being manhandled immensely, which turned me the fuck on. I applied pressure, inhaling the scent her body released for me and me alone. She was already drenched with need; her body ached to be taken hard and fast, just like she wanted it.

She enjoyed pain, even though she'd never fucking admit it out loud or to herself. Aria was built for savaging, walking the fine line between pleasure and pain with me. She enjoyed the intensity of the fight before fucking. It was why she fought so hard, battling against need and duty.

This slip of a girl had men pining to fuck her, toss her down and take what was mine. Fuck that. I could feel the male's eyes on us; smell his need as certain as he could scent her sex filling with arousal that belonged to me. Every fucking gods damned drop of her arousal was mine now.

"Who the fuck do you belong to?" I demanded, watching Aria's eyes open as the fight burned within her.

"Fuck you," she whispered, sucking that plump lip between her teeth to hide the sultry moan that fought to escape her tight throat.

Fuck that answer.

I lifted her thighs, watching her chest rise and fall with her breathing. I didn't strike, didn't pounce on the fact that I could smell her pussy filling with the need to be fucked. My nostrils flared, sucking in her erotic scent as deeply as I could get it.

"You want that other bitch? Go fuck her and leave me alone," Aria snapped, dropping her knees apart with a silent invitation. Her expressive eyes flared in challenge, and I wanted to remind her what it felt like to be stretched by me, beneath me, where she came alive and roared like a ravenous bitch in heat.

Aria hadn't even noticed she'd done it, opening her body to me for the taking. Her body wanted me, and so did she. She was fucking enraged when she thought I'd fucked Diana, thinking I'd stoop that low to fuck a parlor whore when I had her? Fuck that. Aria's pussy was the best I'd ever had or tasted, and I wasn't afraid to tell her either.

"You think I want her?"

"She's like us!" Aria snapped, and I heard it. Worry and fear etched in her voice, and it pissed me off. I hated her fucking family.

Hell, I hated Aria on most days. I hated that she thought she wasn't worthy or wanted for more than her fucking power. I'd made her believe it because I was a fucking prick. I'd put that idea in her pretty head, and I couldn't make myself remove it.

"And?" I demanded, and her eyes flicked to the side, hiding the pain that filled them while threatening tears I could smell in the air.

Lifting my hand, I cup her chin, bringing her eyes back to mine. "You think I'd want her when I have you?" I asked, searching her eyes, and finding the agony burning in them at feeling inadequate.

Aria did not understand how truly beautiful she really was. She was delicate and yet fierce. Her eyes didn't allow her to hide the emotions she felt. It drove me bat-shit-crazy, watching the lust pool within them. It drove me insane to see her mind working as her body heated, imagining us doing deliciously wicked things together.

I'd allowed her to ignore her needs, forcing myself to give her time to heal from the shit she'd endured since entering the Nine Realms. In doing so, she'd had time to believe the shit I'd told her. I fucking hated it, and yet I couldn't make myself correct it, no matter how much I knew I should.

"I don't care if you want her or not. That isn't my business," she responded, but there was insecurity burning in her tone.

I laughed soundlessly, gripping her nape before slamming my mouth against hers, kissing her hard enough to get my point across. Our teeth scraped against one another's in our need to get closer, deeper into the other's skin. We were like two storm fronts meeting and colliding against one another.

The sheer force and velocity of it caused us both to shudder with the need and desire that ripped through us, deep down into the creatures we carried. They dueled for superiority as much as we collided. They dug into one another, trying to learn the other in their primitive forms.

It made everything a capricious mess of emotions that none of us knew how to handle or process.

Aria's moan pulled at my balls. She made the most erotic, delicious noises when I touched or kissed her. Her screams and cries were my favorite song, and it was one I craved to hear play on repeat.

I heard her gasp, knowing she needed air, but I didn't fucking care. I couldn't get close enough, drink her in deep enough, or get enough of her to sate the never-ending need I felt growing for her.

She was like a drug through my system, one that I craved more than anything else. I fucking hated the need I felt, knowing it was the biggest betrayal to my family that hers had taken from me.

She pulled back, and I allowed it, letting her suck in air before my arm snaked around her, and my finger pushed into her cunt, groaning the moment it clenched and sucked ravenously around the single finger.

Her eyes dilated, her back arched with need while she rocked against my hand, pining for her release. Aria was my greedy little monster who didn't care how it looked when need took control. She fucked like she fought, and she fought fucking hard and without mercy.

"To whom do you belong, Aria?" I demanded, my air getting stuck in my throat at her needy moan that ripped from her lungs the moment I added another finger. Scissoring my fingers in her tight sheath, I watched her quiver with need. She tightened around them, sucking them deeper as her body chased the orgasm.

"No one!" she ground out through clenched teeth.

Aria's eyes locked with mine, oblivious to the other male watching me bring my girl to her release. He could fucking watch her come this once, see how she succumbed to my control and touch. Her pussy was already soaked with the need for my cock, and fuck if I didn't want to give her everything she needed at this moment, and that need was visceral.

"Wrong answer, pretty girl," I groaned, pulling my fingers out before slamming them in, harder and harder until she was gasping and meeting them with her need. My hand released her ass, slipping around her throat lazily, cutting off her airflow. "You're not coming until you admit to whom you belong to."

Her eyes held mine, and I felt her pussy clenching, tightening with her impending release. A moment before she could claim it, I pulled my fingers out, holding them against her pussy that was clasping air with need.

It was demanding to be fucked, yet I wouldn't cave to her cunt's sweet pleas. I wouldn't fuck her until she was crazed and wild with need. I wouldn't be fucking Aria until she was begging to be fucked, and her need was undeniable. I also wouldn't do it with the asshole watching me getting her sweet, tight pussy off.

"Knox, you bastard," she cried, her body tensing, clenching, and trembling with violent need.

"That's not the answer I want from you." I pushed her legs apart, dropping to my knees, lapping slowly around her drenched opening while she watched me.

It took everything within me not to grab her thighs and wrap my arms around them and bury my fucking cock in her cunt. I've craved the taste of the little bitch since the first lick in that library.

She'd come over my face, dripped down my chin, and I'd fucking loved every moment. I'd forced orgasm after orgasm to drain every single ounce of come and strength from her until she'd stopped fighting me to get away from the pleasure she'd endured.

Aria had roared her release in that library. I'd never wanted to fuck anyone more than I had her. I'd come in my fucking pants like some bitch instead of spreading her willing thighs and pounding into her haven that begged me to take what she so willingly offered. Fucking magic.

Her thighs clenched my head, and I chuckled huskily against her cunt. I lifted my eyes to lock with hers as I wrapped my arms around her thighs, holding her there for me to fuck her with my mouth. Her pussy was soaked, drenched for me already.

I dragged my tongue from one end to the other, feeling her trembling with need. Her body was so close to coming, so fucking responsive to me that I had to force my mouth away from her, waiting out the orgasm she'd been chasing.

"To whom do you belong, Aria?" I demanded again, craving to hear her whisper it in passion almost as much as I wanted the prick behind me to hear her scream it.

I'd given the bastard my back, a show of disrespect. I showed him I didn't fear him, nor did I care that he was behind me. It was the lowest form of not giving a fuck that a king could illustrate to another male. To turn your back on another warrior told them you weren't afraid of them, and that you didn't find them a worthy opponent. It was a show of disrespect.

I wasn't afraid of him, nor did I care that he witnessed Aria come for me because he didn't even exist in our world. He'd told her he wanted to mate her. Not keep her, not treasure her, just wanted to breed her needy womb.

Not that I'd said much better. I was a cold, unfeeling prick to Aria, unable to tell her how much I craved her.

"Please!" she screamed, her pussy clenching air, arousal dripping from it with her creature adding to it so she could take me in my true form. I fucking loved the taste of her arousal on my tongue, covering my lips.

"Say it, and I'll make you come so hard you'll paint my face with your orgasm," I chuckled, peering up at her through hooded eyes, turned on by my own fucking game.

Her silver hair was bathed in sweat from my denial to allow her release. Aria's eyes were fucking blown, her pupils fully dilated from lust. Rosy, pink nipples pressed against the thin dress she wore, begging to be nibbled.

My fingers trailed over her slick, wet opening, and her body released her heady scent in welcome for me and me alone. Her womb begged me to fill it, and fuck if I didn't want anything more than to oblige its desperate need to be coated in my release.

"Never!" she growled, and I smirked, hearing the challenge buried in her tone.

Standing, I cupped her face and peered into her eyes, sensing her creature watching me. I could feel her power threatening to unleash and take what her pretty shell denied her. She was so fucking close that I could taste the orgasm thick in the air between us.

"You want to bet?" I asked, pushing my fingers into her pussy, but only to the knuckles.

Her body jerked, tightening, and her eyes rolled back as the sexiest noise I'd ever heard in my entire life escaped her throat. The sound was half-moan, half-purr, and so fucking filled with her wanton need that my balls sucked into my stomach, tightening with the need to spill my seed.

I kissed her hard, so fucking hard that we both panted and gasped for air when I pulled away. My knuckles ran over her opening, and I made sure to bump her clit, watching her eyes widening while she lost the fight to me.

"Admit it to you and me, woman. We're the only ones here who will hear it," I murmured, flicking her clit several times, teasing her with the need to watch the orgasm unravel her.

When Aria came, it was the rawest, intense show of pleasure and pain mixed together. Her body shuddered, writhed, and her pussy got wet with her arousal until my cock was soaked with it. Her back arched, and her nipples got so fucking hard that my teeth fucking hurt with the need to bite them. Best of all? When she came, she roared my fucking name like I was the only male she'd ever wanted or needed. Like in her world, I was the only male who would ever fucking matter.

However, she wasn't getting it easy this time. She needed to learn to listen, to be obedient, and take commands. Aria was wild and unwilling even to meet me halfway. She challenged me; stubbornly ignored the need we both felt, and now she had more motherfuckers trying to claim her enchanting fucking pussy.

"You want to come for me, pretty girl? Tell me to whom you fucking belong. I want to hear you admit it to me, and to yourself," I growled, rattling until her body tightened with the call to my creature, hearing him through the red-haze of need burning her to ashes. "Tell me so I can give you what you want, what you crave."

"You!" Her voice echoed through the cave.

My stomach clenched with the need to free my cock and hear her screaming as I stretched her full, taking up every ounce of space in her tightening cunt until I'm pushing against her womb painfully.

"Good girl," I murmured, flicking her clit while I threaded my fingers through her hair. I yanked it painfully, hearing her gasp of shock as the pain and pleasure dueled for precedence. "Look over my shoulder, into the shadows," I demanded, forcing her to look where the male was watching us together.

I could smell his arousal. I knew he was about to explode from her heady scent and her sexy fucking noises that escaped her tight throat. I listened for her whisper of shock, and when I heard it, I pushed my fingers deep into her soaking cunt and pounded into her body without mercy.

I let loose of the control I held, freeing my need to hear her screaming my name. Her pussy tightened, clamping down hard as I hit every nerve against her tight channel. My thumb snaked up, working her swollen clit until she was about to explode, and right before she did, I lifted her against my mouth, claiming her clit between my lips.

I fucking destroyed her cunt with my tongue, pushing into her tight, soaking wet pussy. I feasted on her come, releasing as I rubbed her pussy against my mouth until she screamed my name, uncaring that we still had an audience. Her hands held onto my hair, and I laughed against her clenching sex, drinking her arousal down as she stared into his eyes. My girl, motherfucker.

I knew the moment the male exploded in his pants, because I fucking came too, hard. Her hands were in my hair, holding me where she needed me. Aria fucking slammed her pussy against my mouth, hard and needy. Her arousal painted my lips, my chin, and the moment she moaned my name, I lost my shit and came too. Her pleasure drove me to madness, and she fucking knew it.

I didn't let her orgasm end. It went on forever. Aria bucked against my mouth until my lips swelled from slamming against my teeth while she fucked my face greedily. Her blood was there too, and I couldn't figure out which one I like more, the fact that she fucking rode my face so hard she hurt us both, or that she came so hard I had to fucking swallow her down with the blood.

I released her, allowing her body to trail down mine until she could feel my hard cock already needing more of her, to be buried within her tight cunt. My hand snaked up through her hair, and I forced her to watch me licking my mouth clean from her arousal.

Aria moaned, her body continuing to tremble as the orgasm echoed through her. I smiled at her, but it wasn't friendly. It was cold and unfeeling, and she knew I was pissed.

I leaned down, sinking my teeth into her shoulder before she exploded violently. Her body belonged to me. I knew it. It was why she always exploded without a choice when I bit her shoulder, marking her.

Drawing away from her, my tongue snaked out to seal the wound. My hand captured her throat, and I held her stare. "If you ever flirt with another creature in front of me again, I'll bend you over and fuck you in front of him so he can see how hard you come for me. I'll let him see how primal you are for me when you are naked down to your bare bones, woman. Do you understand me?"

She didn't reply. Her mouth opened and closed, and I smiled before laughing low and huskily. "Now you know what I mean when I say I'm about to lick the attitude out of you. Be a good girl, Aria. Walk, we have a long trek back to camp."

I turned, staring straight into the other male's turquoise gaze with an open challenge. Aria's come still painting my face, I licked around it, letting the beast peer out beneath the veneer I wore.

The male stepped back, his eyes burning with turquoise fire and embers. My smile was all serrated teeth and bite that promised to sever head from throat. He smiled back, his eyes burning with something I couldn't discern. I rattled, but he didn't return the call because Aria answered it, her sultry fucking noise making both of us turn and take notice of her presence.

"Are you coming, asshole? Or do you expect me to suck your cock first?" She purred, and we both groaned before her eyes slid to the silver-haired male, and her lips thinned. I almost smiled at the anger burning in her stare. "You know what? On second thought, you can suck each other off." She didn't bother waiting around to see our reply before she started up the stairs, forcing me to follow her.

I watched Aria's hips swaying up the steps, smelling the arousal I'd placed on her, heady and addictive. The rose shampoo was doing little to hide her scent.

As I'd suspected, Aurora had added shit into her shampoo and body wash to hide what she was from the others. Aria hadn't had any fucking clue, or she'd have commented that the shampoo I had given her was missing something.

The fact that she had men with similar coloring chasing her pissed me off. I'd encountered no one else with her coloring within the Nine Realms until her. Now they seemed to coming out of the shadows, and were showing up around her, often.

It made it damn hard to figure out which breed she was, other than something similar to us. I had a general idea, but her blackening claws weren't something I'd ever seen before, and that was dangerous considering I'd seen every breed within the Nine Realms. Even the oldest ones.

Aria's taunt haunted me. Her need to be loved and create life wasn't something I could offer her. I knew it, and yet I couldn't let her go. It had socked me in the gut that she thought she could leave me to find someone else who would love her. It shouldn't have fucking stung as much as it had.

Not fucking happening.

She was mine.

I ground my jaw thinking about it, and her pretty eyes turned to look over her shoulder, locking with mine. My nails pushed through my fingers without warning. Teeth elongated, slamming through my gums with the need to fucking mark her violently.

Everywhere.

My stomach clenched again, imagining her middle swollen with another's child growing within her. The thought of her lips touching theirs, and Aria kissing another male as she had kissed me in the pool, enraged me.

I barely contained the urge to slam her against the wall and mark every inch of her skin with my teeth. The rattle within me was about to explode, and once it did, she'd be fucked.

We barely made it out of the cave before I pushed her toward Greer and Brander, and I vanished with Killian and Lore on my heels. I almost marked her. I almost just claimed my enemy.

They didn't question my sudden need for space either, just fucking zipped into the jetstream, and we disappeared into the passes. Once I was out of the range of Aria's scent, I stopped and slammed my fist into the side of the rock slab, watching it crack and spider web.

"What the fuck?" Lore demanded.

"Shut up, Lore," Killian warned, seeing the war I was battling against my primal need and urge to claim what wasn't mine to claim. Not like my creature wanted.

That couldn't fucking happen.

"I need distance before I do something I can't take back," I warned, and Killian nodded. "I need to know who the fuck is chasing her. We need to end that shit now."

"A runner came when you were bathing with her in the pool. I blocked his entrance into the valley. It seems there's been an attack on some of the faction. I'm uncertain which, since he refused to give me the message. It was marked for your eyes only with the rebellion's seal. This sounds like a good distraction. You have also been summoned to the council to hear from the other heads of the Nine Realms. There's unrest in some places where the witches have attacked while we chased Aria around the realms."

"Good, that should give me time away from Aria. I need you with her, Killian. Keep her close and don't let her out of your sight. That asshole isn't afraid of us, and he wants her. I probably just made that need of his more primal and more problematic. We'll get back to camp, and I'll speak to the others before leaving at dawn."

The sound of Greer's laughter made us all turn. Peering at the cave they were all walking from, turquoise eyes found mine and held them as Aria paused, swallowing hard.

I could hear her heart thundering, even from the distance in which we stood apart. My nose lifted, inhaling her need, which caused my pulse to echo hers. Her teeth captured and worried her bottom lip, and she started walking again slowly with a blush painting her cheeks pink.

My stomach clenched with need while my balls tightened, moving into my stomach as Greer said something that caused her to laugh loudly. I narrowed my eyes to slits, watching the way her eyes danced with amusement. Yet the moment they came back to me, it washed away.

I was so fucked.

I wanted her unlike anything I had ever wanted before.

She was my enemy.

And none of that mattered when she got close to me and washed it all away with those pretty blue eyes that dared me to fight her.

Aria fucked me harder than life ever could.

She turned me inside out and sank her talons into my chest, demanding my cold, dead heart beat once more.

I feared what would happen if it did. I worried if I allowed it to feel just one single thing, I would unleash everything at once. She'd be the target for whatever I felt, and I was sure she wouldn't survive it, but then neither would I.

Chapter Fifty-Six

Soraya

I walked to King of Norvalla's camp, slipping into the large group of people entering it. My eyes search for the king, finding him within the group coming in beside us. The woman in his arms doesn't seem happy to be there. Yet something in her eyes pissed me off.

She's delicate in form, her silver hair flowing to her waist in subtle waves. Bright, beautiful turquoise eyes slide over the witches brought into camp, and she rattled. Her eyes roamed over the group, slowly coming back to rest on me and the young witch I held to me. I hadn't even realized I'd stopped, not until the guard behind me snarled and pushed me.

The shove sent me and the witch I'm bound to sailing to the ground. The slight woman dismounted, even as the male snarled. Her head whipped back, and she rattled, causing my eyes to round. The subtle hint of magic exuded from her, causing my skin to break out in goosebumps before she picked us up and righted us back on our feet.

"Are you okay?" she whispered, her eyes searching mine before moving to the younger witch.

"Fine, My Lady."

"My Lady, my ass," she snapped, irked at the title.

"Aria," the king growled, and she turned. "They're witches."

"So am I," she snarled back, and I watched his eyes narrowing to slants before he exhaled.

"Come," she stated, baring serrated teeth at the guard when he moved to intervene. "Try me, motherfucker," she warned, and I swallowed the urge to smirk.

Esme was right. There's fire in her eyes and blood. But how long before Ilsa turns it to nothing more than smoke and ashes? I silently took her in, noting she wore the king's cloak. Her shoulders were back, and her head was high. She doesn't look like much, but Esme was right. She's powerful. *Very powerful*. I could feel the power, but it wasn't right. It wasn't ours.

She's something else, yet the same. A warrior stepped closer, and her eyes turned toward him, filling with a sea-green color. Fiery embers burned in them, and I'm struck stupid with the rarity of what that meant. Only a few within the Nine Realms could change. Only a few of the strongest breeds survived past Hecate's rage and the war she waged when she entered this realm and laid claim.

"You aren't with the other witches. Why?" I asked, watching her eyes slide back to lock with mine.

"Because the king knows I'd start a rebellion, and he'd get his ass handed to him," she offered, giving me a smirk before winking.

"Aria, this way," another male called, sliding his eyes down my frame before dismissing me.

"Coming, Lore," she snorted.

I watched her vanish with the men, entering the king's tent before the guards hurried us to the center of the camp. My fingers worked through the flesh of my palm, telling Ilsa that I had eyes on her target. I don't look down as soldiers gathered around us, or when the skin on my palm burned painfully.

Once I was among the witches, I peered down at my hand, reading the runes that covered my palm. My heart thundered in my chest, echoing the blood flow through my ears. My attention moved to the largest tent, watching as Aria slipped inside with the king. I frowned, peering around the large camp filled with warriors, camp followers, and witches.

"Name?" a woman asked, and I frowned. Her gaze lifted, and she paused. "Send this one to the herb tent. We will use her to create potions," she announced without waiting for me to speak.

The guard held out his arm, and I followed him, turning to stare at the tent surrounded by guards protecting the king. Ilsa had said to stand down, that Aria was already dead. It didn't make sense to send me in if she already had another plan in action. Not unless something had changed for Aria, or even for me.

My gaze turned to a group of rowdy men, taking in the lords with three witches naked on their knees. Swallowing hard, I hurried my steps toward the herb tent, moving inside before releasing the breath I'd held.

"You look like you've seen a ghost," a woman exclaimed, her cloudy blue eyes searching mine. "So, have you?" she asked, moving closer to examine my face before reaching for my hands, which still burned. I yanked them away, causing her keen eyes to lift and hold mine. "I'll see your hands, girl."

Swallowing bile, I held my hands up with the backs to her, but she grabbed them, turning them over to stare at bare palms. I slowly blew out the air I'd held, sliding my eyes away from hers. Once she was satisfied, she lifted her eyes.

"You've brewed before, yes?" she questioned.

"Many times," I admitted.

"You look like you've been through it," she stated, and I frowned. "The war. It haunts your eyes. You've seen too much for your age, girl. They call me Maize. You can call me Maize, or you can call me Old Crone. I care not which one you prefer. I am both."

"Old Crone only means you're brave and smart. You're a survivor, too."

"That we all are," she huffed, turning to the cauldrons that were boiling. "If you're smart, you'll stay out of the notice of the guards unless you plan to earn your way on your back."

"I heard the king has a thing for witches," I snorted, moving to one of the brewing potions, cupping my hands to bring the smoke to my nose.

"Not since he brought the Hecate witch to camp, he hasn't. Heck, even before then, he stopped taking them to his bed."

I paused, turning to look at her. "So he's bewitched by her?"

She scoffed and grunted. "No, just today she was beaten by the guards. She attacked another witch who was hurting one of the witchlings. I say she did what we all wanted to do to Bekkah for a long time. Goddess bless her. Aria gave her an ass-whopping she won't soon forget. She might even think twice before beating another witchling within the camp."

I turned that over in my head, frowning at the idea of Aria accepting a beating to protect a witchling.

"Was she fond of the witchling?" I asked snooping.

"Had never clapped eyes on her until she watched the poor thing hit by Bekkah for not casting, or so they say," Maize stated, shrugging. "I don't heed rumors. But she hadn't been here more than a day before she defended the chit. Couldn't have known her for long enough to care if she lived or died."

"And the king allowed it?" I asked, watching her eyes growing sad.

"That he did, and we have not seen her since."

"I just saw her entering the tent. She couldn't have been hurt that badly," I stated, and watched her shaking her head.

"She had blood pouring from her face and a lame arm that hung in her chains. Bekkah made certain everyone knew how badly they had beaten Aria. If she wasn't bad off now, it's because the king took her up to the village with the healing pools."

Why would he care if she were hurt? Why take her to the village unless he cared? The king was notorious for bedding witches, uncaring if he harmed them in his playtime.

Why stay with only her? Better yet, had she felt the power hidden within the caves? If so, was that the loss of power I'd felt? If Aria was strong enough to free those souls, she might just be strong enough to face Ilsa.

Not that it mattered. Nothing mattered except getting Julia out of the Kingdom of Vãkya and away from Ilsa. I couldn't trust someone I hadn't met.

I wouldn't play games with my sister's life. Not even for a Hecate-born witch, especially not one who was dumb enough to sleep with the opposing side's king. If Ilsa's message was right, then Aria would be dead soon enough, anyway.

Chapter Fifty-Seven

Aria

I stared off into the early morning skies, recalling Knox's loathing look as he rode out of the camp. He had left before the sun rose two weeks ago, leaving me with Lore, Killian, and Greer. I'd spent most of the first morning stuck inside my head, trying to ignore the pang of unease and regret that I'd felt.

Knox wasn't happy since I'd refused to discuss the other male in the cavern, but I was still pissed at his caveman antics, bringing me to an orgasm as the other Aden had watched. It may have made total sense to Knox to lay claim and put on the alpha display, but that didn't mean I was happy about it.

I'd slept that first night, cuddled in the furs that held Knox's scent, bathed in their warmth as my mind rushed with what had happened in the cavern. How had I ever thought the sliver-haired men were trying to protect me?

They'd set me up to battle against a female like me, but older. They hadn't cared if I survived, which meant they were no better than Knox, or anyone else for that matter. No one around me cared about me, which sucked. I'd gotten so used to thinking of myself as a tool to be used that I'd stopped seeing that I was worth anything more.

On the second week away from Knox, I'd started to wish for his return. It was one thing to be here with him, and another to be among his people watching me with unguarded hatred burning in their stares without him to protect me.

I also missed him being near to keep the nightmares at bay, which seemed to reoccur nightly without him. The warmth of him against me as I slept was something I'd enjoyed. That also bothered me.

Then there was Lord Andres, who seemed to watch me, nonstop. It became increasingly uncomfortable in the second week, choosing to hide within the tent more and more to escape the lust-filled stares he sent my way. Killian and the others had noted it and kept the lord occupied and away from me, luckily.

It was midafternoon on the first day of the third week when Lord Andres found me alone with Greer. He sat beside me, grabbing me from where I had sat, placing me onto his lap as Greer turned toward me, silently sliding his gaze between us.

"Aren't you a pretty little thing," Lord Andres chuckled, running his nose over my shoulder. I rattled, causing his focus to shift to surprise long enough for Greer to grab me from the lord's lap. "I'd back off, asshole. Do you know who I am?" Lord Andres sneered, and I tilted my head, purring low in warning at the man threatening violence toward Greer.

Lord Andres's green eyes narrowed on me, and before I could duck, his fist shot out, slamming against the side of my head.

I darted forward to attack, only for Killian to slam me back as Lore caught me, rattling low in his throat. Lore pushed me toward Greer before he stepped beside Killian, creating a barrier between Lord Andres and us.

"She's not to be harmed. The king himself protects Aria, and I doubt you want Knox returning to find his protection violated. Do you? Because to harm those under his protection is treason against the king himself," Killian said smoothly.

Lord Andres sized up Killian and Lore, sneering before his stare settled on me. It sent unease slithering through me with the look of hatred and borderline obsession that banked within them. His mouth twisted into a cruel smile before he reached up, pushing his oily hair away from his forehead.

"She's a witch and his whore according to the guards. Tell me, Lord Killian, does the king intend to breed the bitch too? Oh, that's right. He can't, considering his queen already provided him with a son which this whore's bloodline murdered. Yet he fucks her and gives her his protection? Interesting choice of bedmates. Wouldn't you agree?"

"What the king does with his whore isn't our business, now is it?" Killian countered, his anger smothering as his power slid through me.

I tried to step back, but Greer held me in place, noting that Lord Andres's sharp stare shifted to me the moment I tried to move away. Greer tightened his hold, squeezing my arm as if he were silently trying to ask me to remain in place.

"I just found it strange that she is kept away from the other witches, and sleeps in his tent even without him present to use her. She's guarded rather heavily, and it is making my men curious as some wouldn't mind bedding the whore a few times before we take our leave."

"The camp followers are welcoming your men to their beds often. The other witches were given the option as well. Aria isn't among the ones offered to satisfy your bodily needs, nor is that changing. King Karnavious doesn't wish her to be used yet. When that changes, some of us are already in line for that position, Lord Andres. This argument and inquiry are finished. Wouldn't you agree?" Killian's tone brokered no room for argument. His eyes didn't blink as he pulled power to him, blanketing us with it as Greer held me tightly, protectively.

Lord Andres rattled loudly, and Lore and Killian both stepped forward, echoing the noise until my own slid free, low, and deadly, causing all three men to turn and stare at me. It wasn't a friendly sound by any means, more of a *'fucking try me'* rattle that had Killian smiling devilishly as if he considered taking me up on the offer.

Well, shit.

A rider entered the camp and approached the tense situation unfolding with apprehension. Still, he moved forward and handed Killian a sealed letter that held a black circular wax seal. He accepted and opened it before turning to Lore.

"Pack the king's tent and his witch. We're leaving to meet him and the king's guard on the passes. I need to give orders to the men to follow behind us," Killian announced. "I guess this is where we part ways, Lord Andres." Killian moved to make his way toward the men when Lore stopped him.

"Just us?" Lore asked.

"And a large group of men, but we will meet up with Brander and Knox before the passes. He stated that he's impatient to tell us what he discovered. Any other questions, Lore?" Killian asked impatiently, his eyes daring him to speak more in front of the lord's presence. "No? Then pack up as we're leaving directly."

When Killian said we were leaving directly, he meant it. Less than ten minutes later, we watched Lord Andres departing with his men, while we went in the opposite direction.

No one spoke as we rode the horses at a rapid pace into the dark, narrowing road that would take the army hours to navigate, which was why we were leaving them behind and heading out in front of them.

The ride through the countryside was silent, or it was until we approached a fork in the road covered in downed trees. Killian slowed the horse he and I rode on, holding me tighter as we stopped in the road.

"That is a problem," he grunted, turning to peer down the other direction.

"It looks like someone placed that tree there," I

stated, and he tightened his hold on my chest painfully.

"We're taking the alternate road into the pass," Killian announced.

"That will add an hour to the ride," Lore grumbled.

"We'll cut through the forest and slice off the time we added. It'll be midnight before we reach the woods, and the weeping willows will be asleep, right along with the flame-tailed foxes and miscreants that hide within it. It is, after all, the witching hour."

We moved down the road at an easier gait, and I adjusted my rear in the saddle, causing Killian to tighten his hold. Anytime I moved even the subtlest motion, he would pull me closer against his enticing scent.

"Hold still, witch."

"My ass hurts, not to mention other parts of me."

"You keep moving against me like that, and this ride will take a very dark turn, woman. I'm fighting your scent, and everything within me wants to dominate you something fierce after you issued your little challenge, which was fucking stupid to do."

"I don't understand half the noises I make, Killian," I admitted softly, feeling annoyed at being forced to endure his company for the trek to Knox. Killian seemed to deflate a little at that, realizing I really didn't have any clue what sounds my beast made.

I also hated that I was excited to see Knox after being away from him for nearly three weeks. It bothered me more than anything, the butterflies at the idea of smelling his enticingly male scent that both calmed and soothed my unease like a balm against my soul. I also welcomed the thought of a full night of dreamless sleep, where the nightmares couldn't touch me.

A thick fog slipped from the forest floor, flooding over the path. Killian slowed the horse, following the fog with his eyes into the dark forest. Growling erupted from the surrounding woods, gradually growing in volume.

We sat in the middle of the road, staring at the downed trees that once again blocked our path as shadows slipped from the forest, moving toward us.

Killian turned to Lore, speaking in the language they used when they didn't want me to understand what they were saying.

All at once, Killian, Lore, and Greer dismounted with the other men in the group, closing in around the horse where I remained until Killian reached up, pulling me down beside him.

"One wrong move, Aria, and you're dead. I won't hesitate to end you. Do you understand me?" Killian warned with a low purr, enhancing his meaning. "Don't give me an excuse, woman."

"I understand."

"You better pray that this isn't a rescue party coming to get you." He watched me, drawing his sword as he and the others formed a circle around me.

Power slithered through the area, enhanced by magic, sending it rushing toward us. My eyes moved to the source, finding a hooded figure standing deeply within the shadows, surrounded by red eyes.

A singsong voice echoed a chant, and the fog increased as giant dogs lunged toward us. Knox's men all swung together in synchronized movements as they fought off the attack. An arrow shot from the woods, slicing through my arm as it grazed me.

Men rushed forward from the side of the road in an ambush, and I felt my nails sliding into place as Knox's men moved apart, swinging their swords as the other men lunged, deftly attacking without fear.

I felt witchcraft in the air, the call to use my magic against the hooded woman as she watched me standing like a stick in the road, unable to do anything other than watch.

A hound broke through the line, and I leaped, slicing through him as Killian turned briefly to assure himself that I had it handled before he attacked the nearest warrior charging us.

We were outnumbered, and the witch standing in the woods wasn't just powerful; she was a dark witch who commanded beasts with rows of blade-like teeth and crimson eyes.

Lore cried out as a sword sliced into his arm, and I moved, shoving my hand through the male's chest, swinging the blade, pushing Lore away as I defended him. Greer used dual blades, slashing them low and rapidly as the men with us tired from fighting endlessly, while the witch's magic fueling the others. I turned as one warrior in our party swung wide, barely missing me as something slammed against my head, knocking me to the ground.

I screamed, fighting against the hand that pulled

me away from the small fighting group. I couldn't see past the stars that filled my vision, or the magic choking me while it held me in the thrall of its endless power. I couldn't fight or release my power to help the others, either. I felt something slamming me down as a blade moved forward, Killian's scent hit me.

He fought to get me free, to keep them from dragging me into the woods. I felt his magic, but the dark magic oozing through the woods that rushed over us was intensely stronger. Air entered my starving lungs, and I gasped, feeling it sucked out again by force. Whoever the witch was, she starved my lungs for air, holding me powerless and in the thrall of despair while starving my body for oxygen.

I was grabbed, lifted, and dragged painfully away from the sound of the swords still meeting in battle. Killian growled, shouting for me to fight, but I had nothing left without oxygen or magic to assist me. They dropped me on the forest floor within the fog, and I gasped for air as a sliver was allowed into my throat.

I held my pounding head as I sat up, only for someone to grab my hair, yanking me backward into the darkness. I watched Knox's men fighting off overwhelming odds.

Killian rattled, continuing to fight as three armed men swung blades at Lore, hitting him before he could deflect all three blows. I screamed, turning as a hooded figure aimed a silver-tipped bow in Lore's direction, fully intending to end his life with the arrow.

I moved without thinking before the arrow was shot, slamming into the archer with inhuman speed. Someone placed a hood over my head as I heard the ancient language of the witches spoken. I went limp, fainting as if I'd passed out from the words. I'd used every ounce of strength I'd had left to save Lore, and in doing so, I'd fucked myself.

The sound of screaming rattles and battle cries filled the night as the warriors fought while I was carted off deeper into the woods. The assailants moved me away from the fighting, and I was unable to see anything past the hood covering my eyes.

I could smell the sick scent of dark, rotting magic mixed with spices to hide the smell of decaying flesh. Black magic slithered over me, alerting me that there was more than one witch present. Heartbeats sounded around me, and I counted them, calculating my odds of escape.

"Mistress, the men will die if you leave before the fighting ends," a deep voice announced, disturbing my calculations.

"Leave them to their fates. They're not our men. They're Lord Andres's hired hands that he found along his way after slaughtering his army when he switched sides. Come, the king will hunt this one down. We must put miles between us and his dead men. Finding them dead will probably slow him down. Lord Andres is waiting in the woods by the falls. We will not waste another hour of nightfall since my power weakens with the light."

"And her?" a man asked.

"She will die a traitor's death for what she has done to our people. She's too powerful to allow the other side to wield and has proven difficult to catch without the

King of Norvalla sniffing her cunt. If what Lord Andres says is true, she is the one thing that can kill our queen, and we cannot allow that to happen at all costs. Even if the cost is her life," she laughed soundlessly, yet I felt her respond.

Hands touched my side, trailing over it while bile pushed against my throat. I was hefted up without warning and tossed into what I assumed was a cart. The thing jerked forward, and the sound of wheels over rough terrain filled my ears.

Tears slipped free as the thought of Lore, Killian, and Greer meeting their end filled my mind. It was a cruel fate and ending for them. Knox would hunt me down, assuming I'd allowed them to be murdered in cold blood to escape him. He wouldn't even realize it wasn't me until it was too late to do anything to save me.

I'd be dead before Knox reached me, of that I was certain. Lord Andres wouldn't leave me unscathed, not after I'd openly challenged him. The witch that seemed to be in charge, well, she wanted me dead so that I wouldn't pose a threat to Ilsa. No one would come to save me because I'd pushed everyone who could, away. I'd wanted to protect them, and in doing so, I'd left myself open to be at the mercy of my enemies.

Ironically, I was currently praying my enemy would come and save me. The enemy of my enemy and all that jazz, right? My mind wandered to Knox, and I fought the tears that stung my eyes, wondering if he'd even care what had happened to me. What hurt the most was I wasn't sure I even mattered to him beyond something he could wield as a weapon.

Would he miss me when I was gone?

Would he care?

Would I survive this, or would I be just another nameless grave within this world?

I would survive. I promised myself.

I would take the heads of those who had harmed my friends and enemies.

I was Aria Hecate, and I wasn't dying like some weak-minded witch.

I'd escape, and when I did, I'd bring them all to their knees and rattle until they fucking shattered while I rose. I didn't need saving. I'd save myself, avenging those who died trying to protect me, facing Knox in the aftermath as his enemy. Only this time, he wouldn't forgive me.

THE END FOR NOW

Ruins of Chaos coming Winter 2020

Nine Realms' CompendIum

Key Players in the Series

Knox Karnavious – King of Norvalla

Brander – Brother of Knox, full-blooded

Lore – Brother of Knox

Fade – Brother to Knox, full-blooded

Killian – Lilianna's brother and Knox's best friend

Greer – Friend and butler to Knox, vampire

Hecate Bloodline Introduced So Far

Freya – Daughter of Hecate Dead

Aurora – Daughter of Hecate, sister to Freya who raised the twins.

Hysteria – Daughter of Hecate Dead

Twins of the Bloodline

Aria Primrose Hecate / Amara / Dead Other half unknown

Kinvara / Valeria – Succubi

Aine / Luna – Alpha werewolf

Sabine / Callista – Nymphs

Reign / Rhaghana – Unknown

Tieghan/Tamryn – Witches, born of human fathers

Alpha Pack

Dimitri – Pure-born alpha werewolf

Jasper – Pure-born werewolf, Fallon's son, and Prince of the Alpha wolves/Dead

Fallon – Pure-born alpha wolf, King of the Alpha Pack/ Dead

Minotaurs

Gerald – King of the Kingdom of Unwanted Beasts/ Dead

Garrett – Son of the King of the Kingdom of Unwanted Beasts

Other People

Neven – The Queen of Nymphs

Ilsa – The High Queen of Witches

Esmeralda – Unmarked witch friend to Aria Hecate

Asil – Witch holding a stronghold against Knox for Ilsa

Tristan – Slumlord

Taren Oleander – The King of Gargoyle's / Keeper of Lightning

Soraya – Witch that works for the High Queen of Witches

Julia – Witch controlled by Ilsa, sister of Soraya

Siobhan – Marked witch under Knox's rule

Bekkah – Marked witch under Knox's rule

Eva – Unknown

Aden – Unknown

Items and More

Grimoire – A book of ancient spells

Scrying – The ability to search a map with magic to find a location.

White Oak Trees – Grown only in Norvalla in the Arcadian Forest of Knowledge

Frost fire – Ice from the Dark Mountains, appears as regular ice until it swallows up anything, or anyone it can touch. Unbreakable by anything other than witches fire, a spell that only rare witches can use. It was used to protect Norvalla from the Kingdom of Unwanted Beasts.

Midnight Blooming black roses – Grown in the darkest passes in the Dark Mountains. A rare type of rose that blossom's in the icy snow caps of the mountain, holding a unique essence that witches covet.

Tonics – medicinal potions for healing

Gargoyles – Protectors of the Library of Knowledge

The visited lands within the Nine Realms to date

Dorcha –The Darkest Realm, realm in which Norvalla sits as capital

Norvalla – Knox's Homeland

Kingdom of Unwanted Beasts – Realm that borders Norvalla

Kingdom of Vãkya – Aria's homeland, where Ilsa currently resides within the Palace of Magic

Valley of the Dead – Land that borders between Vãkya and Dorcha

House of Magic – Formerly known as Kerrigan Keep, now Aria's sanctuary below the ruins of a castle she claimed.

The Dark Mountains – The Mountain range bordering The Kingdom of Unwanted Beast and Norvalla's high passes.

Library of Knowledge – An ever-changing room that only reveals its treasures to those it finds worthy of the knowledge it holds.

About the Author

Amelia Hutchins is the number one national bestselling author of the Monsters, The Fae Chronicles, and Nine Realm series. She is an admitted coffee addict, who drinks magical potions of caffeine and turns them into magical worlds. She writes alpha-hole males and the alpha women who knock them on their arses, hard. She doesn't write romance. She writes fast-paced books that go hard against traditional standards. Sometimes a story isn't about the romance; it's about rising to a challenge, breaking through them like wrecking balls, and shaking up entire worlds to discover who they really are. If you'd like to check out more of her work, or just hang out in an amazing tribe of people who enjoy rough men, and sharp women, join her at Author Amelia Hutchins Group on Facebook.

Stalker Links

Facebook group: https://www.facebook.com/groups/1240287822683404/

Facebook Author Page: https://www.facebook.com/authorameliahutchins/

Instagram: **https:**//www.instagram.com/author.amelia.hutchins/

Made in the USA
Columbia, SC
08 October 2023

24132809R00304